Rockhaven:
Coming Home

Farley Dunn

THREE SKILLET

ROCKHAVEN: COMING HOME, Dunn, Farley L

First Edition

A Katie Carver Novel, Anthology Edition

 THREE SKILLET

www.ThreeSkilletPublishing.com

v.2

ISBN: 978-1-943189-16-8

Contains four complete Katie Carver novels:

Rockhaven Summer

Rockhaven Wedding

Rockhaven Christmas

Rockhaven Spring

Author's Note

Those of you familiar with Mid-Coast Maine will recognize elements of Vinalhaven Island in my Rockhaven series, but only because of my family history and the summers I've spent there. If you do visit Vinalhaven someday, look for Rockhaven. You'll find that magical place strewn all about the craggy shoreline and in the stalwart people that call Vinalhaven home.

Rockhaven
SUMMER

Katie Carver's hair blew across her face, and she pulled it away with slender, delicate fingers. The thick strands were long and dark, and they glistened when they caught in the wind.

They also caught on her broken nails.

When one brushed against her cheek, she tore her eyes from the familiar scenery rushing by at breakneck speed and glanced at it. The polish, gleaming Brandy-wine with an iridescent sheen, was so inappropriate for today's trip, as proven by the damage she'd already inflicted on them. It was proof, in a way, that she was still the island girl she'd tried so hard to leave behind. She was still Katherine Daytona Carver, of the Rockhaven Carvers, one of the moneyed set who no longer had money, just the name that everyone still knew.

"Katie? Or do you go by Katherine, now? Or maybe it's Dame Carver, newest owner of Carver Point?"

The words laughed at her; she could hear it, and she fought the tears. She would not let Jeffrey Ragsdale know he could still manipulate her like a child's toy, even after all these years. He had been Jeff to his island friends, but she had never dared more than his full name. He had only been a year older, but it had been a gap she'd never bridged, with him always staying just out of reach, whether at seven, eleven, or fourteen. He was the wild island boy who knew every submerged rock ledge, every dripping spruce, and just where to find the thickest stands of island roses.

She had idolized him as a child, worshipped him as a preteen, and thought she'd loved him at fourteen. Then her world had been stolen from her. The call. Her grand-mother's house burned to its foundations, and the Boston funeral attended by Boston society. The whole time she'd wanted to return to the Point to cry her desperate tears, but at fourteen, well, who listens to anyone at fourteen?

She hadn't been back. Her parents had blamed the island and its narrow roads for Grandmother Carver's death. Katie knew differently. She had been the cause. She hadn't been there, and for that reason, her world had been stolen from her.

Now Jeffrey made fun of her. *Jeff.* Jeff made fun of her. She would call him Jeff. At the town float, he'd held his tanned hand out to her as she stepped on his boat, and he'd said, "Jeff, if you please. Never Jeffrey. That's a boy's name." He'd grinned as he said it, though, as if he were teasing a little pigtailed girl.

"Call me Dame Carver again, Jeff Ragsdale, and I'll push you over the side." She bit the final word off, but she would. It was hard enough being on this boat with the boy she'd once thought she'd loved. To have him make fun of her at the same time? It was intolerable.

"I remember a little girl who cried when she picked the roses up at Sommer's Ledge."

"She did not." But even as she said the words, she realized she was rubbing at the side of one finger that still carried a scar. One of the thorns had gotten infected, and the town doctor had lanced it in the middle of the night. She'd never told any of her friends for fear of their ridicule.

"Did, too." The laughter was still there. "I picked out a few thorns, and I'm certain I remember a tear or two. Could have been appreciation running down those cheeks, though. Yeah, I bet that was it. Appreciation for the island boy

10

willing to take the time for a little bloody finger."

He was silent for a time. They were crossing the ferry's wake, and as they rode up one side of the swell, things in the boat shifted. Katie grabbed for her weekend case, only to have the nose of the boat fall just as she leaned over, crashing into the sea and sending a wall of spray over the bow of the boat. Water dripped off the wheelhouse onto her jeans, darkening the fabric in expanding concentric circles. The engine revved, and the boat skewed sideways before biting into the sea again and smoothing out.

"That was a blast!" Jeff laughed. "Want to do it again?" He pointed to the far side of the wake, and he whipped the wheel sideways and gunned the engine.

"Stop it, Jeffrey!" Katie looked away. He was still doing it, reaching inside to manipulate feelings she had boxed up and put away over a decade ago. She had given them to God, and now . . . now they were rearing up again.

It seemed she didn't have a choice in the matter, though, because just then the boat hit the other side of the wake, only this time they didn't hit it dead on. The boat twisted sideways, violently, and Katie didn't have time to grab at anything to steady herself.

"Jeffrey!" The word was out of her mouth as she flew across the boat, hitting her shoulder on *something* before her foot slipped from under her and she collapsed—God forbid!—right against him. He laughed as he killed the throttle and reached to lift her up.

"Whoa! So, Jeffrey is here to stay, is he? I remember a pretty little girl who used to follow me everywhere who once called me that. I was fifteen. I don't think I'm fifteen anymore, but I haven't forgotten."

"I'm so sorry, *Jeff*." She emphasized his name, and she laughed to show the incident was no big deal, as she stood and stepped away from him. "A lifetime ago I wouldn't have noticed that little wave. I guess I've lost my sea legs."

"You think?" His eyes watched her carefully. "No damage? Leg? Shoulder? Ego?" He grinned, though.

"The cabin?" She meant the one habitable structure left on her newly inherited property. Her question was a diversion. She needed to get off talking about the two of them. It didn't seem fourteen years were so far gone that she had severed all her emotional ties with that long-ago life. The truth of the matter? That life was another girl's life.

She felt the old bitterness rise, the one that wanted to blame it all on God. She had given it to Him, but only after months of tears and raging prayers blaming Him for not being there when He should have been. The bitterness had been harder to let go.

"So, the ego is damaged." Jeff was back at the wheel, and the thrub, thrub of the engine started up again. "Not *too* damaged, I hope. Not so damaged we can't plan a lobster bake this weekend."

He wasn't looking at her, but she could see the side of his face. As a boy, he'd been quick-footed and taut, with slabs for cheeks that crinkled into dimples when he smiled. Now? The dimples were deeper, and the sea had taken its toll. It had improved him, though, with laugh lines at the corners of his eyes, and windblown hair that whipped at his face but didn't quite block his vision. She glanced at his hand, the left one. Bare finger with no tan line. Well, at least they had something in common. She laughed sourly. Not by her choice, but there it was, anyway.

"I called Marc at the Paper Store. He said he'd send someone out." They were between Rockhaven and Settler's Island, and the water had flattened out. She watched the rocky shoreline speed past. Carver Point was at the north end of the island, and it was a good twenty-minute ride.

"He did."

"And?" She glanced at him. It was so easy to slip into the old patterns, with short answers that were mere suggestions of responses, leaving things half said and half understood at the same time.

"Just that." The laughter was in his words again.

"Okay. I'll find out when we get there." They passed the De Groot dock, a massive granite monstrosity that half the island envied and the rest decried as a blight on the shoreline. The house, an ancient shingled bear of a manse

12

tucked into the trees, was visible just for a moment, then it slipped into the overgrowth and was gone. Even the dock with its undulating float soon disappeared into the rocky outcrops that broke up the shoreline. She had visited there with her grandmother on occasion, the gas lamps and cedar-paneled walls making it so very dark inside. She wondered for a minute who owned it now, if it had been sold or if it was still in the family.

Whatever, at least it was still there. She dreaded seeing the Point with its bare stone foundation. What memories would that bring? Running up the stone steps with Jennie hopping up after her? She smiled at that. She'd forgotten about her Flemish giant, as big as a small dog, cuddling in her bed at night. Who'd have thought a rabbit could reach upwards of fifty pounds? There were also all the things she had stored up from fourteen summers of memories, things she dreamed about every winter until she could get back to the island each year. Her grandmother had always been the lucky one, going out after the last snowfall, often in late March or early April and staying until the first real cold snap, sometimes in mid-November.

"At least I have the cabin." Katie let out a mournful sigh.

"You have what?" Jeff leaned over and called the words too loudly into her ear.

"The cabin." She placed her hand on his chest and pushed him away, and this time she smiled a real smile. "You heard me fine, and you keep your distance."

"Yes ma'am, Dame Carver."

She turned, ready to carry out her threat only to see a wide smile and deep dimples on his face. That had been on purpose. Well, she could give as well as she got.

"Just you wait, Jeff Ragsdale. You've got one coming." She pointed a broken fingernail at him.

"Yes, ma'am. This weekend will do fine by me. I'll even bring the lobster."

She laughed out loud at that one. "I'll bet you will." They were on his lobster boat, after all. That was the one thing he had more than enough of, lobster.

13

She contented herself for the rest of the journey to take in the shoreline. It was as familiar to her as her childhood, and it was as distant as a vengeful God could make it.

She had loved it once. She wouldn't let God take her memories, too, no matter how hard He tried.

She felt the tears rise again, and she tried to push the bitterness away. Why, God, she let herself think one harsh time. Then she allowed the beauty of her Maine island to fill her senses and force the pain away, at least for a while.

And Jeffrey. Why had he volunteered to bring her out? How odd was that? They hadn't seen each other in fourteen years. Well, she'd been firmly in control, she hadn't let her emotions slip, and once he dropped her off, with luck, she wouldn't need to see him again.

It was best that way, she told herself. Then, when she thought of him again, she told herself one more time, it would be better all around that she didn't see him again.

"This . . ." Katie stumbled over her words. "This. Who?" She felt her throat choke up. The dock . . . and the float. She had expected it to be . . . what, she didn't know, but not *repaired.*

"What, Dame Carver?" The laugh was still in the words.

"You know what I mean." Jeff's continual use of the term "dame" grated on her. "All this. No one's set foot on the Point for more than ten years. I expected this to be falling down."

Still, she was pleased. Boards had been replaced on the ramp, and the remembered lintel leading into the box at the top of the ramp still had the bell with its rope cord that had been there forever. At least she supposed it was the same. The wood looked fresh, though. All of it.

The crescent-shaped beach and the trees rearing up from the shoreline were the same. They were the very ones she and Jeff had clambered through over a decade of childhood, him always showing up with his friends the week she arrived, and like a pack of island wolves, prowling the shadowy nooks and crannies during the glorious months of summer.

15

The top of the hill was empty, though. Carver House should fill the skyline, a white canvas of porches and gables, with Grandpa Carver's rosebushes lining the foundation walls. All that was left was the sky and the wispy outline of clouds in the distance.

The boat glided up to the float, and the engines died away. She reached for a rope coiled on the float and looped it around a cleat on the boat. The movement felt as natural as if she'd left the island the previous summer and she was picking up where she'd left off.

"This one, too."

She turned, and Jeff held another line to her, this one to run from ship to shore. She reached for it, turning her head towards the float as she did, only to feel the warmth of another's fingers brush hers for a brief instant as the rope was dropped into her hand. She leaped onto the float and looped the line around a cleat in the old loop-loop-and-under fashion she'd learned as a girl, and at the same time glancing at the man who'd brought her out. He was turned away, his shirt tight across his back, as he pulled her few bags from the floor of the boat.

So, she thought. The touch, accidental, was just a careless brush of finger to finger as a rope is passed from one hand to another. Nothing had been meant, and she would make nothing of it. Besides, there was nothing to make of it. If there had been anything to make of it, Jeff had missed his opportunity over a decade before.

She stood, aware of the sea smell, one of salt water and spruce, overlaid with wild roses and the sweetness of new-mown clover. That made her frown. New-mown clover. Then she saw it. The path up the hill, trimmed and green. Why was the path trimmed?

"Jeff?" She called to him, still searching with her eyes for anything else that didn't seem right. There. The old swing on the apple tree. It was still there, and it shouldn't be. Rope rots, and in fourteen years, it rots completely through. And the boathouse. There was still a boathouse right where it had always been. The doors were open, and it was empty, though.

"Yes, Dame?" The float rocked, and he stood at her side.

"I told you to stop that. Look at this." She swept the scene with an outstretched arm, stopping to point at the things, the odd things that weren't right. "What's wrong with this picture?"

"It's a pretty picture. I see nothing wrong with it. Why?"

She looked at him, her argument already rising in her throat, only to see his face right next to hers, watching her. His eyes, electric blue, and his laugh lines crinkled in a half smile. In that flash, she remembered the last time she'd seen him all those years ago. August was playing its final tune, and in the heat of the afternoon, the gang had taken over the local swimming hole at the quarry. Jeff had been the wild boy of the bunch, in his cut-off jeans and bare shoulders, screaming like a cougar as he leaped from the rocks to thrash the water below.

She looked away, the intensity of how much she'd worshipped him then filling her with longing for something lost that could never be returned. The old anger at God gripped her, and she brushed her palm against her face to wipe an impending tear away.

"This. Someone's been out here." Her voice barely wavered, and for that she felt grateful.

"I should hope so." He chuckled. "It seems you did call Marc. Am I correct?"

What did that mean? Her call had only been to make sure the cabin was usable. Storms did happen on Rockhaven, and the cabin was right at the water's edge. Grandfathered at the water's edge. And if it were gone, it could never be rebuilt. She hadn't heard back, but if everything was okay, she hadn't expected to. It was the island way.

"I have a friend coming."

Why had she said that? It was none of Jeff's business. He wouldn't be interested, in any case. He was just a delivery service, dumping her on her rocky outcropping, and then he'd be back to his lobster pots and earning his living like an islander should.

She knew, though. She was diverting the conversation. It surprised her he didn't ask about her friend.

"Up?" The float shifted again. Jeff held her bags and nodded toward the ramp, his feet moving that direction.

"Oh, right." She touched him on the shoulder. "Let me get one of those."

"I think you have enough baggage to carry already." He didn't turn, but he did pause for a moment. "Let me get this, and you try to leave the rest here on the float."

Katie stood frozen as he moved ahead. Had he really said that to her? And, God forbid, had she heard a smile in those words? Was he laughing at her? She wanted to call out, Just who do you think you are? The moment of rebuttal was gone, though, as he was half up the ramp and leaving her behind.

"Is my cabin still there?" She called to him as she looked up the ramp. It was across the Point on an isolated cove, and they would have to hike to it.

"Yes, ma'am, it is, at least until the next storm. What say you come along and we'll try to find it?" He set one of her bags down and reached to the rope to jangle the bell several times. He turned to look at her and laughed. "I remember you doing that every time I rowed up to your grandmother's float."

Katie remembered, too, although only after he reminded her. That last summer the bell had been her way of telling the entire island that Jeffrey Ragsdale had come to see her. Now it reminded her of the years it had been silent, and all that she'd lost so long ago.

Jeff had already turned, though, picking up the bag, and heading out of sight down the dock. She stood with one hand on the rail, closing her eyes for a moment. She couldn't go back. She couldn't afford to let herself go back. Not ever. She had to be strong.

The distant clang of a sea buoy caught her attention, and she focused on it, looking out towards the open water. Off in the distance the ferry plied the waves, returning to the mainland to pick up another set of intrepid seafaring islanders, either that or day-trippers come to enjoy the summertime delights of island life, imagining that it was really theirs to claim forever.

Seals, she thought. There should be seals. I used to see seals in the Cove, and I need to see seals.

That made her laugh at herself. Fourteen years gone, everything changed, and she wanted to see seals. What did seals have to do with anything?

She knew, though. The seals were always there, a thing that could be trusted. As long as the seals came to Rockhaven, then life would continue. It was permanence she needed, and the seals were that. The seals meant empty foundations and faded teenage crushes didn't matter so much. The seals meant she could go on, and all because they went on.

"Seals," she yelled at the empty ramp. "Where are the seals?"

The answer echoed back at her, "At the cabin," and she laughed. She truly laughed. Of course he would say that. Growing up, they'd always gathered at the cabin to watch the seals. And the whales. And the occasional dolphin. Of course the seals were at the cabin.

How could she have forgotten something as obvious as that?

"So, what is this? The scenic tour?"

They had followed the shore path rather than directly up the hill by Carver House. It was three times the distance, and there were several times they'd had to duck under low-hanging branches.

"I thought you'd appreciate missing what's missing." Jeff glanced at her out of the corner of his eye, and he winked. "If you get what's missing from what I'm not saying."

"My grandmother's house." The pain cut: the hugs upon her arrival each summer, the pies enjoyed, and the love she'd sensed so strongly nowhere else.

"Smart girl. Best not to be reminded of what's missing. Better to be reminded of what's at your side."

"Like you?" She couldn't believe she said that, but she couldn't take it back now, could she? And yet, with her words she felt her grandmother's ache ease into the background.

"Among other things. We're here. You go ahead." He stepped to the side of the path and nodded with his head. "It's yours. You deserve to be first there."

With him holding her bags, and the overhanging trees,

it would be tight, but there was room for her to squeeze by, if barely.

"I deserve to be first, do I?" She took a deep breath. Fourteen years gone. Did she want to be there at all? Oh, she did, or she wouldn't have come, but what evil monsters was she opening the door to? There were a lot under there, too, ones she had barely buried all those years ago.

"Do you still see Ritchey and Janine?" She didn't move forward, and she knew her question for what it was. She was putting off seeing the cabin. If it were falling in, she would be heartbroken. If it weren't, she would be very surprised. A decade and a half wreaked havoc on abandoned island buildings.

"Ritchey and Janine?" Jeff laughed and threw his head back. "Yeah, Janine's still on island, but Ritchey? He got a degree at A&M. Said Texas was as cold as he ever wanted another winter to be, and he wasn't coming back."

"Never?" Ritchey had been Jeff's best friend, inseparable that last summer the boys were fifteen.

"He lied. Once, with his new wife. She complained of the boat rides every time they went into town. I think Ritchey let that be his excuse to abandon us forever."

Us. She heard that. Did us mean us, the islanders, or us, Jeff and her? Was she still a part of the island anymore, or just a tripper, come to soak up the summer's best, then go home to remember how wonderful life could be?

"Poor Ritchey." She smiled as she said it, though. "I'll need to get with Janine while I'm here."

"Four kids, the oldest eleven? Think about that before you call her up. All four are hellions, and I mean that with a capital H. Trust me."

"And you weren't?" They were teasing, like old times, and Katie felt herself slipping back into the familiar rhythms of easy interactions, like the time one of her seals had been sunning on the Carver House float, and when she'd come to take a picture, it had slipped into the water without a sound or ripple.

"I weren't. I was a good boy." He nodded down the path. "I've got your bags, still, and they aren't getting any lighter. If you'll move ahead."

"Sorry. Sure." She touched him on the arm as she stepped past, just enough to make sure he kept his distance from her. A branch caught in her hair, and she ducked lower, attempting to pull it free.

"Here."

She heard a bag drop, and she knew Jeff was untangling her hair from the branch. When he said, "There. All good," she stepped forward, murmuring, "Thanks."

When she emerged from the overgrowth, she felt her heart stop. In that pivotal moment, all her years of mainland life faded away. It was the summer she'd turned fourteen, with all the specialness of life on Rockhaven Island rolled in.

The stone path, half of exposed island granite, and the rest revealing odd-shaped stone pieces carried in one at a time and now surrounded by mossy soil, meandered toward the shore. Giant spruce rose up on the island side, and wild roses blanketed the seaward outcropping. Sheltered down the hill, just at the edge of the water, was her cabin, with shingled walls weathered to gray, the wooden roof brown and mossy with age, and wild ferns and white turtlehead along the foundation. Beyond stretched the sea, with a glimpse of Dyer's Rock to the left and Spurgeon Light to the right. The rush of water against the rocks whispered memories that carried her back to a happier time.

"Beautiful, I know. It's not changed, has it?" Jeff's voice brought her back to the moment.

Katie got herself under control. It hadn't changed, and that was what was wrong. Even the trim was painted a neat and orderly white, and it should be weathered and peeling. No paint lasted so long in the harshness of brutal island winters and blistering summer days.

"It's too perfect." She snorted at that, hoping he got her question. How was it too perfect? That's what she wanted to know.

"Think your friend will enjoy it?"

There was the laugh again, wrapped up in his words. His question told her more, though. He hadn't missed her comment from before. That was the boy she remembered, one who wove himself in and out of others' conversations, at ease with skipping his attention over the surface of whatever was going on, and never missing anything. It seemed that hadn't changed.

"Anyway," he continued, "I can see you already do. Go ahead. See if the inside's changed much."

"You're having fun with this, aren't you?" She glanced at him, not sure if she was amused or not. She wanted to be, if she could just figure out what was going on. The dock, the path, and now this? Not after years of disuse, it shouldn't be like this. She wanted it to look like this, but it shouldn't. It should be abandoned, like her feelings had been all those years ago. Then she could clear it all away, make it new, and make herself new in the process. This, though? This didn't allow her to change at all. Instead, it made her a teenager once again, and that was very bittersweet. She couldn't have one without the other, and the second half of her fourteenth year hadn't been memorable, not in a good way, anyway.

"Yes, I am." The laughter again, as Jeff answered her question. "Besides, I'm still holding your bags."

"Let me take one of those." She reached and grabbed the handle, only to find the side of her hand was now pressed against his. "Please?"

"How can I refuse please?" Still the laughter in the words. He released the handle.

"Thank you." She caught her breath and let out a long sigh. "Follow me that-a-way, sailor boy." She stepped down the path, the sweetness of moss and crushed clover rising with every step she took, letting herself be drawn into the picture.

"Sailor boy?" His voice was just behind her.

"You like bellboy better? I can give you a tip, then." With her free hand, she pushed her hair back from the side of her face and turned to him. As she did, she caught the sun glinting off the water, and she stopped, looking out to sea. "I remember this. Where have I been for half my life? Oh, this is beautiful."

"I know. I ask myself that question every day."

"You've been here every day. What do you have to miss?"

"You are something else." He grinned. "Every question you ask is exactly the one in my head. You and me? We're on the same page all the way."

Katie shook her head. She didn't know what page Jeff Ragsdale was on, but she'd closed that book long ago. He was on her page for today, but only by accident. Get her bags settled in, and she wouldn't need to see him again. She had her cell phone, a portable solar charger in her bag, and the number for Dyer's Delivery ready to go.

Yeah, Jeff, she thought, as she turned toward the cabin. What could you possibly have missed? You had the island all this time. You had everything I didn't. It was when she stepped onto the deck, swung the screen aside, and opened the cabin door that her underpinnings were blown wide. What she saw inside wasn't what she expected, by any measure.

4

Katie took in the cabin, but that meant she couldn't take it in at all. She stepped in and dropped her bag on a rush-bottomed bench at the foot of the bed, and she laughed.

"You don't like it?" Jeff followed her inside, setting the second bag on the floor beside the bed.

"What's there not to like?" She turned as she looked over the room.

That's all it was, too, a simple one-room cabin, with exposed studs and open rafters; and every wall filled with double-hung windows. The chest she remembered, hand-painted French, brought over by her grandmother from her native homeland. It had endured nearly a century of abuse by Katie and who knew who else, but it was pretty, still. The bench was one she'd picked out at an island tag sale when she was eleven. The chair and desk facing the water had been a grandfather's she didn't remember. The bed, though. It was a queen, at least, with cream-colored linens; a thick comforter and matching dust ruffle; and four plump pillows. It had been two twins before. One for her, and the other for her friend Winnie Catron due on the first ferry in the morning.

"The bed, it's just a blowup." Jeff lifted the corner of

the comforter to expose a hard plastic base with plastic legs. Above it was a quilted mattress. "The mattress looks real, but I had to blow it up with a hand pump."

"A hand pump?" She teased him. It seemed the culprit for all this was coming out.

"It's got an electric one, but I didn't think of that. Out here, no electricity. If it goes down—" He pushed on the top of the bed, his face turning red. "—it'll have to be hand pumped again."

"Oh, my!" She pushed on the bed, then sat on it. It was quite comfortable. "Are you going to come running when I call in the middle of the night? Hey, bellboy, I need my mattress pumped up?"

"I should have planned it better." He brushed his face with his arm and took a deep breath.

"I shouldn't tease. I'm sorry. You did this?" She stood and walked to the windows facing the water. They were open to the sea breeze, and she chuckled. They were clean, too. Of course, he had.

"Um, well, Marc knew I always kept an eye on the place. Squatters, you know. They see a place empty, and they think they can just move in. So, I came out from time to time to give the cabin a presence." He was still on the opposite side of the room.

"Come see this." She tapped the glass. "What's that out there?"

"The Lil' Dude, if I'm not mistaken." He was at her side. "With you coming, I thought you might like to see her out at the mooring."

"My Lil' Dude?" She felt the excitement rising. Lil' Dude was her sailing skiff, a white twelve-foot catboat, to be precise. She'd learned to sail her at nine, and she and Jeff had explored the coves, inlets, and nearby islands with as many people as they could pile aboard. They'd tipped her a few times, too, but that had been part of the fun, if they'd only thought so afterward.

"The same." He sounded pleased.

"You." She looked at him, unable to keep the smile from her face. "Now I can sail to town for groceries. I want to go out and see."

"You gonna swim out?"

"Swim?" She'd done that once at thirteen, but it made her think. "Where's the skiff?"

"Tied to the tree. Go see." He opened the door for her.

Down the gravel beach, there was a small boat, not over eight feet, just out of the water. A rope ran up over the rocks where it wrapped the base of a giant spruce.

"That's not my skiff." She walked across the gravel, calling back, "Where did this come from?"

"An extra. Yours was damaged the first winter you were gone. Nobody remembered it down here, and it was broken up when my dad and I came to check on things that spring. Sorry."

"It's plastic?" She tapped the hull and laughed. "A plastic boat? How brilliant is that? It'll never rust, and it can't leak. Where'd you get this? Bean's?" She reached in and pulled out an oar. It was made of plastic, too.

"Lots of people have these now. Just don't forget to tie it up. Want to row out and see the Dude?"

"Of course I do. Life jackets?"

"Oh, yeah." Jeff stepped into the trees and returned with two orange jackets. He tossed them into the bottom of the boat. "That's taken care of. So, are we off?"

Another thing Katie had forgotten, the wooden locker in the trees. It held life jackets, spare rope, and at one time, even dry towels that her grandmother insisted be changed out every Sunday evening. What else had she forgotten from her distant past?

She didn't get to worry over it, though, because Jeff had the line loose, and he slipped the small boat back until all except the bow was on the water. He held it while Katie climbed inside, then he gave it a shove and leaped in after her.

"Hey!" She grabbed the side of the boat. It rocked seriously sideways before Jeff found his seat. "Careful, big boy."

"I thought it was bellboy." He clipped one oar in, then the other. Pulling, the small boat began moving toward the white sailboat moored in the cove.

"Big boy, bellboy, sailor boy, just get me there high and dry. I don't have a washer. Remember, it burned up over a dozen years ago. It's hand wash while I'm out here this trip."

Then she could see the stern of the boat and the words written in the block script she remembered so well. Lil' Dude. The name had been hers. Her idea, anyway. She and Jeff, and probably Ritchey, had gotten a can of paint that first summer, and pulling the boat up on the float, Jeff had sketched the letters out with pencil, then laboriously, they had filled in the words one painstaking stroke at a time.

The letters were still fresh and perfectly sharp.

"Did you do this, too?" They were coming up beside the catboat, and she grabbed a varnished gunwale. That, too, was perfect. It hadn't been perfect the last time she'd seen it. It had borne five years of harsh, preteen use, and the "crew" hadn't been kind. Someone had put some elbow grease into her.

"My dad and me. We knew you'd be back some day, so we took care of her." He sounded proud.

"Your dad, how is he?" She remembered a weathered version of the way Jeff looked now. Gruff, but then that was the way of island men. The sea and long winters made them that way. The island hadn't turned Jeff, it didn't seem, but then maybe it had, and she was seeing him as she remembered him, rather than as what he was.

"Four years ago, we had an ice storm. It killed power to Otter's Reach." He was tying up to the mooring, and it seemed that was all he had to say.

"Your dad was helping?" She prompted him, watching his strong hands working the line, loop-loop-and-under. When he looked up, she understood what had happened.

"They needed him, and he went. He never came home." His eyes were red, but he shrugged and smiled. "That's my dad. Stuff happens, and you go on. Now, onto your yacht, Dame Carver."

"I *am* going to push you overboard." She gave his shoulder a shove as she stepped into the Lil' Dude, laughing when the small dinghy rocked dangerously. "It's your own fault if you fall in, you know."

"And it's your own fault if I take you in with me. Let's go for a sail."

He leaped into the Dude, light-footed as Katie remembered him all those summers ago, and he landed with the preservers in one hand.

"For you," he handed her one, "and for me." He dropped his at his feet.

"Take me out, Captain." She smiled, enjoying the breeze and the memories of good times forgotten. She waved her hand at him permissively as he stood at the mast untying the sail.

"Thank you, Katie," he said. "I think I will."

She heard his words, and she heard her name. It was the way he said it, as if she had given him more than just permission to sail her boat. She groaned inside. What had she promised herself? Just this one day, and she didn't have to see him again?

She hoped she hadn't just tied an anchor around her heart, one that would sink her when it was time to leave the island. And she would leave. She had no place to stay, not for more than a weekend, anyway. All that had been stolen from her over a dozen years ago.

As she took the line from Jeff and looped it through a pulley on the stern, the wind caught the sail, and the small boat surged forward. Grinning, Jeff dropped beside her and took the line, pulling it taut, and sending the boat flying. It was wonderful to be back on the water, but Katie couldn't help but wonder, how would it feel when it all came to an end? Everything did. Nothing was forever, especially the things she loved the most.

If not for that reminder, her day out sailing in her prized and much-loved sailing skiff would have been absolutely perfect, the sort of day most people wished for and never got.

It had taken Katie fourteen years to get it back, and now, she wasn't sure just how it was going to end. Once they hit open water, it was the spray that made her forget all that. The boat leaped over a swell, and when it came down, the shower of sea water flew over the boat, dousing them both.

"Jeff, no!" she cried. "I can't get wet!"

"Sorry, Dame. Already done."

He was laughing, and she couldn't be angry. She was laughing, too. She let her self-control relax just a bit. Today, she told herself, just for this one afternoon, I won't wish for it to be over. I'll just enjoy myself as much as I can.

She was home, after all. She had been away too many years, and she had finally returned. For that, she could give in for just this one fun and irresponsible afternoon.

Real life could come calling later. It always did, one way or another. Just not while she was out in the Lil' Dude.

The Lil' Dude was meant for fun, and that's what she intended to have.

5

"Winnie! Winnie, Winnie, Winnie!" Katie squealed with excitement only to hear her own name yelled back at her.

"Katie! Katie, Katie, Katie!" Winnie Catron was exiting the ferry, and she dropped her two cases and raised her arms overhead to wave them back and forth. The man behind her was talking into his phone, and he barely avoided tripping over the abandoned luggage.

Katie grinned as her friend apologized profusely to the man—probably much more than precisely necessary – before yanking her far-too-large luggage out of the way and running clumsily her direction on too-high heels.

"Winnie! You made it, finally!" Katie threw her arms around her friend.

"Sweetie, I couldn't *not* make it. Too bad I couldn't bring my car over. I'm mad at you about that, you know. These bags, whew!" She turned one on its side, and sitting on it, she worked one of her shoes off. "And these, not a good idea for that boat out there. Did you know it goes up and down the entire time it's moving? Can't they pick the smooth spot to drive on? I'm not getting on another boat until I leave this island, you can bet your bottom dollar."

31

Katie could see the problem. Her friend's shoes had six inch spikes, with straps that wrapped the ankles. At least no one would miss seeing them. They were neon blue. However, there was another issue, and she thought she'd better address it right away.

"Honey, I don't think that's possible." Katie grimaced at what she knew was coming. After all, she'd barely convinced her friend to join her. Family estate; summer vacation; you owe me this; she'd pulled out all her favor cards to convince her friend to tag along. And now she thought she wasn't getting on another boat until she left the island.

"You don't think what's possible?"

"The boat thing." Katie grabbed the handle of one of the cases and extended it, glad they put wheels on them. They had a ways to walk back into town. And they were walking. The parking lot was emptying as she spoke. If they waited much longer, they'd be the only ones in sight.

"So, where's our taxi?" Winnie had her shoe back on, and she stood, pulling her own case up and popping out the handle. "And I need somewhere to do my hair. It's out of control."

"Out of control?" Katie laughed. "Honey, your hair is never under control." If anything, her friend's hair was bigger than she'd ever seen it, an exuberant strawberry halo only tamed by two giant blue combs that matched her shoes.

"Anyway," Winnie sniffed, "about that taxi. I'm ready to get to the manor house. I need some R and R after that little boat ride over here."

"You want to stop in town and get a lobster roll?" Katie had begun making her way out of the parking lot by then, and Winnie was following. She hoped to get as far as possible before she had to reveal all her bad news.

"A lobster roll?" Winnie slapped one leg and hooted. "A lobster roll? What a punch line! Now tell me the joke. What is it, something like, how does a lobster get off a mountain? He does the lobster roll?"

"Don't be silly. It's a sandwich. We need to get

something to eat before we head out to the house." Really, they did. She had yet to pick up any food. Breakfast this morning—in town, thank you very much—had been truly breaking a fast. She'd gone without eating since boarding the ferry the day before.

"I'll get a sandwich when we get to your grandma's."

"The kitchen is, um, has limited facilities. There." They had made it to Main Street, and Katie pointed to a little take-out window. "That's the local sandwich joint. They have fried chicken, too. My treat." She held up her pocketbook and waved it in the air.

"Sweetie, what did you do to your nails?" Winnie grabbed her hand and held it still. "I know these nails did not rip themselves off without your help. Clams. Have you been digging for clams or something?"

"The ferry driver hit a rough patch in the road, and I forgot my file. I just haven't chewed them even, yet." She shook her hand loose. "Lobster roll or fried chicken?"

Winnie shrugged. "Taxi's my choice, but if you insist, I'll roll the dice. Get it? Roll the dice?"

"I get it." Katie rolled her eyes. She stepped up to the window. "Two lobster rolls with drinks and fries."

"Sauce?" came the reply.

"Sure," she said before handing over her money and collecting her change. "We'll be here at the tables." There were four picnic tables lining the street. Winnie was already parked with her shoe off again.

"We'll bring it out." The girl smiled and waved Katie away.

"Not much to it, is there?" Winnie called to her. "I mean, it's pretty and all, in a *Perfect Storm* sort of way, but who would want to live here?"

"Keep your voice down." Katie slid in next to her. "All these people want to live here. Me? I lived here every summer until I was fourteen."

"Oh, you poor sweetie! No wonder you are like you are!" Winnie put her hand on Katie's arm and clucked in a reassuring manner.

"Stop that!" Katie shook her off. "Wait till we get out to

the Point. You'll see how beautiful all this is."

"So, tell me. Your grandma's house. Is it rebuilt?" Winnie's eyes sparkled. "You showed me those pictures. I imagine it brand new, with white clapboards, and a grand piano in the living room. Maybe a jetted tub in the bath. Could I ever use a jetted tub about now. And a feather mattress. That would make that boat ride out here worth it."

"We have to discuss that feather mattress." Katie was interrupted by the arrival of their food, and she spread it out between them. "Here, one Harbor View lobster roll deluxe, and one caffeine-spiked soda, for your island enjoyment."

"All right, I cave. This actually looks good. Coming in I thought I saw a white steeple. Is that church for Sunday?" Winnie took a sip of her drink, and then she bit into her sandwich. She wiped mayo from the corner of her mouth and smiled. "Oh, never mind church. I'm already in heaven. Thank you, Jesus, for bringing me heaven on earth, right here with my good friend Katie."

"Thank you, Winnie. With that sacrilegious talk, I'm making sure to have you in church on Sunday. Maybe even Sunday school." She grinned. If anything, her friend was more faithful than she was. Now, though, she eyed her friend's cases. Two of them, and they were very big. Too big to get back to the Point. Way too big.

"So," Winnie crumpled her paper wrapper, "I'm finished. Do you want to call the taxi, or shall I?" She pulled out her cell phone and held it up. "What's the number?"

"Call all you want." Katie reached and pushed the cell phone to the top of the table. "No taxi's taking you to Carver Point."

"No? I'll pay double. Else how'll we get there?" She tapped her phone. "Siri, find me a local taxi." She smirked in satisfaction.

"So, what's the number?" Katie peered at the phone's screen. She knew what it'd say. This was an island. A very small island. How many taxi companies did her friend think did business on an island?

The response finally came through. "Dyer's Delivery is

all I can find, open Monday, Wednesday, and Friday. Would you like to schedule a delivery tomorrow morning?"

"What?" Winnie shook the phone. "Has Siri gone stupid or something? Okay, here I go again. Siri, find me—"

Katie covered her phone with her hand. "Honey, that *is* the taxi company. It's a boat, and it only runs three days a week. The other two it's over on East Haven, our sister island. Sorry."

"No taxi?" Winnie shook her head back and forth, setting her hair vibrating in the sun. "You brought me to a place with no taxis?"

"Not much else, either, I'm afraid. Those are very big suitcases. Do you need them both at the house tonight?" She refused to say cabin. Winnie needed the bad news metered out in very small doses.

"I packed light." Winnie huffed. "My blow drier and hair care supplies, along with my electric blanket." She tapped one of the cases with a smug smile. "See? I was paying attention. You said it might get cold at night. Oh, and extra shoes for Sunday. And in this case," she tapped the other one, "fresh clothes for each day, and I brought a few movies and my tablet. You do have WiFi, right?"

"Ri-ight." Katie drew out the word and rolled her eyes. She hoped Winnie took the bad news well. She didn't have a bed for her to sleep on, not a real one, anyway.

"Is this seat taken?"

Katie froze. She knew that voice. She caught Winnie's eyes, to see her grinning and pointing with a poorly concealed finger behind Katie.

"No, this seat is not taken." Katie called her response without looking. She had looked yesterday and given in. Today? She was avoiding that pitfall at all costs.

"Good. The busboy needs to sit." Jeff did, and he slid a plate of fried chicken tenders onto the table. "I see you two ladies had takeout. I prefer the dine-in plate, even if I take it out."

"Ooh, Katie. You know this man?" Winnie's words were buttery, and she winked. "If so, you can introduce me anytime."

"Winnie, Jeff. Jeff, Winnie, my friend here for the rest of the week." She still refused to look.

"Winnie." Jeff held his hand over the table to shake. "Katie told me about you, and it was all good."

"Oh?" Winnie's face brightened. "That's different. I'm glad to meet you, Jeff." She reached back and took his hand, holding it definitely longer than was precisely necessary.

Katie kicked her under the table before she let go. After their sailing expedition, she had sent Jeff on his way, showing him her phone and solar charger, that and the number for Dyer's. With the Lil' Dude, she'd chirped, she'd be fine on her own, so he needn't give her another thought.

She'd been fine for about three hours. Then she'd climbed between the sheets in her newly-made bed, and all she'd been able to think of was Jeff tying the knot on the mooring, Jeff reaching to untie the sails, Jeff laughing as spray doused them repeatedly. She could have had that, she knew, a lifetime of years ago. Now he was a fisherman, she had her Boston life, and she wasn't an island girl any longer. They could pretend, but they could never put back together what had been stolen from them.

By the time she'd thrashed herself to sleep, she'd blamed her parents, herself, and God. And she'd vowed she'd go out of her way to avoid Jeff the whole time she was on the island.

Now he'd found her out. This was not the place she needed to be at this time.

"So, for the third time, Katie Carver, how long have you known this handsome hunk?"

Katie blinked. For the third time? Where was her brain? And hunk? She blurted out before she knew what she was saying, "Hunk? Are you sexist? Good heavens, Winnie. He's just a boy I knew when I was a kid. Give me a break."

She stood and turned away. She still hadn't looked at him. She couldn't, not and walk away, and she had to walk away. She had to.

36

"I can move to a different table."

It was his voice. The same voice that had teased her the day before, the same voice she'd laughed with and that had made her feel so good. Would he haunt her entire week on the island?

God, why send him my way after all these years?

"No, you can't. I don't know anything about you, and you know all about me. It's not fair for you to leave now."

Katie knew *that* voice, too. It was her friend who would soon be her so-called friend if she kept butting in.

"Stay, Jeff. The lobster disagreed with me, and I need to catch some air. Winnie, toss the trash when you're finished." She reached for her wallet only to find empty table, and she cringed at having to turn and find it. Her eyes were burning, and she didn't dare let Jeff see. Then, someone slid the wallet under her fingers, just for moment touching her skin to skin before pulling away.

"Later, Katie, maybe?" It was Jeff again.

"Sure. Maybe. Thank you." She hadn't kept the quaver out of her voice that time, and she fled, walking across the street and through the town parking lot to stand at the water's edge.

The town was spread before her, hugging the rocky shoreline. Many of the shorefront dwellings had colorful shutters, some with contrasting doors. A number wore white clapboards, with just as many covered with weathered shingles. Summer boats of all sorts were attached to moorings leading toward the mouth of the harbor. It was so idyllic, she could not imagine she had stayed away her entire adult life.

She felt her control break. Why, why, why, God? How can I forgive you for what you took from me? This was mine, and then it was gone. Now you tease me with that man back there. It's not fair.

"Sweetie, are you okay?"

She felt an arm across her shoulders, and she straightened her face. She couldn't do anything about her burning eyes, but she could put on a good show. "Hey. I guess it's my hay fever. It gets me on the island every

37

summer." She sniffled her best hay fever sniffle, and she laughed, hoping it didn't come across as too forced. "I should have brought my inhaler."

"Well, we're all taken care of. I told Jeff you were worried about my cases, and he said he'd bring them out. Sweetie, I don't know what bad blood there is between you two, because he seemed really sweet, but I know an old wound when I see one. You need me more than I thought. I'm here for you, no matter what, for the rest of the week. I won't leave your side." Winnie spoke softly and patted Katie's arm the entire time. "Remember, God loves you no matter what flowed under all those long-ago bridges."

"Sure. God loves me. I'll keep telling myself that. See that boat down there?" Katie pointed at the town float below where they stood.

"Which one, Sweetie?"

"The white one. It says Lil' Dude on the back end."

"Sure, that little bitty one. What a cute little toy. What about it?"

"That's our taxi ride home." Katie felt her eyes well up. First Jeff, and now having to tell Winnie this? How bad did she have to feel before God quit squeezing her heart in his hand?

Winnie took a deep breath and let it out. "Okay, Sweetie, if you say so. Jeffie told me I might be riding back on a little bitty boat, no thanks to a warning from you. At least it's a cute one. Shall we get started?"

"Oh, you are a good friend." Katie gave her friend a big hug, even ignoring the mass of hair that got in her way. "I wouldn't trade you for anyone."

"I hoped you'd say that. Right now I'd trade you for a taxi with real wheels, though. How 'bout that?"

"Oh, you!" Katie pushed her friend away. "I'm sorry about that. The last time I was here there was a road to the house. It's impassable now. Everything becomes overgrown almost overnight. You really don't mind riding out with me? That's the boat I learned to sail on when I was nine."

"Sure! That's makes it even better. I'm scared of a boat even a nine-year-old can sail. What can be worse than that?

Oh, and your Jeffie is gone. You can turn around now."

Katie frowned at that. Jeffie? Her Jeffie? Somebody had to be straightened out, and it had to happen soon, just not before she got Winnie onto that boat. This might be a trip to scare the devil out of a person, or Jesus into them. Dear God, she breathed. Please let this be the easiest trip I ever made.

After all, if He couldn't answer the hard prayers, maybe He would give in and answer an easy one. Besides, this was for Winnie's sake, not hers.

For Winnie, please God? For Winnie's sake?

Then she remembered. Before they sailed away, they had to have food, and the store was right behind them.

"Honey, want to go shopping with me?" She smiled at her friend.

"Oh, Sweetie, I thought you'd never ask. I adore shopping!"

I bet you do, thought Katie. I really bet you do.

6

Katie had forgotten about the tides.

Her excuse was fourteen years off island. No matter her reason, the result was a wild fight once they approached the little cove in front of the cabin. The tide tugged the Lil' Dude one way, and Katie fought to force her another, the way of the mooring where the little dinghy was tied.

Poor Winnie wailed the entire time.

"We're going to die!" Winnie had her head between her knees, and her face was green in the gills.

"No, we're not. Keep your head down." That was important, too, because tacking repeatedly meant the sail had to swing to port, then to starboard, then back again, even as Katie forced the rudder left and right to offset the push of the wind.

Equally hard was keeping the small craft upright with a dead body, er, dead weight sitting next to her.

"Duck! We're almost there!" Katie threw the rudder to the side and yanked the canvas sail over Winnie's head.

"I am ducked! I can't go any lower! Oh, I'm going to die!"

"Hold this. Pull it tight." Katie pushed the line into her friend's hand and leaped forward. "I'm tying off. You survived, you know."

"I did?" Winnie looked up.

Katie had hold of the mooring buoy, and she was pulling the line from the bow and attaching it to the mooring, loop-loop-tuck. She grinned. She stood and bunched the sail next to the mast and began securing it. "Now we get to switch boats."

"Here, in the ocean?" A new level of green painted Winnie's face. "I, I might fall into the water. Oh, oh, oh! Something's in the water." Her eyes grew wide as she looked to the back of the boat and tracked something up the other side.

"A seal! Oh, Winnie, this is so wonderful. I knew there had to be seals!" Growing up, Katie had looked for them every year, and she never felt like she was on the island, really here, until she saw her first one, and here it was.

"Will it, oh, oh, it's back! Will it . . . turn us over?" Winnie held to both sides of the boat, and her knuckles were white with fear.

"Not if you sing to it. They like *Hush-a-bye Baby*." Katie refused to roll her eyes, but she was tempted. Seals were the gods of the sea, and there was nothing better, at least not to her.

"Hush-a-bye baby, don't you cry . . . down in the meadow, with little round eyes . . ." Winnie tracked the seal, her voice high-pitched and whispered.

"Not exactly, but it's working." Katie grinned. "Keep it up while I move our groceries." It was helping her friend stay occupied, at least. She dropped four shopping bags into the little plastic boat, and then she motioned to her friend. "Now, before the big, bad seal gets us. Hurry, Winnie!"

"Oh, it's back! I have to keep singing. Hush-a-bye baby . . . oh, it's looking at me! Can it tell I don't know all the words?"

"I can tell you don't know *any* of the words." Katie held Winnie's hand, but she was over by that point. "Now sit so I can come over."

"Okay. Hush-a-bye baby, sweet little seal. I don't want . . . to be your next meal . . ."

"He's gone. You can stop, now." Katie snapped the oars in place and gave the line one last tug to free it. Then she pulled, and the boat surged slowly forward.

"Oh, he's following us." Winnie pointed. "Oh, oh! Hush-a-bye sealie, go go away . . ."

"He's your friend for life, Honey. You bewitched him with that voice." About then the little dinghy crunched gravel, and Katie snapped the oars loose and dropped them in the floor. "Sit still while I get out."

"Don't leave me!"

"With all our groceries? No way. Now hold still." She jumped over the bow, her feet crunching the wet stones, and she yanked the small boat forward. "Now, your hand, Honey. I'll help you out."

"Please. Oh, I've never been so scared in my life." Winnie grabbed Katie's hand and stumbled out of the boat, still in her blue heels.

"Me, either. I was out there with a mad woman."

"Who? I didn't see another boat anywhere." Winnie patted her hair, taking a deep breath and looking around. Back on solid ground, her color was quickly returning to normal.

Katie tucked her chin and looked at her friend. "Who? You have to ask who? Who was singing a bedtime song to a fish?"

"It was your idea, and a seal is not a fish."

"But you *were* singing." Katie grinned.

"And these are groceries. Can we talk about a refrigerator, and a stove, and maybe hot chocolate with mallows? Now, that's a good conversation." Winnie reached into the boat and looped the bags across her palm, lifting them up to hold them over her shoulder. "Is there anything else I can help you with, Sweetie?"

"Step out of the way. I have to tie up the boat." She yanked it across the gravel, barely missing her friend's legs, and causing her to jump sideways with a screech. "Don't be a baby. I missed you by a mile."

"An inch. You can pull that boat all by yourself?"

"It's just plastic. It's not heavy."

"Plastic?" Winnie kicked it with her foot. "You had me in the ocean in a plastic boat? That's dangerous! How could you?" She sniffled. "I should have ridden back with your nice Jeffie after all. He offered, you know."

"Well, he's not my Jeffie, so it doesn't matter." Winnie had finally gotten on her nerves, and Katie let her cross feelings be heard. "I told you before, I knew him growing up, and I haven't seen him for fourteen years."

"Oh. Then it doesn't matter that he likes you." Winnie slipped out of her shoes and held them in one hand, with the bags still in the other. "Or did you even notice?"

"There's nothing to notice." Katie busied herself with a knot tying up the small boat. The thing was, she had noticed.

"Okay. I'll play your game. Well, that hunk you haven't noticed is coming out of that little building down the beach." Winnie pointed with the hand holding her blue shoes. "I think he's looking this way, and I think it's right at you. I bet he notices." She giggled.

"Heaven help me." Katie closed her eyes and shook her head. If Jeff was here, there was no way to avoid looking at him. Why didn't he just stay away? Oh, she'd forgotten. It was thanks to her friend who had packed two bags of electronics that were useless here on the Point.

"Katie! Winnie!" Jeff called to them, his hand in the air waving. "Or are we back to Dame Carver?"

"Don't you start, Jeff! I mean it!" Katie put her hands on her hips and glared at the raggedy-haired man standing on her deck.

"Dame Carver?" Winnie giggled again. "This is almost worth that boat ride out here."

"I dropped off your bags, and I left a few other things, too. I'll leave you two ladies to settle in. I haven't forgotten our lobster bake this weekend." He waved cheerily, and with a grin, he turned and took off running up the hill.

When he was gone, Winnie stepped to the water's edge and looked up and down the beach. She turned back to Katie with a frown. "No boat. Where's he going?"

"The dock's on the other side of the Point. He's

43

probably over there. Trust me. Jeff can find his own way home." Thank goodness he had taken off, too. Then it hit her. A few other things? What things would he have left for them? "I want to see what he's been up to. Follow me." She motioned to Winnie and started toward the cabin.

"Not so fast. This place is cute." Winnie followed her to the deck and dropped her shoes before turning to take in the ocean view. "A lighthouse and everything. I can't imagine how super your grandma's house must be."

"Oh, my!" Katie had the door open by then, and she could barely get out the words.

"What's inside that's so special?"

"Lights." Katie laughed, and it was rather high-pitched and manic, even to her. "We have lights."

"That's special?" Winnie stepped up and peered over her shoulder. "Oh, this is so cute. Who stays here?"

"How can we have lights?" Katie stepped inside. There were two floor lamps, one on each side of the bed, both glowing with yellow electric light. "We don't have lights. I can't have lights."

"Sweetie, I hate to tell you this, but you do have lights. One, two. You can count them on two fingers." Winnie held up her hand, lifting one finger, then a second. "At least that's the way I learned in kindergarten."

"You don't understand." Katie moved to the far side of the bed to see a large plug box on the floor and pushed up against the wall, with an equally large black cord disappearing underneath the bed. "We never had electricity on the Point. Just candles and oil lamps."

"Well, these are the real things." Winnie looked under one shade. "Yep, glass bulbs and all."

"Shush!" Katie put her fingers to her lips. "What's that?" A low sound, one that shouldn't be there, made the floorboards vibrate. "Turn that light out." She flipped the one on her side of the bed.

"Whatever." Winnie shrugged and flipped the light off. The vibration stopped.

"Now, listen." Katie turned hers back on. The vibration started up again. "That's a generator, if I know my electricity."

"Okay, and that means?"

"It means I'm finding that generator." Katie stamped out the door and circled the little cabin. Sure enough, there in the shadowy darkness, resting on four blocks at the back of the building, was a little gasoline generator humming away. "Ooh, Jeff," she growled.

"Jeffie did this?" Winnie was at the corner of the structure with her arms crossed and her giant mane of hair silhouetted against the light coming off the ocean. "If that means I can run my curling iron, then he's a better man than you give him credit for. Yea, Jeffie!" She began to clap her hands.

"He wants something, that's all." Katie brushed past her to stand in the light. Why can't he not do stuff for me? she pleaded to God, if no one else. All she wanted was to be here for the week, try to find what she'd lost, and move on with her life. She didn't need mired in the past all over again.

"Like a lobster bake?" Winnie draped an arm around Katie and put her chin on her shoulder. She whispered, "What's so bad about a lobster bake? That sounds pretty good to me."

What was so bad about a lobster bake? Nothing, Katie thought, looking out to sea at the lighthouse, brilliantly lit on one side, and shadowed on the other. It's what's in the shadows that's the problem. It's feelings that I had to bury half a lifetime ago, and I don't know what might boil back up if someone scratches hard enough. She grabbed her friend's arms and squeezed them. Then she forced a laugh, pulling free and turning back to the cabin.

"This is it, you know. You keep asking about my grandmother's house, and this is all that's left. We get to share it for the week, just you and me." She was bright; and she stepped to the deck, threw back the screen door, and struck a pose. "Welcome, mademoiselle, to my humble abode. Underneath this roof is where we'll spend our time for our week on the island." Then she felt her face crack, and the tears began to flow.

"Sweetie, what?" Winnie reached to her to put her arms around her friend.

"I lied to you. Well, not lied, but I showed you those old pictures, and I let you think all that was still here. Well, it's not. It burned down a long time ago, and this is where we're staying. We don't even have a bathroom!" She began to sob.

"You got a tree?"

"A tree? There are tons of trees. How's a tree going to help?" Katie sniffled and wiped at her eyes.

"You got a tree, and that's all we need." Winnie giggled. "Well, not all, but we'll manage. We're women, after all. We can do this!"

"Thank you, Winnie. I'm being melodramatic, and I'm sorry. I can do better than a tree." Katie smiled at the idea of using a tree. Men, yes. Women, no. "There's an outhouse just down the path."

"Oh, then we're high style. An outhouse *and* electricity. What can be better than that?" Winnie primped her hair. "Now, where did you say the kitchen is? We've got groceries to put away."

Katie shook her head. "That's something else I didn't get a chance to tell you . . ."

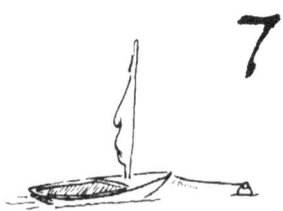

7

"Jeffie" had been more than a "dear." In spite of herself, Katie had finally admitted that to Winnie. She had groused the whole time, though.

It was the tiny refrigerator that won her over, more than the lamps and even more than the folding bed they'd finally noticed nestled behind the door.

Now, though, Winnie's electric blanket was keeping both of them warm.

"Another one, there. See it, Winnie?" Katie pointed overhead. In the city-free sky, the stars were brilliant diamonds on velvet. There was a meteor shower in place, and they were snuggled up on the deck, trying to be the first to see each one.

"That's six for you, and none for me." Winnie pulled her tablet from under the electric blanket and tapped another checkmark by Katie's name.

"Just watch. They're there." Katie jabbed her finger at the sky. "There, I think. Maybe . . . no, maybe not." She giggled. "Sorry. That's an airplane. See the flashing light?"

"I don't know if any of them are real. I think you're making them all up." Winnie tucked the tablet back away and pulled the blanket tighter under her chin. "I mean, like, it's summer, and it's cold out here."

"It's Maine. What'd you expect? I love it like this."

"Oh, I guess I expected a big white house, a claw-foot tub, and maybe a footman and a scullery maid." She giggled. "I didn't get any of those, did I?"

"You got me." Katie pulled her friend's arm close and squeezed it.

"So, are you ready to talk?"

"Talk?" Katie suspected she knew what about. And no, she wasn't ready to talk.

"Come, girl. We've been friends for a hundred years, and you never told me you once had a boyfriend who looked like your Jeffie. Now I want to know everything. I deserve it after you tortured me with that boat ride out here."

"He wasn't a boyfriend. We were a pack of wild animals, prowling the dark undersides of the island." If she made a joke of it, it was easier to tell, and she laughed at the idea of the island having any dark undersides at all. It had been fun and adventure to her, trailing after Jeff and his friends all summer long.

"That just makes it better. Two don't make a pack. Who else was there?"

"Besides me and Jeff? Janine. She's still on the island, and with four wild animals of her own, according to Jeff. Jeff's best friend Ritchey is in Texas. He said he needed to thaw for a few decades."

"Thaw?"

"Remember? Maine? You think it's cold now. It's summer. Try January and ten below."

"No thanks. I want the warm months only. Anyone else?"

Winnie really did sound interested, and the names began coming back to Katie. She told of them all. Apple Dumpling. They laughed, and Katie assured her friend that was really her name. She was conceived under an apple tree or something.

And Austie Williams, tall and lanky, the oldest of the bunch. Maybe a year older than Jeff, but with the presence of a high school boy. He wanted to be a pilot, but she had no idea what had become of his dreams. Yes, she could find out, but after so long, he wouldn't remember her, anyway.

The Reynolds twins were the pranksters. Bennie and Bobby, they wore matching shorts, and they'd switch shirts all day long, until no one knew which one was which. Heaven help them if they both married. Their wives would never know if they had the correct husband. Ritchey could always tell, but then Ritchey had an eye for faces that no one else did.

Babes Baker was the beauty of the bunch. A year younger than Katie, she'd gotten in trouble that final summer. Just a kid, her parents had sent her off island so no one would know. Maybe the adults hadn't clued in, but the gang all knew. It was Babes, and that meant it was obvious.

"How sad. Thirteen and saddled with a reputation." Winnie sat up, pointing. "There, I see one. A shooting star, and a big one."

"Good for you." Katie cheered her friend's success. "I told you they were up there."

"So, you and Jeffie. What was your connection back then?"

"There was no connection. We were part of the same pack, and at the end of the summer, we all went our separate ways, except the islanders, of course. They never talked about their winters here. Summer was summer, and that's what we were, summer friends."

"Oh, don't give me that. You said he's a year older. He must have been like a big brother, or a crush or something. You've got to tell me what it's about. Make it up, if you have to, but I want a juicy story."

"You're a hopeless romantic. That's your problem." Katie smiled. She had so admired the boy she'd known back then. And she had mourned when he was gone. She couldn't go through that again.

"Did you ever hold hands in the moonlight?" Winnie nudged her.

"Oh, you! We might have dug clams in the moonlight, but that's all, and trust me, there's nothing romantic about digging for clams, either in the moonlight or on a sunny day. It stinks, because the mud you dig in is the same mud they defecate in."

"Ooh! TMI, Sweetie. I'll never eat another clam again." Winnie visibly shivered.

Katie laughed. It served her friend right, probing for information she had no right trying to dig out of her past. Anyway, it was time for bed, and there was a nice, soft mattress calling. With the generator, she didn't even have to worry about phoning for a bellboy in the middle of the night. Jeff had hooked up the electric pump. She was going to be safely ensconced, wrapped up in her island dreams all night long.

"Okay, Honey, let's pack it in. Dawn comes early on the island."

"Sure." Winnie yawned. "How early?"

"Five-ish, right through these windows. Visit the potty if you need to. I have a flashlight."

"Five-ish, huh? What happened to seven-ish?"

"Move to Florida." Katie pulled the blanket to her and unplugged the cord. Absently, she began to fold it in half then half again. "You want this tonight?"

"Sure." Winnie took it. "You don't mind the fold-away?"

"Yes, I mind the foldaway very much. Good try." It was already set up with Winnie's things. They'd pushed the big bed to the side, and that left just enough space for the smaller one. It was the lack of blinds that was going to be the problem. There were none. The roll-down shades Katie remembered from her childhood had apparently rotted clean away. The hooks were there, but the shades were nowhere to be seen.

Happy sunshine in the morning! It would be, too, whether they liked it or not!

8

It was the smell of food that pulled Katie from her island dreams. Then, maybe the smell of food was part of her island dreams.

She pushed the covers aside, only to have a fragment of morning sun hit her in the face. The trees to the east were some protection, and moving her head sideways was all it took to find relief. The cold? It was freezing outside of the bedclothes. Only the midday sun would provide any relief for that.

"Winnie?" It really was food. She could still smell it.

"Umm." The sound moaned from under the tumble of electric blanket rumpled across the small bed. There was a click from the controller, and outside, the generator whirred on.

"I smell food. Have you been up?"

"Umm. Takeout, maybe." The mound moved, but no one came out, and the words were muffled.

"Via helicopter, if so." Katie pushed the covers aside and stood, finding her slippers for her feet. The floor was cold. She pulled an old pink terry robe around her, the one concession she'd made for the cool nights. She'd remembered how cold it got even on the warmest summer days, and it was worth the baggage space.

Out across the water, the top of the lighthouse was just catching the sun. The Dude was still in full shade. The cabin didn't catch the sunrise, and from here, she had always judged the time of day from the top of the lighthouse. She guessed five-forty, give or take fifteen. The thrub thrub of a motor floated across the water, the sound finding its way in through a window that hadn't wanted to close completely the night before. In the distance the wake of a lobster boat cut a path in the ocean.

"Island morning," she whispered as she yawned. "I still smell food."

"Breakfast?" A hand peeked out of Winnie's covers, the fingers wiggled, and it withdrew back into its shell.

"I sure didn't cook." Still, while the smells of cooking sometimes carried from houses across the cove on the south side of the Point, from this side? She'd never noticed it before. Then, she'd rarely overnighted in the cabin, either, so maybe it was something that was always here, and she'd never been around to smell it.

She stepped to the door and pulled it open. The smell of spruce and pine and clover—and the barest continued hint of breakfast—surrounded her, and she smiled. "I'm stepping outside, Honey. Stay warm."

"Kay." The fingers wiggled again before disappearing. The control clicked, and the whirring from the generator died away, leaving the lapping of the water against the rocks as the only song of the morning.

Outside was where she found the cause of the smell. An insulated bag sat on the deck with a note attached to the handle. She turned it over to read, "Thought you might like a hot breakfast." Out of the bag came the wonderful smell of sausage, eggs, and muffins, just like Harbor View had served up on cool summer mornings all those years ago.

"Your fairy godfather's been by. There's hot food when you're ready." Katie stepped inside to set the bag on the desk before moving back to the deck. Stuffing her hands in her pockets, she removed her slippers and stepped to the rocks just off the deck. The tide was high this morning, and it lapped right at her feet. Down the beach, the little plastic dinghy floated at the end of its tether.

She wasn't happy. She knew where that food had come from, the same place as the generator, the extra bed, and the little fridge. She didn't intend to eat a bite of it, either. What made it worse was that she should be grateful. She wanted to be grateful, but she couldn't. Every little thing was like another string connecting her to a past she was desperate to forget, tying her down and refusing to let her go. She saw the checkmarks lining up in her head, a whole row of favors Jeff could call in. Each one made it more and more difficult to push him away. She didn't want to be in his debt. She didn't want to be in anyone's debt.

She found a spot where the sun hit her face, and she closed her eyes and pulled her arms around her. For a moment, she let the sounds and smells of the island push the painful connections away: her old summer friends, the house she hadn't yet found the courage to explore the remains of, and the God she had yet to forgive for not taking care of something that had been really important to her. None of that mattered; the important thing now was being here at this moment in time. The island was forever, like her seals, always the same, the waves returning hour after hour, just waiting on her to remember them.

Carver Point had waited, too, fourteen years. It had waited, welcomed her back, and wrapped its arms around her. It was the in between that got in the way.

"Look at you out there." The screen door opened and slammed.

"Hey. You're awake. Find your breakfast?" Katie didn't look.

"I'm eating it." Winnie crunched the gravel beside her, one hand wrapped around a partially eaten muffin sandwich, and the other holding her phone and doing something with her thumb. She held it in front of her, and the device made several clicking sounds. "There, got some pictures I can post. Took one of you. See?"

"In this old thing?" Katie looked, and sure enough, there she was, in her pink terry, looking out across the water, with the lighthouse in the distance. "Feel free to erase that."

"No way." Winnie wiggled the sandwich. "This is good. I liked the note. I guess, Jeffie?"

"Probably." Katie kept her tone even. Jeffie. Harrumph was what she thought. "Lobstermen get out early, and I guess he thought he was being kind. You know, your first morning. Eat it all, but don't expect it again." She would make sure of that. Anyway, when he realized she didn't want to see him, he would fade out of the picture fast enough. Silly summer girl, didn't even have a house or money anymore. She had nothing to offer him, and that wasn't going to change.

"Here." Winnie forced the uneaten part of her sandwich with its paper wrapping into Katie's hand. "It's cold out here, and I've got to visit the potty. Feel free to eat the rest of this. There's another back inside." Her footsteps crunched on the rocks twice, then the sound from her feet was swallowed up by the moss along the path.

Katie looked at the sandwich with its one bite missing. Steam rose from the still warm meat inside, and she felt her stomach rumble. Taking a bite, she let the warmth slide down her throat.

"This is good," she murmured. "Okay, *Jeffie*, just for this morning I forgive you. For not coming to find me all those years ago, I forgive you, because I am really, really hungry; and bringing this by was exactly the right thing for you to do."

She licked the fingers on one hand when she was finished, and she wadded the paper and held it tightly in her fist. She still couldn't figure out exactly why Jeff was doing all this. No one waits around fourteen years, and then picks up where they left off. No one, and she wouldn't believe it if anyone claimed it to her.

Anyway, she'd just been the summer tag-a-long, and he'd barely paid her any attention back then. Maybe he was sorry for her because of losing everything. Yeah, his dad was probably the reason. He remembered that, and that was why he was trying to make things easier for her.

Somehow that made her feel better, and when Winnie called to her from the path, she turned and waved. "I have something I want to show you. Come see."

"Sure. You still have my sandwich?" Winnie readjusted one of her blue combs as she walked across the deck, using it to pull her tresses from her face to form a halo at the back of her head.

"I have the wrapper. I couldn't resist. Look there." She pointed to the lighthouse. "The sun, it's halfway down the side. That's about six, July time. When it hits the rocks at the waterline, it'll be about six-fifteen. It's like my own personal sundial."

"Six? In the morning?" Winnie looked aghast.

"No, in the evening. Of course in the morning, you silly goose."

"This is awful! I'm going back to bed. I'm glad I brought my electric blanket." Huffing, Winnie marched back inside, letting the screen slam on the way in. Her voice filtered out, "Why does God make the sun come out at this time of the morning, anyway?"

Katie smiled. She didn't mind. She enjoyed island mornings, ones just like this. The Dude moved in a swell, and something onboard clanked, the sound carrying easily across the water. When she looked farther, the double tracks from the lobster boat were closer. She caught sight of the familiar shape of the vessel at the head of the tracks, smiling to see the lobsterman standing just outside of the wheelhouse, with one hand in the air. Then she narrowed her eyes. It was! She turned away. It was Jeff Ragsdale, out there spying on her, and proud to be doing it. He was waving at her, as if she should be excited to see him. Waving!

That was the final straw. All she had was this one little beach left to her name, and he was taking even that away. He'd better not show up for any lobster bake on her beach. She'd bake his little waving hands right in the coals, just to make her point.

She felt her eyes burn, and in her frustration, she tried to find fault in the scene before her: the cabin with its freshly painted trim, the walk, neatly trimmed, and the dappled sun through the trees falling across the roof of the cabin and onto the outer edge of the deck. As she stood there, the little gasoline generator kicked on, purring quietly in the morning air. The deck! Why hadn't she paid attention to that before? None of the boards were rotted. Not a one. How had that happened after being left to the weather for years and years?

Guilt wrenched her. She had to pay him back. That was it. Even if he'd done this for his father, she had to pay Jeff back, whatever it took to get the money to do so. If only the Rockhaven Carvers weren't as broke as a tree branch after a spring snow storm.

Rockhaven Carvers? Rockhaven Carver. There were no others. She was the only one left.

The overwhelming responsibility brought tears to her eyes, ones she didn't know if she could ever brush away.

9

"Have you started a love affair with that thing?" Katie lounged in the sun on a cloth and metal chaise. Next to her, Winnie hunched forward over a cell screen, occasionally tapping something only she could see.

"Sweetie, with anything that loves me back. It's why I like you so much." She smiled and kissed the screen. "We did it, girl! We're there!"

"Did what?" Katie's question was less of a question than verbal support for her friend. Right then, she would support almost anything Winnie did, just for these lounge chairs. When Winnie had pulled the first one from her biggest suitcase, Katie had shaken her head in dismay. Unfolded on the deck, she had changed her mind. Then, a second had appeared, its twin, and Winnie had become the best thing she could have possibly brought with her to the island.

"Got a hundred likes. See?" She held out the phone.

"Let me see." Katie shaded the screen, and it was dim in the bright sun, but there she was in her pink robe with Spurgeon Light in the distance. "Get real. No one would want to see that old picture."

"Not over a hundred people, anyway." Winnie

snickered as she took back the phone. "That bumps you to the top of the list. Everyone'll see it now."

"Who would want to look at me?" Katie worked her fingers into her hair, and she pushed it back from her face. Winnie was the lucky one, with her vibrant head of hair. Sure, her friend complained she couldn't do anything with it because it was so coarse, but while she got its thick texture from her father, from her Irish mother, it was a beautiful strawberry blonde. Against her dark skin, it was stunning.

Katie knew *she* wasn't stunning. Not ugly, no, but not stunning, not to get calls for catalog modeling like the friend at her side. No, Katie depended on neatness, nicely manicured nails, and good manners to get her through. After all, she continually told herself, when your hair is board straight and your body is too, you'd better have a wonderful personality.

She wasn't sure she had mastered that this weekend.

"Oh, oh, there. Look-it that!" Winnie held the phone out again.

"Just tell me. The sun's too bright."

"Your Jeffie likes it, too." Winnie giggled.

"My Jeffie? Are you on Facebook?"

"Of course. Where else? It's how the world stays in touch. It looks like Jeffie wants to stay in touch, too."

"Give me that phone." Katie grabbed it and stood, walking over to stand under a tree. Shading the screen, she enlarged the image to read the comments underneath. She growled when she saw his name.

"You like-ee?" Winnie had a very pleased expression on her face.

"I do not *like-ee*. How is Jeff on your Facebook page?" She stalked back over and tossed the phone in her friend's lap.

"He's my Facebook friend, number, um," and she tapped on the screen, "1,203 out of 1,203. I looked him up yesterday and friended him. He friended me right back."

"You friended him." That took Katie aback. Winnie had friended him, and there he had been. Why had she never thought of that? What about Ritchey, Apple, Austie, and the others? How many of them were out there ready to be friended, and she didn't know?

"Sweetie, I friend everybody." Winnie held her hair out of the way and gave Katie a peck on the cheek. "Besides, I asked him yesterday if he had a Facebook account, and he asked me to friend him. See? Be friendly to the natives, and they'll be friendly to you. Are we going to town today? I want to watch another lobster roll down the mountain."

Katie looked, and Winnie's eyes sparkled with amusement. "You mean that?"

"Well, I can sit here and be beautiful all day, but there's only you to see. If you can keep from drowning me, I can be beautiful all the way to town and back again, and everyone will get to enjoy me." She smiled brightly.

"After your complaints yesterday, you must have an ulterior motive." Katie pursed her lips in thought. "I just can't figure out what."

"Isn't it obvious?" Winnie pulled up Katie's hand. "I looked for my nail file, and I can't find it anywhere. I can hardly file these down with a rock, can I? And I promise not to scream but a little bit."

"Okay. I get it. It's all about my broken nails." Katie pulled her hand away, pleased at her friend's concern, and aware of the smile on her own face. "And I promise to pay attention to the tides. That was the real issue yesterday. Today will be much better, I promise."

"I hope so, but just in case, I have a new background on my phone."

"9-1-1?" Katie thought that was funny.

"Better. Matthew 14:25. Jesus walked on the water." She held the phone up again. "That's what I'm going to do when you sink us, and then I also have Verse 31 for after we sink. Jesus saved everybody. See? I'm all set."

About then, the sound of the generator broke the quietness of the morning, and Katie questioned, "Winnie, did you turn your blanket off?"

"Of course, Sweetie. Why?" Her head was already back in her phone once again.

"It takes gasoline to run that generator, and it's running now. I don't know how long the fuel will last." Then she remembered the little fridge. It might have kicked on. "It's probably the refrigerator. I forgot about that." Katie sank back into her chair.

After a moment, she began to smell something. She sniffed. "Winnie? Is something burning?"

"Oh, that's me!" Winnie jumped up and handed Katie her phone. "The signal's not great, but feel free to play. My curlers are ready. See you in a bit!"

The screen slammed, and she was gone.

Katie stroked the slim wooden armrest on the folding chair with one hand and held the phone in the other. Glancing back in the cabin to see Winnie preoccupied with working giant rollers into her hair, she tapped the Facebook icon. Under the Friends section, she scrolled until she found Jeff's name. She felt guilty, like a voyeur, secretly peeping where she hadn't been invited. With her heart pounding she tapped on him.

There he was, his page, all the things he had posted for the world to see. Photos. She tapped and began to scroll. Rockhaven Town Church. There were lots of those, tag sales on the lawn, what seemed to be picnics and dinners on the grounds. Some of the same people were in a number of pictures at the quarry; the younger ones wore swimsuits, with one adult floating on a blowup ring in the water. What looked like parents were sitting on chairs to the side. She enlarged that picture, realizing it was Jeff on the ring. He was waving at the camera; it reminded her of her last summer on the island, except he was wearing a black suit rather than cut-off jeans.

Scrolling further, there were more of Jeff: at the family home she'd visited once or twice out on Moffat Cove; several on a lobster boat she recognized as his dad's old one. He had his arm across his dad's shoulders in one, and he was laughing and holding up a live lobster.

Jeff kept getting younger as she went. He had on a Rockhaven High basketball uniform, and his hair was wet with sweat; he stood around a bonfire on the rocks, in shorts and athletic shoes but wearing a heavy jacket.

She almost passed the picture of her, going on before she recognized herself and went back. She looked at the image for a long time, the memories flooding back. She didn't know who had carried the camera, but Austie and Ritchey had cooked up a scheme to harvest clams to sell to trippers at the ferry terminal. They'd gotten the twins excited with all the money they'd make, but they'd needed a boat. The best mud flats were at the head of Carver Cove at low tide. Katie's little rowing dinghy was convenient, so she was roped in as the only girl on the expedition. Jeff had been enlisted to talk her into it.

They'd towed several long boards behind the boat to lay out on the mud. Otherwise they'd sink to their knees. In the picture, she was in the boat leaning over the bow with a long trowel in her hand. Mud smeared one cheek. One of the boards, mostly brown but sprinkled with flaking white paint, stretched to the side out of the picture. Jeff was on it, his arms covered with mud to his elbows. He was looking at the camera, and he held a giant clam up to show it off.

The camera had focused on Jeff. He was sharp and clear. His eyes sparkled with laughter, the flat planes of his face broken with his dimpled grin. He had pride written all over him.

Her? She looked up at Jeff, grinning stupidly. The color was faded a bit at the edges of the photo, as if it had been displayed in a window or on a wall, and the sun had worked its fingers over the image day after day. One corner had a little tear.

That was the moment she had known she was in love.

Just fourteen, there had been no doubt. During her childhood she had followed him, worshipped him, and wished to be an island child like him. She had never thought of it as love, although in retrospect, she didn't suppose she thought of it as love even that day. In that moment, just when that picture was snapped, everything in her life had taken on a different focus. That muddy boy digging for clams had seemed just about perfect to her. Who wouldn't fall in love with a muddy island boy with dimples the size of the Grand Canyon?

Then September had come calling, the bad news had come calling, and Jeff—her Jeffrey—hadn't come calling. She'd known that if she loved someone enough, he'd feel her need for consolation, and he'd come to find her, wouldn't he? And when he didn't, she'd trusted in a God who could do anything, even magic, as long as she believed in it. She had believed, and watched the phone, and checked her mailbox.

She clicked the phone off and turned it upside down. You can't have back what you never had in the first place. Just because one person falls in love doesn't mean the other person even knows. Does it?

And just because you ask God doesn't mean He answers, does it?

Well, she had picked up the pieces, and she had moved on. God still had a place in her life, but it was a carefully regulated one. After all, if He couldn't do what she had asked of Him, why should she go out of her way for Him?

She did envy Jeff in all those pictures with his Rockhaven Town Church friends. They seemed so happy together. If he had come to find her, she could have had that, too.

She closed her eyes against the sun and listened to Winnie humming inside and the soft slap of the water against the hull of the Dude. If the breeze picked up, Winnie might get quite a ride back into town.

The wind shifted, and she caught the clover and the roses, the fragrance wafting over her in waves. She didn't need Jeff and all the laughter in those pictures. She had this, and how could life get any more perfect than Carver Point?

It was a slice of heaven right here on earth.

10

"Are you sure about this?" Katie stood at the tree serving as an anchor for the plastic dinghy. The air was motionless where they were, but far out, the wind pulled white feathers from the surface of the water. Any location unprotected would be risky in a boat as small as the Dude.

"I can only post so many pictures of the same rock, Sweetie. Fresh air! Besides, I want to see what the coastline looks like."

"You just traveled it yesterday. It's not any different today."

"My head was between my knees yesterday. I didn't see any of it." Winnie had a bag across her shoulder, and she dropped it to the rocks and pulled out her phone. "Look at that. Seagulls. Hold a minute. I have to make a post."

Katie watched the Dude and the direction she pointed, still concerned. Follow the tide out, and later in the day, follow the tide back in. If Winnie knew how to sail, it would be manageable at any time, as long as they had wind. But, as she couldn't resolve that issue, tide out and tide in was very important.

Anyway, if push came to shove, they could tie up at the dock on Carver Cove and hike overland across the Point.

It'd only save them about ten minutes sail time, but it would save them a lot more if they were blown all the way to East Haven.

The hike? That would add twenty minutes.

"Ready!" Winnie dropped her bag in the dinghy. "You want me in now, or should we push it out a bit?"

"Out just a bit." It was twenty feet from the waterline. Yeah, it needed to go out a bit.

Katie undid the rope, and grabbing the boat's stern, she dragged it down and dropped the back end into the water. Holding the line, she called to her friend to jump in. Within two minutes, they were transferring Winnie's bag to the Dude.

"Is that seal still here?" Winnie had the two boats gunwale to gunwale, as if the previous day's seal might find even an inch an open invitation that it couldn't refuse.

"I have an oar. I'll beat it into submission if it shows up." Katie held one up, but she smiled.

"I'm not teasing." Winnie began to sing very softly as she climbed over, "Rock-a-bye baby . . ."

Katie took a deep breath. Maybe this was not a good idea. Even so, once they were settled inside the Dude, Winnie looked around, got out a scarf, and tied her hair into a bundle at the crown of her head. As Katie readied the boat to leave, her friend became very animated, even asking about how the boat moved without a motor.

"How much do you want to know?" Katie was pleased at her friend's change in attitude, and she leaned forward to untie from the mooring.

"Talk to me like I don't know anything." Winnie took the line from her while she stood to release the sail, and she dropped it on the floor.

"Easy enough, because I suspect it's true. Okay, mast." She patted the tall pole the sail attached to. "That was the painter I just handed you, and you just dropped the painter on the keel. That's the low spot that runs up and down the length of the boat."

"Oh, oh. I'm following you, Sweetie! Mast, keel, painter. I think I might even get this. Why painter? It looks like a rope to me." Winnie smiled, very bright eyed and interested looking.

"So you don't tie up the boat with this one. It's the mainsheet." She held up the one attached to the corner of the sail. "Or this one. It's the reef line." She pulled at a series of small cords attached to the center of the sail.

"I get that one. In case we hit a reef, we tie up with those." Winnie grinned.

"Not exactly, but you're getting closer. Each one gets a different name so we know which one we want to use." Katie had the sail untied, and she handed the loose end to Winnie. "That's the clew of the sail, but that's probably TMI. I'll say back, top and front."

"Good. I know those terms." Winnie pulled on the sail, only to have it catch the wind and tip the boat sideways.

"Whoa. Keep it loose until I'm seated." Katie dropped beside her friend. "Now grab this line and feed it through here." She touched a metal eye with a pulley attached.

"The mainsheet, right?" Winnie held it up and smiled. "See, I do listen."

"Yes, you do. Feed it through, and I'll let you control the sail. I'll operate the rudder."

"That thingie?" She pointed to the wooden stick at the back of the boat.

"Yep. When you're ready, pull that rope just until you feel the boat start to move forward. Not too tight."

The boat started to glide forward, the sail tightening; and the water slipped by under them. It made a low-pitched whooshing sound as it disappeared out of sight.

"We're sailing!" Winnie hooted. "Me! I'm sailing!"

"You are. Very good, Honey." Katie turned the rudder just a bit to keep the sail trimmed. "You want to go faster? Pull the mainsheet a little tighter, a tiny bit at a time. Let it off if you want to slow down."

She aimed for the inside route that ran between Settler's Island and Rockhaven. That would avoid most of the wind, and hopefully it would die down by the time they returned. Not too much, because then they couldn't return at all, but enough not to kill Winnie's fun.

As they passed the Point, and Carver Cove drifted by on their port side, she pointed the dock out to Winnie, telling her it was hers, and they could walk over and dive off it if they wanted. At the De Groot's, she pointed to the old house as it revealed itself, giving a little history. She steered expertly around ledges that had exposed themselves with the falling tide by paying attention to the masses of seaweed billowing just under the surface of the water.

By the time they reached town, Winnie had given up control of the sail, and she sat to one side trailing her hand in the water. It seemed the dangers of the marauding seal were forgotten, and Rockhaven Island might have finally captured her friend's heart.

"Is this how we get to church on Sunday?" Winnie had her phone out snapping pictures of the shorefront houses lining both sides of the harbor. A ferry was docked, and cars were moving off and onto the island.

"It's a twelve-mile walk if you want to come the other way. But sure, this is how I'm planning on coming."

"In our dress clothes?"

Katie found that amusing. "No, we bring our things in a waterproof bag, and then change before church."

"You're teasing." Winnie turned her phone and snapped a photo of Katie holding the rudder. "What about our hair?"

"You comb it out. Get parked. We're coming to the float, and I have to drop the sail and dock without killing you, me, or anyone else's boat. Head low!" She snapped the sail to the opposite side of the boat, held the rudder with her foot for a minute, and began to gather up the sail as she walked forward. Wrapping the mainsheet around the mast, she snapped up the painter and stepped off the bow onto the float just as the Lil' Dude came to a rest.

"That was good. You know your stuff, Sweetie!" Winnie clapped several times.

"I grew up doing this. It was learn or be stranded on the Point for three months at a time. Let me help you off." She already had the boat tied up, and she held the stern against the float for Winnie to climb out.

"Katie? Katie Carver?"

Katie looked up to see a plump, round-faced woman with a baseball cap and light brown hair walking across the parking lot above. She went blank for a moment, trying to place the face, when a boy about nine ran up and threw his arms around her.

"Make Kevie stop, Mom!"

A bigger boy, maybe two years older and looking very much like the woman, ran up and grabbed his arm and yanked him loose.

"You weasel. You didn't either see me kick that dog. Come back here." He pulled the smaller boy by the collar and dragged him away, with the first boy stumbling to keep up.

With that, Katie knew who this was. She had been thin as a kid, but with those boys, it could be only one person.

"Janine Roscoe? How have you been?" Katie waved.

"Not Roscoe in a long time. I'm Peavey now. Those were two of my boys. It's good to see you back. Are you still a Carver?"

"That's me, always a Carver. How've you been?" From Jeff's description, she had a pretty good idea, but it was polite to ask.

"Too many kids. Too many winters cooped up inside, but other than that? It's a life. You. You look good. You haven't shown your face here since the day your gramma's place out there burned. Are you rebuilding?"

Janine waited for them, talking down from the lip of the ramp. As Katie and Winnie reached the top, it was clear that Janine, short when they were kids, had already reached her full height even then.

Katie laughed. "Not this summer. Janine, this is my good friend Winnie from Boston. Winnie, meet Janine Peavey."

"Pleased to meet you." Winnie took her hand and pumped it several times. "You live here on the island, right?" She glanced at Katie for confirmation.

"Katie told you about me?" Janine seemed very pleased. "I was born on the mainland, but I've been here since I was three months. When I got married, I knew I was here forever." She laughed as if it wasn't what she'd intended, but rather what had happened. "Is this your first time out?"

"Yes. I left my car back on land, and I came out on the boat. Now we're using that little boat down there." Winnie pointed to the Dude tied up to the town float.

"The Lil' Dude. Jeff took it out for you." Janine laughed. "I kept telling him he should use it, but no, he had it in his boat house, working on it every summer. He said you'd be back some day, and now he's proved right. I remember us out in that little boat a few times."

"More than a few." Katie laughed along with Janine, hearing in the woman's words what she wasn't saying. *He said you'd be back.* And he worked on it every summer?

"Surely you brought your car out." It was Janine again, talking to Katie. "Did you make it down the drive all right?"

"It hasn't been cleared. It's the Lil' Dude or nothing for us, I'm afraid. Jeff took me to the Point, but we're afoot the rest of our stay."

"Oh, no. You could've made it down fine. I was out there in my car just last week. I'm the one who cleaned the cabin for you." A boy down the street darted from behind a building and yelled, and Janine said, "I'm sorry. Those boys! I've got to go. Maybe we can get together before you head off island again. Bye. You, too, Winnie!"

She turned and ran toward the screaming boy.

"Driveway?" Winnie put her hands on her hips. "We have a driveway, and I left my car there?" She pointed with her hand out the harbor the direction they'd sailed in.

"Actually, it's that way." Katie pulled her friend's arm around to point towards town. "Over the island and past Carver Point. But yes, you left your car there."

"Can I go get it?" Winnie huffed. "If I can drive, I want my car."

"You can, if you want to pay nearly a hundred dollars to bring it over."

"How much?" Winnie's eyes went wide.

"But you don't need to." This, Katie found amusing.

"Why not? I do need a car, so I can get to church Sunday, to church without changing clothes when I get to the door." She said that with emphasis.

"Why not?" Katie took her friend's chin and pointed her face towards the other end of the parking lot. "Because that's my car there."

"Oh! Beetle, Beetle, I love you, in red, white or the color blue!" Winnie clapped excitedly. A bright blue Volkswagen Beetle sat in the very last space.

"There is one issue, though."

"Not if we have a car." Winnie threw her arms around her friend and gave her cheek a quick peck. "We've got a car!"

"But the keys are at the cabin."

The dismay on Winnie's face was truly hilarious, and as hard as she tried, Katie could not keep from laughing. Even when Winnie slapped her on the arm and told her it wasn't funny at all, she continued to laugh until tears ran down her face.

11

"Jeffrey Ragsdale!" Intentionally, very intentionally, Katie walked up behind the man she was trying so hard to avoid, and she poked him on the shoulder.

"Katie!" A smile broke out on his face as he turned to her.

"Don't you smile at me. I just talked to Janine Roscoe. Peavey. I just talked to Janine Peavey, and you didn't want me to talk to her, did you? Four kids? Nah. I met two of them, and they were perfectly nice. You didn't want me to know she'd been out there at my cabin. Well, she told me. What do you think of that?"

Katie stepped back just enough that they weren't touching, but she refused to retreat. The pecking order was out of kilter here, and Jeff needed to be set straight. She might not have been around the past fourteen years, but she wouldn't be lied to the moment she returned. She would not!

"They are hellions, Katie. I didn't lie about that." He turned to the older man he'd been sharing a plate of food with, and he explained. "The Peavey boys."

"Ah. Janine and Al's brood." He nodded with a smile, as if that explained it all. "They do have energy to spare."

"Why didn't you tell me the drive was cleared? Winnie and I have been sailing back and forth in the Dude, and I have a car here on island." That had her irritated as much as anything. She'd endured that ride out in his boat. Now, Winnie. Was he trying to make her life difficult?

"You used to enjoy the Dude." He didn't seem perturbed. "I thought you'd enjoy having her out there to use."

"I do, and thank you, but that's not the point. I have my car here, and you didn't tell me the drive is cleared."

"You didn't ask." The man with him chuckled, and Jeff held his hand up to quiet him. "Not now, Roker."

"Okay, but you brought this on yourself, if you ask me."

"Jeff! What about my drive?" She had left Winnie at the Paper Store looking at magazines, because she didn't think she needed to see her take on Jeff Ragsdale, but she was about to get angry.

"I told you I'd kept up a presence at the place." He had one arm on the back of the chair by then, and he was sitting sideways in his seat. "Would you like some shrimp? It's from Harbor View."

Roker pulled his hand away. He'd almost emptied the plate.

"When I called Marc—"

"When you called Marc, you told him you needed a boat out to Carver Point, and would he set something up. He set me up. Were you unhappy with the service? I'll be glad to offer you a full refund on my services."

"I didn't pay you anything." With her words, the amount she owed blossomed into the ride out, the work he'd done on the Dude, the Point, for Janine's cleaning. All of it.

"Okay, so if you didn't pay me, and you're dissatisfied, then I can only give you a refund by paying you. All my money's wrapped up in lobster, so I guess that means we have to have that lobster bake out at your place. I've got it penciled in for tomorrow about seven. Are we still good with that?"

"I—" She had worked herself into a corner, but she wasn't sure it was one of her own making.

"Careful, Jeff." That was Roker, and his amusement came through just fine.

From down the street, Winnie called, "There you are. Oh, hi, Jeffie! Are we still doing our cookout?"

"Are we, Katie?" He still had his arm over the back of the chair, and he was fighting a smile. From the other direction she caught the sound of Janine chewing on one of her boys.

"Stop it, Konnar. That's my friend down there from when I grew up, and I refuse to let her see you like this." He kicked her and ran off down the street.

"Will you bring Janine? No kids?" Then it would be like a gift to her old friend, a gift of a few hours without her trying children. It wouldn't be a date in any form or fashion.

"Janine? Al won't be happy babysitting." That was Roker again. By now, the plate was completely empty.

"For you, done." Jeff held a hand out to shake.

"No you don't, Jeff Ragsdale. Right now I don't trust you to the end of this street. I'm not shaking any hand you hold out to me."

"Smart girl." Roker chuckled.

"Jeffie! How sweet!" Winnie appeared at Katie's side, and she took Jeff's extended hand in both of hers. She massaged it for a moment, her eyes going wide. "Sweetie, you need to feel this man's hand. It's all muscle, like a real man's hand."

"Oh, you two are made for each other!" Katie turned and walked away. She crossed the street and stopped at the edge of the lot overlooking the harbor. It seemed she'd developed an ongoing exit strategy. Blow up, cross the street, and stop at the ramp down to the town float. She couldn't even be creative, maybe go in the Paper Store and slam the door, or get in her car and speed away.

Now, she'd invited him to her beach for an entire evening. If she'd just stayed away, then everything would've been fine. She wouldn't have seen him again, and . . . and . . .

That wasn't what she wanted at all. She wanted what she'd seen in that picture from over a dozen years ago. She wanted fourteen, and to be in a dinghy on the mud flats with all her friends, and to be looking into the eyes of a boy who'd just dug up a giant clam in hopes of making a boatload of money.

The other thing she remembered, their venture had gone south in a heartbeat. No one had wanted to buy their clams, they'd begun to stink in their tub, and they'd had to throw them all into the harbor. For a week after that, no one had come to the Point, and she'd felt useless and abandoned.

It was that same feeling now. Her trip to Rockhaven was heading south in a heartbeat. All the people she knew, all the places that had been so familiar to her weren't quite the same as they had been.

She wasn't the same as she had been.

She was stronger. She had her place in Boston, she worked with people she liked, and Winnie was her best friend. She could hang on to that, couldn't she?

The float below caught her eye. She still had to sail back to the Point, and the tide didn't turn for another four hours. How could she stay in town with Jeff Ragsdale right behind her for another four hours?

The ferry horn blew, and across the harbor, its diesel engines began to roar. The massive ship with its half-empty deck pushed the water aside to the complaints of a dozen or so birds. Several people, probably daytrippers, had gone up top already, and one figure had a camera out. He paused, shifted position, paused, and shifted again. He was memorizing Rockhaven. To him, when he looked at his pictures, it would always be exactly the way it looked today.

What about her pictures? In her pictures, Rockhaven was a big white house, friends she couldn't wait to return to every summer, and a life that was more of a dream than the best dream possible.

Where had those pictures gone?

Her only answer was the sound of Winnie's voice, loud and laughing, and Jeff's deep-throated laughter in return.

Those weren't the memories in her pictures, and she didn't have any way to change the pages in her photo album and make them new.

She didn't even have the help of God, not really. He had left her to go her own way a long time ago.

Five more days. She could do this five more days, and then she'd be gone. She was that strong, strong enough to do this five more days. And Winnie? That girl had better be her right hand man. After all, she was sleeping in the bed next to hers. They were a team, and not even Jeff Ragsdale was going to break them apart.

She took a deep breath, turned and began her walk across the parking lot, determined this time to be the strong woman she knew she had become.

If Jeff didn't like it? Tough. That was just the way it was.

12

The sky had hunkered down, and heavy rain threatened. The wind spiked the water with jerky little hats of white foam, and anyone normal would avoid open water.

That was fine with Katie. It matched her mood. It did something else, also. It had convinced her soon-to-be-ex-friend to hitch a ride with her new Jeffie-friend to the cabin.

It also kept either of them from seeing the tears she refused to wipe from her face.

She had been mortified to find herself greeted by Jeff Ragsdale when she had arrived on the island, and she had rebuffed him at every opportunity. Then she had lashed out at him in town, making her position as clear as pie on his face.

Nothing had fazed the man. Nothing. It was like that boy from the picture. It didn't matter how much mud he had to dig through, or what was in the mud that was splattered all over him; when he had a goal in mind, the goal was the only thing he saw.

What did he expect from her? She wasn't an island girl, no matter how strongly she'd wished for that very thing all those years ago. Her time away had been just long enough that she'd seen the way the world really was. It was a high-rise apartment, a cubicle in an insurance company's claim division, and regular car payments every month. Islands were for summer vacations and the occasional free weekend. Life on an island? That was for Janine trapped during the brutal months of winter with four wild animals. It was probably the reason they were wild in the first place. Winter and too many hours of darkness could do that to a person.

Now Katie flew from the harbor. The Lil' Dude did what she did best: She surfed along the tops of the waves, the centerboard holding her true, and the tiller vibrating against Katie's hand. She had reefed the sail, and still, the wind was a fist that drove the Dude forward.

It was glorious, it was hard, and it was just what she needed to bleed out her anger and frustration. She wrapped the mainsheet around her hand, and she pulled it taut, the tell-tales straight out and perpendicular to the mast. Occasionally the bow slammed into a swell, and a fine mist wet Katie's clothes. It also wet her face, filling her eyes with moisture.

Of course she admitted nothing otherwise, that the moisture might have been there even without the ocean spray. It was the salt that made her eyes burn, because salt water did that, didn't it? She had to watch for remembered underwater ledges, to dart between seaweed-covered outcroppings, and to pull up sailing skills from a childhood that had been snatched from an innocent girl just when her life was truly taking form. How could she worry about damp eyes at a time like this?

She was halfway to the Point before she realized the water hitting her face was there whether the Dude was flinging spray through the air or not. Slipping into the passage between Settler's and the island only made her mast lines buzz with intensity, and the little Dude became a frisky mare, filled with fight, and ready to spar with her jockey.

Katie sparred back, giving the controls the one-two. The sail was already reefed, but she had a few remembered skills up her sleeve. She tucked the boat next to Settler's, with the mast barely clearing the low-hanging spruce that would brush the water at highest tide, and just before the little boat crossed in front of the massive De Groot dock, she gave the tiller a hard push and skimmed around Little Goose Ledge, skirting the hidden rocks and their seaweed icing before they slammed into the bottom of the boat. For years, she remembered the tales of those who had holed their craft on Little Goose, but never Katie. She prided herself in that.

It was going across the mouth of the Cove that could be dangerous. The tidal bore was in full throttle by now, and it could easily pull a craft as small as the Dude right inside. That was what she would have normally done as a girl in weather like this, dart in through the tumbled fists of massive stones that gripped Carver Cove in its embrace, and landed her craft, cowering against the elements under the safety of the sturdy granite pillars that were the entrance to her grandmother's oceanfront home.

No, not today. That home had been taken from her. The cabin was hers now, all that was left from a life that had been ripped from her, and she would master the voyage to the life she now lived. The wind might beat at her, and the waves might pummel her craft, but she was master of the seas, and none could best her skills.

She was adrenalin charged and so pumped up by the time she saw the little plastic boat that her victorious conquest was all that mattered to her. It was when she released the sail to grab the mooring that she realized a storm had truly overtaken the sky. The rain was steady, and it bit into her skin with icy pricks that could only come in a northern summer gale.

"This might get bad," she muttered, loop-loop-and-tucking the line. If so, she had one more job to do. She reached under the seat and pulled out an oiled, waterproof canvas sheet. After Janine's comments in town, she had known it would be here. Jeff would have made sure of it. Along the outside edges, rope was strung through grommets. She expected it would slip over the top of the cockpit perfectly, and the lines would mate up precisely with the cleats around the boat. Keeping water out meant keeping the boat afloat in weather like this.

Securing the sail, she shook out the canvas cover and began at one corner. Looping the rope, one cleat at a time, she was pleased to make quick progress. The rain was getting heavier, and her adrenalin-infused enthusiasm was wearing thin. She wanted to get in.

She was now chilled, too.

Finally reaching the shore, she dragged the plastic skiff into the trees, turning it upside down and tying it tightly. No good losing a good boat, and she didn't intend to swim out to the Dude, not in this weather.

She ran toward the cabin, her feet slipping on the wet stones. Once she nearly went down, and she laughed at her own clumsiness. The lights were on, and that made her happy. When she started from town, she hadn't wanted to see Winnie when she arrived. She had wanted to be alone. Now? She would appreciate the company.

The door opened as she jumped up on the deck, and Katie laughed and waved at the familiar head of strawberry hair.

"Winnie! Am I glad to see you!"

"Hurry, Sweetie. I'm getting all wet. We worried you might not make it." Winnie gabbed Katie's elbow as she darted through the door, brushing water from her face.

"We?" Katie patted her friend on the cheek. "You, maybe. I didn't doubt myself for a minute."

"Me, mostly." The deep voice was resonant, complementing the pattering rain on the roof. There at the desk sat the very nemesis that had driven Katie to the sea in the first place.

"Jeff." Katie brushed her face again with her hands, then pulled her hair back to squeeze out what water she could. "Did you bring the lobster out? I don't think they'll fit in the fridge." She smiled and shrugged.

He rolled his eyes and stood, looking out into the fading light. He was still for a short time, his shoulders broad under his heavy shirt, and his hair a wild tuft of dark, shining moss careening from a stolid mound of ancient stone. Then, he shifted, and he was alive once again, as he turned to face her.

"Is that the only reason you think I came out?" His mouth seemed to want to smile, as if he found his question amusing, but there was redness in his eyes. He glanced at Winnie, then back to her, but he didn't say anything else, as if it was her turn to talk.

"Maybe?" Katie looked to Winnie to see if she was any help, only to see her friend shrug. She tried again. "To bring Winnie back in warm, dry comfort, maybe?" She looked back to Jeff.

He pressed his lips tight, and he looked away with a sour chuckle.

"What's that for?" Katie knew she'd missed something. It was warmer inside, but not much, and she shivered.

"A decade and a half, and you're the same as you were back then." He glanced at her. "I should have expected it, but I guess I made you into what I wanted, and that's my fault."

"And that means?" She was serious. How was she the same? She had been a happy-go-lucky girl then, one that was willing to fall in love when it landed on her doorstep each June, and willing to wait for its return when she left each fall. She wasn't that girl anymore. She was strong and independent, and she would tell anyone who asked her so.

He looked at her and shook his head. He stepped to Winnie and took her hand, then he patted it and said, "See you tomorrow. It'll be fun." He turned to Katie. "The weather's just a squall that'll blow over by morning, so your car won't be a problem. Full sun the rest of the day. I'd like to come out early and set up if you don't mind. I've invited a few people you might remember. I want you to have fun. You'll try?"

He grabbed her hand as he stepped by, releasing it as he moved into the blustery rain. The screen slammed, and the floor began to darken with increasing spatters of moisture. Katie closed the door.

"Okay, Winnie. What did you say to him?" Katie crossed her arms and tried to look severe, although she was pretty sure the sound of her wet clothes every time she moved didn't do much for an angry look.

"You're dripping." Winnie giggled and pointed to the floor. "Somebody's got to clean it up."

"That's not what I asked. What did you tell him?"

"Sweetie, he just gave me a ride home, that's all. Oh, we stopped by his house." Her face brightened. "It's on the water, and it has a real kitchen, and a bathroom and everything. You should try it here at your place sometime."

"And? All that was for?"

"Towels! We brought towels!" Winnie opened a large bag on her bed, and she pulled out two towels striped in cream, blue, and red. "Here! One to dry your hair, and the other to dry everything else. Jeffie is so sweet. He thinks of everything!"

"I bet he does!" Katie grabbed the closest towel, and she began to work it roughly over her hair. She couldn't help but be thankful in some small way, because she hadn't brought any at all. What really bothered her was what Jeff said.

How was she the same? After her long, uphill climb to find out just who she was, and learning to be strong in the process, how could she be the same in any way, fashion, or form?

Maybe Jeff was an idiot, and she'd never figured that out all those years ago. Yeah, that was right, the island idiot that couldn't find a rock ledge in broad daylight, and that had been God's plan all along. God had rescued her, and she hadn't even known.

She laughed at that idea, because it hadn't felt like a rescue back then. Now? She'd take any help she could get to get her out of this pickle.

"I knew it would be just fine." Winnie laughed and put her arm around Katie. "See? You're happy again. I got you a file, and I posted another picture of you." She pulled out a fingernail file from one pocket, laying it on the bed, and her phone from the other. "See?"

The post was her in the Dude just leaving the town float. One arm was back, pulling the sail taut, and the other held the tiller. A small bow wave curled up the side. Her hair was tossed by the wind, and she looked angry.

"You can unpost that, you know." Katie turned away and continued to rub her hair. She should be smiling and happy in her pictures. Then she would remember Rockhaven as a happy time in her life. That picture? Who would find her life attractive if they looked at that?

"Oh, I don't know." Winnie sat on her folding bed, her face buried in her phone. "I might wait to see what Jeffie thinks."

"What Jeffie thinks?" Katie looked at her and snorted.

"Sure." She laid back, holding the phone in the air. "There! He came through, just like he said he would. That's the Jeffie I like so much!" She turned it for Katie to see.

"Did he tell you he loves you?" Katie was down to her arms, and she smirked at her friend.

"Well, I think he means you, so I'm not really sure."

Katie grabbed the phone and she looked under the picture. There by his name was a little yellow happy face. She held the phone back out to her friend.

"See? You make him happy." Winnie held the phone to her chest, just where her heart would be. "Happiness is so hard to find."

"Especially in a cabin in the woods." Katie began to strip her wet things off. "Sometimes good friends are hard to find, too."

"That's why I'm glad I found you." Winnie stood with a bright look on her face. "I need to visit the potty. I'll be right back." She pulled an umbrella from behind the door.

"Where did that come from?" Katie knew she hadn't brought it.

"This? From Jeffie." She smiled, opened the door, popped the umbrella open, and disappeared down the path, the bright sound of rain on the fabric quickly fading away.

Of course. Jeffie. Katie had to admit, he was doing all the right things. He was checking every box, and Winnie was eating it up. Her? She couldn't figure him out, and that bothered her. After what he said earlier, it bothered her more than she liked to admit.

13

Everything dripped with the remains of the night's downpour, but the sky was clear. The sun would be fully up before long, but for now, Katie enjoyed her lighthouse sundial being completely shaded. It gave her something to look forward to, like she owned a part of Rockhaven that no one else knew about.

She unfolded the lounger from the day before and positioned it at the best viewing angle. Pulling her robe tight, she slipped out of her shoes and pulled her feet up and covered them. Now all she had to do was wait on the sun.

She closed her eyes for a minute to soak in the sounds of the fresh island morning: the dripping branches shedding last night's rain; the water undulating against the rocks on the shore; even the occasional ding, ding of a buoy bell. It was so peaceful she felt she could stay in this one spot forever.

"Sweetie?" The word was whispered, and the screen door bumped closed quietly with no more than a soft thump.

"Yes?" Katie didn't want the morning disturbed.

"I came to keep you company." The second lounger clicked softly as it unfolded.

"Sure. Quiet, though. I'm waiting for the lighthouse to light up. I finally made it out before the sun hit it."

"You've been up a long time." Winnie's chair creaked, telling that she had sat down.

"No, I just got out here." She had been about to open her eyes and check on its progress when her friend came out. Now she was having trouble opening them at all.

"You better hurry if you want to catch it before the sun's to the bottom. It's about to ring the magic daytime bell."

"It's what?" Katie sat up, forcing her eyes open. "Oh, Winnie! I missed it! My third morning here, and I still haven't seen it at first light."

"Shush! Shush! It's okay, Sweetie. I got it for you. It's already posted." She held out her phone.

Sure enough, shot through the screen on one of the windows were several grainy photos of the lighthouse, the first one with the sun just lighting the very top, and several more as it slipped toward the water.

"You got up to do this?" Katie looked to see if there were any likes, but they were all blank. It was early, though, so that didn't mean anything. Every other normal person was still asleep.

"Almost. My arm got up." Winnie was snuggled under her electric blanket, although it wasn't attached to a cord. Her hair was a fluffy halo of a pillow, and her eyes were closed. "I heard you, and I knew you were having a little love time with your beach, so every few minutes I held my phone up and took a picture. But me? Nah! I like nine o'clock too much to get up just for a sunrise."

"You're here now. Why the rush?"

"I was lonely, and I like your company. I thought maybe you like mine, since you invited me here. Do you? After yesterday, I wasn't real sure."

"I couldn't be here without you." Katie reached over and patted the electric blanket. When she found Winnie's arm, she squeezed it. "Who else would stay with me in a cabin with no bathroom, no running water, and no curtains?"

"We may have a little company after a bit." Winnie said the words carefully, as if she was afraid they might not be taken well.

"Not your Jeffie, please." Katie took her hand back. She hoped she hadn't lied. She laid the phone on the top of Winnie's blanket.

"We do need the car." Winnie looked at her imploringly, her eyes pleading.

"I put your phone there."

"I feel it. Is the car okay?" She smiled.

"Is it Janine?"

"Oh, she could have done it, I suppose, and I bet she wouldn't mind. Then she could visit with you and make up for old times. That would be so sweet. I didn't even think. So sorry." Winnie had begun to smile, and her eyes were closed again.

"Okay, Cheshire Cat. Spill the beans, or I'm taking a picture of you sleeping and post it on the Internet."

"Here." She took the phone and held it out to Katie. "I look cute when I sleep."

"What makes you think that?" Katie took the phone and found the camera, held it up and snapped a picture.

"I have to be. Just look at me." She shrugged under the blanket, but her eyes remained closed. "I can't help what I am. Want me to post it?" She held out her hand.

"Oh, you. Sure. You post it." She slapped the phone into the open hand. "It is Jeff, isn't it? You can have him, you know."

"He's not my Jeffie. He's your Jeffie. I asked him for a ride to pick up your car last night, and he said it had to be early. He has to take the ferry to town."

"He does, does he? I guess I need to get dressed. First ferry's at seven."

"Thank you, Sweetie. I think I'll go back to bed now."

"I thought you were here to keep me company."

"Only until you said yes. You've done that now." She stood with her blanket wadded in her hands. "I might leave the lounger, if it's okay with you."

A horn caught their attention. Katie sat up. "He's here,

already?"

"Be kind, Sweetie. I told him you said for me to ask. That's probably why he was so confused last night. Sorry. I didn't get a chance to tell you." Winnie scuttled inside the door and was gone.

So that was what he meant by "her car wouldn't be a problem."

"Katie? I can't take long. I'll miss the ferry." The words echoed in the quiet, carrying over the Point.

She guessed there was no time to change. She stepped inside and grabbed her purse, and then she headed up the path, pink housecoat and all. The ferry didn't wait. That she knew. If she wasn't there when Jeff needed to go, he would drive off without her. He had no choice.

She was curious about why he was headed to the mainland. He'd been insistent about the lobster bake being at seven, but anyplace off island was an all-day venture. One way was nearly an hour and a half, and that didn't count the wait time in line before the ferry loaded. Without a reservation, two hours was the minimum for getting there early. The spots were first come, first served.

As she topped the rise, she passed by the old foundation of her grandmother's burned-out house. She cringed and refused to look, more than just a glance. The stone still rose above the ground several feet on one end, and nearly a full story on the other. Left through a gate were the parking area and the drive. Just past it would be Jeff, waiting to hustle her to her car.

The gate, an old wooden one, was the first item she'd seen on the Point that was in poor repair. It was cocked open, and the paint was peeling. It looked like the main post had rotted completely through at the base.

Past it was a shiny green Jeep with fat tires and a fabric roof. That made her smile. Who on the island would waste money on such a frivolous car? A truck, or an SUV, perhaps, because off-road capabilities were in demand during the long winter months, but even she found the Jeep a bit showy.

Jeff had his door open, and he stood on the sill looking

over the roof. "Good morning, Katie. I know it's early, but I didn't know it was that early."

"I expected you later." She waved. Like five o'clock in the afternoon, but she didn't say that. There was no point. He was here, the ferry was leaving, and to get her car, this was the only logical way.

"Hey, I don't care. I'm just glad you asked for my help. I'm glad to do it. Climb in." He dropped into his seat and shut his door.

"I bet you are," she muttered. Here she was again. She had started out the week in his boat, bumped into him every time she went out, and now she was riding in his car. If she wasn't careful, people who saw her would think she'd gone totally native.

However, Janine Roscoe Peavey was not what she wanted to become. Four marauding kids and a look on her face that said "What have I got myself into" didn't cut it for the city girl Katie'd become. Coming back was on her own terms, and this place had better plan to deal with it.

She slammed the door when she got in, and she glared at Jeff.

"Okay," he said. "Fine by me. I won't say a word." He shifted the Jeep into reverse, and in a few moments, they were headed down the drive, the big tires and soft suspension swaying a whole lot more than was exactly comfortable for anyone just out of bed.

Katie hoped she didn't lose her stomach, and she was very glad she hadn't had anything to eat. And Winnie thought being on the water was bad. For a second time, she glared at Jeff, but she found he refused to look her way.

She couldn't get satisfaction even from that. This was not going to be a fun day.

"You remember your keys?" Jeff said the words very softly.

Katie grabbed her purse from the floor and dropped it on the console. "Yes, I have my keys."

"Okay. My mouth is closed." He ran a finger over his lips, zipping them up, but he had a smile underneath.

"Oh," she growled, looking away. What really irked her

was that he'd gotten better looking in the years she'd been away. How did that happen, and why to her? He should be fat and bald, and then she wouldn't care.

She couldn't wait to get to her car. It wasn't safe for her being cooped up with Jeff Ragsdale, not safe at all.

14

Katie listened to the sounds of the Jeep as Jeff downshifted one gear at a time to slow for town. Once they were past the potholes and granite rock heaves that made up much of the driveway, he had pushed the off-road vehicle to nearly sixty. It was heart stopping on the island's narrow roads.

"Ferry's not loading yet." She noted the line of cars, two very small ones, and a truck filled with blocks of granite.

"It wouldn't be." He tapped the clock on the dash then pressed in the clutch and pulled the shifter into a lower gear. The engine growled its complaints.

"Thank you for doing this." She had her purse back in her lap, now uncomfortably aware of her pink house robe. Out on the Point, she'd pictured slipping from one vehicle to another and driving back to the cabin totally unnoticed. She was irritated at herself for not remembering how early island life started. Lobstermen didn't wait on eight o'clock to start up their boats. They ran by the great time clock in the sky. Daylight was their alarm, and they were in full force on the docks.

They seemed to know Jeff's car, too, calling and

waving. One or two whistled, and as low as she ducked in her seat, she knew she couldn't disappear altogether.

"All you had to do was ask. Thank you for asking, by the way." He flipped the blinker on to turn in the town lot. With a slight rev of the engine, he coaxed the big tires over the low curb. The puddles from the night's rain splashed as he gained speed across the tarmac before stopping just in front of her car.

"How do you know this one's mine?"

"That's a silly question. Who else has Mass plates around here?" He turned the key off and shifted in his seat to look at her. "You know, I'm twenty-nine, and this is the first time I've ridden in a car with you."

"Your boat doesn't count, huh?" His remark was just what she'd been thinking. How many times had he driven these familiar roads, either alone or with a girlfriend, and she'd been attending high school, later college, and now working for half-a-dozen years for the insurance firm?

"Ah, my boat always counts." He leaned forward and wrapped both arms across the steering wheel, resting the side of his face on them and looking at her. "You've enjoyed the Dude, though?"

She looked at him, so boyish. She could see the fifteen-year-old from her last summer looking out of those eyes. She laughed and looked away.

"What?"

"You. You haven't changed at all." Her eyes burned, and they shouldn't. All connections with this man had been scoured away years ago. It was just a memory she'd seen in those eyes and nothing more.

"Then what has?"

She looked back at him. There on his cheek, just where his face dimpled when he smiled, was a crease. It was small, but it told her he smiled a lot. "Everything. Did you notice the big hole where my grandmother's house stood? That one's pretty obvious."

"Nah, the house doesn't mean anything, unless you let it." He leaned back, keeping one arm still on the steering wheel, and his back against the door.

"How can you say that? It changed my life."

"Stuff doesn't change your life. Not the real changes that are important." He looked out the back of the car the direction of the ferry landing. It was too far to see from the town lot, but something caught his attention. "I remember the girl who rang the bell every time I rowed up to her float." He smiled and shifted his eyes to look at her.

"You told me already."

"Right. I did. That first day." He laughed and looked away. "I guess I'd better get to the landing. They'll be loading up in a minute."

"I'm glad you haven't changed." The words slipped out before Katie could cut them off. She put her hand on the console, an ordinary gesture for an ordinary situation, but one she was aware of as very risky in this situation.

"Oh, I doubt that's true." He looked at her hand for a moment, then with a deep breath, he turned his head to look through the windshield. "Tonight, then?" He readjusted his position and started the engine, working the gearshift into neutral. With his left leg, he let out the clutch. The engine idled noisily.

"Early, you said. Still?" Katie found she didn't want to get out. This was a small taste of what she'd enjoyed so much with Jeff all those years ago: half saying things and knowing you didn't have to say the rest; the easy pauses; and the way he moved, comfortable in himself and with the world around him. He'd been a natural on a boat; and the cornerstone of the gang. Then he'd become a hole in her life she'd never been able to fill. For this one moment, she felt some of it back. It wasn't an opened floodgate, by any means, but the trickle was nice.

He looked at her and winked. "You better go. Town's coming alive, and that's a really pink bathrobe there. Don't want anyone talking."

"Oh! I didn't even think." She was now, though. Jeff, delivering her to her car at the crack of dawn, and wearing this? Could it look any worse?

"Just go. I'll be on time." He was smiling by then.

"Let me get my keys." She dug in her purse, finally

coming up with a bright yellow sunflower attached to a ring. "Don't you move until I get in that car." She looked at him hard.

"Yes, ma'am." He nodded. He did wait, but only just. Then his tires spun on the wet asphalt, and he was gone.

It didn't do much good for him to stick around, because just in front of her was Marc from the Paper Store. He waved with a smile and gave her a thumbs-up on a raised hand.

Oh, she was going to die. She was absolutely going to die!

Mortified, she started the car, working out the best way out of town to avoid being seen. Turn right, and that took her by the school. It also took her by the soccer fields and the high school track. She expected they were in use even this early: summer soccer games; joggers taking July seriously. Left were the docks and the ferry landing. Either way she was sure to be seen. Her car color didn't help. The bright blue stood out like a sore thumb.

She gritted her teeth and shifted into drive. One direction was as bad as the other, and she turned on her left blinker. It was at least shorter.

Before she got past the docks and the ferry horn sounded, more than one arm had waved to her. As she passed the landing, she felt relief no one was arriving this early. Word would be all over town. Only one man was walking the side of the road facing away from her, and he didn't look up.

Rounding the corner, she could see the ferry exiting the harbor with a whitewater tail trailing after it across the surface of the ocean. It had filled up after all, including two large trucks. At the very back of the deck was a green Jeep with a black fabric roof. Its brake lights flashed once, as if someone had shifted position inside and brushed a foot against the pedal, then immediately moved away.

It was just a glimpse. No more. Yet, as her car moved on down the road, Katie felt an empty sadness surround her. Like she'd had something, and now it was gone. Taken. Slipped through her fingers. Carried away by the ferry into lands unknown, with no news of just when it would return.

She knew what it was. It was fourteen years erased with the brush of a man's smile. It was fourteen years she wished she could live over again.

One more chance, God. Why did you take my life from me?

He hadn't. Not really. She had admitted that years before. The real problem, the real reason she couldn't forgive God was that He hadn't done anything at all. He had left her alone to learn to swim on her own, and she'd nearly drowned.

She wasn't jumping into the water again. One lobster bake and one ride to pick up her car didn't make a life preserver. If she was going to survive, she had to lock up her past tightly and keep it right where it belonged.

Sorry, Jeff, she determined. Bring lots of people, because you're going to need someone to talk to.

Her determination didn't stop the tears, though. She knew what she was giving up. However, safe was better than sorry, and when she got back to Boston, she'd be glad she'd been strong.

She just didn't feel glad now, and she didn't bother to wipe away the tears.

15

"You cannot expect me to do this." Katie held up the two strings Winnie had handed her, and she made a face. "I tie my shoes with bigger cords than this."

They weren't exactly strings, but Katie didn't consider them much more. The fabric amounted to little more than patches compared to what she usually wore.

"Okay." Winnie didn't sound offended. "Those were just freebies from a Macy's shoot. Toss them if you want. What about this?"

She pulled out a one-piece still on a hanger that was half black and brightly flowered over the rest. An extra strap was attached to the hanger. "I'm just not sure how we'll tighten it up to stay on you. The stringy thing is easier to adjust."

"Here's our solution." Katie lifted the strap from the inside to show it was a belt.

"Oh, you are so smart. Of course!" Winnie giggled. "Go put this on. You think soap will be okay in the water? I don't want to *pollute* or anything."

"The fish will live." Katie had jumped in, soaped up, and rinsed off by diving back in more than one time in her life. It had never done any damage that she was aware of.

She was glad Winnie had suggested this on her own. It was a sorely-needed distraction after the drive back in the car. She had been in control by the time she'd walked to the cabin, but the day seemed to stretch emptily ahead; and even the brilliant sunshine hadn't seemed to repair the pain.

Swimming off the float would be just the thing.

"Sweetie, look at this." Winnie stood at the window looking out towards the Dude. "We have water right here."

Katie had explained it once. At the float, they could leap in. Here? To get deep enough to swim meant wading in. What she didn't say was why jumping was better, but Winnie would learn. She might not be happy afterwards, but she would learn.

"See? The water's going away." Katie pointed to the exposed stones that still shimmered with water. The tide had started to turn, although it was still high. Yet, it had dropped past the edge of the deck, and it would be out several hundred feet before it finished.

"Still, we have to hike all the way over there?" Winnie already had on a two-piece, one that was conservative compared to the two strings from earlier. She held one of the striped towels under one arm.

Katie gave in a little, giving the bad news to her friend as gently as possible. "Water temperature. The sun warms the Cove, but open water is too deep, even on a day like today. Swimming off the float can mean a twenty-degree difference." It didn't mean it would be warm, but twenty degrees could mean the difference between invigorating playtime and hypothermia.

"That's a lot, I guess. Are there stickers?" Winnie wasn't wearing shoes, and the walk over the Point covered a lot of grass.

"Probably. What do you have?" Besides the blue spikes, Katie meant. Her shoes were more sensible, but she only had the one pair plus her house shoes.

"These?" Winnie pulled out a thin-soled pair of sandals, with jeweled beads for straps.

"Perfect. Just stay out of the tall grass."

"Are there snakes?" Winnie's eyes went wide.

"No. Just killer seals. They sleep in the grass." It was a mean thing to say, but Katie's emotions had been stripped bare, and she couldn't help herself.

"Now I know you're teasing." Winnie grabbed Katie's arm and laughed. "You take such good care of me, how can anything go wrong?" She gave Katie a soft peck on the cheek and walked out on the deck, humming to herself.

Katie ran through the list of things that could go wrong. They could slip and fall on the way down to the dock. The water might not be as warm as she hoped. Then there were sea urchins, the prickly kind that bloomed infections across the bottoms of your feet. There were all sorts of things that could go plenty wrong, like hearts stripped bare, old flames that had flamed out, and heavenly Fathers who hadn't acted very fatherly.

Oh, no, Winnie, she wanted to say. I can't take very good care of you at all.

Instead, she slipped on the suit, found it fit rather better than her friend had suggested, and cinched the belt up around the waist anyway. She had packed a bar of soap in her bag, and she dug until she found it. For a wash cloth, she pulled out a clean sock to drop the soap in. With the second towel in tow, she exited the cabin to join her friend.

"Ready?" She nudged Winnie who lay supine on one of the loungers.

"Sweetie, I was thinking. You know, you said that about the water temperature. Did I see a motel in town?"

"No, no. We are not renting a motel room just to take a shower." Katie pulled Winnie up from the chair. "This is the real Maine experience, and you get to live it all."

"How cold will it be?" Winnie had found sunglasses from somewhere, and she slipped them on her face. "Very much colder than Key West? I was swimming in the ocean there once."

"Oh, Honey. Maybe a degree or two. But, hey! We have sunshine and soap." Katie held up her sock and soap combination. "What else do we need?" Besides hot water, she thought, but the less warning given about that the better.

"And towels, from Jeffie's." Winnie held hers up and

smiled.

"Sure. And Jeffie's towels. Now, about tonight, the tide won't be all the way out when everyone arrives, but by the time we set up the cookout, we'll have quite a bit of room on the rocks. It's safer with the fire that way." Katie talked as they headed across the Point. The trail would lead right past Carver House's empty grave, and the turn in the conversation was to get them to the other side. She needed time to get used to the hole. She should have considered that her friend's inquisitive nature would lead her right to it.

"Your grandmother's house was big." Winnie stopped the conversation in full swing. "What are these steps going down?"

"They led to the basement." It would be easier if they walked on by, and Katie made a try to move her friend along. "It's probably filled with raccoons and mice now."

"Ooh! They won't get me if I look over, will they?" She walked through overgrown grass to peer into the sunken cavern. "I thought there would be boards and stuff inside. Where's everything that didn't get burned?"

"Everything got burned." Her parents had received the bill for clearing away the debris, from a local man suggested by the town council and hired for the job. With the disaster that had happened, and six months later to have to pay for cleaning up everything that was left? That had been the final straw for them, and the property had sat unloved and unused for all the intervening years.

"Janine said you could build a new house on top of this." Winnie smiled brightly, as if that resolved the whole issue.

"Maybe, if an engineering survey tested it out as sound. Somebody could rebuild, anyway. I work and make a car payment, remember? I have no money."

They moved on, and just ahead the dock came into view. So did the Cove. The water sparkled in the sun, and the trees lining the shore looked unreal in their perfection. There was just enough of a breeze to put the swing on the old apple tree in motion, and it was beautiful.

"Forget that old motel in town. This is my bathtub." Winnie pushed her hair from her face when the breeze caught it. "This is *Sound of Music* beautiful."

"Or *Under a Tuscan Sun*." Katie knew how her friend felt, though. She had lived this for all of her childhood, and it had always felt that way to her.

"Me first!" Winnie took off down the path, her beaded sandals catching in the sun, her towel held high in one hand. "Come on, Katie! This will be fun!"

"I have the soap," Katie called after her. It was fun watching someone else finding so much enjoyment in this place she'd loved dearly. Walking more slowly down the path to the dock, she idly ran a finger over the nails she had filed nearly completely away. When they were still broken, she'd at least remembered how beautiful they were. Once they were filed, they didn't catch on stuff anymore, and she was able to put them out of her thoughts. They had become nothing, not a nuisance, not beautiful, nothing. But the thing was, she didn't enjoy them anymore. They would have to grow out before she could appreciate them again, and that was something she couldn't rush. She would have to file them, shape them, and it would happen a little at a time. Yet, if she was patient, she would have her fingernails back again, just as beautiful as before.

She saw the connection, one that she would have once attributed to a caring and almighty God. Her relationship with this island and with Jeff was her fingernail. It had been torn and made ugly. She had improved it, but only by slicing away everything she had loved. It no longer hurt, but only because it was no longer there.

In the process of repairing the pain, she had lost something very beautiful. The only way to get it back was to give it a chance to grow once again. If she continually filed away every entreaty Jeff made, all she would ever have would be nubs on her heart, and that wasn't very appealing at all.

The in-between stage wasn't enjoyable, though. That's the part she dreaded. Anyway, she only had four days. How much could a fingernail grow in only four days?

Lots of luck there!

Just then she heard Winnie scream, and Katie took off running down the hill.

16

Winnie's scream was a serious false alarm.

Katie found that out only after slipping once on the grass and racing to the end of the dock to look down at her friend standing on the float running her hands up and down her arms.

"What's wrong?" she called down, still catching her breath. "Are you hurt?"

"Do you know how cold the water is? I have chill bumps all up and down my legs. You should have told me." Winnie sounded particularly peeved.

"That's why I didn't." Katie patted her chest, glad to have her heart under control. She started down the ramp, seeing that there was even a ladder on the side of the float. Good. It was easier to exit the water with a ladder. Someone, meaning Jeff, had been very thorough about keeping things in good repair.

At the bottom, she dumped her things on the float, and she pulled out her sock and the bar of soap. "This early in the season, I would have suggested soaping up before you jump in. Then, if you're freezing, you don't have to take another dip." She had the soap slipped into the sock by then, and she dipped it in the water and began scrubbing her leg. She made a face. "That *is* cold."

"Yeah. It is." Winnie didn't sound very forgiving.

"You warm up while I go first. You have to do this, though." She pointed the soap at her friend then dipped it back in the water and continued working on the grass stain on her leg. "See this green spot? This is where I slipped when you screamed. Maybe I should make you go first."

"Not me. My chill bumps are still bumpy."

"Who cares about your funny little chill bumps?" Katie grinned impishly, reminded of long-ago friends on the island joining her on summer adventures, one of which had been tag on this very float. The goal had been to force your target to leap into the water.

She dipped the soap in the water and went for Winnie.

"Not my hair!" Winnie screamed and ran toward the ramp. She got about halfway up before Katie pretended to give in.

"You are such a baby. I'll leave you alone, if I must. If you're lucky, maybe the mean seal will swim away when I jump in the water."

"He's back?" Winnie scanned the water. "Where . . . where is he? Maybe I don't need a bath after all."

"I'm sorry." Katie apologized, holding the soap behind her back. "I forgot how scared you were the other day. There's no seal out there. I was just teasing." By then she was nearly to Winnie, and when she was close enough to grab her, she wrapped a hand around her wrist and began smearing soap over her arm.

"Katie! That is so mean. Now I have to get back in the water." Winnie wiped at the soap, but it was hopeless. Her hand was dry, and none of it brushed away. Instead, she spread it around.

"That's right. Now, what happened to Sweetie?" Katie held the soap over her head, flouncing a bit as she walked toward the float. "I like it when you call me Sweetie."

"Sweetie's for good friends who don't smear soap all over my arm. You smeared. You're Katie from now on."

"Oh, Honey. I apologize. Forgive me?" Katie held out her arms for a hug.

"Okay. Just don't do it again." Winnie smiled, and she held out her arms in return to give Katie a hug. Just as they touched, Katie rubbed the soap vigorously up and down her back.

"Gotcha!" Katie hooted.

"No!" Winnie tried to pull away. "Stop! You apologized!"

"I was teasing! No! No!" By then they were off balance and far too close to the side of the float.

With arms flailing, and hands grabbing each other and empty air, Katie's foot missed the edge of the float first, and she stood off balance for several seconds as she realized what was about to happen. Winnie tried to disengage to save herself, but it was no good. Katie had a firm grip on her arm, and when she went completely off balance, the two women tumbled into the sea.

Neither one saw the splash, as they were underwater, but they both swam for the ladder as soon as they came up for air.

"It's cold," Katie grabbed at her towel. "I had no idea!"

"I told you. Listen next time." Winnie grabbed at the soap still in her friend's hand. "Give me that. I might as well get this over with."

When she got it, though, it didn't happen quite as Katie expected. Winnie was ready to give as good as she got, and she chased Katie across the float until Katie dove off the side to save herself.

"Chicken," Winnie called when Katie came up for air. "Here. You might as well use this. You can clean up your behavior, too, and be nicer to me." She tossed the soap into the water.

Katie swam for it with several strong strokes. It would sink if she didn't grab it fast, and it was the only bar she'd brought. She did take time to soap up before climbing out. She called out that on the second time in, the water was much more bearable, and she tried to sound very encouraging.

Winnie was having none of it, and she pouted, dipping her fingers into the water and brushing at her arm.

As she climbed out, Katie tossed Winnie the soap. Either she would or she wouldn't. For now, she planned to dry and catch some sun. In Maine, that was the only way to warm after a swim.

It was the splash as she lay with her eyes closed that told her Winnie had followed through. Good, she mused. You can sleep inside tonight.

It was a pleasant and satisfying thought.

The water her friend splashed over her before she climbed out was far less pleasant. However, rather than giving Winnie the satisfaction of complaining, she sat up and laughed. It was a vacation, after all, and she was here with her good friend. If they couldn't take a little teasing from each other, then what was the point of it all?

Heading back to the house was their first big bombshell of the day. Walking past the old basement, from beyond the broken gate, a voice hailed them.

"Katie! Winnie! Hi!"

"Janine?" Katie looked at Winnie and shrugged before calling back, "We didn't plan for anyone to be here so early. But come on in."

"I know, I know, and I apologize." She came through the gate, her hands up in apology. "Oh, you've been swimming. Am I interrupting?"

"We've been bathing." Katie laughed and held up the soap. "With no running water, we have to depend on the island to keep us functioning."

"I'm so sorry. I should have remembered your gramma making you do that. Old memories are good memories, right?" She leaned in to Winnie, smiling. "Makes the city look pretty good, right?"

"Janine! Don't encourage her. I barely got her in the water." Katie drew a finger across her throat with a grin.

"Sweetie, what's that?" Winnie touched Katie on the shoulder and pointed through the gate, to where two boys were throwing sticks at each other.

"Oh, I should have said. I brought help." Janine yelled out, "Boys! Boys, get over here, and I mean pronto. And I better not see any black eyes when you get here."

"Are they here for the cookout?" The very idea worried Katie. That was specifically not what Jeff had promised. Katie planned to give him a fistful if he'd fallen through on this.

"Don't you worry about that. I roped their daddy in for the evening. However, he's off island for the day, so they're mine till the last ferry. I'm just putting them to work to keep them out of trouble. Boys! I said now!"

Two tow-headed boys came running up, both small, and wearing jeans and sneakers. Both had on striped tees that looked like the boys weren't the first owners. One bumped into the other when they stopped, and the first one kicked his brother on the leg.

The next two Katie recognized from town. The bigger one, Kevie, she thought, had the smaller one, Konnar, by the neck. Literally by the neck. He had his arm around his head, and he was giving him what she thought was a noogie, with his knuckles scraping his brother's head right on top.

"Stop that." Janine pulled his arm away, grabbing the smaller boy's face in her hand. "Are you okay, Konnar?" When he nodded, she pointed her finger sternly at Kevie and made a demanding face. When she turned back to Katie and Winnie, she brightened with a smile. "You've met my olders. The two younger ones are Karlton, but he likes to go by Karl, and Keithie."

The youngest boys waved. The older two continued to wrestle with their mother's back turned.

"What can we do for you?" Katie questioned Janine as she waved at the four boys.

"Take these home with you when you leave? No, I'm teasing." She laughed as if embarrassed she had said that, looking at her boys before shaking her head. "Thank you though for insisting I come tonight without them. I've needed a break, and this will be nice. Now, though, I have a job for them to do."

"Doing what?" That had Katie mystified. She'd done lobster bakes. There was nothing to it. Build a fire, let it die down, and throw in some lobsters wrapped in foil. Even easier? Boil a pot of water on the fire and toss the lobsters in. She didn't have a pot, but since Jeff had made the plans, she assumed he'd provide the pot. Or pots, as it may be.

"You'll see." The boys had turned restless, and two now wrestled on the ground. "We have stuff to unload. If I don't keep them busy, they'll do this all afternoon. Al has the truck, so I borrowed Roker's for the day. You'll know it by the roll bars." She shrugged, as if the roll bars embarrassed her. "You just go on about whatever you were doing. We'll be out of your way in no time."

She had turned and was already heading towards the gate as she finished, her words fading as she reached to pop one of the boys on the back of the head before chasing them into the parking area.

"Sweetie?" Winnie was wide-eyed. "We have company."

"I know. She did promise they weren't staying long." Katie laughed. "And she's a very good friend from a very long time ago. Be patient, just for the day?"

"I suppose." She made a sad face, before letting it break into a wide smile. "For my very best friend? Absolutely!"

"Are you looking forward to tonight?" Katie wasn't sure she was, although it seemed it was happening one way or another.

Winnie made her viewpoint perfectly clear when she grabbed Katie's arms and squealed. "Lobster bake! I've never been to a lobster bake on a real beach. I'm so excited!"

Katie laughed. They were going to have a very good time. Winnie's reaction cinched it. Janine's boys? They'd be gone by then, and that was the icing on the cake . . . or maybe it was the butter on the lobster. Either way, if Winnie was this excited, it was going to be the best day of their trip.

17

"We can have cool air, if this window will just work." Katie wrestled with one beside the bed. It had raised several inches then stuck. She had her hand underneath it, shaking it in an attempt to force it up. The sun was now fully on the cabin, and with open rafters and no insulation, fresh air was paramount.

"I'm no good at windows, but I know we need some flowers in here." Winnie picked up her sunglasses from the desk. She had on pale blue shorts and a bright pink sleeveless top. The colors matched the beads on her sandals exactly. "Want to go looking with me?"

"Later. I'm working on this window." Katie was also in shorts, tan, with a teal-trimmed pocket tee. She wore her sturdy island walking shoes. She was down to inspecting the tracks on each side of the window frame to see what was blocking the movement of the glass panel. "In any case, we have to find a vase to put them in."

"Done. One water bottle emptied and ready." Winnie stepped out the door, and it banged shut after her. The sound of water splashed the deck.

"You could have left the water in. Something to cut them?" Katie yelled after her. "Most of the flowers up here have thorns."

Frustrated, she rapped the recalcitrant window pane with her knuckles, and got on the bed to open one of the two just above it. She bumped the wooden frame on the new window with her palm to get it started, and it slipped up with ease the rest of the way. "Why can't you learn this lesson?" she muttered at the partially opened window next to it. She could see Winnie already out in the woods, water bottle in hand, searching through the underbrush.

"The big purple ones are pretty," Katie called through the screen. "They're called lupines, but the best ones grow in full sun."

"I found some little white ones. There are so many I can't choose." Sure enough, there were several already waving from the mouth of the bottle. Winnie held it out with a smile for Katie to see.

"There's one place you have to see while you're here." Katie called through the screen again. "When you get all your flowers collected, we can drive there if you want."

"I'm ready now." She tucked something in her pocket and headed toward the cabin.

Once inside, Winnie set her collection of flowers on the desk, and she pulled her nail file from her pocket. "I love this." She held it up to show Katie then laid it beside the flowers.

"You love a nail file?" Katie reached to pick it up, and she held it in the light. "What in the world for?"

"It does everything. Like just now, I used it to saw off the flowers. Don't leave home without it. Do I need to change before we leave?" Winnie ran the comments together, fluffing her hair at the same time by running her fingers through it, and at one point, pulling out one of her blue combs and adjusting its position. She looked into a large hand mirror as she did so.

"We're going on a hike, so only if you're worried about stickers."

"We've hiked already this morning." Winnie let the mirror fall to the bed. "All the way to swim and back again. Besides, you said we could drive." She smiled prettily, as if pleading for leniency.

"We drive there. We hike up."

"A lighthouse? It must be a lighthouse. I've never been up a lighthouse." Winnie brightened.

"A mountain, although, before you panic, it's not a real mountain." Katie had to smile at the expression on her friend's face. "It's called Lookout Ledge, and it's got the best views anywhere around."

"Okay." Winnie sounded like it was somewhat less than okay. "No chairlifts, I suppose." She flipped the mirror over, toying with the handle a minute, before lifting it up and primping her hair again. "Still, if we can see everywhere, then everyone can see me. I can't complain about that. I'm ready." She dropped the mirror on the bed and walked to the door.

On the way to the car, just as they got to the gate, they found the few things Janine and her boys had unloaded amounted to a truckload, and not a small truckload at that. There were numerous folding tables leaning against the good gatepost, three galvanized metal tubs, and an enormous stack of metal folding chairs with slightly rusted joints. Four large and covered plastic bins apparently held *something*, but what they didn't know.

"Oh, my!" Katie was taken aback. "How many people are planning to be here?"

"Oh, it's like a real party!" Winnie grabbed Katie's arm and squealed. "Thank you, Sweetie! I'll climb any mountain you want me to, because I get to go to a party tonight!"

"Sure. Just for you." Katie smiled and patted her friend's hand in congratulations. The feelings running through her were a little different.

So, she thought. She was getting her wish. Jeff was bringing lots of people to talk to. Well, she had wished it, so she shouldn't be disappointed. She guessed somewhere in the back of her mind she had hoped for a little bit of her childhood back for this one evening. Oh, she knew in any case it wouldn't be more than a tantalizing tidbit of a time that had evaporated with the smoke rising from the remains of all that had been taken from her, but it might have been fun, anyway.

With her memories in tow, climbing Lookout Ledge was bittersweet. It was a designated town park, but parking was a grassy spot under the trees. To get to the ledge was a climb up a root- and moss-encrusted series of steps, with thick branches for handholds. The reward was a bare granite outcropping falling off into Carver Cove and offering unrestricted views across Rockhaven Island, showcasing the island's three massive wind turbines, and several large homes that topped spruce-covered ridges in the distance. They turned to take in East Haven Island behind them, and undulating hills visible on the mainland in the misty distance. All of it was held together by the deep blue of an ocean that reflected a brilliant and sunny sky.

Winnie oohed and aahed, and with her phone in her hand, she clicked and posted all that she saw. She posed herself with Katie, sending several selfies to the Internet kingdoms in the sky, and seemed enraptured with her mastery of this mountain throne.

Katie saw more. She pictured Babes at twelve, the summer before her final one, already buxom in her exuberant leap for adulthood, bundled up in a purple hoodie, with Apple at her side, trying to create a successful s'more over an open flame. They weren't supposed to build fires on the top of Lookout Ledge, but as kids, well, rules were made to be broken, and they had broken a few.

The sky had been heavy that day, with the wind filled with pending rain. It had spit at them occasionally, but it had yet to really open up on them, and being kids, they would only give in when forced to retreat.

Austie and Jeff had stood at the tip of the Ledge, flapping their arms and crowing like Jack in *Titanic*. King of the World, they'd called. We're King of the World.

They had been, too. Katie guessed Benny and Bobby must have been there. They were with the gang constantly all summer long, so she couldn't imagine them anywhere else, but she couldn't picture them that day. Ritchey and Janine had been off island participating in some long-forgotten summer school function. No, that day had been just Babes and Apple, and the Kings of the World.

Austie. Katie remembered him as tall, in spite of not being much older than the rest of the gang. College tall, a real man, in body, if not in behavior. At least not that day. He had crowed, after all. Jeff, still fourteen, and looking very much fourteen. A head shorter than Austie, he could have been his midget twin, thumbs under his armpits, his face pointed to the sky.

They had called her over to join in their brash declarations of godhood to the entire world, but the edge of the ledge had warned her away, and she remembered being very cold. She'd escaped her grandmother's house with a jacket but left it on the gate as she ran down the road with her companions-in-mischief-and-mayhem leading her away.

Astray, she now thought might be the better word. They had done things she would be embarrassed to admit. The fire on Lookout Ledge hadn't been the worst. Oh, nothing too terribly serious. They'd been kids, but they'd explored what wasn't theirs to explore, houses with drives roped off for the earliest months of the year, boats moored and unused for the entire summer, and the occasional hidden beach, where they could laugh and be silly, and no one besides them would ever know.

It was Babes' last full summer on the island. In retrospect, Katie should have seen it as a warning, as the handwriting on the wall. *Watch out, Katie. I'm taking it all away. You've enjoyed this too much, and I don't like you having this much fun.*

So, there on Lookout Ledge with Winnie on a bright, sunny afternoon, there were two events taking place. One was two adult friends, snapping perfect, beautiful pictures and sharing laughter with each other; and a second, of a faded childhood that had been perfection, and those living it out hadn't even known what they'd had.

It wouldn't have mattered, anyway. When God decided to take it away, it evaporated completely. What was, what is, and what might be are three very different things. You can't hold to one, you have to live out the other, and the final one? That's a dark mystery that no one can plan out or depend on, and sometimes it never shows up at all.

That was Katie's day on Lookout Ledge, and she soaked up both memories, because they were both hers to claim.

18

Katie awoke from her nap to the sounds of screaming boys and large stones being tossed from the beach into the changing tide. She sat up to see her friend still asleep on the foldaway bed at her side. Outside the three younger Peavey boys ran rampant on her beach.

"No," she said. "They cannot be here."

The oldest, she thought. Kevie. Where was he? She'd seen them in action, and not being able to find one was disconcerting. She stood and slipped her shoes on, exiting quietly and hoping to let Winnie sleep.

At the edge of the deck, she snapped her fingers and called, "Boys!" They stopped and looked at her. "Where's your brother? Kevie, right?"

They all shrugged, but Konnar, the second in size, said, "We dunno. He took off." They stood and looked at her, like they were waiting on something.

"You're Konnar, right?" She smiled, but she didn't feel a smile inside. Them not knowing? That was ominous.

"Yes, ma'am." He nodded, as if he was used to being just one of the bunch, and he rarely got his name used by outsiders.

"Thank you, Konnar. You may play now." She looked

down the beach, and it took a minute before she noticed what wasn't there. When she did, it leaped out at her. "Konnar, where's the dinghy?"

He was picking up rocks a quarter his size and lobbing them to make them splash, and he paused just long enough to huff out, "Kevie," before he let loose his next volley.

"Oh, my word," she said. She scanned the water, hoping to see him on Dyer's Rock or at the lighthouse. There was no plastic dinghy. She took off down the shore path, knowing she would catch glimpses of the water all the way around the Point. If he had headed for the Cove—and where else would he have gone—she would find him at some point.

She pictured the lighthouse. The sun had been shining on the west side, and it was fully lighted. She figured in her head. It must be after five. Jeff had said he was coming early, and he hadn't been specific, but with the ferry times, five had stuck in her head.

Where was Jeff?

At every opportunity, she ducked past the greenery to see if the small boat was visible. With the tide high, the massive rocks dropped off sharply into the ocean, and she had no idea what she would do if she saw the boy, but at least she'd know where he was.

She was nearly to the path down to the dock when she got her first sighting, and it wasn't what she expected. Jeff appeared first, coming up from the dock, and then the boy appeared, his collar firmly grasped in Jeff's hand. Jeff didn't look pleased, either.

"Katie! I hoped to see you. Kevie here and I have been having a discussion, and I need you to clarify a point or two."

"She did, too!" The boy tried to wrench free from Jeff's hand, but he was eleven, and Jeff had a lobsterman's big hands and strong arms.

"I did what?" The boy's claim caught her off guard. She'd waved at him earlier when Janine had been there . . . and then she knew. This boy had been telling Jeff she and Winnie were bathing off the dock. How embarrassing! It had been perfectly innocent, but had the boy been spying? With what she'd seen, she thought it entirely probable.

"Hold that thought." Jeff held up one hand to her, his palm out. "Now that you're here, I want to ask Kevie my question again. Kevie, did Katie give you permission to take the dinghy?"

"Yes!" the boy spat.

"I—I—Jeff!" The boy was lying!

"Just a minute, Katie." Jeff leaned over and got right in the boy's face. "Kevie, she's right there, and whatever you tell me, she's going to hear. Make sure you tell me what really happened. Now, again, did Katie give you her permission to take the boat out?"

"Well, she didn't say no!" His words still stung with their arrogance.

"Jeff! I was—"

He held his hand out to her yet again, interrupting her rebuttal. Instead, he asked Kevie another question. "Did you ask her?"

"How could I? She was asleep in there with her pink friend."

Katie was flabbergasted. She'd seen the younger boy kick his mother, but how could anyone be so bigheaded? She had no idea kids could be so awful. It pleased her to see Jeff grab him by his ear as he stood.

"You little weasel. You know I don't put up with that nonsense. I should tie you to a tree until I take you home tonight. You don't deserve any lobster."

The boy barked back, "I don't want any lobster."

"Then I'd better not see you eating any, and I counted them. I know how many I brought." Jeff released him, and the boy took off over the top of the hill. He turned to Katie. "I'm sorry. There's nothing I could do. I had to bring them."

"All four of them?" She had spoken with Janine, who said her husband was keeping them. "Why the change of plans?"

"Al is why I was off island today. His truck had to go to Bangor, and I was supposed to be bringing him back. There was a fender-bender on the way, and he's having a broken arm repaired. Janine's on the ferry now to go pick him up." He laughed and shrugged. "Island life."

"But, you said you were taking that boy home tonight."

"Maybe. That one thinks I am, anyway. If Al gets out of surgery—"

"Surgery? My word, how bad was it?" The boy's antics with the boat seemed to pale in comparison to this. If it required a hospital stay, how long would that be? Poor Janine.

"You know fender benders. His arm was inside the steering wheel when he got hit, and it snapped it clean. Right through his shirtsleeve. The doc said he could probably be released tonight but driving would be out of the question for a week at least." He laughed.

"It's not funny. You can't laugh just because Al's not here." She didn't know Al, but laughing at him seemed insensitive.

"No. It's what he said in the doctor's office. Doc, he said, I can't drive, anyway. My truck's wrecked. I can still pilot my boat, though? I got lobster traps to haul." He laughed again, shaking his head. "That Al. They had him on something by then, so I suppose he can be excused."

"How will they get back, if he does get out?" She knew what last ferry meant. It meant last ferry, and that meant they were stuck on the mainland no matter what.

"I'll run over. I can take Janine for her car in the morning. Not a problem, as long as I go early." He made a motion with his hand, as if to brush it all off as old news. "Are you ready for a real lobster bake, one to shout out summer to the entire island?"

"I suppose?" She said it like a question, because she wasn't sure. "I saw all those tables. I don't know that I have room—"

"Come, now. There's lots of room."

"My deck won't hold all that stuff Janine and her boys unloaded. Just those tables alone . . ."

"Ah! Come here." He held out a hand, and when she offered hers, he pulled her to him and pointed down the path to the dock. Along the beach, the glistening stones shimmered in the afternoon sun. Roker from town and another man were unfolding the tables from up by the old gate. "We'll position the tables, and as soon as the tide moves completely out of the way, we'll set up the bonfire. More tables are already set up in the boathouse. You'll see later. Right now, how's Winnie doing?"

She pulled her hand free. Just for a moment, she'd let herself be lulled into thinking that fifteen-year-old boys matured into respectable men, and she really ought to give Jeff a chance. He had handled that boy masterfully, and to spend the day on the mainland to help a friend, only to have to go further and do more, including babysitting his children and taking his boat to the mainland to get him? Twice? That would be very expensive.

She remembered he had taken Winnie's hand the night before. His words rang out in her memory. *See you tomorrow. It'll be fun.* He told Katie he hoped she'd have fun. He'd known Winnie would have fun, or at least that he would have fun if Winnie was around.

"Why so many tables?" Her question was a distraction. What she wanted to ask was more along the line of, Why are you here? Why am I here? Why haven't you found a wife yet, Jeff Ragsdale?

Then, maybe the real questions should be aimed at God, as in, Why are you putting me through this again? Wasn't once bad enough?

Jeff was explaining with enthusiasm, though, all the people she would meet, and how they were excited to finally meet her. He didn't seem to notice she'd pulled her hand away when he mentioned Winnie's name. And why, of all things, would anyone on this island be excited to meet her? It had been half a lifetime, she had just been a summer girl, and the Point had sat abandoned and forgotten forever. Who knew and who cared? Not Katie, not God, and certainly not Jeff Ragsdale, who was more interested in Winnie Catron's happiness than he was about hers.

Just when she had been willing to at least give all this a try, and now God had to step in and bungle it one more time. Or, Katie was perfectly willing to admit, maybe it was like before. God wasn't stepping in, and that was the problem. He wasn't stepping in, and that's why things were falling apart, just like they had all those years ago.

19

The first few people arrived through the rickety gate, and somehow, that's how Katie expected everyone to come to the party. About six, the first boat showed up. It was a dinghy about the size of her plastic one, and there was a middle-aged couple in it. They looked like summer people, him in a paisley summer sweater and boaters, and her wearing a light jacket and chinos. They laughed when they shared that they had seen the bath on the float. They were glad their new neighbors across the Cove were taking advantage of the warm summer sun.

More came by motorboat, most small, but several lobster boats and one cabin cruiser tied up at moorings in the cove. Jeff set up a teenager with a small motorized skiff to ferry them to shore.

After a time, the float looked like the one in town, the small boats stacked three and four deep, the latest arrivals walking over those already docked to get to the float.

Ashore, adults corralled children, and teens explored among the trees. Someone had put bright yellow tape around the old foundation, with signs that said off limits. It seemed to be keeping most people out, although Katie knew that as far as the teens wandering the point went, they would see it as a challenge hiding something too good not to explore.

Jeff even had an athletic-looking teen girl giving the younger children rides in the plastic dinghy out and around the Lil' Dude. A stack of orange life preservers was in one of the plastic bins delivered by Janine that morning.

At the crescent-shaped beach by the dock, Roker and the friend from earlier had a driftwood fire roaring, with a large bucket of banded lobsters to the side. They would go on as soon as they had coerced a good bed of coals from the flames.

Jeff seemed to be the center of it all. He directed, he pointed, he requested, and things moved just the way he intended. The children knew him, and he knelt and played with the younger ones; the older crowd he called out to, and they called back. The adults seemed to think him a friend, as if there was a very real connection between him and each one of them.

Most surprising to Katie was the number of people who spoke to her. They were very polite, introducing themselves as living on this cove, or on that harbor, or on the road that led to yet another part of the island. A surprising number mentioned that they hoped to see her in services the next morning.

The fire had been knocked down, and the lobsters were being prepared, when Katie caught what Jeff was doing. As he greeted people, he shook their hands, or sometimes gave the women a formal kiss on the cheek. Then, invariably, he searched until he found her, and pointed them her way.

She wanted to roll her eyes at that. She didn't appreciate being the poor summer waif whose home and chance for a lifetime of enjoyment on Rockhaven had been stolen away by a freak late-season fire. Let it go, Jeff, she thought. This was all your idea, and I gave in only because you forced me into it. I don't want to be singled out. I don't want people to feel pity for me.

For a distraction, she searched for Winnie. She had been angry at her earlier, yet she hadn't been at Jeff's side at all. She hadn't seen her anywhere, and that worried her.

Winnie liked to be at the center of everything. The young woman was a dear, and Katie adored her, but her natural beauty had shaped who she was. She was so used to being admired that she expected to be admired. Ignore her, and she didn't understand why the world was behaving as it was.

Prowling, carrying a glass of clear soda in her hand, Katie finally found where her friend had gotten herself to. As she neared the cabin, she caught the sound of giggles and high-pitched laughter. Once she stepped on the deck, she saw the culprit. Inside, Winnie perched on Katie's bed, and she was surrounded by probably a dozen preteen and teen girls. Spread out before her were all her makeup supplies, haircare ointments, and other pretties for making herself beautiful. At the desk, an island girl with medium length hair was trying—not very successfully—to work Winnie's curlers into her hair.

"Winnie?" Katie knocked and opened the screen. "Are you having fun?"

"Oh, Sweetie, more than I ever thought possible! Your Jeffie said I would, and I am. I really am." Several of the girls giggled when Winnie called him Jeffie. She didn't seem to notice, though. She reached to point to a girl who was putting eyeshadow on with one of Winnie's application pads. "Oh, right there. You missed a tiny spot."

Katie laughed. "Enjoy, Winnie. I'm going to mingle." She turned away and stepped outside, not sure if her friend had even heard her. She had been wrong about Jeff and Winnie. She had to have been. They didn't seem to have spoken more than a dozen words to each other the entire evening, if that. Her good friend Winnie was still her good friend Winnie, and she was glad.

It dawned on her that she hadn't seen Janine's boys creating havoc the entire evening. She frowned, wondering how bad the damage would be if those boys had found a way to escape observation for any length of time.

"Katie, there you are." Jeff stepped on the deck, and he walked up to her with a smile. "I see Winnie's doing what she really enjoys. I know you especially like her, but I can't imagine spending my life with someone who likes makeup better than the outdoors. I'd rather dig in the mud any day."

"I remember you digging in the mud." Katie smiled.

"Seriously? After all this time, I thought you would have forgotten anything like that." He seemed very pleased with her remark, and he rocked up on the balls of his feet with a smile.

"It's on your Facebook page, remember?"

"Oh. Right. You and Winnie are friends, and she probably showed you. I didn't think. Man, you scrolled a long way down if you found that picture."

"That was a long time ago, wasn't it? I also noticed it was faded around the edges. Torn in one spot, too." It felt good to talk to him. Not to worry about what she said. Not to have to explain herself. Just to say what came to her.

"It was my mirror you." He bumped her arm with his elbow. "You were there smiling at me when I got up in the morning and when I went to bed at night."

"You didn't know I was alive." She teased, but it was true. She had been the summer friend who slipped in and slipped out. The others had been the true twine, all wrapped into a ball, one, and complete. Except Babes. She unraveled first, then Katie, then she supposed Ritchey was the final straw. She hadn't heard anything about the other four.

"Oh, I knew. I just didn't know how to talk to you."

"Hokey-smokey. That's nonsense. You talked to me all the time. Can we borrow your boat, Katie, or you knock down the hornet's nest first, Katie. You talked all the time." She laughed. She had forgotten much of that until now. Being here with Jeff, with the people milling around, offered a kind of security. She could relax, because it was safe to let her guard down.

"We did used to say that, didn't we? Hokey-smokey. I'd forgotten. Yeah, I said that stuff, but only because I didn't know how to say anything else. I talked to you like a boy because I didn't know how to talk to a girl." He took a sip of his soda, and without warning, he pointed. "There's one."

"One what?" She looked for a hawk, or a deer.

119

"A Peavey. I have them all assigned to church members, one per boy."

"Like wardens." Katie laughed, then she looked away, embarrassed. "Oh, I'm so sorry. Don't ever let Janine know I said that. I had wondered why they weren't running rampant over the landscape. You, you have a fix for everything, don't you?"

"I hope." He looked at her and smiled, raising his eyebrows and letting them fall down again. "Have I fixed everything?"

"I don't know. What needed fixed?" It seemed to her that he had fixed a lot of stuff already. Her dock, the cabin, the Lil' Dude. "The gate. The gate's not fixed. One post is rotten through."

He laughed. "Not exactly what I meant, but I can do that, too. If I do, will you promise to come back to enjoy it?"

Katie knew what that meant. Come back and enjoy him was what he meant. She didn't answer. She didn't know how to answer.

"Okay. I'm pushing too hard. So, have you enjoyed my church?"

"Your church?" It hit her. Not just some, but almost everyone had invited her to church the next day. She'd not thought too much of it. She and Winnie had planned on going all along. Now it made sense. "These people are all from your church?"

"Mostly. A few attend sporadically, but we are kinda a one-church town. If someone attends, yeah, they're from my church." He motioned to where one of the smaller Peaveys tugged against an older woman's grip on his arm. "That's why I take so much interest in Janine's kids. Not because they're wonderful, because they're not, not to spend time with, anyway." He chuckled. "Don't you tell Janine I said *that*. Still, those boys are part of my church, and I've always felt responsible for them. It's why I step in when Janine and Al need a hand."

Katie felt her eyes burn, and she chewed her lip. Why was he saying this to her? No man could be this generous

120

with his time and emotions. This evening, all clearly planned by Jeff. The Point, all clearly maintained by Jeff. Janine's rough and tangle family, all clearly kept functioning by Jeff. When did Jeff do *Jeff?*

She was angry, too. Look at these people. They clearly enjoyed each other. They were well-mannered and polite, but they were here, and they were having a good time. This was what she'd wanted all those years ago, why she had looked forward to returning each summer. This was what God had stolen from her.

For her the knife thrust even deeper. This man standing next to her. What could have grown between them if they'd had a lifetime to get to know one another? What could their lives have become?

"Katie? Is everything okay?" The words were soft and caring.

Katie knew them for what they were, though. They were the same soft and caring words he had offered to Janine and all these people around her on her beloved Point: You need a hand. Can I step in?

That was not what she needed from him. Her emotions were on quicksand, and she was about to go under. She did the only thing she could think to do.

"Peachy. Hokey-smokey." She waved her hand in the air between them, wriggling her fingers, and she laughed. It was to keep from looking at him. "You throw a fine shindig, Jeffie. I think it's time to head to the bonfire and see if those lobsters are all fired up." She turned away from him and headed up the hill. She continued to wave her hand over her shoulder, waggling her fingers as she went.

She heard him call behind her, "Jeffie?" but she didn't dare slow down. She was afraid the tears would fall if she did.

20

Katie traced the rafters in the dark.

Well, the almost-dark. A sliver of a moon was out, and it cast just enough light that she could make out almost everything in the small cabin. With no shades, and windows running completely down each wall, a lot of light came in.

She had done her best to avoid Jeff the rest of the evening. He had cornered her once or twice, and she had adroitly skidded the conversation onto safe ground, bringing up old times to laugh about, or telling him funny stories from Winnie's modeling gigs. The last hour she'd been surprised not to find him at all. She'd looked, but he was nowhere. She'd seen Roker at the fire, tamping out the final bed of coals, and getting ready to spread them out on the stones to let them die. The incoming tide would do the rest, and in the morning there would be nothing left. She asked about Jeff, and he was surprised she didn't know. He'd left early to get to his boat. He had received Janine's call that they were on the way to meet him.

The rest of the evening had been on her shoulders. After Jeff's remarks about Janine and her boys, she went out of her way to say farewell to them, one at a time, from the smallest to the largest. The order had been intentional;

as she was afraid she would lose her nerve if she approached the oldest first. If he kicked her, she would run in terror from the others.

Poor Winnie. She'd learned a new lesson today. Beautiful can't be given away. It's a gift to some people, and those who don't have it sometimes want it so badly it devastates them. The girl with the curlers had expected her hair to turn into Winnie's brilliant halo of perfection. Instead, she'd still sprouted a poor haircut, split ends, and drooping curls. She'd cried at the end, and Winnie hadn't known how to console someone in a situation she had no familiarity with.

She imagined Jeff on his boat, alone, gunning his engine just because he could, with the spray from the biggest swells flinging itself over the boat. His broad shoulders and his flyaway hair would be the silhouette Janine and her husband would see from a distance, and they would know their friend had come to ferry them home.

Did they know what they had, how special Jeff was? Who did that sort of thing for other people, just because they needed him?

She looked at the moon out the window. The day had been warmer than most, and the window was open several inches. The smell of the sea mingled with spruce and crushed clover swept in on the sounds of a tide that even now, in the peace of the night, brushed silken fingers along the rocky shoreline. All those years ago, she wondered, did I realize what I had, how special Jeff was? He said he hoped he'd changed. What had he meant by that? What was she missing out on? What had he been trying to fix, if not the Point and the damage of fourteen years; if not the Lil' Dude, the boat on which she'd learned to sail?

Come back to enjoy it. He'd said that to her, and it had sounded like an invitation. Of course she'd be back. This was her home, even if her grandmother's house was long gone. Rockhaven wasn't gone. Carver Point wasn't gone.

The next one she whispered out loud. "Jeff's not gone."

Ritchey was. He was gone to Texas. Babes? She'd been gone longer than Katie. The rest, except Janine? Not a word, except Austie, maybe piloting airliners across the friendly skies.

Jeff was here. She was back. That picture on Winnie's phone, Katie and Jeff in their mud-streaked youth, and smiling just because they were there, in that place, and at that time. In that picture, to those people, they hadn't looked to the past and asked it whether they had permission to be happy, and the future hadn't been on their radar. That moment was all they had, and they had grabbed at it, and they had been happy. That picture said so.

Why was this so hard for her? Forget the past. Brush aside the future. Grab today.

She wanted to, but that burned-out hole still loomed, she had to be in Boston next week, and she still had a car payment to make. How could she toss all that away for the memory of a boy she'd once known?

She turned in her bed, trying to find sleep. The mattress control on the little table at her side lighted up, and something clicked. The generator outside hummed, and she felt the mattress adjust itself underneath her. It reminded her of Jeff. Everything reminded her of Jeff. Even the sound of the generator humming her to sleep in the dark.

Somehow, she was aware of the world fading around her, and then the rafters turned dark, and she was gone.

21

Sunday morning shrouded the little cabin in a blanket of fog, and the misty swirl of sea air muted the sounds of the island. It was a morning for coming to life slowly, and life under the weathered, shingled roof whispered.

"Did we survive the lobster bake?" Did they survive over a hundred people and more food than should be served at any one time was what she meant. Katie rolled over and pushed at the lump on the smaller bed. "Are you alive under there?"

"Spa!" A hand appeared from underneath the electric blanket. "Spa! Warm bath! Please, Katie!"

"Oh, you!" She pushed the hand back under the blanket and pulled her own bedding to her chin, seeing the window still open next to her. "It's chilly this morning."

"It's chilly every morning. Next summer, I want an inside potty. Mark that on your list."

"Sure." Katie smiled at that. She might as well go it all. "And a jetted tub. How would that be, with marble counters and heated floors?"

"Seriously?" Winnie's face appeared from underneath her blanket. "You would really do that?"

"Honey, my family once had money, but it's been gone

a long time. I'm lucky to have this."

"And your potty." She disappeared once again.

"That, too, and I think it's time." Katie threw back the covers and pulled on her robe. She might as well be warm.

By the time she returned, the first rays of sun were trying to beat away the fog, and the sea could just be seen beyond the deck. The trees dripped with the silky touch of a summer Maine sky that had come to brush early morning earth.

"Honey, sun's coming out." Katie shook Winnie's shoulder. "Church in a couple hours. Time to climb out of bed."

"Oh, I do have to go." Winnie threw back the covers and stretched. "My turn."

Once she was out the door, she called to Katie, and she began to sing, "Rock-a-bye baby . . ." One hand knocked on a window.

"Are you okay, Winnie?" Katie looked out at her. "What is it?"

She pointed to the water, starting up again, "Rock-a-bye baby—oh, Katie! Come save me! Quick!"

"What, Honey?" When Katie stepped outside she laughed. There was the seal, just out of the water, warming in one of the few sunny spots on the beach.

"Shush! Be quiet as a mouse, Katie. It might attack us. Sing with me. Rock-a-bye . . . oh, I can't remember the words!" Winnie shook her hands in frustration.

"Watch." Katie leaned off the deck and picked up a big stone. She tossed it close to the seal to where it would make a lot of noise. She took a surprised step backward when the big creature turned its head their way and barked at them.

"Katie! Be careful. Stay right there while I go inside. I'll call 9-1-1 for you." Winnie sidled sideways, while starting up again, more softly, "Rocky-bye-baby, don't come this way . . ."

"Stop it, Winnie. It's scared of us, too. Just wait a minute." At least she thought it was. It hadn't run, though, and she knelt for another rock. She picked a bigger one this time and tossed it just beside the seal. This time, at the clattering sound, it rolled, twisted, and slipped into the water.

"Oh, girl, I was so scared! I really have to go now." Winnie tapped Katie on the shoulder to move her aside, and with her arms in front of her for balance, she gingerly danced down the path to the outhouse.

"What next?" Katie hit her forehead with the palm of her hand. She stepped back inside just as the sun broke out, fully lighting the edge of the deck, and sending shards of light lancing into the room. "Oh, how beautiful!" She turned to the window and looked out to the water, the Lil' Dude just visible in the wisps of fog still encircling everything out at sea. It was gone at the cabin, though, and it seemed she was in a magical fairyland, like something absolutely wonderful was about to happen. A change in her life, perhaps. Whatever, she knew it would be just what she needed.

A ferry horn sounded, and Katie realized the fog had thrown her timing off. They had slept through the sunrise, and that meant they were going to be in a rush.

"Is it still gone?" It was Winnie calling from the far edge of the clearing. "Can I come across?"

"Come on. You're safe if you run. Hurry!" Katie opened the screen for her friend.

"Why? Will it chase me?" Winnie ran through the door, her hands in the air like a criminal surrendering after a holdup.

"No, it's not that. It's something more important than any old scal. The fog messes up the time, and now it's later than I thought. We have to prep for church as fast as we can." She threw her big case on the bed and flipped it open. Her church best was inside. It wasn't actually very dressy, but it also wasn't shorts and a tee. A pressed denim skirt and summer shirt would have to do. It was just right for her island walking shoes.

Winnie was at her side, and she had a difference of opinion. "No, no, Sweetie. I cannot let you torture everyone in that cute little church we drove by. We have to get you something better to wear." Winnie began to drag one of her cases over.

"Honey, we never drove by the church." They'd seen the steeple, but that was all. Katie was pretty sure of that.

"You're right. That was Jeffie and me that went by the church. Now, let's choose you something pretty." She situated her case next to Katie's and snapped it open. She pulled out a blue silk dress with a burgundy thread woven through it and held it up to her friend.

"This is too much." Katie laughed, shaking her head. "Even if it fits, I didn't bring shoes to go with this."

"But I did." From underneath the dress, Winnie pulled out a pair of blue sandals with burgundy beads that just matched the threads in the dress. "See? Just like mine."

"If they fit." Katie held them to her feet. "I don't know."

"You think they fit me? Of course not. See this strap?" She pulled at a thin strap across the heel. "I can get three sizes out of this. A freebie from a Neiman's call."

"They are pretty together. I'll give it a try." If Winnie wore something equally flashy, Katie was pretty sure they would be the most overdressed pair at church. Still, it was sweet of Winnie to offer, and she did appreciate it.

"We'll knock their socks off. Now, let's see about your hair . . ."

Katie decided to give in and go with it. It seemed she would be beautiful this morning whether she liked it or not.

Arriving at the church was the first surprise.

"Look, Winnie. It must be a special service today." It did look that way. The church sign out front was low to the ground, and it had a large, hand-lettered sign wrapped around it. In block letters it spelled out WELCOME BACK.

"How sweet! Reunion Sunday." Winnie pulled out her phone. "Let me see . . . um, Rockhaven Town Church. They do have a website! Give me a second, yes, it is a special Sunday. Oh!" She looked up.

"What?" The lot in front of the church was very full, except for one spot next to the door. Katie pulled in. "Nice. The best spot."

"It may be somebody else's. It says Reserved." Winnie held out her phone. "Maybe we should come back another time. We might be intruding."

"Intruding? It's church." She took the phone, though, and she read the website banner for that morning. CELEBRATION SUNDAY – DON'T SPILL THE BEANS! "So it's the pastor's anniversary or something. It'll be fun."

"What if this is his parking space?"

"Or hers. The pastor could be a woman, you know. By

129

this time, if she's not here, she's not coming." Katy undid her belt and let it retract. "Look, Jeff's car." Sure enough, just around the corner sat the green Jeep with the black fabric roof.

"Think he saved us a seat?"

"Let's go see." She would be surprised if there were any seats to save. She'd attended here numerous times growing up, and it wasn't that large. With all the cars, she expected it to be standing room only, and they weren't late.

Before they reached the door, the first couple from the evening before greeted them, this time in coordinating summer suits. Katie felt more an honored guest than a one-time visitor, but it was nice. She attributed it to the party the night before, and it had been a party. Perhaps the enthusiastic greeting was gratitude for allowing the church to use her property.

In the foyer, she was surprised to find the Peavey Four neatly dressed in suits and ties. The eldest, Kevie, handed her a red rose, and he bowed his head and said, "For you, Miss Katie." The other three echoed, "Welcome, Miss Katie."

"How cute!" Winnie held up her camera and snapped a picture of them. "You boys are adorable."

"No, we're not." Konnar growled those words, barely getting them out before Kevie elbowed him on the shoulder.

"Not so cute," Katie whispered to her friend. "I've spent time with them."

The second surprise of the morning was the huge banner across the front of the church.

WELCOME BACK KATIE CARVER TO ROCK-HAVEN ISLAND

"Look." Winnie pointed.

"I can see. I'm not blind." Katie was startled to have Roker take her arm and lead her to the front of the church. Arms reached out to them as they walked by, people saying hello. She recognized most of them. Janine was one, and a man stood beside her with a cast on one arm. She waved and smiled. Two empty seats were waiting, and Roker deposited them on the first row.

So, Katie decided. All this must have to do with last night. Why would it be a secret, though? She hadn't talked to anyone. Who was there who could spill the beans to her? She hadn't known anyone before last night. She laughed, hiding it behind her hand to keep it quiet.

"What's funny?"

"This. I'm trying to decipher if we're the guests of honor, but we can't be. We parked in the honoree's parking place, though. Of that I'm pretty sure."

"That's you up there. I can read, you know." Winnie's eyes were on the banner.

"Small churches do this. They save seats for guests, and the sign? I did host them out at the Point. Believe it or not, even I know that's pretty special out here. People don't just show up on private land for lobster bakes."

They had been whispering, and the organ started up, drowning out their conversation. They stood as the ministerial staff walked in from a side door. Their third surprise? Jeffrey Ragsdale wore the ecumenical vestments of an ordained minister. He caught her eye and smiled at her, giving her a nod.

A lay leader came forward first, asking the congregation to stand, and together they sang a familiar song, calling the faithful to Christ. Afterward they were asked to bow in prayer as special thanks were offered for fourteen years of prayer that was being answered on this glorious celebration day.

Katie frowned as she glanced at Winnie, but her friend had her eyes closed. This couldn't be what she thought it was. Still, fourteen was a number that was too coincidental for her comfort, and there was all the rest: Jeff sending his "parishioners" one by one to greet her yesterday out on the Point; the parking space she now suspected had indeed been reserved for her; and the signs that weren't just for the average visitor. Dear God, she breathed. You had better not let this be what I think it is.

The first few lines of the prayer told the truth of the matter, though. The words thanked God for keeping watch over their good friend Katie and allowing her to spend time

131

with them once again; for protecting her from the dangers of the world, and allowing the devastation of the past to be wiped clean.

The words reached deeply into Katie, and they awakened old pain that was worse than anything she had felt in years: her grandmother, her parents, her friends that had been lost forever. How could he use the words *keeping watch, protecting,* and *wiped clean* about her life? God had done no such thing. No. He had left her in her hour of need, and He had not been there for her since.

She would burst if she listened any longer, and in a moment of desperation, she slipped past Winnie. She tried to walk, but she was running by the time she reached the door. She broke into the sunlight and felt the tears burn in her eyes.

Ooh, she thought, clenching her fists. If only she'd stayed in Boston, gone to the Bahamas, maybe. Anywhere but here.

"Katie?"

She turned to see Jeff walking toward her. She laughed, sensing it sounded a bit manic, but feeling the frustration she fought welling up and not knowing how to disguise it any longer.

"I don't understand. What does that mean?"

"Why didn't you tell me about this?" She pointed to the sign, then to the church. She fought to keep the tears inside. "How could you expect me to have that thrown at me and not be offended?"

"How could I stop what I didn't know about? I realize this caught you off guard. It caught me off guard, but they did it because they are wonderful, caring people."

"But you told them. How else would they know about me?" That ripped at her inside. All these years, and she had told no one about Jeff. He had been her pain, and she had let no one know. She felt violated.

"How could they know? Because I told them? Yes. I did that. That's wrong? If so, yes, I was wrong. Since you left that final summer, I've waited for you to come back. You were all I talked about to anyone who would listen.

Katie Carver this and Katie Carver that. Everything we ever did, they know. I've loved you since we were kids." He looked away at that, and he took a deep breath. "I'm sorry. I shouldn't have said that. But I won't take it back."

"What about my privacy? How could you do that without me knowing, without asking me if it was okay to tell my life to people I don't know?" She'd heard his words, though, the ones she'd wanted to hear all those years ago. Could it ever be enough, after all she'd endured? She'd hurt so much!

"You may not know them, but trust me, they know you. And Katie, how could I keep it quiet?" He took her hands in his. "I spent the entire summer I was sixteen on the Point. My dad and I put the float out, and I walked the drive with a shovel, filling in the low spots. I hoped you'd come that year, maybe with your parents, and you never did. My dad said to give you a year, let you turn sixteen. You'd be able to drive then. Keep the cabin up, and one day you'd be back. Every year I thought it would be the year. Then I went away to college, and when I returned, I didn't think you'd remember me any longer. I hardly remembered me. That first summer back, I went to the Point, and it was a wreck. I knew then that if you ever showed up again, I'd make sure it was ready for you when you did."

"Why?" The tears really did flow this time.

"Just in case, Katie. You might come back, and I did it just in case."

"That's not what I mean. Why didn't you come find me for all those years?"

"I tried. I tried so many times. I called. I left messages. Your dad, and your mom, too, told me I was just an island boy, and I had no place in your life."

"No. They wouldn't. Not Mom and Dad." It made sense, though. Their refusal to return, cutting her off completely from the island. She suspected they would have sold the Point if her grandmother's will hadn't left it to her, something she'd learned only in the past year.

"I want to show you this." Jeff reached into his vestments and pulled out a worn, stained envelope. It was stamped and sealed, and across the address had been printed *Rejected. Return to sender.* "I was eighteen when I sent you this. It was the first time I was brave enough to tell you I loved you. I invited you back to the island to live here forever. This is why I went away to school. I couldn't bear to be here where I was reminded of you every day."

"You came back, though. Why the change?" Her emotions were a pendulum. She wanted this, to believe in all of this. She really did.

"I did. I came back. I went away because I couldn't bear to live in this place that reminded me of you everywhere I went, but I came back because I had to be in this place where I was reminded of you every single day. I had to have as much of you as I could get, even if it was only memories."

"And if the Point had been sold? My parents wanted to."

"The island has tax records. They list the owner. Your name automatically went on the deed when you turned eighteen."

"A transfer-on-death deed from my grandmother. I only learned that last year. I had to be eighteen to gain control, and my parents chose to never tell me. Even then, it still could have been sold. All your work would have been wasted."

"As long as you were on the deed, I had hope to hold to. If hope was all I ever had, I couldn't let go of you." His eyes were red, and they pleaded with her. "If I had said nothing about you, these people still would have known. Everything I did out at the Point was out of love for you."

Katie looked away, trembling with the emotion that overtook her. All this time she'd tried to lock her memories of Jeff away, and all this time, he'd been soaking up every one. How could she have skewed so far away from the one thing that had ever been really important in her life? She wiped at her eyes, trying to blink them clean.

"Katie? Was I wrong? You did love me. I know you must." He was silent for a time before he stepped forward to look in her face. "Do I have permission to still hope?"

"You know, I blamed God. I could never forgive Him for everything I lost. You. For losing you." She looked into his eyes, understanding now that love worked in more than one way. All those years that she had pushed the memories of Rockhaven away, Jeff had been here preparing Rockhaven for her return. "I know better now. God brought me back to you."

Jeff smiled. "I knew that from the moment Marc called and said you were coming back to the island. I never doubted God for a single minute."

She wiped her face, finally understanding her estrangement truly hadn't been God's fault. All those years, and He had kept her chances alive, in spite of her. He hadn't stolen them from her at all.

When Jeff wrapped his arms around her, this time she didn't push him away.

From the church, cheers and clapping broke the quiet of the island morning.

Katie looked up at Jeff. "Do they always know everything that goes on around here?"

"When it comes to you, yes. I couldn't hide the way I feel about you if I wanted to, and trust me, Katie, I don't want to."

It was a hand on Jeff's shoulder that broke up the intimate moment. Roker said, "Son, you've got a lifetime for this. The rest of us in there? We want lunch, and we want it on time."

Katie enjoyed the service, more than any she had ever attended before. When the final prayers were said, she had something of her own to say, even if no one else heard.

"God, you didn't take my life from me. You kept it for me until I was ready to return. I can never thank you enough for that."

"And for your good friend, Winnie. Thank Him for that, too." Winnie put her arm across Katie's shoulders, whispering her words softly.

"And for Winnie, even if she does snore at night." Katie smiled.

"Eh! I do not." Winnie was smiling, though.

Katie looked up at Jeff, so proud and fine in front of the entire town, and she was convinced of one thing. Her Rockhaven summer was turning out to be the best one she'd ever had.

Rockhaven
WEDDING

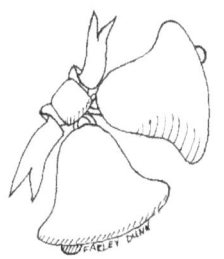

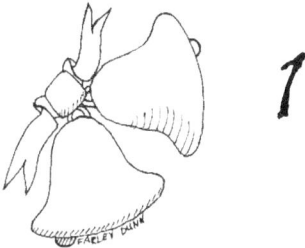

1

Katie Carver's delicate fingers flew across her keyboard. She typed with immaculately manicured nails, the black letters appearing out of nowhere, blocky and dark, and they glistened when they caught in the wind.

Caught in the wind?

She smiled and closed her eyes, aware how silly that was, letters caught in the wind. Instead she pictured a sailboat with the words Lil' Dude neatly painted on the back, the ocean off a Maine island, and catching the wind with a sail humming in the stiff breeze. The picture was complete with Jeff Ragsdale at her side, as he had been just weeks before.

She shook her head and pulled her hands from her keyboard. She knew one thing. Her letters had better not catch in the wind, not if she was to get her deadlines met. Yet, at the same time, she wanted them to do exactly that. She pulled a single sheet of paper from a chrome-plated letter tray on her desk, one containing a printed email from Jeff. She stroked the words gently with the fingertips of one hand. The black ink spoke her fiancé's love carried across two hundred miles of wire and cable, sent from Jeff to her. These were the words she wanted to catch in the wind.

Her thoughts of Jeff were interrupted by something a little less endearing.

"Katie? Are you awake this morning? You have a call on Line 3." A trimly dressed woman holding a company-issued black tablet stood at the entrance to Katie's cubicle. She leaned one elbow casually over the low cubicle wall.

"Oh!" Katie laughed guiltily. There her phone was, blinking red on Line 3. "Sorry, Connie. I was distracted."

"Dear, you deserve to be distracted. You've other things on your mind besides minivans and SUVs. Better get that call, though." She winked, and she pointed at the phone.

Connie was Connie Rivera, Claims Specialist for ALDMass, the fastest-growing discount auto insurer in New England. Auto Liability Discount was on the letterhead, but say "Old" Mass, and it was instant brand recognition. *Stability is our middle name.* Well, actually, Liability was the company's middle name, but the ads worked. They were the fastest growing in New England, after all.

Connie was Katie's immediate supervisor.

"Katie Carver, Old Mass Claims Department. How may I assist you?"

"Come to Rockhaven for the weekend?"

Katie looked up at Connie, still hovering over her wall, to see her smiling broadly. "Told you you better get that call." She turned and stepped away with a brief wave.

"Oh, Jeff, I miss you so much. I want to. I so want to, but Fridays are tough. Especially this Friday." And she did want to go. After the week so recently spent on the island, and finding that the daring and adventuresome boy she'd loved years before still waited on her, coming home had been the most difficult thing she'd ever done.

"What's there for you?" His words laughed without laughing. "After all, I'm here."

She pictured him as she spoke, his dimples crinkling, or the wind in his flyaway island hair on his lobster boat, and the completely different man who donned clerical robes and lovingly guided Rockhaven Town Church's members and attendees past life's rocky ledges. Yes, she wanted to be there.

Or him to be here.

"Think you can make Friday's 2:45 ferry? If not, I can make the 10:30."

She sighed, shaking her head. He knew better. For her to make the 2:45 meant a crack-of-dawn exit from Boston, and Jeff on the 10:30? With city traffic, he was getting to Boston about midnight. Then to turn around and return? He couldn't miss Sunday services.

"I heard that sigh, Dame Carver. Does that mean you're turning me down?"

"I really thought I could just walk away." From her Boston life, she meant. *Hoped* was a better word. *Wanted to* was also pretty accurate. Old Mass had to hire a replacement, and there was paperwork to file, retirement accounts to settle, and that was just with her job. Her apartment lease and her car? She hadn't had time to think about those.

"What can you not walk away from? I miss you, Katie. A lot. I get you for a week, and you disappear again. Phone calls aren't enough." He chuckled, but it sounded like his throat caught. Like there was more emotion there than he was willing to show. "I can't hold you or smell your hair over the phone. One Friday. This Friday. That's all I ask."

"If only I could. I'm one of the principal presenters. I can't just not be here." Getting in the way this Friday were the Old Mass regional reps from across New England who would be gathering at ALDMass' Boston headquarters. The meetings had been in the works for months.

"You're breaking my heart, Dame Carver." He teased her again. "I had hoped. That's all. Maybe next weekend?"

"Jeff, you're going to make me cry if you keep on. You know the office has a shower planned next Friday. They want you here, but I explained about the ferry, and you having to be back for Sunday services." She said that to show him she cared, that even in this, she was watching out for him.

"I'm off the hook, huh?" He didn't sound like he

wanted to be off the hook.

"I got your email." She pulled out the paper from earlier, touching it lovingly. It was a distraction from the weekend's discussion, and she knew it. Still, the email had touched her, all ten times she'd read it.

"You did, huh?" His grin came through in his words.

"How long did it take?" To sail around East Haven Island, she meant. Jeff would get that. He'd mentioned it in the letter.

"You know how fast the Dude is."

"I know how big East Haven is. What about the tide?" Again, half said, understanding the shared thoughts better than most couples understood a whole discussion.

"Might've scraped a board or two."

"Jeff. Don't tease." Hearing him talk about the Dude, the twelve-foot catboat she'd learned to sail at nine, made turning down his offer especially hard. He had it there. She didn't have it here. There was nothing easy in that.

"Gotta tempt you with something. Is the 2:45 sounding pretty good, yet?"

"It sounds too wonderful to imagine. I want to be there, but this is real life. Six weeks, and I can be there all the time. I can't do it any faster. I'm so sorry."

"I love you, Dame Katie. I'll be thinking of you every minute. I'll call you at home tonight."

"You'd better. I love you, too, Reverend Jeff."

Placing the phone back in its cradle, Katie gave her heart a minute to settle. Being separated from Jeff again after thinking she had lost him for fourteen years was one of the hardest things she had ever forced herself to do.

In addition, there was one more thing. She had a wedding to plan, and there were fifteen miles of ocean in the way. She could only hope she didn't drown somewhere along the way.

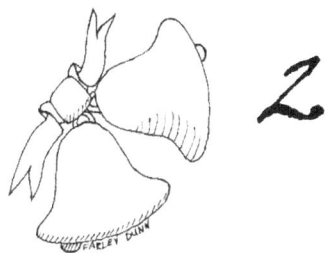

"What's this?"

Half the office staff blocked Katie's way out. She had shut down her computer, and for the first time in days, she thought she might actually get out of the building on time.

"What's what?" The reply was more a giggled tease than a real answer, and it came from Ashlynn Seabourn, a thin blonde with tightly curled hair.

"Eight of you hovering around my cubicle like summer butterflies around a stand of milkweed." At the five o'clock notification bell, office personnel normally evaporated like sea mist in the sunshine, and Katie had hoped to be one of them.

"We have something for you."

That was sung in chorus by two sisters who had worked on the Old Mass insurance circuit before ALDMass had become Old Mass. They looked less like sisters than friends who had similar tastes in jewelry and makeup. Isabelle Lawton was the elder, short, dark, and round; while her sister Lesly Buchannan was trim and svelte. One was married, but Katie had trouble remembering which. Lesly, she thought.

"What?" Katie shook her head. It was now after five.

"This!" River Sopko, a dark-haired petite Asian beauty waved a card in the air. Katie's name was in bold print on the front.

"That's sweet of you." For this, she didn't mind being trapped. Not as much, anyway. She reached for it.

"No, not so fast." River pulled the card away.

"Friday's!" The final four women sang out the name of the iconic restaurant in four-part harmony. Lisa Vickers sported long, Cher-like tresses. Kambri Green peered through ever-present gold wire frames. Michelle Jeter matched Kambri's wires, except she wore her gold in great hoops in her ears. Ellie Reese's signature was an old-fashioned pageboy that gave her a cuttingly contemporary look.

"I can't." Katie laughed with them, but she didn't have time to spend an entire evening out on the town. Especially tonight. Jeff was calling.

"Oh, yes, you can." Michelle in her hoops pulled the group's trump card out of her purse. "Look what we have!"

It was a key ring with a large, yellow smiling face attached. Katie's key ring.

"How . . ." Katie opened her purse, to find hers missing, only to hear Ellie tease her.

"How many sets of keys do you keep in there, because we have one."

"How did you get them? I've had my purse with me all day."

"*Almost* all day. Connie's such a team player. Remember that emergency report she had you run to her?" Isabelle looked smug. "I was right outside your cubicle, and I waved to you. Remember?"

"Izzy, and I thought you were my friend." Katie wagged her finger at her.

"And Lisa's friend, and River's friend, and Kambri's friend—"

"I get it." Katie grabbed her arm, laughing. "You don't need to name everyone here."

"Oh, but I do!" Isabelle was in full swing by then, pointing around Katie to the other women. "And Ellie and

144

Michelle and Lesly and Ashlynn. There. Got 'em all."

"I have my husband's van today!" Lesly shook a set of keys attached to a dark leather fob, the sort a man would carry. "It's a surprise wedding shower! We're stealing you away for the evening. Off to Brookline!"

"I tried for the Dedham Friday's on Boston Providence Highway. It would be less crowded, but who cares! Party!"

Katie wasn't sure who said that, but by then, they were tumbling out the door into the late July heat, and into the parking garage. It was Fenway that might be the problem. They'd be driving right past. This was the city. Catch game-night traffic, and they'd add at least an hour to their drive time.

At least she had her cell. If the events of the evening went on too long, she could text Jeff and let him know where she was. Yet, right then, she could barely hang onto her purse. She had eight friends, all excited as summer magpies, strong-arming her to a waiting van to cart her off across the city.

They survived the van ride, making it to Friday's in record time, although four had to crowd the last seat. Lesly pulled to the door and shooed the rest out, offering to go and park the van. Isabelle took Katie's purse and dropped it in an underseat bin.

"No, you don't." She waggled her finger at Katie. "You don't need any money, and we won't have anyone calling for a taxi. You're all ours tonight. No distractions allowed."

Katie shouldn't have been surprised to find they were expected, and a large table was set up for them. There were balloons, streamers, and even flowers in the middle of the table. It was Connie Rivera that made sense of it all.

"Did you guess at any time today, my dear?" Connie took Katie's hands and led her to the seat of honor. "We've been planning this since the first day we heard of you leaving us. Oh, we are going to be so sad you're gone." She patted the sides of Katie's face, and she had red rings around her eyes.

"Oh, I do love you so much, Connie." Katie threw her arms around her supervisor.

"Then stay." Connie pushed her away and held her at arm's length, looking hard in her eyes.

"Connie! Connie!" Katie didn't know what to say to that.

"I'm teasing. A good man is so much better than a good job." Connie squeezed her hands and motioned for her to sit. "Now, Katie, we've taken up an envelope to cover tonight, so you order whatever you want. Don't even look at the prices. Tonight is our treat."

Katie laughed when Connie handed her a menu. It had been prepared beforehand with all the prices taped over with blue painter's tape.

They had a waiter and a waitress step up and seat everyone else, and within minutes, menus were in everyone's hand. Tea and sodas appeared, with water for Isabelle, and coffee for Connie.

The ladies had prepared special cards, and each one stood, reading, singing, or acting out their written sentiments. Katie laughed and cried, sometimes at the same time, as she reconnected with remembered events, joys, and experiences shared with those around her.

River reminded everyone of her brother, visiting from Vietnam, now married, but once a blind date for Katie. It had been a disaster, with raw seafood that Katie claimed had climbed off her plate.

Ashlynn told of her mother's illness, and long talks with Katie, who understood because of the way her grandmother died.

Izzy and Lesly had never traveled abroad, and Katie had borrowed the money for them to go, never expecting it to be returned. It had become the down payment on her new car.

Kambri was her Saturday lunch date on cold, winter weekends. Katie had kept Lisa's bird on more than one occasion. Michelle's latest boyfriend had been suggested by Katie.

Ellie? They wore the same iridescent Brandywine nail polish, often borrowing from one another at work.

The evening slipped into small gifts opened, and that

card held so high by tiny River? It was much more than just a card.

This was the real wedding shower, they hooted and called out, waving the card in the air before turning it over to her. The shower planned the next week at work would be a meet-and-greet. Cake and cookies. Just another boring shower for the boring crowd. The juicy stuff was coming tonight.

Of course, they were teasing about the upcoming shower at ALDMass, but they were serious about one thing. That card? It was a generous gift certificate to a high-end boutique, one aimed directly at the honeymoon crowd. When Katie opened that, the entire group erupted into hooting catcalls, and even more fun was had by all.

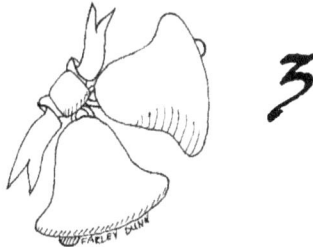

3

"I need my purse!" Katie had enjoyed the meal, but it was well past Jeff's time to call, and now she felt guilty. Her phone was in her purse, and her purse was in the front seat.

"No, no! You go in the back!" Ellie and River jostled her into the rear seat. "That purse isn't going anywhere."

"Why are you doing this to me?" Katie saw her purse out and tried for it. She really did, but she was trapped by her coworkers, and within minutes, they were headed down the street to drive the most impossible roadways in the state. She was laughing, but she knew how close she was to tears. "I need my purse. My phone's inside."

"Here. Take mine. I get free nationwide minutes, even off shore." It was Kambri.

"Yeah. *Off shore.*" Several voices chimed in, and in the glow of the interior lights and occasional passing street lamp, it was impossible to tell just who it was. However, it was clear just what they meant. She could call *Jeff,* and they could listen in to every word.

"Okay. I give in." Katie took the phone with a chuckle, her palms already sweaty. Some of it was anticipation. Behind that was the guilt. She'd known he was going to call, and yet she had let her friends pull her away for a night on the town, having fun, doing all the city things she would no longer be able to do on the island. Calling Jeff was like turning the Boston switch off and shutting her friends out of the life that would soon be hers.

Or shutting herself out of the busy city life that she'd come to love as part of who she was.

At this particular moment, surrounded by these particular friends, she didn't want to let go of her stimulating city life. Rather, she did, but she was aware of exactly how much she'd come to depend on her friends and how much each one meant to her. It would be hard. Very hard.

"How do I turn this on?" Katie tapped the flat panel and only got a pattern of dots that quickly faded away once again.

"Oh, here." Kambri tilted the phone her direction and traced her finger in a pattern, then pushed it back to Katie. "Just punch in the numbers and hit call."

"Hit call, girl!" Izzy and Lesley tittered and clapped wildly.

She typed in the first six numbers, and the last four, well, who could forget J-E-F-F? It wasn't really JEFF, but that's how she remembered them. 8-6-6-6 were the numbers just under J-E-F-F.

"Is it ringing?" Ashlynn pushed the phone to Katie's ear. "I know what I hear. Two little lovebirds, sitting in a tree. K-I-S-S-I-N-G. First comes—"

"Shush! He's picking up." Katie held her finger to her lips. She giggled, feeling stupid, and yet not feeling stupid at all. It was her friends huddled around listening, and the apology she knew she needed to make. It was finding the words she must choose to explain not being at her phone that twisted her stomach just the tiniest amount.

What she heard was not what she expected.

"Jeff Ragsdale. I'm either away from the phone; doing the Lord's work; or my battery's gone dead. Whichever, leave a message. You'll hear from me ASAP." Then the line beeped. Katie frowned and looked up, totally off kilter.

That was one thing she had not expected.

"What did he say?" River waved her hand in front of Katie's face. "Wake up, there. He said something, or you wouldn't have that look on your face."

"He said I should leave a message."

"I can do that for you!" Kambri grabbed the phone. "Kissy, kissy, Jeff!" With a wink, she pursed her lips and made several kissing sounds, and then she dramatically tapped the off button and dropped the phone in her purse.

"Oh, Kambri, you are so wicked!" Ashlynn was wiping her eyes by that time, she was laughing so hard.

"Wicked good! That's me, wicked good!" Kambri fluffed the ends of her hair as if primping. "Since Jeffie's not home, we have more hours to kill."

"Whoo, whoo," Lesly called out, starting up the van. "My husband's out for hours, yet. Where to, girls?"

"A movie! Let's go see a movie!" Ellie and River chanted together. "Brad Pitt! Brad Pitt!"

"Somebody younger!" That was Isabelle, with a petulant look on her face.

"Oh, Izzy, not a Jonas brothers' movie. You're not a tweener anymore, so I forbid you to see even one additional tween heartthrob flick. So, there." Lesly waggled her hand over the seat, pointing to her sister, as if that were it, and she'd not hear another word about it.

Katie didn't want a Jonas movie, and she had no desire to see anything else, either. That phone call bothered her. How could Jeff not have picked up? He always picked up. It had been twelve hours since she'd spoken with him, and his words reminded her of how dependable he was: *I'll be thinking of you every minute. I'll call you at home tonight.*

And she hadn't had her phone to answer. She hoped he wasn't upset. She could explain that it was her friends that had distracted her. Yet, that seemed almost like betraying her friends, as if they had become a hindrance in her life. The reality was that she would miss them, and terribly; and as much as she loved Jeff—and wanted to be with him on the island—she knew she would grieve for all she was leaving behind.

She didn't want to grieve. She wanted love, she wanted Jeff, and she wanted her friends, too.

She guessed she wanted it all. Who didn't?

Her purse began to ring, and she felt her heart surge inside. It was Jeff! Who else would call this time of night?

"My purse! Where's my purse?" Katie reached over the seat, took it from her friend's hands, and pulled it into her lap. Digging frantically, she saw a flashing light and pulled it out, tapping the answer icon without looking, afraid he would hang up before she could tell him how sorry she was for not being there to catch his call.

She put the phone to her ear, and covering the mouthpiece with her other hand, she breathed, "Oh, I miss you so much. I love you more than anybody."

The reply was not quite what she expected.

"You do, Sweetie? Well, I love you, too. You know you're out of peanut butter, and oh, I'm taking your couch for the night. I used the embroidered cases, and thank you ahead of time. Oh, one last thing. Have you heard from Jeffie tonight?"

"From Jeff?" Katie heard the undertones in Winnie Catron's voice. This might be her best friend on the phone, but Winnie never asked anything innocently. If she wanted to know about Jeff, there was something going on.

Katie got distracted, though. Ashlynn had heard Jeff's name, and she grabbed the phone, calling into it, "Jeff? Hi, Jeff! All our love!"

Katie never did get her phone back. It began the rounds, in spite of her protests. She did manage to convince the girls she had to get back to her car. A movie was simply not in store for a Monday evening, not with work the following morning.

And Winnie spending the night? Now what was that all about? With that phone call, it couldn't be good by anyone's measure.

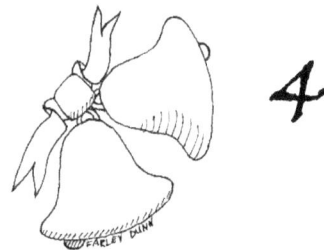

4

The overhead numbers in the elevator changed smoothly. In the background, Elvis sang about blue suede shoes, which meant it was after ten. Muzak commanded the airwaves between six and the bedtime hour. Oldies played until two, and the deep hours of the night were for the heavy metal freaks.

Katie's arms were filled with packages. Tissue paper overflowed one sack, and one crinkled red-and-gold bow she especially wanted to save kept falling to the floor. She couldn't leave any of it behind. She had to keep every piece to remind her of how much she had enjoyed the evening. She smiled when the King belted out "one for the money" a second time.

She leaned her head against the wall of the elevator and smiled. The trouble with money was that she didn't have any. Her grandmother once did, but Katie had been no more than a summer visitor on a craggy point running with an island pack of regulars. She had loved it every year, but she'd never considered how her grandmother paid for it all.

Now, the money was gone, her grandmother's house was gone, and she was heading back. She hoped for a lifetime spent on her favorite rock, one with Jeff Ragsdale, who had been her one-time childhood crush and would-be boyfriend.

It was all good, though. Who needed money when she would soon have Jeff forever and ever?

The car hushed to a stop, and with a gentle ding, one so well-mannered that Elvis paid no notice as he sang on about his wonderful shoes, the doors whooshed open, disappearing without any effort into the walls.

The hallway to Katie's apartment was tastefully appointed, if somewhat modern and stark. Directly in front of the elevator was a massive modernist painting, something with red and orange slashes partially covering a thick, black scribble, a vibrant, visual feast that she'd come to look forward to when arriving home. It was like a jolt of life, no matter how tiring the day had been.

She turned left, past two chrome and leather Breuer-designed Wassily chairs, wondering idly why no one ever sat in them. She'd been here for half-a-dozen years, and she'd never seen them used.

The hallway jogged past a dark-green slash of a window, one that hardly had a view of anything except a deep-set brick-and-stone cavern as it groped for a view of the city, but that was okay. The real windows were in the apartments, walls of them.

Then she was at her door, a post-modern slab made of layers of metal and wood, pierced by thick stained glass wedges that glowed with light from the other side. She frowned at that, as there should be no lights on in the apartment. Her friend Winnie knew better, as there was an electric bill to pay, and Katie had moving expenses to cover. That wasn't cheap.

When she went to unlock it, it slipped open easily, already unlatched.

"Winnie?" Katie pushed the door wide, irritated to see the overhead light blazing away full strength. She hit the switch and opened the alarm panel, cringing to see it wasn't set. Yet, nothing looked out of place, with not even the sofa pulled out for a bed, and she laughed softly in relief, calling out, "Shut the door next time, girl!"

Pushing the door to with her foot, she dropped her things onto a chair before stepping back to secure the apartment.

"Winnie?" Katie headed toward the bedroom. Her first evidence of her visitor's presence was on the bed, a jumble of vividly colored fabrics strewn across the foot. She groaned when she saw the bathroom door closed and light bleeding from underneath.

The floor began to vibrate, a sound Katie recognized, and she stepped to the bathroom door and rapped loudly. "Winnie! I hear you in there!"

The noise stopped, and after a moment the door opened. A shock of strawberry blonde hair appeared through the crack, and below it, a strikingly thin woman wrapped in a plush towel smiled at Katie.

"Hey, Sweetie. I didn't know how late you'd be, so I borrowed your tub. Do you need anything before I climb back in?"

She smiled disarmingly, but Katie pushed through, anyway. Yes, she did need in. Her toothbrush was alongside the sink, not in the hall bath. Without her toothbrush, she wasn't going to bed.

"See?" She held it up to Winnie before she walked back out the door. "Never come between a girl and her toothbrush. Oh, and I do have the loft, you know." As in, why did you tell me you were sleeping on the sofa? There's a bed up there.

"Oh, not tonight." Winnie pushed on Katie's shoulder to move her along with a giggle. "I can't let anyone see me like this. It just wouldn't do!"

The door shut in Katie's face, and she stepped back, confused. Who was there to see? The bathroom door made a noise, and Katie frowned, ready to bark at her friend when it began to open.

"Welcome home. I hope you enjoy your surprise!" Just a hand came through, it waved, and as it withdrew, the door closed with a click after it.

The floor began to vibrate again, and Katie knew she wouldn't get back in for at least an hour. Back in the living room, she pondered. It didn't make sense why Winnie had told her she was sleeping on the couch when it wasn't made up. Yet, there was Winnie's pillow in a chair, and neatly folded underneath, a set of sheets. She looked up, considering whether to sleep in the loft for the night and let Winnie have her bed. It was quite private, as long as she closed the French doors opening onto the living room; and there was a twin bed in the space, although the guest bath was on the main floor, and to hike down during the night for emergency visits wasn't very enjoyable.

Clearing her things away, the sound of running water from the hall bath got her attention. Tossing her belongings back onto the chair, she ran down the hallway to find the door closed, locked, and light shimmering from under the bottom edge. The shower was going full blast.

Winnie! How could she have turned the water on and then locked the door? It was a pair of men's shoes beside the door that suggested otherwise, and they caught Katie off guard. This wasn't like her friend at all.

Then Katie got angry. Bringing a man into her apartment? What was Winnie thinking?

The shower quieted, and Katie heard the curtain rumble back, the rings skittering on the metal rod. As angry as she was, she would be horrified to be caught eavesdropping. Once he was dressed, she would send him on his way, and then Winnie would hear what she thought about it. She headed to the bedroom to find out just who this was.

In that moment, the reality of the situation dawned on her. The alarm had been off. The door hadn't been latched correctly, and Winnie had already been in the bathroom. Did her friend even know a man was inside the apartment with her? She stepped to the bath door, ready to knock, when the blower kicked in on the tub. Katie dropped her hand. There was no way her friend would hear anything now.

9-1-1! Except . . . her phone was in her purse, and her purse was in there!

She jumped when she heard a cabinet door in the kitchen slam shut. Then the rattle of knives sliced into her awareness.

Her heart pounding, and tiptoeing carefully across the floor, Katie made sure the bedroom door was closed and locked. Breathing raggedly, she climbed on the bed and pulled the comforter up around herself. The front door . . . it had been open, and Winnie hadn't known. It frightened her that her friend might have been killed already, and it would have been Katie's fault, for living in Boston, for having this apartment, for not having a doorman to screen everyone who entered the building. He could have come in when another resident buzzed in a guest. Who knew? Dear God, she prayed, how will I ever forgive myself if another person I care about dies, and all because of me?

It was the television on the other side of the door that told her she might be stuck in here a very long time. The intruder was waiting on her to get home. He would probably wait all night. What would she and Winnie do?

She hugged the bedclothes tighter and hunkered down to wait. She had only one option: Pray and trust God to keep his hand on them, to keep her and Winnie safe from those that might harm them.

She was still frightened, though. God might help, but that man was in her living room, and that wasn't reassuring in any way, form, or fashion.

What she really wanted was to cry.

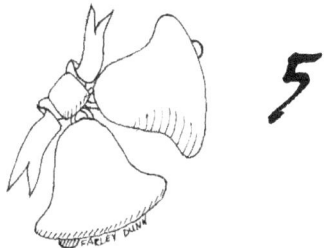

5

Katie jumped when she heard a door open. The remembered panic of the unknown intruder put him in the bedroom with her, even though she had securely locked the bedroom door.

It was Winnie that entered in a billowing cloud of steam, coming through the bathroom door with a white towel twisted around her hair, and wearing Katie's old pink bathrobe, the one Katie loved so very much.

Katie cringed when her friend headed directly toward the bedroom door.

"No, Winnie!" Katie tossed the covers aside and leaped from the bed, calling out in a strident whisper, "It's not safe!"

"Safe?" Winnie paused with her hand on the knob. "How can it not be safe?"

"There's a man out there. With knives." Katie still had her pillow with her, and she hugged it. She moved beside the door, afraid that if they were heard, the intruder would force his way through. The sound of the television still came through the wall, so she was certain he hadn't gone anywhere. Things couldn't get more dangerous than this.

"Oh!" Winnie struggled to keep a smile from her face.

"A man, and it's not safe. I see. It's not safe for you. For me? Sweetie, I adore men."

"No! Not this time," Katie hissed. "He even took a shower, like the whole apartment was his. There's no telling what he wants."

"You, apparently. It's your apartment." Winnie twisted the knob, only to find it locked, and she grunted in frustration when Katie grabbed her hand to keep her from unlocking it. "Swee-*tie!* Come on and let me though. I'm hungry."

"Me?" Katie's mind filled with fog, her thoughts closing in on what her friend had said to her. "What does he want with me?"

"Love, maybe." Winnie forced Katie's hand free, unlocked the door, and pulled it open. She leaned through, looking at Katie the entire time and calling out, "Jeffie! Katie-poo's crazy in love with you, with a strong emphasis on the crazy part. Come get her!"

"Winnie!" Katie whispered tersely, "You don't know who's out there."

"Sure," she laughed. "I let him in, silly goose! I'm your chaperone. This is your surprise." Winnie patted Katie's face and walked through to the other room, calling out, "What are you watching, Jeffie? *Love* Boat?"

Mortification washed over Katie, and she felt her face burn. Jeff! How could she have thought . . . and she had hidden from him, not knowing he had driven to Boston . . . and it hit her. The missed phone call. Her extended evening with her friends. She wondered if he'd planned this all along, maybe had even been on the road when she'd talked to him that morning. That was so sweet if so, but it irritated her a bit, too. She would have been here, prepared for him if she'd known. She had a life, after all. She couldn't be expected to sit waiting on him, telling her coworkers, "Oh, Jeff might call. I have to sit by the phone."

And Winnie! That was mean, setting all this up, and then not telling her Jeff was here when she knew all along. Had she thought it was funny? Katie didn't.

Even so, Katie felt her eyes begin to burn. What was

she thinking? Jeff, her Jeff had come to see her. Her Boston life might be unraveling as she stood here, with her pending resignation at ALDMass, the upcoming termination of her lease on this apartment, and even her friendships all going on hold for however long, but how many years had she dreamed of Jeff, her perfect Jeff riding up on a white horse to rescue her from a life of abandonment and loneliness? Well, maybe not on a white horse, but certainly piloting a white lobster boat. Then, just months ago, they had been reunited with her first trip back to the island in fourteen years, only to find he'd waited on her all that time.

And he was here! He was here!

"Katie?" It was Jeff's voice, deep and masculine. "Dame Carver, are you coming out? I did drive a long way, and all to see you. I've prepared a late supper, if you're hungry."

"One minute!" Good heavens, but she was an idiot! The knives. He'd been cooking! She couldn't let him see her crying! She darted for the bathroom door, closing and locking it firmly. The mirror was still fogged from her friend's extended bath, and Katie wadded a hand towel and wiped a spot clear. There her face was, surrounded by a halo of misty effervescence, her long, dark hair standing out in contrast against the cloudy mirror. Having Jeff here unexpectedly juxtaposed him vividly against her Boston life. To her, he was always her island man, handsome and rugged, and perfect in his island setting, whether digging for clams in the mud or sailing on the water with the residue of salt spray rimming his hair with white. Her Boston life was sidewalks and streetlights, with elevators, restaurants, and people who had only seen the ocean from the protection of double-glazed windows or driving I-90 on the way to Logan Airport.

The problem was that tonight, after being on the town with her friends, she knew what she was giving up.

She also knew what she was gaining—Jeff, her treasured memories of Rockhaven Island, and the life she'd always dreamed of—but what was being left behind tugged at her. Winnie, her best friend, always at her side. Connie, always calling her "dear" in a motherly way. Ashlynn and River, Kambri, Ellie and all the rest. They were her family, and she knew what would happen when she was gone. It had already happened with the island friends of her youth. They'd taken off in new directions, their lives diverged from hers, and rightly so. Yet, it meant they were no longer a family, and for the first fourteen years of her life, those island chums had been her family, as much as her grandmother and more than her parents ever could be. Why? Because they had loved something Katie had loved— and something her parents hadn't.

Her work friends loved their Boston life, even if some days they wished to sleep in or spend the day anywhere but at work; and although the ongoing slush of melting winter snows continually soaked their shoes, to live in Boston was to live at the center of the world. There was no better life than one lived in the finest city in America.

Katie knew what she was giving up. She was choosing to let go of something she loved, but that didn't make it easy. She hoped Jeff understood. He'd never loved city life, running back to spend his life on Rockhaven after his years in college. Katie was running back, too, but her reasons were different. She wasn't running from Boston. She was choosing something she loved better. Jeff would never grieve for the loss of all this. She would grieve for a very long time.

"Sweetie! Jeffie's waiting!" Winnie tapped three times very softly on the door. "The food's getting cold. Are you coming out anytime soon?"

"Just making sure I'm perfect. Be right there."

"Okay, Sweetie. I have some lemonade all made up. I used all your lemons. So sorry! Come on out before Jeffie and I finish it all." She knocked another three times. "You are coming, please, Katie?"

"I'm there." Katie flushed the unused toilet. "Let me wash up."

"Um-kay. Don't take too long."

Katie took a deep breath in the silence, and she laughed. It was like an old song her dad used to listen to, something along the line of being torn between two lovers. Well, she didn't have either one, not as lovers, but she certainly had two loves. She was in love with Jeff, head over heels, and she wanted to spend every minute of her life with him. She had come to realize she was also in love with the life she had built for herself to stand in for the man she once thought she'd lost.

She was torn between two loves, and how was she ever to be happy with just one?

"Oh," she groaned aloud. Then, with determination in her backbone, the same determination she had sailed her skiff the Lil' Dude with during many an island gale, she grabbed the door knob and thrust herself through the door. Striding to the living room, she threw out her arms, and she let a smile spread across her face.

"Jeff, Winnie cannot have you one minute longer. Oh, I have missed you!"

It was when he swept her up in his arms and gave her a kiss that she knew she was making the right decision. She let herself melt into his embrace, certain that there was no choice at all. There never had been. Jeff, her island boy grown all rough and handsome, or her work friends, out for a night on the town? The only answer was Jeff, of course, and she'd known that all along.

Winnie had no problem inserting herself into the situation, though, laughing and calling out, "Break it up, you two. I'm still here."

Jeff chuckled, backing away, but Katie didn't let him get too far. Arm's length was about the right distance, where she could look into his eyes, and imagine never looking away again.

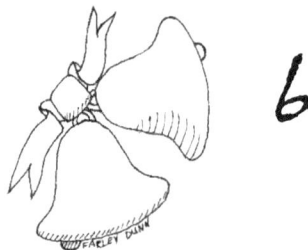

6

The Berkshires, Western Mass in all its mid-summertime glory, with flowers littering the shrubs like too-early Christmas bows, hinting at a distant but magical future coming quicker than anyone could imagine, spread the undulating landscape with vivid green.

The top was down on Jeff's Jeep, and the breeze was gentle as it whisked away the warmth of the afternoon sun. Katie waved her hand through the open window, letting it catch and dance in the onrush of air.

She smiled at Jeff in his wrap-around shades. He was tall enough that his hair caught and lifted in the breeze, giving him an engagingly boyish look. Out on the highway, the top had been securely up, but once they moved onto the back roads, Jeff had pulled to the shoulder and adroitly dropped the canvas covering, leaving their carriage for two open to the sky.

"We need sun," he'd laughed.

It was shade they mostly received, from the towering trees that crowded next to the road. Now Katie held his hand, and she enjoyed the warmth of his muscular grip.

"There." She pointed. It was a sign that directed them to their destination, an off-roading mecca, one with more muddy bogs for rampant wheel-spin than the green Jeep had ever seen in its life, or so Jeff had claimed.

"One day off, for me," Jeff had whispered in her ear the night before. "Surely they can give you one day."

"One day? That's all you want?" She'd laughed at that. He wanted her entire life. One day was only an appetizer, and not a very long one at that. "What could we do in one day here in Boston?"

What came to her mind was Fenway Park. Any man of any worth would be fascinated by the best sports facility in the Northeast. Or, a museum, maybe even the Museum of Fine Arts or the Gardner Museum. Then there was the Old North Church and the ship USS Constitution. And restaurants! LaGrassa's or Atlantic Fish. Her tummy rumbled just to think of it.

"Mud bogging." He'd grinned. "With you."

She'd pushed him away, shaking her head. He was teasing, right? Mud bogging?

"My Jeep. You know, I brought it with me, and Berkshire East is letting vehicles on a few lower trails."

"Berkshire East?" She'd looked across the room at Winnie. "Is that the one . . . ?"

"I think so, Sweetie. Two years ago with the church. Remember Roberto's broken wrist?" Winnie spooned a bite of ice from her lemonade into her mouth and began crunching away before turning back to the television.

"No self-respecting ski resort would let you bog on their trails. Seriously, now—"

"Seriously, now, yourself, Katie. They're rebuilding the trails, and this is a once-in-a-lifetime opportunity."

"You won't bog if it doesn't rain." Winnie wagged her spoon at him. "But we've already discussed that." She had her feet up under her, and she swung them to the floor, standing and heading for the kitchen.

"Before you got home," Jeff explained to Katie. "She's right, though. Mostly we'd be navigating the slopes, but I understand it's all dug up, so if it rains . . ." He smiled brightly.

"Thank John Deere for bulldozers." Winnie giggled

from the kitchen.

"It's a long way." Katie saw the glossy images of Fenway and LaGrassa's fading away, to be replaced by towering trees, dusty jeans, and a very long ride back. She guessed it would be hot dogs and roadside hamburgers for their gourmet dining options, if they did this.

"Two hours, maybe three. If we leave by eight, we'll be there by lunch. Say yes. I've never had the Jeep on real trails before, and this might be my only chance until next summer."

"I will need to call my supervisor. Old Mass does still own me for several more weeks." Katie tried to shift gears quickly, sorting out in her head if she could do this with the presentation on Friday. "It's too late to call Connie tonight."

"Connie?" Jeff looked mystified.

"Her boss." Winnie was back in her chair, with a bowl of baby carrots in her lap. "And no, you don't."

Katie unwrapped Jeff's arms, and she stood, feeling she had to admit, just a little perturbed. Her job was her responsibility, and she had done it well for half-a-dozen years. Just because she'd given notice didn't mean she could walk away from what she'd contracted to do when she hired on. "Winnie, what are you doing?" Her friend had pulled Katie's purse into her lap, and she proceeded to turn it over and dump it out.

"Just looking. Goodness, you keep everything in here, you know that? What would Calvin say if he saw what you did with his creation?"

"Calvin?"

"Klein, Sweetie. I should take you on a fashion shoot someday. You might learn something." After a moment she pulled Katie's phone from the disarray. She turned it on and unlocked it, tapping several times before holding it up for everyone to see. "Listen to this."

"Katie, dear, it's Connie. I just spoke with Lesly, and I'm so glad you girls had such a good time. It's after ten, and I think you need a day off. We'll see you on Wednesday, my gift to you. Tootles!"

"So we're all set?" Jeff had come up behind her,

wrapping her in his arms. "My outdoor girl, in my outdoor world. What could be better than this?"

Well, it was Tuesday now, and the mountains were beautiful. They weren't Fenway, and the lobster roll they'd enjoyed hadn't quite been to LaGrassa's exacting standards, but she was full, and she'd enjoyed her lunch with Jeff.

What was wrong with her? Katie couldn't pin an exact tack into it, but she suspected her evening from the night before had something to do with it. No, not the evening with Jeff, but the one before that, with all her friends from work. It had been totally unexpected, had caught her completely off guard, and it had been exactly the sort of thing only the closest of coworkers would do for a good friend.

The part where the tack fit? Katie was shelving this part of her past voluntarily, choosing to close it up in a book, leaving the pages of her life high on a shelf to open from time to time, hoping to relive some of the best times she'd ever known in Boston. It was the same as on Rockhaven when she'd seen that picture of her and Jeff digging for clams that final summer before her grandmother's house burned to the ground.

The events of her childhood had been locked away in that photograph, and while it could be remembered, it could never be lived out again. It was tidily tucked away, to be pulled out for a rainy day, and while that was nice, it wasn't quite the same.

Ellie, Michelle, and the gang weren't rainy day friends, and she didn't want to lose them.

She laid her hand on Jeff's arm, and when he turned to her, she smiled at him. She pointed to a second sign, this one leading into a grassy field. Off through the trees, glimpses of brown dirt lifted skyward. To the left they came to a sign attached to a tall pole, telling them if there was no attendant, to drop $50 into the attached lockbox and stay on the marked trails. The gates were locked at dusk.

That day, more than dust covered Katie's jeans before Jeff had his fill of off-road trekking. Four-wheel drive low was just the thing for maneuvering around newly cut tree stumps, snowless moguls, and Jeff's pride and glory, a mud pit.

Katie laughed harder than she ever thought possible. Only once was she attentive enough to be frightened when the off-road vehicle careened down a slope toward a patch of trees, but Jeff hooted, and throwing the gears into low, and gunning the engine, he left debris flying all the way to kingdom come.

One time during the day they saw someone else on the course, several teens in a lifted truck, bouncing crazily down the trails. Katie noticed a boy in back, holding to a roll bar, with his face lit up in excitement.

She knew just how he felt, except better. She had her best friend, excepting Winnie, of course, at her side. She and her fiancé were off for the day, just the two of them, doing something he loved—and that she was finding she thoroughly enjoyed, as well. Most of all, they were doing it together.

Afterward they found a family barbecue stand along the side of the road, enjoying a plate together at an old picnic table under the trees. Now, with the top still down, and the wind whipping Katie's hair, she held Jeff's hand with one, and toyed with the air with the other.

She had a wedding on her mind, one that wasn't that far away. Watching the Christmas-ribbon bushes flash by in their bright sparks of summer color, she imagined how it might be, Christmas on the island. She'd never done that, been there for the holidays.

That was in the future, and Jeff was in her present. She pulled the hair from her face with her right hand, and she turned to him, catching his profile against the late afternoon sky. He was everything she'd ever imagined him to be, and they might not have dined at LaGrassa's, but they'd dined together, and for that, she'd ride the slopes with her man any day of the week.

She smiled at that, turning back to look through the dirt-splattered windshield. She'd rather ride the waves in her sailing boat, but whatever was fine with her, as long as Jeff was at her side.

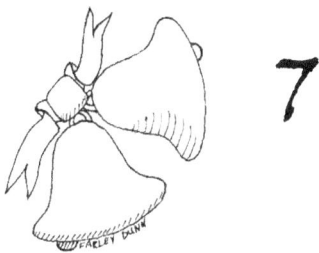

7

"For one hundred sixty-five, that's right." Katie turned the florist's brochure over, pointing to one picture, although it couldn't be seen over the phone. "Baby's breath, can you do that, too? White mixed with baby blue, maybe a fifty-fifty mix?"

Part of the difficulty in planning her upcoming wedding was the fifteen miles of ocean between the shore and the island. There were ferry schedules to coordinate, caterers to organize, and decisions to make on where to bed down those from off island!

"Yes, there is," she responded to the phone. "Dyer's Delivery can pick up from the mainland. Will the flowers need refrigeration? This is an island we're talking about, and I'll need time to set things up."

Another twenty minutes and an explanation that Styrofoam refrigerator packs would do quite nicely to preserve the exquisite beauty of Katie's preferred blooms had her almost rolling her eyes. Still, if she was paying for them, she wanted everything to be perfectly beautiful on her wedding day.

The flowers had been the easy part, though, she was finding out. The cake? Corrine's Creations, an on-island bake shop, had seemed to fit the bill nicely, until Katie learned they mostly did cookies and cupcakes for birthdays and school functions. This was their first wedding ever, and they had never done a wedding cake. However, over the phone the mother and daughter team had been so enthusiastic that Katie hadn't had the heart to break theirs. Besides, she accepted with resignation, she would soon be living with these people. She had already contacted them, and she couldn't back out gracefully, not with the wedding being a major island event.

Later, Jeff told her the two women attended his church regularly, and Katie was horrified that she might have driven a wedge into her life on the island even before setting a permanent foot on its shores. For days afterward she wondered what other mine fields she would have to maneuver within island politics to keep her future life glued together properly.

The clock on her desk spoke of her lunch hour slipping quickly away, and as she pulled out her microwavable soup from her desk drawer, the phone rang.

"Katie Carver. How may I help you?" Even during lunch, she wouldn't refuse to answer her line. All incoming calls routed through the switchboard, and if it came through on her time, it was personal. Suzie on the switchboard was good about that.

"Katie? Is this little Katie, from Boston Katie? Oui?"

"Yes, this is Katie from Boston. Who am I speaking with?" *Little* Katie? She hadn't been called little Katie in twenty years!

"I am so pleased to make this contact with you once again. I hear this most happy news, and I will be soon arriving at your JFK Airport. I would be making reservations for my stay at a very good location. You may have a suggestion, s'il vous plait?"

"You need a hotel room." Katie stated it as a fact. What else could her caller mean? The "happy news" could only be her upcoming wedding. But her JFK? She didn't live anywhere near JFK. That was New York.

"Oui."

The speaker at the other end of the phone was so animated and pleased-sounding that Katie hated to suggest she might be coming in to the wrong airport, but Boston would be a better choice. She still didn't have a name, although Katie had an idea how to draw it out of her caller.

"What name should I register you under?"

"Ah, your grandmamma always say I am so empty-headed. You do not remember me from so many years before. I am Nicolette, my little Katie. You remember, now? From your party, when you were cinq, non, five year of age. You must be remembering Cousin Nikki, non?"

"Nikki!" Nikki? The name seemed . . . somewhat familiar. Then she pictured an elegant woman with a fur collar on every item of clothing she wore, even her swimsuit. The party. The party! Yes, she had been five, and her parents had come to the island. It was the Fourth, and the grounds had been crowded with people. Katie remembered wanting them all to go away.

"You remember Nikki! Oui?"

"The Fourth of July, right?"

"Ah, I knew you could not forget. I gave you a little ring, one with a very small stone. You have it still, oui?"

"Oh, I do remember." And Katie did. She had left the ring on the windowsill that last day on the island, knowing it would be in the same location when she returned in the spring. "You do know my grandmother's house was destroyed in a fire when I was fourteen. Nothing was saved."

"Ah, ma chère! How could I be so silly! Of course, of course. You have nothing but your grandmamma's love remaining. I am so old a fool. Now, to business. I need rooms, and for quite some time. I have not been to America in many years, and to fly, well, is not so good on me anymore. I will take this chance to enjoy your country's fine hospitality for the extended period. You will help me, ma chère?"

"That will be wonderful. I'll set things up. If I can get a return number?" Katie's clock was winding lunch down, and her soup sat, unopened and unheated. She sighed, but

169

she would live. She wrote down Cousin Nikki's information, promising to get back with her soon, making sure she got the dates of her flight.

It was after she hung up that she kicked herself. With the flower worries, the cake, and then the surprise of a second cousin she hadn't seen in over twenty years, she forgot all about JFK. Nikki needed to fly into Logan. Perhaps her flight could still be changed. She reached for the phone to call her back when it began to ring.

Katie glanced at the clock. Lunch was over, and that meant this was work-related. Suzie was good, and that meant Suzie was with the clock. Anything personal now would jump directly to voicemail.

"Katie Carver, Old Mass Claims Department. How may I assist you?"

"I need a repair."

"Ah, yes. We will get you back on the road in a jiffy. As we say here at Old Mass, you only have to call us once. Have you already had your car looked at by a claims specialist?"

"Sweetie, it's not my car that needs repaired." The caller giggled.

"Winnie?"

"Of course, silly goose." Winnie giggled again.

"I'm working. You can't call me now." Katie put her hand over the button to cancel the call as soon as she made herself clear. She was not allowed personal calls during business hours.

"Oh, that's why I have a repair. Otherwise, I get that machine, and I can't talk to you then. Now, I've been think-ing about those bridesmaids atrocities you plan for us to wear, and I have a better idea. There's someone I know—"

"No, Winnie. I'm not going there. Enough is going wrong as it is. Now I've got my cousin coming in, and I've got to find her a place to stay."

"Your cousin? Now that's a horse of a different color. What cousin?" It sounded like Winnie was chewing gum and popped a bubble too near the phone. "Maybe she could help plan the new dresses. Or is it a he?"

"She." Winnie sounded more hopeful than Katie

170

thought she should, and she decided she'd better set her straight. "She's from France, she's really old, and she's flying into JFK."

"New York? That's hours away!"

"Are you offering to pick her up?" Hope lit up Katie's mood.

"Sweetie, I don't have the time. Remember, I've got this dress mess to untangle. I will not wear an atrocity for anyone, not if other people can see me. Sorry, not even for you."

"Ooh, Winnie! Why do I keep you for a friend, anyway?" One more thing going wrong, and Katie felt she would shatter, and she still hadn't had lunch. She wanted to snap someone's head off. Winnie had better be glad she was on the other end of the line, and not here in person.

"Because I love you. So I can go now. Thanks for letting me redo all the dresses. I've got everything under control." The line clicked, and she was gone.

"Winnie?" Katie tapped the line, but all she got was the dial tone. She dropped the receiver heavily into its cradle. She had not given her friend permission to redo all the dresses, had not even hinted at it.

The phone rang again, and Katie grabbed it, prepared to bark at Winnie for assuming entirely too much. When she pressed the button, her remarks were preempted by her supervisor.

"Katie? This is Connie. We've got a situation. I need you here in my office, dear, ASAP."

"Certainly. I'll be right there."

Katie placed the phone down gently, and looked longingly at her uneaten cup of soup. What fun they could have had together. Oh, well. Soup, soup, come again another day. She opened her desk drawer and dropped it inside; and pushing it shut, she grabbed her pen and tablet and stepped from her desk.

Before she headed outside, she double checked the cabinet securing her purse. Satisfied, she flipped off the lights and walked away, leaving her office silent and in the dark.

8

"Hey, Kam. Free for lunch today?"

It was Saturday, and the meetings at work the day before had run long. Katie had worn out long before the sessions had ground to a close. Being presenter at many of them hadn't helped. She needed out and about; a change of scenery.

A nice lunch might help, she had decided. And company. She desperately needed company. A good friend, someone just to sit with and talk about nothing at all. Kambri was her Saturday regular, mostly in the depths of winter, but Katie wouldn't be here this winter, would she?

Katie had her phone in front of her, watching the screen in speakerphone mode, her friend's picture smiling back at her.

"I'm watching my nephew, today, so it might be a MacDonald's run. How 'bout that, Harry? You want to go to Micky-D's and play in the bounce room?" She could be heard calling to someone Katie couldn't see.

"Kambri, don't tease. He'll expect to actually find one."

"Nah, he's three. Kids retain one minute for every birthday they've had. So, in three minutes he's rebooted and ready for something new. If more parents realized that,

172

they'd do a lot better job parenting." In the background, it sounded like the boy threw something that banged against a glass object. "No, no, Harry. Micky-D's. There we go, give Auntie Kammie the shoe. Thank you. Want to go see Auntie Katie?"

"Yah! Auntie Kay-Kay!" He screamed so loud Katie heard him just fine.

"On Massachusetts? Will that do?" Katie had cringed at the sound of the three-year-old's excitement, but she needed company. A super-charged three-year-old explosion on steroids might not be her first choice, but still, today she'd take what she could get.

Before she hung up, she had instructions to pick up her friend and to bring along a cookie, if she had any. Harry's visit had been a surprise to Kambri, and the boy was ravenous. Sugar or peanut butter? Katie had asked. Anything the child could eat, Kambri had replied.

"Oh, no," Kambri moaned when they drove around the block towards the restaurant. "You would come here. We'll never get the kid away."

It was the Boston Fire Department, their Arson Squad.

"All little boys love fire trucks." Katie put on her blinker, her little Beetle slowing to a stop as she waited for three cars to pass. The sun was in her eyes, and she lowered her shade just as an open spot appeared. Pulling through the gap in the busy Saturday traffic, she slipped smoothly into the lot.

"Yeah, and they scream when you drive away." Kambri turned to the back, and reaching over the seat, she pulled the remains of a cookie out of the boy's hand. "No more for you until after you eat."

"We see fire trucks?" He pointed out the window where the front of one, bright red, could just be seen.

"Sure, Harry. See? Now you've seen a fire truck." She glanced at Katie and shrugged. "You do what you gotta do. Let's get the little guy inside and some fries inside him."

"You know, we could walk over and look at one." Katie whispered as she opened her door, leaning Kambri's direction. "They've got several parked outside."

The building next door to the restaurant was huge, and Katie was pretty certain the Boston Fire Department loved kids. Who knew but what one might grow up and join the ranks. Anyway, she'd done an insurance claim for a captain at this location. If he were here, she was pretty certain he'd be glad to talk to the boy.

Kambri just laughed and took off after her nephew, catching him by the collar when he almost ran in front of a car backing out of a space.

Inside, with Harry's child-oriented meal keeping him occupied, and the women's more adult fare spread before them, they finally had a chance to talk.

"So," Kambri began, "what about this?" She motioned with her forkful of salad at the building around them. "You have this? On the island?"

Katie laughed, and then she apologized. "You don't know Rockhaven."

"Okay, then tell me." She dug into her salad and hefted another load of greenery. "How do you keep kiddos happy without one of these?"

"We put them in boats and let them drift in the tide."

"Get out, girl! No way!" Kambri waved her hand dismissively.

"Get out, girl!" Harry repeated, smearing a fry into his catsup and sucking the condiment off before repeating the action.

Katie laughed. "Would you like half of this?" She had a sandwich, but she'd cut it in two and didn't think she'd be able to eat it all.

"Me? Just my salad. Thanks."

"I'm going to miss all of you more than I expected." Katie hadn't planned to say that, but it was true. "Monday was so much fun."

"Nah! You'll have a man, and you'll forget all about us, and you're welcome about Monday. It was mostly Connie, though." Kambri reached out and patted Katie's arm once.

"Have a man," Harry intoned, picking up on his aunt's words, before sucking another dollop of catsup from his increasingly soggy fry. He smacked his lips and said,

"Forget about it."

"Harry's cute." Katie smiled, pointing. "Forget about it. He's not paying us any mind, and still, he hears every word."

"And repeats every single one to my sister. I have no secrets when the little nephew's around." Kambri laughed, sucking a smear of dressing off one finger. "I found that out when he was two, and my sis knew every detail of a phone call I made. He's got tape-recorder memory, my dad says. With no erase mode."

"Any juicy details to embarrass you?"

"Listen. Harry?" She reached over and tapped his table.

"What?" He was sucking the French fry all the way in, and he began to chew.

"Hi, Rosa . . ."

"Did you run the 'thon this year?" He was on a fresh fry, and it looked like he wasn't listening at all.

"Watch this," Kambri whispered, pointing. Louder, she said, "At the gym . . ."

"I met a cute guy." Harry sucked, and red catsup disappeared. He went on, sticking the fry back into his catsup, and mumbling on about something else.

"You poor girl." Katie shook her head. It was amazing, though.

"Just be careful what you say. At odd moments, something'll trigger his memory, and he'll say whatever he's heard, no matter what it was." Kambri was finished by then, and she set her plastic bowl on the tray, pushing the whole thing to the side. "Now tell me, what did you do with your honey the other day? We all know that's where you were on Tuesday."

"I should have known I couldn't keep it secret. You had to have learned that from Winnie."

"Of course. We're friends, and I get all her Facebook posts. You and Jeff were so cute there on your sofa. Now, Tuesday. You don't post, so I never know unless I ask. Where'd you eat? Please say Island Creek. That's the yummiest place in the city."

"Not exactly. Try roadside barbecue." At Kambri's

175

look of dismay, Katie explained. "He brought his Jeep up, and we took it to the Berkshires mud bogging."

"No! Mud bogging?" Kambri began to laugh. "Are you sure you found the right man? I can't imagine you in a mud bog, ever. Did Jeff get in, too?"

"We both did."

"I bet Jeff had fun." Kambri winked.

"Bet Jeff had fun," Harry repeated, now on his third fry.

Katie rolled her eyes, the wink explaining a lot. "Not mud wrestling, Kam. Mud bogging. We were in the Jeep driving through the mud, perfectly clean and dry." Well, not exactly clean and dry, but certainly not rolling around in it. What was her friend thinking?

"I like my version better. Oh, well." Kambri sucked on her straw, only to have it gurgle with air. She set the paper cup beside her salad bowl and put her elbows on the table, resting her chin on her hands, and watched Harry smearing red up and down the side of his drink cup.

Marching music broke the moment of silence.

"That's me!" Kambri pulled her purse up and dug out her phone, laying it flat on the table. Tracing a design on the face, she tapped an icon, and two seconds later, she spoke to it. "Hey, Sis. What's going on?"

"Jeb and I finished lunch, and now we find the movie's sold out. You want we should come get Harry?" The voice was gritty over the speaker phone, but it was loud enough to get Harry's attention.

"Mommy?" He was licking his fingers, and he looked up.

"Hi, Baby. Want Mommy and Daddy to come pick you up?"

"Get out, girl!" He laughed, reaching for the phone.

"Kambri, what's that about?"

"We're with a friend out by the fire hall, the one for arson. He overheard us talking."

"Off Mass Ave?"

"Sure, I think so." Kambri glanced at Katie, waiting until she nodded. "Yeah, that's the one."

"We're not too far. We'll be there in ten minutes. Sit

tight."

"Kay. See ya." Kambri tapped the phone to turn it off. She smiled at Katie. "That was easy."

"That was easy." The boy was down to licking the side of his drink cup, and he had catsup smeared across one side of his face.

"Your sister's sweet. Should you clean Harry up before she gets here?"

"Probably." Kambri stood and held out her hand for his. "Let's go potty with Auntie Kammie. It'll be fun." She looked at Katie, made a face, and shook her head before laughing. The boy grabbed her hand with his catsup-covered one, and they headed off down the aisle.

Katie looked out the window at the traffic passing by. A car very much like Jeff's, except red, pulled in the service station across the road, and two young women got out, both wearing denim shorts and tee shirts, looking like they were headed out to enjoy a summer day that was quickly approaching hot. From the main dining room, she couldn't see the fire department, but that was just as well. Her friend was apparently right, because three minutes after stepping inside, Harry had forgotten all about the fire trucks, and he'd become engrossed in his catsup. Perfect, since his parents were on the way.

Mud bogging. She'd had a good time with Jeff. There was no doubt in her mind about that. Without him? Tuesday's activities wouldn't have been on her radar. It was Jeff she'd enjoyed.

She missed him. Immensely.

He should be with her here. Today. At this family-oriented, child-friendly restaurant. Then they could tour the fire trucks together, and they'd be building memories here in Boston.

She wondered if that was part of the dark mood she seemed to be under. She loved Jeff; more than anything she loved him. She needed him mixed up in her Boston life. The Berkshires? That had been nice. Rockhaven? Even nicer. However, her Boston life was separate, all her own, and while she loved Jeff, she loved Boston, too, the traffic, the restaurants, even the big red fire trucks that tooted their horns when navigating the crowded streets.

Her friends? They'd meet Jeff for one fun weekend, and they'd never really know him, except Winnie. And she'd only met him in July, and then, of course, letting him into her apartment and serving as a good chaperone for the night.

Come back, Jeff, she called mentally. Come and get me, my love. I need you to be part of all this, so I can turn it loose when it's time.

He didn't hear her, though. He was a day's drive away, probably on the island, out of range of her phone.

She made up her mind. She was phoning him today, once she dropped Kambri off. If the call didn't go through, she would try and try until it did. She needed the sound of his voice to keep her on track. She had two worlds, both tugging at her heart. She knew which one would eventually claim her, but it would be easier with Jeff's voice in her ear.

She looked back into the restaurant to see Kambri and Harry heading her direction. Kambri had her face twisted in a frown, and Harry was dragging hard behind her.

"Is everything all right?" Katie moved the boy's things off his table to where he couldn't reach them.

"It will be when my sister gets here." Kambri smiled brightly.

Katie knew that look, and she fought a smile. She'd seen it on her friend Janine Roscoe Peavey's face out on Rockhaven, but in reality, there was no comparison. Kambri had been penned up with one boy for five minutes in the restroom. Janine was penned up on an island in the freezing weather with four boys all winter every winter.

Even so, Katie felt better, somehow, like she'd made a connection between her Boston life and her island home. In that moment, she was certain Jeff was the right choice, and she relaxed.

In fact, there was no doubt in her mind. She'd known it all along.

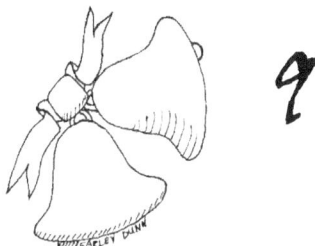

9

"Rain." Katie stood at the window holding her phone in her hand, and she could hear it ringing on the other end. Drops of water splattered against the glass, melting into the moisture already coating the slick surface, and giving the scene outside a distorted, otherworldly appearance.

It didn't brighten her mood much. She was meeting Winnie for breakfast before morning services, and she was having trouble getting moving. She was dressed, though, and ready to go, if only after much moaning and complaining.

"Winnie, here." The voice on the phone's speaker sounded out of breath, as if she had been running up a flight of stairs.

"Hey, Honey!" Katie brightened her tone, in spite of the gray world outside. "Are we still on for breakfast?"

"Let me see." Winnie's voice grew faint. "It's 8:40 now, and services start at 9:00. My hair, and nails . . ." She grew louder, even more out of breath. "Oh, oh, there's no way I can make the next service. I'm so sorry, Sweetie. I forgot to plug in my rollers. How about 10:40, Wendy's or Burger King?"

"Sure, either." The choice of restaurants didn't matter.

Both were right across the street from Trinity, Winnie's current church of the moment. "Why so late? I'm hungry now." What she meant was that they might be attending the 11:15 service, but they could meet for breakfast anytime.

"Sweetie, I have to be beautiful, and it has to be the real thing, not just crawl-out-of-bed beautiful. Now, my treadmill's saying I'm burning calories, and I'm not even on it, so, see you on the way!"

The line clicked off, and Katie set her phone aside. Immediately she picked it back up, finding her recent calls list, and pulling up Jeff's name. She wanted to phone him now, but he would be in services of his own by this time, and she couldn't interrupt simply because it was raining outside.

Last night's call hadn't been all she'd hoped it would be. She'd gotten through, but Jeff had been in his car—an Al and Janine emergency—and the call had cut out twice. She'd returned it once, concerned that one of her old friend's four rowdy boys might be ill or injured, and the second time? He'd been nearly to Janine's, telling Katie Al had called, and he didn't really know what it was about. When that call dropped, too, she'd let it go. He'd sounded horrendously busy, anyway, and she supposed his parishioners needed him pretty badly.

Her husband, a preacher. Did she know what she was getting herself into?

Tapping the face of her phone, Katie knew she could not remain in this apartment. Heading out, she pulled an umbrella from the entry console and made sure this time the door was firmly shut and the alarm engaged. Someone called to her from down the hall.

"Miss Carver!" The voice was cracked, and it wavered in an ancient soprano. "Are you headed to early services?"

Katie turned to see a petite woman, maybe five feet if she tiptoed, with white hair swirled around her head. Anabelle Rosenbaum, although Katie had heard her friends call her Annie. She sprouted an off-center pillbox hat enveloped in rose-embroidered netting. She was really quite an adorable sight coming down the hall, the perfectly coifed

180

little old lady in this ultra-modern building.

"If I can make it on time. It's Anabelle, isn't it?" She hadn't thought about attending the earlier service alone, just intended to get out, but she might at that.

"Annie, if you please. Or, as my old auntie used to say, s'il vous plait." She smiled, her bright-red lipstick cutting a pleasant slash across her face. "She was French, you understand, old money and all that. She gave me this hat, you must know, in the forties; brought it from France. Vichy. There was a war on."

"World War II." They were at the elevator by then, and Katie tapped the down button. "Germany."

"Don't forget Japan, my dear, but that was the other side of the world." Anabelle tapped her chest just at the throat with the fingers of one hand. "Ah, I should not confuse the two. Japan was very different. They wanted manufacturing materials. Germany wanted to kill the Jews. I am Jewish, you know."

"I didn't know that." Katie tapped the lobby button, and the doors closed them in. "Are you headed to the synagogue?"

"Not practicing, dear. Just Jewish. It's a race, not only a religion. Dear, I am converted, a good Christian, as are many of my fellow race. I do believe I attend at your fellowship." Her voice brightened when she said that.

"Trinity?" Katie never would have dreamed. Boston was so large, and Trinity was just one church out of the many throughout the city. "You're attending the 9:00 service?"

"Every Sunday, my dear. I've seen you there once or twice, with your friend." She motioned with her hands in a circle around her head. "The pretty one? With the hair?"

"Winnie." Katie smiled. "She travels for work, but when she's here, we attend together."

"Not that you're not pretty, my dear. You are, and very young. I've seen your friend. Macy's. Only the prettiest girls model for Macy's. I get their ads, you see, and I look at them. I like nice things."

The elevator sounded, and the doors opened into the

lobby. Katie smiled, and she held her hand out to Anabelle.

"S'il vous plait."

"Oh, oh, my dear," and Mrs. Rosenbaum tittered. "No need to speak French to me. I'm not French at all." She tittered again, and it was obvious she enjoyed hearing Katie say the words.

"Then, if you please." Katie motioned and followed her new friend into the tall, spare, and neatly organized foyer. "You do speak French, though. You sounded so fluent earlier."

"Oui." Mrs. Rosenbaum tittered. "Oh, my dear, I haven't said that in decades. You, dear? Are you French?"

"Hardly." Katie laughed. At the door, she glanced at Annie. "Your umbrella?"

"No, no, dear. I don't carry one. My driver, he will have one for me." Annie smiled, stepping through the door to stand under the overhang. "He should be here any minute."

Katie smiled. Driver? Anabelle wore a hat that was counting down to a century old, and she had a driver?

When the van pulled up at the curb, Katie understood. On the side it said Senior Transport, LLC. A tall man in a uniform exited the driver's door with a black umbrella in his hand. When he got to Anabelle, he opened it and held it waiting.

"We have to hurry if we're making the 9:00, Miss Annie. Stand next to me. We can't have you getting your hair wet." He smiled at her, as if he knew her pretty well.

"Carl, this is my friend, and she is attending with me this morning. May she ride along?" Anabelle patted Katie gently on the arm, smiling brightly at Carl.

"Well," Carl started, hesitating. "You are my only passenger, so I guess it's okay. Afterwards, though, I can't promise. If I'm full—" He let it go at that.

"I appreciate it, Carl." Katie was quick to express her gratitude, although she would have been glad to walk or catch the subway. This was about Anabelle, though. With an invitation like this, it would be rude not to accept it wholeheartedly. "If you're full afterward, I can find my way to the T with no trouble."

182

"Yes, ma'am," he said, nodding his head. "You understand how it is. If I'm empty, and a qualified rider wants to take a guest, I can sometimes accommodate them, but if I'm full or almost full, then I have to allow for those who qualify." He'd said the word twice, telling Katie he was reiterating company policy, not his own. "Sundays aren't usually full, so if you want a ride back, as long as Miss Annie's with you, well, I'll be glad to have you along." He shrugged and smiled.

At the van, a step extended beneath the opened door, enabling Anabelle to enter slowly but carefully, and once she was aboard, Katie climbed in after her. Carl pulled out smoothly, navigating the nearly empty streets, and in only minutes, they were at Trinity Church. He reversed his procedure, stopping out front, providing the protection of his black umbrella, and walking Anabelle to the door.

He thanked Katie for her understanding, and closing his umbrella, he stepped back into the rain, flashed his brake lights, and pulled smartly away from the curb.

Katie didn't normally attend this particular service, and now she wondered why. It was the family service, with peppy music and active participation by the youth and the choir.

The service was just starting as they entered, and Anabelle seemed to know everyone, stopping to shake hands and to pat small children on the head. She went so far as to introduce Katie to several people, most in Annie's age bracket, but several younger.

They sat four rows from the front, under the massively domed ceiling. With the rain outside, the light from the gigantic stained glass windows was softened, and the whole place had a charmed, fairy tale feel.

This close to the front, Katie was reminded of a summertime service not so long ago when she had sat at the front of a similar service, honored as a special guest, and even found the man she wanted to live with for the rest of her life. Winnie had been there with her that Sunday, but this wasn't too bad. She had Annie with her as a stand-in, and with her little gauze-infused pillbox hat with its rose

183

embroidery, who could say but this wasn't as fine a friend as anyone had ever had.

The minister was somewhat different, though. That summer Sunday, her minister had been tall and handsome, with slab-sided cheeks that broke into the most endearing dimples. His fly-away hair had hardly been tamed, even in his ecumenical robes, and when she'd run in frustration from his wonderfully supportive congregation, he'd chased after her, leaving his church leaderless and confused.

What would this minister do if she ran out the door in the middle of his service, only to stand on the steps with tears running down her face? Would he come running after her?

Well, actually, she hoped not. She would be mortified; but she didn't intend to run from this man at any point. Rather, it seemed she would be sitting through his ministry two times this morning. After all, she was here now, she would be having brunch with Winnie afterwards, and she would return for yet another service after that.

This had better be good, she thought. Her stomach was rumbling, and she was missing Jeff about as much as she could miss anyone.

She was also irritated at Janine. She'd really wanted to have Jeff to herself for a little while the night before, and those four wild ones she was raising had taken her place.

It was partly the hunger, Katie knew, but she envied the members of Rockhaven Town Church. They had Jeff Ragsdale, and she didn't.

Miss Annie must have seen the longing on her face, because she patted Katie's arm and whispered, rather too loudly, "It's okay, my dear. I was lonely when I didn't have a man, too. God will bring one your way. Just you wait and see."

Several people looked Katie's way, and she thought about running at that point, but Jeff would not be at the door to catch her, and what would she do for an hour and a half? Then, she began to chuckle. It was funny, in a way. God had already brought her a man, just that he was in Maine, and she was here. Did God see the irony in that, or was

Katie the only one that understood? Her in Boston and Jeff in Maine? What good did that do?

The congregation stood to begin a choral reading, and Katie had to put her self-commiseration aside. It was Sunday, and Sunday was for God, worship, and finding peace in Him. She would eventually find her peace, even if she had to wait until she was in Maine to do so.

She joined in, "The Lord is my Shepherd, I shall not want . . ."

In her mind, though, she imagined a good breakfast sandwich from Burger King, or even Wendy's. She didn't care. She was hungry, and all the psalms in the Bible couldn't feed that.

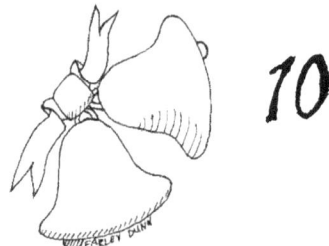 *10*

Katie sat across a dining booth from Winnie, and she chuckled. She had exchanged one brand new friend, for one very old friend. The thought made her smile, as her new friend was very old, and her old friend sported a very new hairstyle. Well, it was as new as a new color could make it.

"You will be back for the wedding?" This was important to Katie. Winnie had done shoots in Dallas, Atlanta, and L.A.; and once in Calgary. That one had been in the middle of winter, and she'd vowed never again, no matter that it had paid better than any other job, before or since.

This shoot was in the Bahamas, for Disney. She would soon be famous, Winnie had giggled over her paper cup of diet soda.

"Sweetie, I'll be back for next weekend. You have a shower on Friday, remember. I plan to be there." She waggled a finger, with a twinkle in one eye. "Might be getting you something pretty special, if you know what I mean."

"So, back to you. When do you leave?" For the photo shoot, Katie knew her friend understood.

Winnie sighed and rolled her eyes. "In the morning.

Who knew planes actually flew at 6:30?" She brightened. "The good thing is I'll be there by noon. More time in the sun is what I say."

"That's the reason for the hair?" It was pulled back to the nape of her friend's neck, tied with a scarf, and woven into a thick braid below that. It was also bright red.

"You know Disney! There's not a strawberry bone in their body. So, I'm red for the week." She smiled brightly and took a bite of her breakfast sandwich. She wrapped the food securely in its packaging before setting it back down, patting it gently. "Stay warm little sandwich, in case I need another bite."

"On a diet? Are they getting you into a swimsuit for the week?"

"If they want, but I think I might be a beach hostess. They're shooting a new brochure. This face is going worldwide. And you knew me before I was famous. Lucky you. Touch me while no one knows me. Say you were the first." She held out her hand to Katie.

"No thanks. You just make sure you get on that plane back home, and make sure you get here on time. The shower's at four."

"Yes, ma'am." She held her hand out to the family sitting at the next table, calling to them, "I'm going to be famous. Touch me while you still can." They looked at her strangely and moved to the other side of the room.

"See? They have the right idea." Katie teased, but she had an eye on the clock, also. It was nearly eleven. "Ready? Second service starts in a few minutes."

"Third." Winnie slurped from her cup, and she dropped it and her unfinished sandwich into the bin behind her. "I missed the second, remember?"

"I didn't. This is my second service. This morning."

"Seriously?" Winnie grabbed Katie's arm and looked her hard in the face. "Are you getting all religious on me? I thought I was the good one."

"Yes, Miss Bikini Queen. I'm getting all religious on you. For your information, I made a new friend this morning, and we went to the 9:00 service together." She

187

peeled her friend's fingers from her arm.

"Oh?" Winnie finally looked interested. "Can I get a name?" She patted her lips with her paper napkin and dropped it in the waste bin, also.

"Anabelle." Let Winnie stew on that. "She has a car and a driver and everything, and she speaks French." Katie grinned wickedly.

"Oh, French! I love French." Winnie grabbed Katie's arm and squealed. "Introduce us. Promise you will! I can practice! Au contraire . . . bon appétit . . . oh là là! Oh, I can say something else. Let me see . . . je t'aime. That means—"

"I love you. I know. Maybe at the shower, if she can come." Katie hadn't yet invited her, but who knew? "Now, though, want to share my umbrella?"

The rain had become a torrent while they were eating, and the sidewalk in front of the restaurant glistened, with bright spatters skipping up every few inches, like little hands reaching for the sky. It would be an impossible dance to avoid every one. Still, Katie figured, if they ran, what with the umbrella, they might just keep their hair relatively dry.

"Ready, Honey? Wet feet and all, but oh, well!" Katie smiled brightly, remembering childhood summers running barefoot in the rain on Rockhaven.

"Almost," Winnie said. She reached down and pulled her shoes off. "Versace. I'll carry mine."

"You silly girl! Barefoot in Boston!" Katie laughed, wondering if she dared. Hose might be twenty bucks, but her shoes were five times that.

"I've got a bag." Winnie pulled a thin plastic sleeve from an invisible pocket, and she dropped hers inside. "I'll carry yours, too."

The rain continued to increase, and Katie kicked hers free, dropping them in her friend's bag. Laughing, they hugged each other tightly, the umbrella stretched over them both, and headed into the torrent.

At the curb, the flood gurgled along nearly six inches deep. By then they no longer cared. Their stockings were soaked, and while they might survive to be worn again, they couldn't get any wetter. Winnie let out a high-pitched wail when they hit the first curb, and Katie joined her by the time they got to the second. Reaching the church vestibule, they realized they couldn't put their shoes back on, not without letting their feet dry, so they smiled guiltily and shrugged when the greeters glanced at their dripping hose; and leaving Katie's umbrella behind, they tiptoed into the sanctuary, finding the first empty seats to remain as close to the back as possible.

Clearly this was a time for worshipping the Lord, but the storm outside had them laughing harder than they had laughed in a very long time, and Katie couldn't help but think God would approve. They were across the building from where they usually sat, and the faces they recognized filed in from the farthest doors. Several couples greeted them, and a family with a trio of preteen girls trailed in. The youngest pointed to their bare feet, and she waved at the two women.

As the final people were settling in for the service to begin, Katie's purse began singing the wedding song.

"What's that?" She held it up and looked at her purse blankly.

"Oh, here." Winnie grabbed it. "That's Jeffie. I reset your ringer at the restaurant. You want to get this call." She pulled the phone out and handed it to Katie. The song was louder outside of the purse, and those closest to them were beginning to turn and stare.

"How do you know . . ." Yet, there was his face on the front of the phone.

"Out. Services are starting. Go, Sweetie." Winnie pushed Katie up and out of the pew.

Moving quickly, so as to minimize the disturbance, Katie swiped the answer icon and pressed the phone to her ear, whispering, "Jeff?"

"Katie! I'm between services, and I hoped to get you. Are you free to talk just for a minute?"

"Yes, always." She was in the foyer by then, and the greeters were shutting the doors. One put her fingers to her lips, and Katie nodded, moving to stand as far from the doors as possible. "I'm in the vestibule, and the services are just getting started. Winnie's inside already. I don't want to make you late." She laughed, glad to hear his voice. She'd needed to hear his voice, and with this being her second service of the morning, she now understood why God had arranged to get her to the 9:00. He knew Jeff was going to call, and this way she could enjoy both.

"I'm in a pinch, Katie, and I need your help." His next words were muffled as if he had the receiver covered. "In a minute, Roker. I'm taking care of it now."

"Jeff, what's wrong?" Katie was growing more concerned by the moment.

"It's Janine. Remember I was headed out there last night?"

"Of course. What?" What now, was what she was thinking. Had Al run off? Had one of the boys set the house on fire? Poor Janine had seemed pretty frazzled a month ago when Katie had last seen her.

"Can you meet her there in town? Al's coming, but it'll be late tonight."

"Sure." But she thought, in Boston? Why would Janine be all the way down in the city? "Will she have the kids with her?"

"Nah, no kids." He covered the phone again and called, "Thirty more seconds and I'll be there. Have them sing one more song."

"Jeff. What is this about?"

"Sorry, Katie. I'm needed. You know, a one-horse show. Mass General at two. She should be there by then. She'll appreciate a familiar face. I love you, Katie, so very much. Coming, Roker." The phone went dead.

Katie supposed the final words weren't for her.

Janine, though, and Mass General. Why in the world would Janine be heading to the hospital in Boston without Al, and the kids . . . and it hit her, was Jeff babysitting again? Would he expect her to take up that job after they were married?

She slipped into her seat beside Winnie, her phone this

time definitely off. She set it on the cushioned bench beside her, right between her and her friend.

"Did you like the ring tone?" Winnie leaned in and whispered. "I set it just for Jeff's number. I thought you would like that."

"Janine. I'm meeting her at the hospital." Katie said it in a whisper, the words making it real.

"In Maine?" Winnie's eyes were wide. "She's the one with the kids, right? That's hours away."

"No, here. Mass General."

"Hm. They're driving all the way down? Bangor has a hospital, don't they? Or Portland. That's even closer."

"I don't know. I'm supposed to be there at two. I don't even know what's wrong." It couldn't be good, though. Winnie was correct. There were lots of good hospitals between Rockhaven and Boston. What could be so wrong that Janine was coming all the way to Boston? Only the highest priority cases came directly to Mass General.

She was distracted by the congregational reading. She was glad it was the same, and she took more comfort in it than this morning. Somehow, she felt it would be important to Janine, also, and she thought of her friend heading to Boston as the people started to rise around her.

She stood, and she took Winnie's hand as she began, "The Lord is my shepherd, I shall not want . . ."

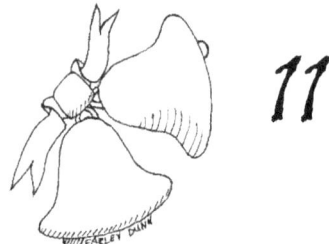

11

"The Children's Hospital. Are you sure? I don't think she's bringing any of her children with her."

Katie held her phone in her hand, messing with it, the screen blank, and wanting to call Jeff for clarification, but urgently feeling the need to be dependable Katie, self-sufficient Katie, the Katie who would do what she was asked in a moment of extreme emergency. It had always worked for her at ALDMass, but she was having trouble with it this afternoon.

"Yes. Even if she has no children, she will be arriving there. All MedFlight and other helicopter services use the helipad at the Children's Hospital." The well-dressed and very polite woman behind the information desk pulled out a map of the Mass General campus. "We are here, and if you follow this arrow—" She had a marker out, drawing in a path. "—it will take you directly there. Two o'clock, you say?"

"By two, I think." Katie wasn't entirely sure, because she wasn't entirely certain why she was here, only that she hadn't been able to get Jeff on the phone after services, and on the way to the hospital with her good friend Winnie in tow, she'd received a text that Janine would be arriving via helicopter. Helicopter! That sounded serious.

The woman—Brendy Barkie, she'd introduced herself earlier—glanced at a large clock on the wall. "I'm not sure you can get there by two. If you don't mind waiting a moment, let me make a call for you." She placed her hand on a phone and smiled at Katie, waiting on her response.

Katie nodded, and the woman picked up the receiver and turned away to begin the call.

Katie stepped to the lounge area, coming up behind Winnie and tapping her on the shoulder. Winnie turned, and seeing it was Katie, she grabbed her hand and pressed it to her face.

"Oh, Sweetie, was it bad? This, and I have to be gone all week, and you with your wedding plans all in a jumble. How will you make it through?"

"The receptionist is checking." Katie sat beside Winnie, reclaiming her hand, and holding her phone in front of her. "Nobody's answering, and that's what I can't figure out. I'm worried."

"Maybe it's simple, like appendicitis. Snip, snip, and she's all better." Winnie smiled brightly as she reached to pat Katie's knee. "Isn't Janine your reception go-to girl? She won't let you down."

"She may not have a choice." Katie looked away, squeezing the phone in her hands. Winnie, God bless her, wasn't making this easier. What she said was correct. Winnie was abandoning her, and Katie depended on her, beyond what Winnie knew. And the wedding. Sometimes she thought she had it all together in her head, the scheduling and the different people to organize to come together all on the same day; and then something would glitch up, and she felt it all coming undone.

Now this with Janine. She was, too, just what Winnie had described—her go-to girl—although Katie hadn't thought of it that way. Katie had been hesitant at first, her friend having to work around four wild island boys at home, but Janine had insisted. "It's something to do that's just mine, and I'll enjoy it, and don't you try to stop me." She had said it with such fervor that Katie had understood.

193

Janine had drawn a line with her family, and she had claimed a slice of her time for her own.

Now, if something had happened to Janine—and it seemed it had—all that her friend was doing filled up Katie's vision until she could see nothing else. The chairs to be set up at the reception, the island women to be organized, even the on-island lodging for those from the city, Katie had let all that slide onto Janine's shoulders, and now she felt it sliding right back. It wasn't a feeling she liked, either.

"Miss?" It was Brendy from the information desk.

"You have news?" Katie stood, and out of the corner of her eye, she saw Winnie do the same.

"We do have a flight coming in. It's a few minutes early, so it's probably too late for you to get all the way there. From north of Portland. Your friend is coming out of Maine, correct?"

"Rockhaven. That's off the coast." Katie licked her bottom lip, her uncertainty making her jittery. "I guess she's coming directly from the island."

"No matter." The woman smiled warmly. "It's our only emergency transport from Maine today, so it's bound to be the correct one. Come with me, and I'll get you a new map. We'll get you and your friend connected."

"Thank you."

"You are very welcome." The receptionist reached a hand to Winnie. "Let me introduce myself before we go any further. I'm Brendy Barkie. How are you, today? Will you be meeting our new arrival, also?"

"I'm so sorry." Katie shook her head, embarrassed at her blunder. She hadn't introduced the two women. "Mrs. Barkie, this is Winnie Catron, my best friend forever. Winnie, Mrs. Barkie, my salvation in time of need."

Brendy chuckled. "Hardly your salvation, but thank you. Feel free to call me Brendy. I'm very glad to meet you, Winnie."

"You, too, Brendy." Winnie took her hand in both of hers, squeezing it for a moment before letting it go.

"Brendy. You told me that." Katie looked away. "I'm

194

sorry. It's . . . I'm distracted, I guess."

"This is a distracting time. Don't you worry yourself about my name. Your friend, though." Brendy had been looking closely at Winnie. "Have we met, before? At a hospital reception or something?"

"I don't think so," Winnie said brightly. "But I'm glad to meet you now."

"I'm sorry. I know what I'm thinking." Brendy apologized. "You look like someone from the Macy's circular. It's not you, though. The girl in the ad has strawberry hair. Otherwise, the two of you could be twins."

"Twins?" Winnie's eyes sparkled. "Hear that, Katie? I could have a twin."

"Dear God, preserve us from the evil that might come our way." Katie felt lighter, though. Like she could get through Janine's trauma, as long as she had her good friend Winnie at her side.

"Oh, it's time." Brendy reached to touch a device on her waist that displayed a blinking red light on top. "They're on the pad and headed in. Let me check and see where you need to meet your friend. Excuse me for a moment."

It turned out Janine wasn't alone. Mass General had an outstanding oncology department that was second to none, able to diagnose and treat the most severe cancers, keeping alive those that other facilities had already written off, and easing the final days for the poor souls that were beyond the help of modern medicine.

The transport had come from Portland, and from Rockhaven, too. Janine was with her father, a man solidly in his fifties, and—his family had thought—in robust health. Indigestion that wouldn't be tamed, then uncontrollable and severe cramping had forced him to Portland. The cause behind the indigestion was what now had him in the hands of the good doctors at Mass General, the best hospital by anyone's measure in all of New England.

Janine was a mess when Katie and Winnie met up with her. Tears ran down her face, and she held a soaked tissue

195

in one hand, with the pocket of her sweater filled with still more. The other hand held a near-empty tissue box that was growing lighter by the moment.

"Katie," she wailed, throwing her arms out. "They've taken Daddy to die! It's already metastasized, and there's nothing we can do!"

"Metastasized?" Winnie mouthed the word to Katie over Janine's sobbing form.

Katie shrugged, making a face to show she wasn't familiar with the word. Right then, the only thing she was interested in was giving Janine all the support she could. And right then, she clearly needed all she could get.

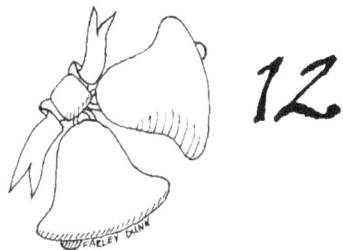

12

"No, I won't even listen to that." Katie held the third box of tissues out to Janine, and as her friend pulled one out, emptying it, Katie glanced inside to be sure, and she set it beside the trash bin. The bin was already overflowing, probably because it was entirely too small for grieving relations come to see dying loved ones in a cancer ward.

"I'm supposed to be helping, though." Janine blew her nose raggedly, wiping at it several times before dropping the tissue onto the already filled bin. "I mean, I can't leave Daddy, and I'm supposed to be up there getting all your *things* organized. Tables, chairs . . . the island guest lists. I haven't even started those. What will you do without me? I could scream!" She leaned her head back and pumped her hands up and down in frustration.

"It'll get done. You worry about your father, because he's all that matters now."

"It was going to be perfect. Island flowers on every table, only to complement the ones you ordered, of course." Janine sat up, her eyes shining with enthusiasm now, instead of pain. "I called the florist, you see, and I've been driving around with the boys. The boys!" She laughed, and it was infused with a tinge of hysteria.

"Were they helpful?" Katie thought not, but her friend needed gentle fingers just now, and to criticize would be to abrade already frayed emotions.

"You know my boys. Helpful as in not. But I did it, pretending we were just on a day jaunt in the car. If I'd let them know what I was looking for, they'd have found a way to trample them all down."

"No. They're better than that." However, Katie remembered a stolen rowboat, and one of Janine's boys claiming Katie had told him to take it, even with her standing directly in front of him. Kevie, she thought. They were toots, and there was no calling that horse by any other color.

"You spent time with them, but thank you. I just . . . this has been good for me, helping you out. It's like old times when we used to do things together. I looked forward to you coming every summer. You were fun, and the gang got together again. It wasn't the same after you left in September."

"Wasn't the same, how?" Got together *again*? They were together all winter, or at least that's the way Katie had always imagined it. It's what she'd envied when she'd sailed away on the last ferry of the summer.

Maybe island life was a two-pronged fork. Maybe the summer folk brought something to the island that they didn't realize, because it was always there when they were present. Some form of authenticity, like they validated the island when they showed up each summer. Their arrival told the islanders that people *remembered* them, and for some islanders—though not all, Katie was absolutely confident—the first summer people were a social waypoint marking the end of a long and sometimes harsh winter, with long nights and very short days.

Odd, she'd never thought of it that way, always imagining summer escapades that surely stretched over the winter months, when even for island children, there were days of unending rain, school, and chores to do before darkness ate the sky at 3:30 or 4:00 each afternoon.

She shivered at the realization, even as Janine went on.

". . . and that was Babe's problem, anyway, having

nothing to do all winter. She told me the summer before your gramma's house burned that if she had to get pregnant, she was getting off the island."

"No." And Katie had felt so sorry for her. Surely it hadn't been intentional.

"Well, she's never been back, and both her parents still live up on the Reach. It's why she was so wild every summer. She said she had to cram nine months of living in three, because the rest of the months on the island weren't worth living." Janine sat back, her burst of energy deflating fast. "I understand now, with four boys under the same roof for six months. I dread rainy days, you know. I try not to watch the forecasts too closely, because I'm depressed two days before, and when it's over, I'm depressed for two more days, because I have to spend at least that long cleaning up the mud the boys tramped in."

"And here you are, with your father at a moment's notice. You are amazing, Janine Peavey. Al is so lucky. Your father is so lucky." Katie laughed, holding one finger up for emphasis, pointing it Janine's direction, and looking intently at her friend.

Janine squeezed Katie's wrist in thanks, giving her a brief smile, but the conversation had wound down, and they sat in silence for a time. Katie thought of her own parents, and wrapped up with them were memories of her grandmother.

She had loved her grandmother immensely, but going to the island each summer had been a tug of war emotionally. Oh, she wanted to go, but her parents thought differently. One year they had argued, with yelling and harsh words, and she had boarded the bus north in tears, vowing never to return to her parents ever again.

Of course, she had. Her home was Massachusetts, not Maine. Her school and her friends were all there, and after cooling down for several weeks, her grandmother had convinced her to call her parents and settle matters between them.

Then, after Carver House and her grandmother were gone, there had been a new round of disagreements, her parents taking the side of mainland life, and Katie wanting to return to Maine. It hadn't worked out, though, and her northern world had been lost to her for a decade and a half. Funny, she'd always imagined the others living on as they had before, perhaps missing her, but doing all the things they'd done together as they grew up on their wild Maine island.

Then her father, older than those of her friends, with Katie being a late-in-life surprise, had developed a cough. Three months later he was bedfast, and her mother didn't last much longer. Somehow, with the home place sold to cover the final medical bills, she'd finally found time to go through all the old paperwork as the auction crew carried the last of her parents' things away. It seemed, although Katie had never imagined it at the time, her parents hadn't planned on her—or any children—and her birth had put a twist in their early retirement and travel plans.

Maybe that was the reason for their emotional distance from Carver Point. Grandmamma had lived the life they lost when she was born.

Katie couldn't undo what was done, and Janine still had her father. She patted her on the knee, and when her friend looked at her and smiled, Katie told her she would be here as long as she needed her, and excused herself to the ladies' room.

There, she looked in the mirror, and she splashed water on her face, pulling a paper towel to pat the remaining droplets clear. She peered deep into her eyes, wondering how prophetic Janine's words were. *What will you do without me?* What would she do without her? Most brides had a mother to help them plan, or a sister . . . a cousin, maybe. Katie had none of those. There was Nicolette, but she wasn't going to be much help, not all the way from France.

It was hitting home to Katie how much she had come to depend on poor Janine, just accepting her offers of help, without thinking of the cost to her time, or how much it must pull from her family. And Al, injured last month in that horrific wreck. How was he taking Janine's commitment to Katie's wedding?

"How are you going to do this, Katie?" She peered into her eyes, as if the person on the other side of the mirror was able to give her an answer that would springboard her off in a new direction. "Fifteen miles of ocean, and now I've lost Janine's help. How am I going to do this?"

She noticed her change of pronouns. The girl in the mirror? She was just a reflection of the little girl who'd wanted to live forever in her summer island life, and now she was getting the chance. Only thing, every pothole possible was getting in her way.

Was God trying to tell her something? Was she not paying attention?

"Katie?" There was a gentle knock on the door. "I don't mean to bother you, but I just got a call."

"One sec!" Katie brushed her hair back with her fingers, and she practiced smiling brightly. Turning, she opened the door, to see Janine was standing behind one of the waiting room chairs, tapping it gently and looking around the ceiling. She had a cell phone in one hand, but it looked off.

"There you are." Janine turned. Her eyes were red, but she smiled. "You are so beautiful."

"Okay. I don't know what that means, but tell me about the call. Was it good?"

"Well, Al's just outside the city, heading in. I thought you would like to know Jeff's with him." She smiled again, but it fell away, and she wiped a thumb under one eye.

"It's going to be okay." Katie put her hands on her friend's shoulders, then she pulled her close and hugged her for a moment, before releasing her with a short laugh. "You've got people who love you, and everything will be just fine."

"I know. I need Al here, that's all. If he gets here, I can make it through this. Really I can."

The news that Jeff was also arriving had turned Katie's thoughts around. She was completely on board with Janine, too. If Jeff were here, she could make it through this. Really, really she could.

201

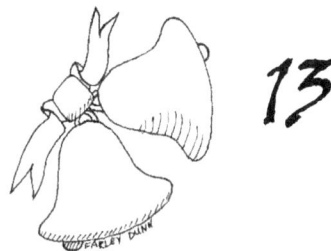

13

Winnie had long since evaporated, off packing for the Caribbean, and Janine was in with her father. Katie didn't know him well, other than as the occasional presence in his daughter's long-ago life, and she had encouraged her friend to spend some private time with the man she rarely saw anymore.

Katie took a deep breath. Poor Janine. From the looks of things, every minute she spent with him could be the last one. How could her own wedding woes hold a candle against what that broken-hearted woman must be going through?

At the window, she placed her hand against the glass. The rain had stopped, although the sun was still wrapped in fistfuls of ominous clouds. When cars passed on the street below, she caught bright, reflected images in the puddles still lingering along the curbs. Glimpses, really, no more. There would be a bright flash of color and chrome, gone before she could really see it, and only recognizable because of the car speeding away.

Those that moved slower allowed her to see them better, her eyes catching with more clarity that wavering shimmer in the puddles that told of what was passing by at just that moment.

Those cars were her life, she mused, as she studied the way her hand left misty imprints on the glass when she moved it away. Through the damp and opaque residue, the world outside looked like a misty Rockhaven morning, with everything that was truth covered up by the fantasy that only the softening of a morning fog could lay across the land.

She had spent a week just months ago rediscovering a boy she'd known fourteen years before, and she'd learned the love she'd hoped for back then was still alive and waiting on her. That week had been a bright flash of shimmering chrome and richly hued paint against the asphalt and concrete that had made up her days.

Then, further down the road she'd caught glimpses of what her life with Jeff might be like in phone calls and letters, and the occasional weekend when they were able to get together to reforge that connection. The distance between each puddle was quite far, though, with the travel time from Boston to Rockhaven.

She recalled running out of the restaurant that morning on the way to service with Winnie. The rain had started to pound, and there was water everywhere: the sidewalks, the streets, even filling the drains along the curbs. Of course, filling the drains. It had been everywhere.

The only thing was that she hadn't been able to see any reflections at all. Oh, shards of this or that, but it was all broken up so quickly, that no one could have made anything of the images seen there. The water had covered everything, but nothing had reflected the world as it was. Rather, it was chaotic, a frightening world in disarray, where one could reach and grab at what might be out there, but only if one could find what the water was reflecting.

The puddles now were fewer, but they reflected more accurately. In them she could see bits of buildings, and the occasional limb of a tree. It wasn't much, but it was real, what was actually there, and not what one imagined to be there.

That was the way of life, Katie supposed. No, not

supposed. She knew it. When life was happening, it was chaotic, sometimes fun, and often like the rain had been that morning. She and Winnie had stepped out of the restaurant, aware of the damage the falling torrent could do, and they had tried to protect themselves from the worst of it. Then, they had given in, and running across the street, they had become drenched with all the "life" that surrounded them.

They had laughed and had a good time, but only because "life" had come at them so unexpectedly, and they had refused to let it trap them. They had gone for broke. They had taken off their shoes and simply gone for broke, pedal to the metal, firing both barrels at the same time.

Katie thought of herself the past weeks, and she saw herself for the first time in a long time as she really was. She had been looking in the small puddles, finding bits of memories in long-ago Rockhaven, here and there seeing her life with Jeff the way it might be, and she had tried to protect herself from the worst of it: the leaving her friends and her apartment; moving for a lifetime to a new and only partially familiar island; and inserting herself into the everyday existence of people to whom Boston was a nightmare from the other side of the world.

"Katie, Katie," she whispered. "You want everything to be picture perfect, and it's not, ever. Life comes at you, messy and unpredictable, and you have to just jump in and hope you can swim. A life jacket never hurts, though." She smiled and thought of Jeff. He made a pretty good life jacket. At least she expected he would.

She reached down and pulled off her shoes, holding them in one hand. She wriggled her toes, remembering the rain. She wanted to run barefoot, with Jeff, of course, but barefoot, nonetheless. Leap into the rain, and laugh with abandon as life dumped itself on her head, bathed in a wild torrent of happiness at times, and the crashing maelstrom of disappointment at others. No little puddles for her! She wanted the whole shebang. She held her arms out and twirled in the silence of the empty room.

"Katie? What are you doing?" Janine stood across the room with a wad of tissues in one hand.

204

Katie froze, remembering her shoes held in one hand, and Janine's awful predicament on the other. Her face warmed. "Being an idiot. I'm sorry."

"I know. You've got to relieve the stress someway. I tell Al now and then I've got to go into the woods where no one can see me and scream. He laughs, but I mean it sometimes. Your idea is much better. Take off your shoes and dance." Her face screwed up again, and she pressed the tissues to her eyes. "I'm sorry. It's Daddy. They can't give me any good news at all. I need Al."

"Oh, Janine." Katie tossed her shoes to the floor and dashed to throw her arms around her friend. "Al's on the way. Come sit. There's only one thing you can do. Give it to God."

"I know. Jeff says that all the time in services. Give it to God. What if God doesn't give it back?" She shook with emotion, sobbing, even as she let Katie seat her on one of the sofas.

"We can't control that. We let go, and God does what He knows is best. So, let's take hands, and if you don't mind, I'll pray, and you listen to what God says to you in your heart."

"You're right." Janine sniffled. "Daddy's had a good life. He's been a bear, never sick, so I suppose if he had to linger, it'd be harder for him than this. Maybe God knows what He's doing in spite of my complaints."

"That's it. Now, here I go. Father, Holy One, we know you hear our prayers . . ."

As she prayed, Katie knew it was true, because about halfway through, unseen to Janine, in walked Al, followed by Jeff. Al started to walk forward, and when he saw the prayer, he stopped, removing his hat and holding it stiffly in his hands. Jeff put his hand on his friend's shoulder, and he dropped his eyes in respect.

"Amen." Katie finished up, and she grabbed Janine in a hug. She looked her in the eyes and said, "How do I know I can trust God? Because during our prayer, He answered it with something you really need. Al just walked in the door."

"Al! Oh, Al, I've needed you here so much!" With the fountains gushing forth once again, Janine turned from Katie, and she ran to throw herself against her husband.

"You're a good woman, Dame Carver." Jeff kissed her on the forehead as he stepped to her and put one arm around her.

"And I told you I'd push you overboard if you kept calling me that." It felt good to have him at her side, teasing her, like everything was going to be all right. "I need a real hug, Jeff. It's been a long day."

"I've got one to give." He wrapped his arms around her, and he picked her up and swung her around in a full circle before setting her down. "You seem shorter than usual today. What's that about?"

Katie laughed. "I'm shoeless. That's worth at least two inches."

"Ah, shoeless. That explains everything." He struggled against a laugh, as if it didn't explain anything at all.

"The rain, Jeff. You have to take off your shoes in the rain." She patted him on the chest. "You never, never wear your shoes in the rain." She knew she was being silly, but she was giddy with him in her arms.

"That really explains everything. Rain in the hospital waiting room. Maybe I should suggest Al transfer his father-in-law to a better facility."

"Don't you dare. Janine's barely holding it together as it is. Let me get my shoes on."

She moved to pick them up only to see a nurse come into the room. She stepped to Janine and spoke to her quietly. After a moment of discussion between the nurse and Al, the three of them exited the room.

"Think that's good or bad?" Jeff had slipped his hands in his pockets, and he made a face, questioning with his eyes.

"Depends on your point of perspective. From what I've picked up, the end of this tale will be very bad, indeed. This particular paragraph, well, I'm glad Al's here now. He's just what Janine's needed."

Katie had her shoes on by then, and she took a deep

breath and let it out. A question had been flitting around in the back of her mind, one she hated to bring up, because it could undo carefully laid plans that might never come together again. Yet, she had to, if she wanted to live with herself.

"Jeff. About the wedding." She stopped, dreading the actual question, and finding the window easier to look out of. It was once again spattered with drops.

"What about it?" He placed his hand on her neck and stood at her side. "Wet out there. Not in here." He chuckled, glancing down at Katie's shoes.

"Should we, what with this about Janine's dad, think about it?"

"Think how?"

"You have to have considered this." She looked up to see him half smiling. "What? You have considered it. I can tell."

"What have I considered?" Still that half smile.

"Rescheduling. A funeral and a wedding that close." She shivered, as if saying it made it real. Janine could never hear her say that. Ever. It would be like a prediction.

"Al and I discussed it on the way down. We're not postponing."

"And if . . ." This was the worst of all. She gathered her determination and spat it out. "What if we have to have the funeral on the same day?"

"Like I said, we're not postponing. Al and I agreed, and he knows Janine will feel the same."

"All right, then." She placed her head against his shoulder. "Everything's on."

"It'll work out. You'll see." He put one arm all the way across her shoulders, and he squeezed her gently before relaxing to stand against her.

Katie wanted to hear Janine say that, though. It was easy for two men to make whatever decisions they wanted, but they weren't the ones losing their father. Janine was, and this was up to her. It was totally and unequivocally up to the one woman to whom today's events mattered most of all.

Then it hit her. Where were the boys?

"Jeff? Where are Al and Janine's kids?"

"Don't you worry about *that*." He laughed softly. "We farmed them out."

"You did, did you?" She remembered him doing that once before. It had worked pretty well, too. It seemed Jeff had a firm handle on just about everything that happened on Rockhaven.

Maybe things would go off without a hitch after all. If Jeff were there, then she'd trust him to pick up whatever pieces might come breaking off their finely crafted wedding plans.

It's what he was good at, after all.

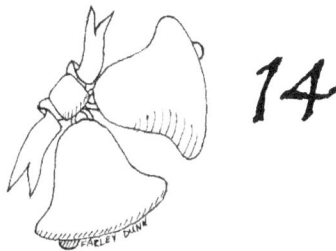

14

Monday dawned bright and clear.

According to the forecast, it would be hot, too. Boston hot, with stifling humidity and early morning traffic. The rain from Sunday had drenched lawns and patios, and all that water had to go somewhere. Once the early morning fog burned away, the sun would grab at the remains of yesterday's deluge and whip it into the air.

It would make the air a wall of water that one would need to swim through.

Katie began the experience while the rest of Boston was still snoozing on their favorite pillows. Winnie was her wake-up call at the unfathomable hour of five. She was off to the islands, she'd quipped, brighter and more chipper than Katie had imagined her friend could muster at such an early hour. She wanted to know how Janine's father was doing, and when did he get out of the hospital? And, oh, did Jeffie come down, too? That was something he would do, because he was such a sweet man.

Katie barely found the answers. Groggily, her head still thick with sleep, she mumbled, "As well as can be expected; yes and no; and yes he did. And thank you. That's why we have a wedding planned."

"Okay, Sweetie. Let me know if anything changes." And she rattled off a phone number that probably belonged to the production company, telling Katie that her phone surely wouldn't work "way down there."

Katie sat up, her feet finding her slippers on the floor. The sofa was comfortable enough. It just wasn't her bed. She'd let Al and Janine have that. It was the only one she owned large enough for two. Upstairs? Jeff was ensconced there. He'd overnighted in the loft once before, and she refused to take that away from him.

She missed her bathroom, though. Yet, she didn't really mind giving it up. In a couple months, it wouldn't be hers, anyway. Someone else would be living in her Boston apartment. Why not start practicing now? More to the point, after the news Al and Janine had received at the hospital, they needed their privacy. And today, they had a decision to make. A very hard decision to make.

It wasn't Katie's, though, and she was glad enough for that. She grabbed up her toothbrush from the coffee table and spoke to it softly, "Thank you for joining me for the night. Come to the bathroom with me, and let's have a little early morning dance."

"Katie?"

She froze. She'd forgotten the loft opened to the living room, and the French doors must have been left open. Her and her big mouth. Why couldn't she keep it closed when other people were around to hear?

"You awake down there?"

"Hey, Jeff. Not really." That was God's truth.

"I didn't sleep well and heard something about a dance. You have company down there?"

"Only my toothbrush." She held it up in the dark, although she knew it was for her benefit, only. Jeff couldn't see it, unless he had Superman eyes. Then, after his masterful performance yesterday with Al and Janine, maybe he did.

A soft light flickered on in the loft, filtering across the living room ceiling, the glow one she recognized from a gift she'd received several years before. It was an egg that when touched shimmered with soft LEDs. It was on a timer that automatically shut off after ten minutes. Touch it twice, and you had light for twenty.

Twenty minutes, she thought. Just enough time to fall back asleep, if only I didn't have to go in to work today.

"Hey."

It was Jeff's warm voice again, and when she looked up, there he was, leaning over the railing, his hair rumpled and wild, and a roughened shadow of beard across his jaw. He was in plaid pajama bottoms with a paisley top. Oops, Katie thought. Al in the bedroom was probably matching, except Al would have on a paisley bottom and a plaid top. She found that funny, and she began to giggle, looking away and covering her mouth.

"So, what's that about?" He yawned and rubbed one hand across his face, and in the same motion, he ran it through his hair, pushing it back from his forehead. It fell right back down, though, and he ignored it, as if he had actually made a difference, and the shock of hair was now right where he wanted it.

"You." She crossed her arms and looked up at him. "Did you even look at what you're wearing?"

He glanced down and pulled at the fabric of his pants, shaking his head. Then he pulled at his shirt. "Looks okay to me. You don't like paisley and plaid together?"

"Oh, paisley and plaid are just fine. It's that you and Al are twins. Depending on whether you like paisley or plaid, he has on your pants or your shirt."

"He does, does he?" Jeff had his elbows resting on the railing, and he looked down at her. His voice was soft and low, and he didn't act as if it were much of a problem. "And whose fault is that?"

Seeing him there, his face shadowed in the dim light, with only his voice floating so easily down to her, it was his shoulders that stood out. They were a man's shoulders, a working man's shoulders. A lobsterman's, to be exact. How could this man be so beautiful?

After too long a pause—way too long, Katie decided—she whispered, "Mine."

"So, I guess I can expect an apology." His words were barely there as they returned to her, but they carried laughter woven into every syllable.

"You are a fool, Jeff Ragsdale. How do you expect me to apologize for mixing up your pajamas?" She would have laughed at him, except for Al and Janine just in the other room. And it was too early for any sane person to be awake, unless they were headed to some Caribbean island for the week.

"Oh, I could think of a few ways. That toothbrush. Are you planning on starting that dance anytime soon? When you're finished, I need to make my way down to your level."

"Oh, oh, right." She grimaced. She wasn't thinking. Four people. Two bathrooms. She didn't have the liberty to indulge staring at Jeff just because he was here. Today, this morning, her bathroom was meant for sharing.

"You go dance. Buzz me when you're through. Oh, and good morning, Katie. I don't get to say that very often to the woman I love." He turned, and gently pushing the French doors closed, he disappeared from view.

"Good morning, Jeff Ragsdale." She whispered it, too softly for anyone to hear. It was something she wanted to say every day, and she wanted to say it with a kiss to the man she loved.

It was a pretty good way to start a morning, she thought. A pretty good way indeed.

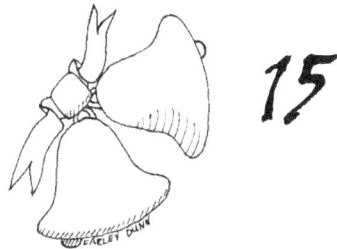

15

Katie hit the humidity when she exited through the glass doors of her apartment building. It smacked her in the face, and it wasn't even hot.

Yet.

It felt it, though. When she caught a ray of sun peeking through two buildings, it was a stab of bright heat across her dark blue blazer. For a moment she considered heading back to change, but then she remembered her bedroom was off limits, and she would be inside most of the day, anyway. All she had to do was walk a short distance, catch the T, and she could relax until late afternoon.

She would need to purchase a sandwich from the food cart, though, if she were out of soup in her desk drawer. Who knew after the hectic jumble of Friday's presentations?

At the stairs down to the T, she felt in her purse to make sure her personal phone was there and on. The hospital was awaiting a decision from Al and Janine on how long they wished to keep Janine's father on life support before letting nature take its course. Already he was unresponsive, and hospice care was their only option. He could go home, if Janine wished, or remain at Mass General for more

213

personalized care.

That had been the final trauma of the evening. How does a person let go, when the week before, her father had been on a golf course, and hosting his partner to lunch at the club? Now, the doctors said the machines were the only reason he still lived.

Katie couldn't imagine, except that she could. Her father had gone in much the same way, only more slowly. She didn't envy Janine's day. Stay as long as you need, Jeff, she'd said before leaving the apartment. Make yourselves at home, and let Al and Janine sleep as long as they need. They're bound to be exhausted.

He was exhausted, he'd replied. But, yes, he would let them sleep, and they'd give Katie a call the first they heard something. He'd hugged her, kissing her ever so gently on the lips, and she'd pulled herself away. She didn't trust herself to stay. Somehow, she thought, maybe it was better he was on the island, and she was in Boston. She was too much in love with him to keep away. She was surviving by the two hundred miles in between. Any less distance, and like magnets, she'd let them be drawn together, never to be separated again.

This morning they were separated, though, as she was working, and he was keeping his friends' lives from falling apart. It was Lesly that Katie ran into first, coming out of the parking garage as she traversed the last of the sidewalks before entering the building.

"Hey, Les," she called, very brightly. "How was your weekend?"

"Busy, and that rain yesterday. Have you ever seen so many dogs and cats fall from one sky? I was glad I didn't have to get out. How about you?" Lesly held her keys in one hand, this time hers and not her husband's. "A couple more weeks, and you'll be hitched."

"I like to call it a merger. Two great corporations linking assets to become one." Katie smiled as she said it. After yesterday, it was good to step into a world that wasn't weighted down by an impending death and a best friend that had abandoned her in the middle of it all. It was nice to joke about something just for the joke's entertainment value.

"Nah. Not a merger. It's the tie that binds, so get ready for it. It's the tie that ties you down, if you want to know the truth." Lesly nodded knowingly.

"Is that a bad thing?" They were inside, where the humidity was cut in half, and Katie's blazer felt pleasantly warm.

"Not for Brian and me. It's the babies that do it. Kids? Wait as long as you can, if you want my advice." They greeted the receptionist before heading to the elevator. Once they were past, Lesly laughed. "If you want my advice, don't have them, but what kind of expert am I? I've got two, and a grandbaby on the way. So, don't listen to me."

Once in the main reception room for the claims adjustment division, Lesly waved as she headed off, saying she couldn't afford to clock in late. She'd see Katie at the morning staff meeting.

The wrapped box on her desk surprised Katie. She picked it up and opened the small card dangling from the ribbon. *Katie, Katie, Katie* was all it said.

"Hm," was her spoken response. There was no hint of who might have put it here. No suggestion of who might be waiting in the wings to catch her response, and she knew there must be someone watching. A prank, perhaps? She still remembered the keys from the previous Monday.

Stepping to the door, she looked up and down the corridor, and seeing no one, she worked her finger under the edge and broke the wrapping loose. If they were watching, she would see they got her response. "I'm opening the gift." She called the warning into the emptiness.

A voice she didn't recognize replied from far away, "If it's candy, I get a piece." Whoever it was laughed, as if they didn't really intend to claim the prize.

"That's what you think," she muttered. Katie, Katie, Katie. She tried to picture who at work had ever called her that, but she came up blank. She could only think of one possibility. This had to have been from three of her friends, joining in to buy her something extra special. It was obvious, one Katie for each of her coworkers.

Her anticipation building, she slipped the wrapping paper free, and she was left holding a brightly worked metal box. Pushing the clasp aside, she raised the lid and lifted it. "Oh," she said, sitting at her desk, and dropping her purse to the floor.

It was a small spiny sea urchin, brightly colored, with all the spines removed. She lifted it and turned it, seeing the bottom was plugged with a rubber stopper. Shaking it, it rattled softly, and the motion brought forth an exotic smell of roses and wild berries. She pulled a note from beneath it and unfolded it.

"Katie. This made me think of your island. Rockhaven's going to be your home, and I'll miss you so much. This is for your desk, so you'll remember Jeff misses you even more. All my love, Winnie, Winnie, Winnie."

Katie's eyes watered as she remembered what this was about. On her friend's first visit to Rockhaven, Winnie had exited the ferry, and they'd done just that, called each other's name multiple times in excitement.

Winnie, Winnie, Winnie, she thought. I'm going to miss you more than you can ever know. She cleared a spot at the edge of her desk, one right in the center, and she placed the sea urchin all by itself, just where everyone who came in to talk to her would see it.

"Knock, knock!" Katie's supervisor stood at her cubicle door, and she peered in, smiling brightly. She held a company tablet in one hand.

"Good morning, Connie. How was your weekend?" Katie stuffed the paper from the gift into the trash bin, and she set the box on the floor by her purse.

"Always good." She looked at her tablet, tapping on it once. "You're here, but don't forget to clock in. I know you're at your desk, but Corporate only knows if you say so on your computer. I see you got your gift all right. I'm glad. That was left with the night watchman this morning at the crack of midnight."

"Crack of midnight." That was funny. Katie laughed as she held up the sea urchin and shook it. "My good friend is

216

on a photo shoot to the Caribbean. She gave me this. Smell."

"Wonderful." Connie inhaled deeply. "Roses. I thought people brought gifts when they returned from trips."

"This is from Rockhaven in July." Not exactly, but close enough. "From Macy's, most likely, but we find them on the island. It's to remind me of Jeff."

"Ah," and Connie nodded her head as if she understood. "Did you get to see him this weekend?"

"I certainly did. Thank you, Connie. I guess I should log in, now."

"Best, dear. We want to keep Corporate happy. Remember, staff meeting in fifteen minutes. Breakfast is provided, and most of your coworkers are already there." She tapped her tablet once more, smiled, and disappeared down the corridor.

Katie hadn't wanted to say that Jeff was still at her apartment. How would that look? It didn't matter that another married couple was with him, or that he was only there because of her friend's father, now dying in a local hospital. To explain all that would sound too much like a list of excuses, when all people would hear was that they had been in the same apartment overnight. Different beds and on different floors? They most likely wouldn't believe that part.

Well, that was the way it had happened. God believed her. But even Katie knew better than to trust her friends with that juicy bit of information.

Thinking of Al and Janine, she pulled her phone from her purse, and she placed it on her desk. Tapping it on, she checked it for missed calls or texts. Nothing. So, either Al and Janine were still sleeping, or they were making their decision as she sat here. She would keep the phone at the ready, even in the meeting, because she didn't want to miss a call this important.

She'd missed Jeff's call the week before. Look where that'd gotten her. She wasn't missing another one. This was her new life, coming to make her part of it. She planned to jump in with both shoes off. It was the only way to live life to its fullest, and that's exactly what she intended to do.

217

 16

"You don't have to do this, Janine."

It was early morning, and it was cool for a change. The sun was creeping over the tops of the buildings, and before long, Katie would say good bye for a time to Al and Janine. Jeff had driven back to Maine the previous Monday, and Al and Janine had continued to claim Katie's bed.

Katie's heart went out to her friend, both for her sorrow and her unqualified generosity. Who else in the whole world could lose a father to an undiagnosed and rampantly aggressive disease, and not wallow in self-pity about it for weeks on end? Now her friend continued to insist that the entire reception was on her plate, and if Katie would let her, she wanted to help with the wedding, too, as much as she could manage from the island.

"I do, too, have to do this." Janine threw her arms around Katie, and she hugged her tightly. "If I don't have this wedding to plan, I'll go crazy." She backed away, sniffling, and she dabbed at her eyes with a tissue. "Once I get Daddy taken care of, then I'm leaping into your wedding with both feet. It's going to be the island event of the summer."

"Not so fast." Al had his one good arm around Janine

by then. The other was still in a cast from the wreck he'd been in back in July. "We don't want to rush the love birds too much."

"Katie knows what I mean. Anyway, it's summer on the island until the first cold snap, and that won't come until October. I can call it whatever season I want, even if it is after the middle of September." Janine was finally smiling. She had made it clear this project captivated her, and her improving humor verified it.

"I see a bus arriving. You know, I could still drive you up."

"We'll be dropped off at the terminal door. I have my tickets, and this saves you a whole day behind the wheel." Al patted his breast pocket and smiled. "Anyway, you have work today."

"Give your boys my best, and when you see him, give Jeff my love." Katie took her friend's hand, and she squeezed it. Al was right, but Katie felt it necessary to at least offer. This afternoon was her shower at work. It had been planned for weeks, and to miss it? Even for this? Al and Janine had refused to allow her to think of it, especially after putting up with the two of them, Al had joked.

When the expected had happened, as bad as it was, at least it happened here, Al had remarked over coffee one evening, and not at home where Janine would be reminded of her father's demise at every turn. He had sipped the final dregs from his cup, and pointed at his wife through the bedroom door, curled up in exhaustion and finally asleep.

"Our boys," and he'd paused, looking out the windows at the shadows cast by the setting sun on the buildings across the street, "take a lot of energy, and Janine bears the brunt. After the second, we intended to stop, but things didn't work out that way. She's envied you, since you've been back. I appreciate you letting her do this for you, in spite of all that's happening now."

He'd taken a deep breath and stood, placing his cup in the sink, and making his way to his wife in the other room.

Katie had watched him go, not wanting to rob him of his moment. It wasn't like Al to be outspoken with her.

He'd hardly said four words to her since she'd returned to the island in summer.

In summer. What a long time ago that seemed, her returning after fourteen years away, only having recently learned her grandmother's property had been willed to her, and all she had to do was claim it.

She'd claimed much more on that trip: time spent with Winnie; faded island friendships restored; and a fiancé, one who had grown handsomer with the years. It had only been weeks ago, and already it seemed so much time had passed. She knew what made the difference. It wasn't the time. It was what filled up the time, and hers had been very full since she'd returned from Rockhaven.

Now, she was sending Al and Janine back to Maine with Janine's heartfelt assurance that Katie had done more than she and Al could have asked. The funeral was to be no more than a private memorial, as her father's will stated he was to be cremated. He wanted his ashes tossed off the ferry as it traveled to the island. Not from, but to, like he was going home, forever caught up in the wake of the boat. When Janine had told her, the long-ago memory came to Katie. As a girl, she remembered Janine's father saying exactly that, thinking it was a macabre joke to send shivers up a young girl's spine. No. Janine assured Katie that her father had always said that's the way he wanted to go. She might one day put a marker for him in one of the island cemeteries, but there would be no one there. He would be in his sea, floating across the world forever.

"I could still come up for the ceremony. Please?" Katie hated thinking she was abandoning Janine, just sending her off, and not being there in her moment of closure.

"Al and I talked about that." Janine had her one small bag's long strap over her shoulder by then, and she squeezed Katie's arm. "Being here in peace and quiet—"

"Without the boys," Al interjected, with an awkward grin.

"Okay, Al. You don't have to explain it so bluntly. Katie understands. He means that without the boys we got to really talk. We want to wait until you're coming up for good. We'll ride the ferry off the island and back. You and Jeff, and the boys, too, can drop a little of Daddy off the side. That's probably all we can get away with, anyway. We don't want to cause a problem with the Transportation Authority."

"You are so sweet." Katie leaned in and kissed her on the cheek. "Have a good trip, and oh, be strong when you think of how much your father loved you all those years he lived on the island with you."

"Bye-bye, blushing bride." Janine giggled before climbing on the bus.

"I'll tell Jeff how much you miss him." Al winked and climbed aboard after her.

It was hard watching the bus drive away, but then it was easier, too. It was just . . . just Katie, then. No Al, no Janine, no Winnie, and no Jeff. She was back in her element, with her blue Bug, her trendy apartment, and her very stable job at ALDMass. For the first time all week, she had a few minutes to herself, and maybe, just maybe she could get back on track with her wedding plans. In spite of Janine's generous offer, there was stuff only Katie could do.

With Winnie, of course, to call on in the tight spots.

Her purse began singing to her, and she frowned, opening it and pulling out her phone. Certain it was Connie, and trying to recall if she'd remembered to let her know she would be late this morning, she held it to her face and answered.

"Katie, here. I'm on my way. Sorry."

"Oh, Sweetie, how'd you know I even needed a ride? How long until you're here?"

"Winnie? Is that you?" Logan! Katie knew that's where her friend would be.

"Of course, Sweetie. Who else would call you at this time of the morning? Did you like my little present?" She sounded tired, but her voice was chipper, anyway.

"Everyone's loved it. It sits right on my desk." What was on the tip of her tongue was something else, though. She was thinking, If you expected me to give you a ride, shouldn't you have let me know? What she said was, "I'm headed to the car. I'm at the Greyhound Terminal, so it won't be long."

"Oh, you're so silly, and that's why I love you so much. But Sweetie, that was a senseless place to wait for me. I couldn't ride the bus all the way across the ocean. Greyhound might be good, but not even they can walk on the water. We'll save that for Jesus." She giggled. "Once you get here, I'm planning to sleep all afternoon. See you in a bit!"

And the line went dead.

Well, Katie thought. So much for Winnie helping out in the tight spots. Rather, she was a tight spot, one that was waiting on her at Logan Airport.

Still, she had what she had, and that little sea urchin had been a nice treat all week long. Every time she felt Janine's father bringing her down, she had shaken her urchin and enjoyed the smell of roses and berries. It had reminded her of Carver Point, and that had reminded her of Jeff.

That was her goal, after all, Jeff and the island. Of course, she couldn't have one without the other, but that was the point, wasn't it? Jeff and the island, forever and ever, amen.

That made her smile as she put her key in the ignition and started her little Beetle up. She imagined what Winnie would be saying if Janine and Al had taken her up on her offer to drive them to Maine.

"Katie, Katie, Katie!" She could picture her friend now.

And her reply? It would be what it always was: "Winnie, Winnie, Winnie!"

Winnie would never change, and Katie felt somehow better knowing that. Her friend was the one constant she had depended on forever, and she was glad to claim her as her number one favorite person.

Right under Jeff, of course, but right up there with the best.

After all, those three words sounded the same in any language.

"Winnie, Winnie, Winnie!"

Katie laughed as she pulled out into the street, not even caring that the parking attendant looked at her strangely as she drove away.

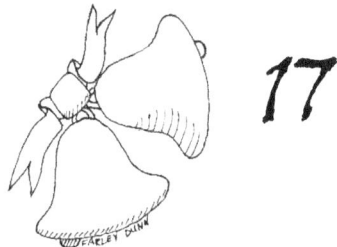

17

Katie held her list of things to do in one hand, and a retractable pen in the other. It was an important list, the most vital one she'd ever made.

The shower the previous Friday at ALDMass had been just what her friends had suggested, a charming meet-and-greet. More of a cake-and-punch social, with the social outweighing the shower. The reason was that ALDMass was huge, and she didn't know well many of those there that day. A collection had provided a money tree, and it was appreciated, but it didn't compare to the more intimate shower given by her friends at Friday's.

Outside the windows of her apartment, the late-afternoon sun washed the distant buildings, catching her attention. The windows were open to let in the perfect September breeze, and she pressed the paper against the tabletop, setting a thin book on top to keep it from blowing to the floor.

She laid the pen on the table beside it, glad to have the afternoon off. The sun might have warmed the sidewalk, but the air carried hints of the upcoming season. The two together? Priceless.

"This is a day to die for." The words came from the

loft. "Hey! Yoo-hoo, down there. Why aren't we out there soaking up some rays?"

"Because I have a job," Katie called up. To herself she muttered, "Unlike some lucky people." Winnie did have a job, but it was sporadic, giving her plenty of time to play. Modeling paid well, but sometimes she had weeks between assignments. Such was the price of being naturally wonderful, her friend had quipped on more than one occasion.

"For one more day. That's not so bad." Winnie adjusted one of the jeweled combs in her hair, pulling the ebullient mass back from her face. "I'll be right down."

"And I'll put you to work. Are you sure?"

Winnie laughed and waggled her fingers over the rail. With a jangle of spangles on her arms and neck, she disappeared. It was only a second before she reappeared down the stairs. She walked to the windows to stand in the breeze. Her thick and permanently curled hair lifted in the inrush of warmed air, a strawberry halo against her permanent tan.

"You are so beautiful. How do you do it?" Katie put her chin on her palm, and rested her elbow on the table. Of course, beautiful was the reason the girl got so many modeling gigs. She was a fairy princess of unimaginable good fortune. Now all she needed was a Prince Charming of her own to have it all.

"Good genes." Winnie looked at Katie and smiled, her bright teeth lighting up her face. "The elliptical trainer at the gym helps, too, and one day, liposuction!"

"Lipo-what? I can't see you ever needing that." Katie picked her list back up, the beautiful spell broken. It was just Winnie, lovable and inscrutable Winnie, and that was all right, if sometimes irritating. Not too much so, though. She smiled at that.

"What's funny?" Winnie pursed her lips as if petulant, but her eyes laughed as she spoke.

"Look at this." The list made a good distraction. "Maybe I should call Jeff and tell him March is a better time for a wedding."

"Girl!" Winnie picked up the list and shook it, rattling the paper, and completely ignoring Katie's suggestion. "You have got to get to hopping. That knot's not going to tie itself. I may actually have to take over some of these for you."

"No, you don't. I will not have Donatella Designs doing my wedding." Katie snatched the list back from Winnie. "Besides, I'm not rich enough to afford anything you'd want to do."

"Donatella Designs." Winnie giggled. "There's no such firm anywhere that I've heard of. When did you become the fashion expert? Now, someday I might have a little shop and call it Winnie's Designs. Think you'll be able to afford what I do?"

"Seriously. Real designers don't give away their goods." Katie knew the better stores often let Winnie have what she wore in the shoots, but designers? Ha, was her thought on that.

"Oh, I don't know. People like me, and I can pull a few favors, if I put my mind to it." Winnie sat and smirked. She tapped the paper on one particular entry. "You can mark this one off. I've taken care of this already."

"The bridesmaids' dresses?" It was an entry that was starred. Katie had thought it was all wrapped up, and it had come apart at the seams once again. All her best friends at work were to be on Rockhaven, attired in identical outfits, the design selected from a Macy's line that was as affordable as Katie could stomach, yet when she'd mentioned it casually to Lisa Vickers the previous Monday, her coworker had looked at her in surprise. "The Macy's dress? Oh, friend, I am so glad you let Winnie take over that little detail. No offense, but . . ." and she had wrinkled her nose and shaken her head. Then Connie had paged Katie, and she hadn't found out what Lisa meant.

That's why it was on the list.

"You don't need to worry, Sweetie." Winnie smiled impishly and tapped Katie on the nose with one finger. "Everything will match beautifully. And I get to wear vintage Oscar. I'm so excited!"

225

"De la Renta?" Katie choked. She might not wear high fashion, but she knew the names of the best designers. "No one in this wedding party can afford that. Remember, we're working girls, not debs out to spend Daddy's money."

"That's why you have me. As I told you, I've taken care of this already. Now, where's a pen?" She picked up the one Katie had laid down earlier, and she clicked the end. With a flourish, she squiggled a line across the page, right through Katie's reminder to find out just what was going on with the attendants' dresses.

Katie took a moment to breathe deeply before responding. "Do I get to see what everyone's wearing?"

"Sweetie, if it's Oscar, you *know* it'll be fabulous. So, you don't worry one minute. You can trust your good friend, Winnie, don't you know? I have never let you down, not once, not ever. Now, before this evening gets away, let me see those hands." Winnie grabbed Katie's hands and began to inspect her fingernails. "Ole Brandywine. Do you ever wear anything else? Oh, well, it'll go with the dress I've picked out for you, so I guess it's okay. This one's chipped, though, so I need to get busy. At least they've grown out from all that damage you did back in July. You butchered these, Sweetie, and I thought your nails were lost forever!"

Katie gave in as Winnie pulled her obviously prepared manicure supplies from a small bag beside the table, and proceeded to happily begin repairing any damage she could find.

However, Katie was pretty sure she had already picked out a dress. She had gone to a fitting at a good but moderately priced shop, although it wasn't paid for yet. The wedding was two weeks away, and with tomorrow her last day at work, she'd planned on getting all the final strings tied together in what she'd come to call her "Detail Week."

"Where's your Brandywine?" Winnie said it absently as she applied filler to one rough nail. The other hand soaked in polish remover. "We're going for a full fresh coat."

"My Brandywine?" Katie shook her head as she rolled her eyes. "You're the manicurist. You figure it out."

"Oh, girl, why do I have to do everything around here?" Winnie set her tools aside, and she stood. "Now, you don't move. You and me? We've got some major repairs going on, and we can't scrimp on this. Tomorrow's your big day, and we want you to go out with a bang."

"With a bang?" Katie smiled.

"Like in a western. Be back with a nice bottle of *po-losh,* quick as a rattler on a rat." She giggled.

"Po-losh? Say it correctly, polish, and what's this rattler on a rat all about?"

"My new photo shoot coming up. It's for a western store. You like that? Sczz-zz-zz." She made a sound like a rattlesnake before disappearing into the bedroom.

Katie was sitting with one hand soaking and the other covered with drying filler when her phone rang. "Winnie? My phone's beside the bed. Can you get it?"

"I'm under the sink. Give me a minute." Her reply was faint, as if she truly was under the sink. The phone had stopped ringing when she returned from the bedroom with it in her hand.

"Was it Jeff?" It was about time for him to call.

"Let's see." Winnie smiled and tapped the play icon.

"Hey, Katie. Jeff here. Busy week." He laughed in the recording. "Out to collect the boys from school. Some after-school something. Detention, probably. Al's at the clinic getting his cast off. Love you."

"Call him back." Ooh! That Winnie! Katie had her hands totally tied up, and there was nothing she could do about it.

"Let's see. I think the number's 1-800-J-E-F-F-I-E. Oh. Not enough numbers." She looked at Katie and tittered. "Maybe it's 1-800-L-O-V-E-J-E-F-F. Oh, that's too many."

"Oh, you. If I had my hands free . . ." Katie growled.

"Oh, I'm scared now. Okay." Winnie tapped the phone. "Now it's ringing. Now. Now. Oh, it's a recording. Wait on it . . ."

"Hold it closer." Katie wanted Jeff to hear her apology for missing his call.

Winnie seemed to think otherwise.

227

"Hey, Jeffie. Katie's on the other side of the room. We're having a girl's night in, and we're doing manicures. Have fun with your little tykes. Love from Katie, and oh, this is Winnie, her bestest friend." She tapped the phone and smiled, plainly pleased with herself.

"If my fingernails were free—"

"Well, I'm glad they're not. You know I always look out for you. Now Jeffie knows I love you, and you love him, and it's all right for him to be out with his little friends. What makes a man happier than that? See? I might not be married, but I know what makes a man happy. They want everything. Even the sweet ones." Winnie lifted Katie's hand from the remover, and she inspected her nails critically. "They pass. Now for polish."

Katie leaned her head back and closed her eyes, letting her friend have full reign for the moment. However, she had a list, and a manicure wasn't on it. Not even in the vicinity. Ooh, Winnie, she thought. If you knew what I was thinking, you'd think me a bad, bad girl.

That made her giggle, in spite of it all, and when Winnie slapped the top of her hand and told her to hold still, she began to laugh. A girl's night in. Instead, it was Winnie's time to play dress up, even if there was a wedding two weeks away, and the list of things left undone was longer than her arm.

At least she had one thing marked off. The dresses. Just what she would see on her special day, she didn't know, but that was the fun of having Winnie for a friend. What you got was what you got, take it or leave it, and Katie knew she'd take it, no matter what her friend handed out.

Even if it was Oscar de la Renta, one of the priciest in his field.

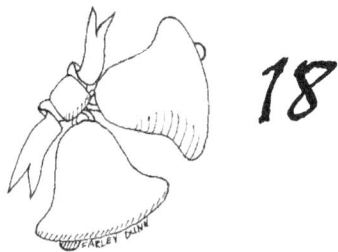

18

"This is the heaviest one yet." Katie held the moving box in two hands as she carried it to set it on top of the three boxes already taped shut and ready to ship to her new home. It was unsealed, and newspaper-wrapped items filled the inside.

It was a full week since her final day at work, a week of sorting through the personal items she brought home from her office and the small parting gifts received from her coworkers. An outsized potted flower graced the balcony, one that she'd lugged home with some difficulty. Managing her unexpected bonanza had eaten into packing her apartment. She'd appealed to Winnie full time to help her, claiming desperation. It was an honest plea, too. She still wasn't finished, and she was scheduled to be gone the following day.

"Oh, no, Sweetie. Mine was heavier." Winnie smiled from across the room, but from the sound of her voice, her enthusiasm for packing was worn thin. She had a bandana tied around her hair, and her white jeans and lemon-colored tee were streaked with dirt. She had cotton gloves on her hands. A fresh manicure, she'd proudly boasted, as she'd pulled on the gloves to protect it.

"Wait till we get to the decorative items." Katie looked at her friend and smiled, holding up the tape. "Get this box sealed, and another one bites the dust."

She attached the tape on one side, and pressing the flaps down, with a ripping whack, she yanked tape across the top and down the other side. Once there, she cut the tape and pressed it firmly down with her fingers.

"Oh, Katie, how many left?" Winnie dropped into a chair, putting her wrist on her forehead. "You bought so many boxes. I'm certain I'm coming down with exhaustion, and it doesn't look like we've done anything in here."

"There's barely another fifteen still leaning against the wall in the entry. You're coming down with laziness, in my opinion. And no, we haven't done anything in here. All we've packed is my personal items."

"I get it." Winnie blew out a strong breath, puffing her cheeks out. "I'm your slave for the day. I'm only half African, don't you forget. You can't make me work all the time. See, I can joke even when I'm on the brink of total collapse."

"When does the work half start?"

"How about I kitchen us up a good meal?" Winnie had one of her gloves off, inspecting her nails. "At least these are still beautiful."

"How do you kitchen up a meal?" Katie had pulled another box from the stack, and she popped it open, folding the interlocking bottom down to keep the sides from closing back up. She flipped it upside down, and with a ripping sound, she applied tape to the seam.

"With these." Winnie held up her car keys, and she jangled them. "You can go, too."

"Oh, Winnie, Winnie, Winnie! I wish I could." Katie set the tape on top of the empty box, and she fell onto the sofa. In reality, she had about done all she wanted for the day, also. "How will I get this done? A week, I thought. I had a whole week, and I haven't wasted a minute of it. Not a minute, and I'm not packed, yet. It's Friday, and I'm leaving for the island tomorrow."

Winnie was smiling broadly.

"What? If you're making fun of me, you can go to lunch and not come back. No, forget that. You have to help me pack. Oh, what is it?"

"You said you haven't wasted a minute of your week, and I've been here all the time. How sweet of you!"

"How's that a compliment?"

"You spent time with me, and not a minute of it was wasted. I'm getting you a cheesecake shake from the place with the drive-through. Do you want raspberry or vanilla?"

"Raspberry, if you must, but something real before I tackle a shake. How about a chimichanga? I like Montecristo on Huntington. I have some money in my purse." Katie pointed to it.

"I've got it, Sweetie. Be back in a couple hours." Winnie pulled a credit card from her back pants pocket and waved it. "My treat."

"Hours? What do you mean you'll be gone hours? Is this your way of bailing on me?" Just that one word, and Katie felt overwhelmed with desperation. With Winnie here, she pictured getting finished. Alone? All she hadn't managed to get done felt like it was about to crash down on her day.

"Sweetie, it's you who wants Huntington. Do you know what the traffic's like today? It's Friday." Winnie smiled and tapped Katie on the end of the nose. She pointed around the room. "And don't you worry about all this. Everything will work out fine. I love you, God loves you, and Jeffie loves you. What more could you want?"

"Oh, you!" Winnie was right, though, and Katie felt her mood lift. She stood and saw her friend out the door, but as she closed it, the collapsed boxes beside the door reminded her accusingly that in spite of Winnie's confident assurances, only about a fourth of her possessions were boxed and ready to go. The rest . . .

She hit her forehead with the heel of her hand. Wrapping paper. Tissue paper, she meant. She had used the last that morning, substituting her used newspapers, but even those were gone. She should have given Winnie money to pick up some.

Before she could get to her phone to call her and tell her, it began to sing a bright and cheerful tune.

When she picked it up, it surprised her that it wasn't Jeff or Winnie. Or any of her friends from work. They might call, as the majority of them were heading to the island in a week to serve as members of the wedding party. No, this was just a number, with no name attached. And that was very odd.

Katie tapped the icon to answer and placed it to her ear. "Katie Carver here. How may I help you?" She cringed at the formality, but after so many years at ALDMass, she guessed it was inevitable.

"My little Katie, dear. How wonderful it is to hear your voice! I should wish to come to see you once again."

Katie recognized the voice, and she felt her day go flat. How could she have forgotten? She was to have reserved a hotel suite for her French relation, one that she understood was to be top-of-the-line. The best.

"Cousin Nikki?" Katie's mind raced on how to rectify her mistake.

"Oui, my dear. You are home, non?"

"Yes, absolutely, Cousin Nikki. Where are you?" Katie brightened her voice. She didn't dare let her dismay bleed over the line. How, though, had this very important duty gotten away from her? She was horrified—and at a total loss as to what she could do. She pictured the better hotels, first latching on Buckminster. No, better, the Boston Harbor or the Ritz-Carlton. The Four Seasons had the best suites, though. Give me twenty minutes, Nikki, she pleaded silently.

"I am here, my dear. May you give me your permission? I will also require a espace de stationnement, s'il vous plait. Non, non, is not right. A place de parking. Non, a parking spot. Place, a parking place. I am so sorry, my dear. Is not used to English for a long time."

"Parking? Here?" Nikki's voice was coming across very warmly over the phone, but she seemed to be stuck on this. A suspicion began to nag Katie, and she walked to the window and peered down. Dismay pulled the light from the sky and the energy from her limbs. Far below was the longest white limousine she thought she'd ever seen.

"Oui, my dear. A few things I have that will not fit, I think, in my rooms. Are you *full up*?" That was said with a laugh.

Sure enough, the driver, in full livery, had several large suitcases and one trunk already on the sidewalk, and he was using a small dolly to move them into a central pile. One of the car doors was open, and an elegantly dressed woman partially emerged. She wore a smart suit in light gray; with fur around the hem, the cuffs just at her wrists, and edging her lapels. Light flashed from her fingers, and there was no question what that signified. Diamonds, beyond doubt, and lots of them by the winking glimmers of miniature suns.

The broad-brimmed hat disguised her face as the driver stepped to her and offered his hand, helping the stylishly attired woman to her feet. It was when he reached back in the car and brought out a walker, opened it and placed it in front of her, that Katie saw deeper into her cousin. Twenty years had passed, and while Katie had grown up, her cousin had grown old.

Nicolette looked up, showing her face, and she peered across the facade of the building. Katie just caught sight of what she thought was a Bluetooth earpiece, when her phone spoke to her once again.

"My dear, now is a good time. We cannot block the street for always, now can we?" She waved her hand in the air, at who it was impossible to tell.

"Oh, I'm sorry, Cousin Nikki. Of course. I'll buzz you in."

"Merci, my dear. And then, s'il vous plait, we will find our way to our American residence for our extended stay in your country."

Katie's heart pounded as she hung up. She had about fifteen minutes to find a room for her cousin. Good heavens, how was she going to get this done? Her life was falling apart around her, and she was getting married in a week.

It hit her in a whole new light. One week. What had she

been thinking? She had to call Jeff and have him postpone. She could not do this in one week.

It didn't help when she called the numbers to the hotels. She found fifteen minutes were fully adequate to resolve the question of a place for Nicolette to stay. However, the news wasn't exactly what she wanted to share with her cousin. They were booked solid. Why? Of course, of course! Oktoberfest. There were 200,000 attendees expected this year, and Harvard Square would be packed. This weekend had been booked for months, and no, there were no extra rooms at any price.

Before Katie could sink any further into her mounting despair, the doorbell rang. Oh, oh, Cousin Nikki, she thought. You are going to be so disappointed in me.

With lead in her feet, Katie forced herself to the door, and brightening her face as much as she could, she pulled it wide, calling out the most energetic greeting she could manage.

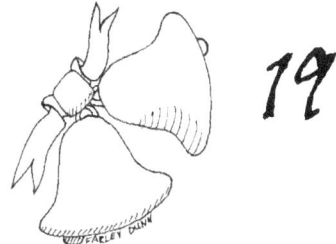

19

"Cousin Nikki!" Katie kept her voice bright in an attempt to hide the dismay that had swallowed her inside.

"Ah, ma chère!" Nicolette held out her arms, and her driver moved the walker out of the way adroitly and unobtrusively. "You, my love, so very beautiful you are. How I miss my own chance at love. Ah, tomber amoureux. To fall in love. It makes one so belle, so beautiful. Give Nikki a kiss."

In that request, Katie remembered that long-ago visit on Rockhaven, the expected kiss, and the exotic way her cousin had conversed half in French and half in English. It also seemed by the end of the visit, the French had transformed itself into full conversations in understandable words. She hoped this would be the same, or she'd be forever trying to figure out what her cousin wanted to say.

At the moment, though, her words had been pretty clear. She expected a kiss, and if Katie remembered correctly, it was more a brushing of cheek to cheek, rather than a true kiss.

Katie smiled broadly and replied, "Of course. Welcome to my home and to America." She stepped forward, and gently touching Nikki's arms, she brought her face next to her cousin's and made a soft kissing sound.

"Comme c'est beau! A wonderful flat. Charming, I believe you must say here in America. Now, the view. Show me." Nicolette wrapped one of Katie's arms in hers and moved into the apartment, rather better than her walker suggested she might.

"Absolutely." Katie glanced into the hallway to see the driver standing against the wall just beside the door, his hands behind his back. At his side was the set of cases Katie had seen on the sidewalk below. Now, she wondered, what's that all about? Out loud, she spoke to her guest. "This way. I have a small balcony you can enjoy the breeze from."

"From which, my dear. But, ah! You young people. You do not use so much the prepositions in the way to which I am familiar. Forgive an old woman." Nicolette tapped her forehead with her fingertips and smiled. "Show me this small balcony of yours."

The breezes were fresh, but they were also a little much for the elderly woman, she declared after a short time of viewing the different landmarks. Once inside, she removed her hat, and offering it to Katie—who had no idea what to do with it except place it on her bed—she seated herself on the sofa.

"You are leaving, are you not, on the morrow?" Nicolette's eyes had roamed the room, and now she looked directly at Katie. She seemed amused, for whatever reason.

"Oh, you saw my boxes." Katie was reminded in that question of all she hadn't completed. Her list! It wasn't getting marked off, and she squelched the panic that tried to rear its head once again. "I have a friend who's been helping me, but she's off on an errand."

"Ah. Je la connais." Nicolette tapped her forehead once again. "My apologies. I forget I am no longer in France. I should say, I know her. Winnie, am I correct?" She smiled as if the answer were obvious.

"Yes!" Katie was surprised her cousin knew her friend's name. "You can't have met before, I don't think. She's just been in the Caribbean, but France?" Katie shrugged.

"Elle est au téléphone." Nicolette waved one hand dismissively in the air. "I call here one day, and your Winnie speak with me. She is a very charming girl."

"Oh, yes." Katie raised her eyebrows at that. "Very charming, I am sure. She's my bridesmaid." She said that brightly.

"Yes, yes. For next week, it is such a wonderful thing to have a dependable bridesmaid. For now, though, when is the compagnie de déménagement arriving to vacate your flat? Surely you must be ready at that time!" Nicolette smiled as if this was a pertinent detail, and she was making very relevant observations.

"Compagnie de déménagement. Um, management company? I'm not sure what you mean."

"Um, l'instigateur, non. Um, locomotive. To marche." Nicolette frowned at her choice of words.

"Moving? Moving company!" Katie grinned. "Oh, there is no moving company. Jeff, that's my fiancé, he has a houseful of furniture. I have no room for this. My friend Winnie is selling it all for me."

"Vendant? You will sell all of this? Why do you not keep your flat, if you must sell your fine things?" Nicolette used the arm of the sofa to stand, and she walked to the kitchen, using tabletops and walls along the way to steady herself. "My little Katie, this is quite nice. You have, shall we say, taste in the most exquisite manner."

"Money," Katie called as she followed her cousin, pleased to see she was really quite capable on her own. "You do know Grandmamma's story, I suppose."

"Of course, dear Katie. It is so very sad."

"I've held a job, and it paid for this, but I'm off to Maine. Tomorrow, as you know." Her cousin's words tweaked Katie's emotions, however. She had thought the very same thing, which was why her personal items had been the first to be boxed, and she'd left the rest of the apartment untouched for as long as possible.

"If you sell quickly, will you regain your money?" Before Katie could come up with a reply, Nicolette had opened a drawer, and she lovingly stroked Katie's flatware. "This, dear, you cannot know, but it is the same as my grandmamma's."

"It's similar to my grandmother's, too. I guess that's why I chose it." Katie reached in and took a spoon. She rubbed her thumb across the ornate pattern in the handle before replacing it. "I like that your grandmother had something similar. It makes it a family pattern, in a way."

"You have the original, still?" Nicolette pursed her lips, as she pulled her hand from the drawer and gently closed it.

"Grandmamma's?" Katie smiled, and she looked through the dining room to the view outside the windows. "If it was in the house up on Carver Point, it was lost. I'm sorry, no."

Katie turned to her cousin to see her eyes red rimmed, and she seemed diminished.

"I hoped always to see it again. When I see these, my heart soars. Now I know they are gone." Then, Nicolette straightened her back, and she said more forcefully, "You are leaving tomorrow, am I still correct?"

"I have ferry reservations at 2:45."

"Your grandmamma's house. It has been rebuilt, non?" Nicolette began making her way to the dining room window. There, she paused, taking in the view from both directions. One hand rested on the tabletop for support.

"Non." Katie smiled at using the French for no.

"Where do you stay?" Nicolette seemed surprised at Katie's response.

"Do you remember the sleeping cabin out on the Point?"

"Oui. By the water, is correct?"

"There. My fiancé put in a generator, and that's where I'll be over the next week."

"Ah, let me think." Nicolette's pointer finger tapped. "This flat, it is one bedroom, I think. Only one?"

"Yes, although it has a loft. There's a bed up there, but I don't think you could make the climb."

"Francois is the one who will be there. Do you own the flat, or is leased year to year?"

238

"Month to month. Well, year to year, but I pay month to month."

"Forgive me for asking, my dear, but a decision now arises. I must have information. Let me ask bluntly. The lease, it is terminated, non?"

Katie laughed in an embarrassed way. That was something that bothered her. She knew she was moving, but she hadn't told the management yet. With her furniture unsold, what could she do? Winnie had promised to stay here until all the major pieces were gone, and the rest they would donate to charity, if Jeff couldn't find a place for them on the island.

"I see. You have not yet returned the lease." Nicolette gently took Katie's hand, and she squeezed it, smiling. "Then we must make arrangements. C'est plus facile à dire qu'à faire to find good lodgings, and I will help you in this." She nodded her head in a brief bob, as if that settled the entire matter.

"What did you just say? Just now in French, I mean?" Katie wasn't sure she was on the same page as her cousin, but then the older woman operated in a different world, culturally and financially.

"C'est plus facile à dire qu'à faire? I am so sorry. I should speak English full time. It means," and she paused, searching, "when something is hard to do, but easy to say."

"Easier said than done." Katie smiled.

"Oui. Very exact."

"So, what are we doing?"

"Ah, we are making a plan. Cancel all my réservations. I will stay here, for as long as you will let me." Nicolette's eyes twinkled impishly. "And I think that may be a long time, as I think you are very in love."

"You want to rent my apartment?"

"Oui, little Katie. It is perfect, is it not? All your fine things. Grandmamma's silver, it will all be here for you to use again."

"Are you sure? And it's not really my grandmother's silver."

"Oh, dear, I am aware. It is the memory I am enjoying.

239

And oui, it is what I am sure of. Francois, upstairs he will sleep, and he is mine always. He will be shopping boy and service ménager. Housekeeper, I intend to say. Leave what you will, and it will be here when you return." Nicolette's pronouncement was matter-of-fact, and she looked around the room, her eyes not missing one detail.

"Rent is still due, Nikki." Katie hoped she didn't think she could live here for free. Katie had saved back enough for a month or two, but that was being reimbursed by the sale of her furniture, she hoped.

"Oui. Is less than one night for Francois and myself at a good établissement. I will have a home in America, and all with saving much expense. Who can ask for better than this? It will be no problem to cancel, oui?"

"Your hotel reservations?" Katie smiled, feeling the tension from earlier melt away. It would be the easiest thing in the world, especially as she'd never made them in the first place. "For you, Cousin Nikki, it will be no problem at all."

"Now for parking for the car. It is very big. How shall we park a very big car in your American city?" Nicolette smiled with that impish look in her eyes. "Perhaps we must find a smaller car?"

"Just not too small, Cousin. That's a lot of luggage out in the hall."

"Non, ma chère." Nicolette looked surprised. "Is not much at all. Is reason for very big car. Is full, how shall we say, to the brim." She laughed at that. "For a very long stay, Cousin Nikki needs all the things that make her happy."

"I expect you will be very happy during your stay, then."

"Now, about this man of yours. When I was young like you, the men to me were as butterflies to a beautiful flower . . ."

"Don't say anything. I have a full explanation." Katie held her hand up to silence Winnie's look at the cases piled along one wall in her living room.

"But, Sweetie, we were packing." Winnie's sunglasses were in her hair, an extra set of eyes just over her forehead, and in one hand she held a plastic sack with Montecristo artfully written on the side. From her other hand dangled her keys, and they jangled with the swinging of her hand as she spoke. "Do we have to move the stuff from this to those?"

Her eyes looked from the four taped boxes to the pile of Nicolette's cases.

"I do have an explanation. I was about to explain." Katie took a deep breath.

"No, no. I get it. I'm gone for one minute, and you have a change of plans. Well, tell me, Sweetie, how you managed to afford these. I know good luggage, and this is the best." She had set the sack on the taped boxes, and with one fingertip, she traced an intertwined Y and S and L on the outside of the closest case. "If you can afford this, you can afford to *give* me all this stuff. Why bother moving anything? Just buy more." Winnie dropped onto the sofa, and she crossed her arms and looked away.

"Okay, I get it. You're irritated. What?" Katie sat on the coffee table, and she took Winnie's hands in hers. "It can't be just this luggage. Now, give."

"On the island." She sniffled, pulling one hand loose and brushing at her eyes. "I used an outdoor potty all week, and you had money to put in a real bathroom."

"Oh, so that's it." Katie laughed, and slapping her hands to her knees, she stood, motioning to the cases. "These aren't mine. Cousin Nikki, the one you didn't tell me you talked to? She was here, and this is all hers."

"Oh." Winnie bit at one finger. "One little-bitty detail I forgot. I gave her your address, and she's coming today. There. I told you. Are we okay, now?"

"Well, you don't have to sell any of my stuff, any-more." Katie smirked. "It's already taken care of."

"Katie! I wanted your sofa. How could you sell it already? I just needed to get the price down." Winnie stood and huffed, then she walked to pull the sack roughly off the boxes and take it to the kitchen. "I'm hungry. I bought me a chimichanga, too. Here's yours if you still want it." She pulled the second one out and plopped it heavily on the counter.

"Honey!" Katie went to her. "You never told me you wanted the sofa. When Cousin Nikki moves out, you can still have it."

"Oh!" Winnie wailed. "Now she's living here, too? Did you give her everything? I wanted to buy your lamp, too."

"Okay, enough spoiled baby. Now you listen like I asked you to when you first came in. My cousin is here from France, my very wealthy cousin is here from France, and she wants to stay for an extended time. I forgot to reserve her a hotel suite, and now she's staying here. It's like a sublet."

Winnie looked at her with a twinkle in her eyes, and she was trying to fight a smile.

"Get it out. What have I said now?"

"You forgot to get your cousin a hotel room, during Oktoberfest? Oh, that's funny. What did your cousin say?"

She giggled, her sandwich forgotten for the moment.

"She doesn't know, and shush, you don't need to tell her. She saw my flatware, and she decided she'd rather stay here than at a hotel. I lucked out."

"Your flatware, hm-m." Winnie opened the drawer and pulled out a knife. "I mean, it's nice enough, but I don't know that I'd rent an apartment just for the flatware."

"That shows what you know." Katie took the knife and dropped it back into the drawer. "It resembles my grandmother's from the island, which I didn't know was Cousin Nikki's grandmother's set from France."

"Who has your grandmother's set now?" Winnie had the drawer back open just a bit to where the ends of the flatware showed.

"You were there." Katie had the chimichanga in her hand by then, and she pulled a plate from the cabinet. The food had cooled and needed a minute in the microwave. She pushed Winnie aside and slipped it in, hitting the Quick Cook twice for one minute total time. She looked back at Winnie expectantly. "So?"

"Okay. There wasn't anything there. I guess it was burned up or sold." She had her sandwich on a plate, and she waited for the oven.

"Sold?" Katie was growing impatient, either that or very hungry. Sold? Hadn't she seen the empty basement? Everything was gone.

"Okay, burned. Nothing was left. I remember you telling me that. I just thought, nothing was left, but what wasn't there had maybe been sold. Some things sometimes are found after a fire. Metal. Fire. Metal things should be okay." She made a face like, duh.

"Well, it wasn't, and I bought this just for the memory. Now with Nikki here, we're finished packing. Want to return some unused boxes with me?"

"Finished? Sweetie, that's the best news I've heard all week. If I packed one more box, I'd be too tired to get in the spa, and I'm never too tired to get in the spa."

They were at the table with their food by then, and for a moment, the silence of the very hungry reigned. Shakes followed, which Katie had to admit were very good, as they tasted each other's, and found them equally satisfying.

As they were finishing, Winnie's attention was drawn back to the luggage filling half the room.

"Did your cousin hire a moving truck? This is a lot of stuff."

"A moving car. A limousine, to be exact." Katie gathered up the paper, and she dropped it in the trash bin under the sink. "They've gone to get a smaller one, one that'll fit in the parking garage."

"They? I thought this was just your cousin."

"And Francois." Katie looked expectantly at her friend, letting her stew on that word.

"Francois? Like, male friend?" Her expression brightened with interest. "I think I like your cousin Nikki, and I haven't yet met her."

"Oh, I give in. He's her chauffeur." Katie sat at the table, letting herself be caught up in the excitement of it all. This had been her grandmother's world, although Katie remembered very little of it. Her grandmamma had always had caretakers at the Maine property, people who put the boats out every year and placed them back in storage in the fall. And in winter in the city, a driver, but it wasn't something Katie had really paid attention to. It had just been Grandmamma, and it was in the summer when Katie spent time with her. On the island, there had been no drivers at all, just the occasional delivery service showing up at the dock or down the drive, as normal as the summer day was long on a Maine island fifteen miles out to sea.

"Your cousin has a chauffeur." Winnie breathed in deeply, an enraptured expression on her face.

"And he does housecleaning, laundry, and grocery shopping. But sure, she has a chauffeur."

"And I could ride in her limousine."

"No, you can't." Katie tried not to laugh. "You missed it. They've gone to get a smaller car. Remember what I said? The big one wouldn't fit in the garage."

"Oh." Winnie shrugged. Then she said, more excitedly, "Oh! Francois can take you to the airport tomorrow. Can I ride along?"

"Sure, Honey, sure." Katie laughed, and gave her a hug. "But I'm driving my car. I'm not flying up."

"Then," Winnie still held on, whispering in Katie's ear, "Can I use him on Sunday?"

"Sunday? To church?" Katie pushed her away.

"Uh! Don't you ever listen? I have a cowboy shoot. They're flying me to Colorado Sunday afternoon." Winnie huffed. "I have to go to the airport sometimes, too, and you won't be here, now."

"You're going to Colorado just like that." Katie shook her head in dismay. How come her friend always took off when Katie needed her most? "And did you tell them your best friend's getting married next week?"

"I wouldn't let 'em forget. My return ticket is to Maine." Winnie giggled. "It's like a free trip up there. And because I'm flying out of Logan, they gave me another voucher from Maine back to here."

"Oh, you bad girl." Katie teased, but she was glad to have this news. If her friend already had her flight scheduled, she might even make it. There was one more question she had to ask. "The dresses—"

She got cut off, though.

"No, don't even ask. I'll have them there when I show up, and not a minute before. Anyway, you know it's bad luck to have the groom see the bride in the dress before she walks the aisle. I don't trust you, so I'm keeping the dress."

"Dresses." Katie wanted that clear, as it seemed to her Winnie had taken them over.

"Dresses. I have them all, and I'll have them there, and I don't want another word said."

Two voices came drifting through the open front door, both speaking fluently in French. One was Cousin Nikki, and they both recognized that one. The second got a frown from Winnie.

"Sweetie, you did say your cousin's chauffeur is named Francois. He. That is a man's name, right?"

Katie smiled. She knew who the other voice belonged to. Her cousin had found Miss Annie from Trinity. Katie was glad. They'd be good company for each other while Cousin Nikki was here.

A man's voice joined the first two. He also spoke in French.

"Oh, thank goodness," Winnie said, with a laugh. "For a minute, I thought that . . . um . . ."

"You thought what?" Katie teased. She could see her friend's face flush. It was hard to pick up on with her beautiful and perpetually tanned complexion, but she was definitely blushing.

"Just that, oh, that Francois . . ." and without finishing her statement, she stood and walked toward the door, calling out, "Welcome to Boston, Cousin Nikki. I'm Winnie, the one you spoke with on the phone—"

Katie sat back and laughed. Winnie was Winnie, and that was all there was to it. She felt better, though. With Nikki's arrival, she'd been able to strike about ten things off her list, from utilities to furniture to who was going to collect her mail. She could even wait until after the ceremony and honeymoon to get to the post office and update her address.

It seemed the storms of change were clearing, and maybe she and Jeff could merge their lives on time after all.

The one thing she couldn't put off this afternoon was to call Janine. If the cabin wasn't ready, she'd have no place to stay. Then there was gasoline for the generator, clean linens, and the drive. She had to have someone to check to see if it was still passable. It had been July when she was last out, and it was now the end of September. No one was going to have a sailboat out there, and few people left their docks out after the middle of the month. It was the drive or nothing.

Katie slipped a sheet of paper from her binder, and she began to scribble. She'd just thought the list was getting shorter. Now it was longer than ever.

What, oh what would she do? Winnie could handle some of these, she decided. Then she remembered Winnie's run for lunch. Her cousin's words came back to her. C'est plus facile à dire qu'à faire. She remembered exactly what it

246

meant. Getting help from Winnie would be easier said than done.

Katie leaned forward and wrote one more thing on her list. *Thank Winnie for being the best friend ever.* Then, with her pen, she circled it three times. If she didn't get any of the others done, that one she would make sure of. She knew now it was the most important item of all.

21

It was the smell of salt and spruce, and the tang of diesel fuel that told Katie she was almost home.

On the drive up I-95, rain had drizzled and spit on her windshield. Yet, once the ferry had broken free of the harbor, and fifteen miles of ocean had stretched in front of her, the clouds had given way to shards of broken sunlight, then gradually evaporated altogether.

Now, seabirds danced across the waves, and the clang of sea buoys drew Katie in. She had always loved the sound of the buoys as they warned seafarers that there was danger if one came too close. Finally, they were hers forever, if she could pull off a wedding in a week's time.

Off in the distance was the misty profile of the upcoming island, and she looked for the spruce-topped finger that ended in Carver Point. She could also catch Spurgeon Light standing tall in the sea if she kept her eyes on just the right spot. It was easy to miss, and she refused to let herself get distracted.

Distracted. She smiled at that. Everything about her wedding had kept her distracted. If she wished for anything, it would be someone to take the planning from her and let her just enjoy this special time. A mother, maybe, and a father. She let herself dream of that for a moment. This week would indeed be easier if she had a mother to plan all this for her, and a father to pay for it. But, that was not her case. They were gone, and if she wanted it to happen, it was up to her.

She closed her eyes to the breeze and turned her face to the sun, smiling. She had her faith in God, her good friend Winnie, and Jeff waiting for her on Rockhaven. That was what counted. The Carver fortune that had once allowed her family to live well? Katie had never shared in it, only unknowingly enjoying the final days of its demise, never realizing that her family had once had money that was mostly gone by the time she'd arrived. What a wedding she could have planned if the Carver riches were still around!

If wishes were fishes. Katie opened her eyes and laughed. The Carver estate had burned a decade and a half before, the money was gone, and she had learned to live with that. Besides, she and Jeff would be living in his house just outside of town. The Point was inaccessible during winter. Snow, fallen trees, it didn't matter. The Point was for summer. Town was for winter. Even if Carver House still graced the rocky promontory on Carver Point, it wouldn't have made a full-time residence.

Now, the islands surrounded her, as the ferry pulled between Settler's Island and Rockhaven. It was as beautiful every time she returned as it was the first visit each summer.

The ferry was mostly empty, with the deceptive weather on the mainland and the lateness of the season, but a family with two small children stood at the front of the boat with Katie, oohing and aahing as each new exposed ledge and island came into view. This close to Rockhaven, a thin layer of fog still hovered just above the level of the sea, reaching like tenuous fingers to wrap the shore in otherworldly vapors. Tree-covered rocky outcrops and undersea ledges breaking through the waves grew out of the mist, washed out and vague at first, then finally coming in plain view to delight the children.

The little girl called, "There! Daddy! What's that?" and

she pointed to a dark object floating in the water.

Katie knew before the man answered, and she took this as a sign from God. An answered prayer, even if it wasn't one she'd specifically prayed. What had she told Jeff back in July? There should be seals. There should always be seals at Rockhaven. Of course, the one that had sunned itself on her little beach out on the Point hadn't exactly charmed Winnie, but still. There should always be seals.

"It's a spotted seal, honey." The father squatted behind his daughter, wrapping her in one arm, and pointing with the other. "See? It has spots on it."

"Does it like swimming?" The little girl's voice was high-pitched and clear.

"Probably." Her father called to the brother. "Levi, come see this. Your sister found a seal. I told you I used to see seals out here growing up."

Katie stepped away, leaving the family to their discoveries. She envied those children. Her own parents hadn't loved the island and had rarely come out. Her children, should she have any, would get the chance to love this place just as much as Katie did. More, even, because they would live here.

The ferry broached the last outcropping, and Rockhaven Harbor came into view, with its boats tied to their moorings and all the houses along the shore, many with brightly painted doors and shutters, and others wrapped in their wooden shingle cocoons.

Many of the pleasure boats were gone, and that was nice. Katie hadn't thought of that. Late September brought the end to the season, and the summer people wouldn't return for another eight months. It felt odd saying that. Summer people. She had been one of those, only here for the best months of the year. Now she would have to rethink herself, becoming an islander.

In any case, the harbor free of summer yachts was a nice surprise, and she let the revelation be her own private moment of enjoyment, sort of icing on her cake. Her wedding cake, if she had her way.

At the change in the sound of the engines as the boat

slowed to approach the terminal, Katie climbed in her car and rolled a window down, preparing to pull onto the island in a brand-new way. In spite of her cousin's assurances that she need take nothing with her, the little car was filled completely. The four boxes? Check. Her favorite plant? Check. Food for her week on the Point? Check. Then there were all the little things she had grabbed at the last moment, thinking, how can I leave this behind? Half the stuff? Probably useless, and she would wish she'd left it. If she'd left it, she'd wish she'd brought it, so here it was.

Her stomach fluttered with butterflies. Jeff would be waiting, his hand offering her a life she'd always wanted and now could see just hundreds of feet away. She wasn't sure if her butterflies were anticipation or a warning, but decisions had been made, and her life was changing.

The ferry shifted roughly, and it was at the terminal. Just in front of Katie, a woman in an orange bib flipped a lever on a post, and the ramp dropped to mate with the front of the ferry. She started the engine, and with some difficulty—the car was very packed—she pulled the lever to release the parking brake. At a signal from the orange-trimmed woman, Katie shifted into gear and pulled forward into her brand-new life.

22

"Janine!" Katie waved through her window. Her friend had one of her sons in tow, one of the smaller two. Her hand firmly grasped the collar of the boy's sweater. Jeff was nowhere to be seen, and Katie felt a moment of deflation. She called to her, "Let me find a spot."

"There's one right up here." Janine pointed to one Katie hadn't seen, waving her forward. "Jeff stepped away for a minute."

"Jeff's here? Good!" A thrill of anticipation surged through her, lifting Katie's spirits. Jeff had indeed come to meet her! She glanced around. "Where?"

"There!" It was the boy, and he pointed before jerking free from his mother's hand, and running toward Jeff. He crashed into him with both fists up and balled into weapons. "Where's my candy?"

"Whoa!" Jeff held a small bag high over his head. "Not so fast, Karl."

"My name's Karlton. Karl's for babies. Give it to me!" He jumped for the hand.

"Not when you're like this. Hi, Katie!" Jeff called to her, waving with the hand holding the package. The other was on the boy's head, keeping him from jumping. With a laugh, he wrapped his arm around the boy, holding him tightly against his side. "Go park, and we'll wait."

Katie pulled in and shut off the car, her heart pounding. That boy! Still, this was Janine, and she had come to greet her. In any case, Jeff seemed to have him under control, even if he was determined to be a crazy little devil. Katie pictured the Saturday morning cartoon character based on the Tasmanian devil, no more than a black whirlwind across the television screen. It was enough to make one swear off children forever.

"A hug?" Jeff called to her from behind her car.

"Coming!" She opened the door and climbed out.

"You get my right side." Jeff's eyes twinkled. "I've got my other favorite person on my left." He pulled the boy tighter before releasing him just a bit, leaning down slightly to whisper to him not very softly, "And if you kick, no chocolate at all. I'll eat every bite."

"Mom!" The boy yelled it out.

"You've got your hands full." Katie took his empty arm and folded herself into it. She leaned to give him a kiss on the side of his mouth.

"Now I've got my hands full. I don't mind, as long as one of my arms is around you." He kissed her on her temple.

"You are so silly. I've got a carload, and I need to get to the cabin. How are the plans coming along?" Wedding plans, she knew he'd understand.

"Shush!" He nodded to the terminal building, where Janine was just coming out the door. She had disappeared inside once Jeff had taken control of her son. "Mostly okay, I think, but the rest? I'll let you discuss it with Janine." He shrugged.

"What's not okay?" That didn't sound good to Katie.

"Mom!" Karlton yelled again. "Jeff's telling."

"You little rat." Jeff handed Katie the package, and laughing, he picked the boy up in both hands, one arm under his back, and the other under his legs, and began walking toward the street. "You may not get another candy bar until you're eighteen."

"Sorry. Restroom break. What's that about?" Janine stepped up beside her, pointing at the boy and the man, now already to the sidewalk. Karlton was waving his arms and kicking his feet, but Jeff clearly had him under control, and he wasn't getting free.

"I don't know." Katie waved the scene off with a brush of her hand. "You, though, how've you and Al been holding up?"

"You mean with Daddy?" At Katie's nod, she continued, "The boys keep us so busy we haven't had time to really grieve. You know how they are. But let's not talk about that. Your wedding. I'm so excited. It's next week."

"Everything's falling in place?" Katie had been on the phone with requests and reminders, but Janine had told her repeatedly that it was all taken care of. Not to worry, Katie. Not to worry. Everything'll be ready.

Well, now, after Jeff's remark, then the boy's response, she wasn't so sure.

"I see your car's full." Janine peered into the windows. "Mine's back in town. Jeff thought Karlie needed to burn off some energy. Do you want to walk in with me, or take this out now? I can bring you back to your car."

"How's the cabin?" Was it ready, she asked. She'd just called yesterday, and on such short notice, she could only hope.

"Okay, I think. I sent Tammie Barker's girl out. You don't know Tammie, but her daughter said she could use the work with fall coming on. Al's been swamped with the boat, now that he's got his cast off. Everything's piled up with him not able to go out properly. Kevie went out a few times to pull traps, but finally Al said it was more work with the boy than alone." Janine barked a laugh and shook her head.

"What's that about?" However, Katie could imagine.

"I could have told him that eleven years ago." Janine smiled. "Town or to your place? Either's okay with me. I just need to get together with you in the next day to sort out wedding details."

"I've got food in the car, and a plant. I really need to

unload. I'll try Jeff on the phone, but if I can't get him, let him know I'll be back in town today. All I'm doing is unloading. You're wonderful, Janine. I couldn't do any of this without you." Katie gave her friend a warm hug before backing away and stepping to grasp her door handle.

"I feel the same, with Daddy and his, um, well." Janine's eyes were red, and she wiped at one. Then she brightened her expression. "You, go unload, and I'll tell Jeff you're coming back in. Oh, I have a great idea. My house tonight. It won't be fancy, but you and Jeff have to come. It's the only day something's not planned between now and the wedding. Okay?"

"I wouldn't miss it." Katie tapped her fingers to her lips and blew Janine a kiss. Then she dropped into the car. Something had her thinking, though. Every day this week? What could possibly be planned every day this week? She had no time for that. She had a wedding to pull together, one she wasn't absolutely sure she could get done.

Starting the car and pulling out of the lot gave her time to think, though, and as she passed the pond, she laughed at herself. Why did she think everything planned on this island was all about her? There could be quilting meetings, maybe a Town Council meeting, or even a meeting of the library committee. Good heavens, it could be the week for the monthly school board meeting. Lots of things happened on the island, and most of them weren't about her.

She had a whole week, she didn't have to clear out her apartment, and Janine said she had everything concerning the wedding under control. Goodness, even her dress was taken care of. Winnie had promised, and when had her friend ever let her down, really let her down?

After all, she was on her island, and she was here to stay. Life was perfect, and there was nothing that could get in her way.

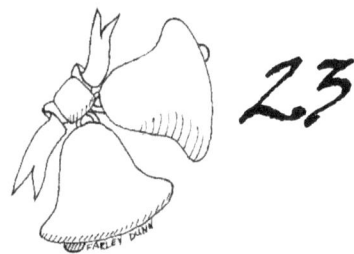

23

The September evening was only slightly cool, and as the horizon dimmed to reds and golds, the four friends sat in lawn chairs on a deck without railings. Beyond the trees, the ocean reflected the colors of the sky. Wire lobster pots filled one side of the yard, and the four boys were off chasing each other in the near darkness. Several dogs, one very large, tried to insert themselves into the action, occasionally barking at the passing bodies.

The meal may have been simple island comfort food, but it was good. Janine had fixed a big casserole of lobster mac with handmade rolls and Indian pudding afterward. Katie was stuffed.

She sat next to Jeff, and they held hands as she soaked up how wonderful life on Rockhaven could be. This was a week to be enjoyed, and she planned to make the most of it.

Janine stepped from the house, letting the screen slam behind her, and she carried four steaming mugs. "Cocoa," she whispered secretly, "for the adults."

"Thanks, Love." Al took one, and he wrapped his hands around it. He looked with creased eyebrows at Jeff. "Lots of empty pots, and best time of year."

Katie knew what he meant. He had a lot of empty pots

that weren't out there catching cash to survive the upcoming winter.

"I'm here for you." Jeff took a cup from Janine, and he leaned forward, wrapping it much the same as Al. "When this week is done, we'll double up and get you up to speed."

"Right there, and I appreciate your time. Janine and I, we need some catching up after this past month. Come, let me show you something. I got this new idea for hauling pots . . ." He and Jeff had risen as he spoke, and they moved off into the dark. After a minute, lights flickered on past the lobster pots, and the men could be heard discussing something or the other that had to do with lobstering.

"Men." Janine shook her head. "That's all Al thinks about, his boat and his pots. With his arm, he's had to come up with ways to keep working. I think he thinks he's become an inventor. Something with pulleys and stuff." She laughed, but not loudly.

"You said you wanted to get with me." Katie shifted the conversation, but carefully. "What do you need from me for extra help?"

"What do I need?" Janine laughed, and it had a manic edge to it. "You know, when Al and I got married, you could say we got hitched. It was less a wedding than a break in lobstering, and not a long one. He'd gotten in his first real boat, and he was about as interested in it as in me."

"I can see he loves what he does. Jeff's the same."

"You're lucky. Jeff has a real life besides his boat." Janine acted like she wanted to say more, but she took a sip of her cocoa, instead.

"So, details," Katie prompted.

"Details. Right." Janine set her cup on the deck at her feet. "Places to stay. You asked me to set up accommodations for the wedding party. I've been working on that." Again, she stopped.

"What do you have so far?" Something, Katie hoped. It was this week that she needed it.

"I haven't tied anything down just yet. People want to hold out for the best prices until they're sure the last summer people are gone. Even then, there's nothing cheap.

Several of the B&Bs are closing this weekend, and the motel is booked, already. Some are your people, I assume. You have eight attendants that need a place to stay, right?"

"Plus a few others." Katie touched the heel of her hand to her forehead. "My cousin. She just arrived yesterday, and I'd forgotten. Then there's Winnie, and Connie—my supervisor at work—to put up. I expect several spouses, so, twenty, maybe twenty-four. Oh, my cousin has a chauffeur. He'll need a bed, too. What about houses? There's bound to be lots empty this late. Can we rent?"

"I'm glad you brought that up. I didn't know if you wanted to try for one big house." She paused. "It's expensive." The smallest boy ran onto the deck, and Janine called out, "Not now, Keithie. Mommy's got business."

"Mommy," he began to wail.

"Kevie! Come get your brother. Five minutes. All I asked for was five minutes." She yelled it into the dark.

"Okay, Mom. It's been longer than five minutes already." The oldest boy ran up and grabbed his brother by the shirt and dragged him off, telling him, "I told you you'd get me yelled at. You're going to wish . . ."

Katie didn't want to hear the rest. As long as all four boys were alive when she drove off, she was good with that. Janine was already going on, though, and Katie turned her attention to what she was saying.

"Briar House is empty. I've talked to Peg Briar, and she said if we'll pay cleaning before and after, she can let us have it at a good discount."

"That big Victorian, the one just in town?" Katie didn't know it rented. "I thought it was a full-time residence."

"After the captain died, the kids opened it up. It's big."

"I was in it once." Katie hadn't toured it all, but her grandmother had taken her there to pick up or deliver something. What, she didn't remember, but it had seemed dark and overflowing with heavy furniture.

"Nine bedrooms, and the attic has been opened up for more sleeping space." Janine sipped more of her cocoa, her hands now wrapped around the cup. The air was cooling fast.

"Done. Briar House it is. I suppose some people must already have houses rented for the weekend, those that aren't at the motel, anyway. We'll squeeze as many in Briar House as possible. You said, and it's Tammie, right? Tammie Baker's daughter is cleaning? Can we use her?"

The talk went on, getting the accommodations settled, and backup locations for lodgings squared away. Jeff and Al returned, sending Janine inside for more cocoa, and they pulled their chairs to the edge of the deck. One of the dogs, the big one, joined them, lying sideways against Al's chair legs, and nudging his foot until Al reached one hand to scratch behind its ears. The light was still on past the lobster pots, casting just enough of a glow that the four adults were able to see each other easily.

The boys' voices filtered in from somewhere, and once there was a loud splash. In the resulting silence, Janine made to stand, softly calling Al's name, but the boys started yelling, and Al raised one finger at a time, naming each boy. When he had all four identified, Janine relaxed back into her seat.

As the evening was wrapping up, Katie was surprised to find she was expected at an event the following evening. Al mentioned it first.

"Ah, ready for the social tomorrow?" He said it offhand, as if he assumed she knew about it.

"Social?" Katie looked to Jeff and Janine. "What social?"

"Oh," Jeff said, grimacing. "I, um, guess I thought you knew It's something that's sort of expected for island weddings." He shrugged.

"I should have thought." They were back inside, and Janine was repackaging leftover food into smaller containers. She laughed as if it was no big deal. "Al and I had one. I forget you've not been here for a long time. It's not a dance, but imagine a big barn dance. It's in the town hall."

"And what goes on, if I may ask?" A barn dance that's not a dance?

"Dancing." Al looked at Janine, and something passed

259

between them. Good memories, perhaps. "If I have my say about it."

"It's an island meet-and-greet. For you, a welcome to island life." Jeff took one of her hands in both of his.

"A church thing? They were at the Point in the summer."

"More." Janine stood from placing food in the fridge. "Everyone comes to this. Sometimes they bring instruments, and impromptu music starts up."

"Electric guitar." Al did an "air" guitar, and he "twanged" it, grinning. "It's fun."

"Sure." Katie smiled brightly. "I didn't know, but sure. What time?"

"Four." Janine. "You don't worry about the food, either. I've already planned what everyone's bringing, the ones who'd listen to me. Just expect lots of pies."

"Lots of pies." Jeff smiled broadly.

"Dancing," Al reminded them.

"This is the biggest thing planned for the week. Everything else? Don't worry. It'll be fun." Janine's eyes sparkled.

Everything else? Before Katie could come up with an appropriate response, the door slammed open, and in came the nine-year-old Peavey, and he was dripping wet and mad as a hornet.

"I'm going to beat up Kevie. This is the second time. Tonight." Without another word, he threw himself up the stairs, taking them two at a time, and disappeared from view.

The other three boys crashed through the door, and their eyes gleamed in excitement, calling out all at once, "Where's Konnar?" Al pointed to the stairs, and in a tumble of arms and legs, they disappeared after him.

"Until tomorrow?" Katie decided it was a good time to make her exit. Asking about the "everything else"? Maybe she didn't want to know.

"I'll see you out." Jeff stepped up and took her arm. He leaned in to whisper, "At least all the island's wild animals are upstairs."

"I heard that." Janine narrowed her eyes at him, but she fought a smile at the same time.

Something crashed upstairs, and Al and Janine took to the stairs together, leaving Katie and Jeff to let themselves out. It also gave them time to say goodnight, which, to say it nicely, needed a little private time.

A hug and a kiss. Who wanted to watch that, except three dogs that only cared about having their ears scratched?

All-in-all, Katie drove home afterward thinking the evening had wrapped up pretty well. Yep, with Jeff as the dessert, it had wrapped up pretty well, indeed.

With Jeff on her mind, who cared about what was happening tomorrow night, or the next night, or the next? Only Saturday counted, because that was the day she was getting married.

24

"Winnie, can I do this?"

Katie stood in front of a floor-length mirror, and her stomach churned. She wore a mid-thigh Oscar de la Renta wedding gown in white and pale blue. It was a princess dress, and she did not feel like a princess bride.

"You are beautiful, Sweetie." Winnie stood behind her and put her hands on Katie's shoulders. "Even Oscar would have to agree, no one could wear this dress any better."

Katie's week had been a whirlwind. Last Sunday's social? That had only been the start. Janine's prediction that the rest would be fun? Exhausting was the word. Monday's lingerie gala? Who knew isolated island women were aware of so many types of unusual undergarments. "What else do we have to think of all winter?" one very elderly woman had murmured to her. Tuesday? Cake testing. No wonder the island bakery came so highly recommended. Icing coated everyone's lips before they were done. Wednesday was the school social, earlier than the others, as the students left at three. Katie met every elementary child on the island, from preschool up, and three of them were Janine's. The teachers, though? Once the children were gone, Katie was their excuse to live it up for several hours. Thursday was spent scheduling the reception tenting on the point. There were chairs to organize, locations to mark, and food! Where was the food to be served!

Then, the night before, everyone she knew started rolling in off the ferry, and that had broken into her carefully apportioned memories, and she had cried half the night.

Of course, being the night before the wedding, she hadn't stayed out at Carver Point. Preparations would be going on out there from the crack of dawn, and she would have no privacy at all. No, she and Winnie had shared the owner's suite at Briar House, and that's where they were now.

"The dress is beautiful, that I'll concede."

"*You* are beautiful." Winnie reached one arm over her head and pulled her wild mane aside to rest her face against Katie's. "If anyone says otherwise, I'll sock 'em sideways."

"Thank you, Honey. Still, can I do this?" Katie felt her eyes grow damp, and she refused to cry. No, she said to herself, looking at the woman in the mirror. You are not allowed to cry.

"What is it?" Winnie stepped around her, dressed in a satin sheath dress that just matched Katie's blue. She had been true to her word, bringing vintage Oscars for each woman in the bridal party. What a search it'd taken, she'd exclaimed, to find coordinating ones, but her "people" had come through. Each one had to be pristine on its return, though. They were just on loan.

All the woman had matching de la Renta pumps, also temporary gifts, just for the weekend.

The flower girls? Not by Oscar, but a good miniature knock-off by a talented seamstress Winnie knew.

"I wanted to spend the week with Jeff. I wanted to look forward to today, and I've hardly seen him at all. Every day something else was planned for me to do. I'm tired, Winnie. That's all."

"I have something to cheer you up. Hold on." Winnie held up one finger, and she bobbed it a few times, like one would while training a pet. As she made her way to the door, she said it again, "Stay."

"I have no patience for surprises. And it had better not be Jeff. He cannot see me in this dress." Katie turned back to the mirror, and she flipped the veil up, only to have it fall back in her face. Once again, she felt the tears rise.

"Surprise!" Winnie pulled the door wide.

Into the room swelled eight blue beauties. Ashlynn flounced in, with her tightly curled blonde tresses highlighted by a blue bow. Winnie had managed to get matching dresses for Isabell and Lesly, the only two sisters in the group. River, with her Asian features, had a blue pillbox atop her head. Lisa touted blue-ribbon curlicues trailing down her Cher-like bounty. Kambri? She was charming with a princess crown in gold to match her wire-frame glasses. Michelle's hoops dangling from her ears more than accentuated her features, but it was Ellie that stunned the crowd. Her contemporary pageboy, her cutting-edge signature look, was lofted and fluffed into a swirling halo filled with glittering blue sequins.

Katie could no longer contain her tears.

"Oh, I have missed you so much!" She threw out her arms, wanting to draw them all in, touching hands, and leaning in to brush cheek-to-cheek. Then she saw Connie, sturdy, no-nonsense Connie, there in the door, with a black-faced tablet in her hand.

"Have you signed in today, dear? I know you're here, but Corporate only knows if you've logged in on your computer. Do you need to borrow mine?"

For a moment, Katie was unsure how to respond. Then, each of the other woman held up their company tablets, and they called out, in a random, not very organized fashion, "Or mine?" "Use mine!" "No, mine!" and on until all the tablets were right in front of her.

Katie clapped in excitement. "I love you so much. All of you. Thank you all for coming."

Winnie was behind her again, and she grabbed her shoulders and pressed her face to Katie's, whispering, "Can you do it?"

"I can do it," Katie whispered back. "Absolutely. I can

do anything."

"Good girl. Let's go marry us a Jeffie."

"Woo-woo!" The rest of the wedding party began to chant and cheer. Occasionally, one called, "Jeffie!" or "Marry us a Jeffie!"

All-in-all, they were having a very good time, and they did exactly what needed to be done. They lifted Katie's spirits, and she felt, for the first time all week, really felt like she could get through this day, and at the same time, enjoy every single minute of it.

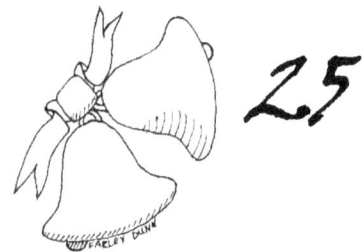

The small Town Church was packed. Cars went up and down the street on both sides, and inside was standing room only. Even people who didn't attend services now knew of Katie Carver, granddaughter of the Rockhaven Carvers, come back to the island to marry Jeff Ragsdale, of the Rockhaven Ragsdales.

Of course, the Rockhaven Ragsdales didn't have quite the social clout of the Carver family, but they were well-respected by the island crowd, nonetheless.

Katie's biggest surprise? Mrs. Anabelle Rosenbaum, her neighbor from Boston. It seemed Cousin Nikki and she had indeed become very good friends, and Nicolette had once again rented the longest limousine she could commandeer for the trip to the island. It created quite a stir coming off the ferry, and when word got out that it was bringing a Carver all the way from France? Katie's social standing went up another four very large notches.

Ten women wearing vintage Oscar dresses? That hardly did any damage at all. How Katie looked in her dress? Stunning. Everyone said so.

Amidst a bevy of tapers and blue and white flowers everywhere, Katie and Jeff clasped arms and knelt before

God. It was when he lifted her veil and kissed her before God and everybody that she knew she was someone different. She would always be a Carver, because the Carver family tree was in her blood. Now though, she was more. She was Katie Ragsdale, the very person she'd always wanted to be.

Exiting the church, with Jeff at her side, and clapping and cheers from the attendees carrying them along, she made her way to the ridiculously enormous limousine for the ride to the Point. "You must, ma chère," Nicolette had insisted, in her fur-trimmed suit, "borrow the car. You must, you must." And she had nodded as if that were that. Once inside, the hush of the luxurious vehicle surrounded them.

"Can any day be more wonderful?" Katie pulled her veil up, attempting to find the pins in her hair to pull it loose.

"Let me help, Dame Carver." Jeff pushed her hands gently aside, and he worked the pins free, smoothing her hair as he set the veil on the seat. "There. All beautiful."

"You're wrong." Katie smirked at him. "You're very wrong."

"You are beautiful. No one can say otherwise." He leaned to kiss her on the top of her head. "I have declared it, and it shall always be so."

"Not about that." Katie snuggled against him.

"What, then?" He wrapped one arm around her, pulling her in.

"I'm no longer Dame Carver. I'm Dame Ragsdale, now." She held up her hand to display her sparkling diamond ring.

"Ah, that's where we differ in opinion. Dame Ragsdale you may very well be, and I'm glad for it, but you will always be Dame Carver to me."

Katie picked up his hand and pressed the backside to her lips, kissing it gently before letting it fall back into his lap.

"What?" Jeff squeezed her shoulder. "Nothing to say?"

"Everything to say. But I can't say it all." Reaching to the door, she pulled out a tissue and held it to her eyes, pressing carefully to avoid smudging her makeup. "I can't cry, not now. Not with nearly two hundred people meeting us at the reception. What would they say?"

"That we love each other very much, I think."

"Okay." Katie took a very deep breath. "I know how to tell you everything I want to say."

"Oh?" Jeff chuckled. "It's only a twenty-minute ride. Are you sure?"

"Absolutely." Katie turned to look him in the eyes. "It's only three words."

"You can say everything you want to say to me in three words?" He laughed. "Okay."

"I love you."

"Wow," he said. "I can do better. I can say it without any words."

Without anything else said, he pulled her to him and kissed her on the lips. When he was finished, he looked at her and raised one eyebrow.

Katie leaned against him with a smile.

"How'd I do?"

"You win," she said, pulling his hand up and kissing it again. "Dame Carver is who I am forever and ever. However, I'm signing my name Katie Ragsdale."

"I should hope so. After all, you are my wife."

It was the kiss he got in return that told what she thought of that. It was exactly who she'd wanted to be her entire life.

Rockhaven
Christmas

1

The languid aroma of wood smoke filled Katie Carver Ragsdale's dreams, and she smiled as she imagined a plump, lightly browned turkey roasting over an open fire. At the sizzle and pop of dripping fat, her stomach rumbled, and in her dreams, apple and cherry and pumpkin pies floated around the room.

Her guests raised their glasses in a toast, downing their eggnog in a single draught before tossing Katie's new stemware into the stone fireplace and shattering glass all over her perfectly roasted turkey.

Katie's eyes jerked open, and she felt the chill in the room as she waited for her breath to slow. It was dark, still, meaning the sun wasn't up. The snowstorm yesterday had become a blizzard, and before the phone lines had gone down, they'd learned the town storage facility had lost half its roof. Jeff had shaken his head, remarking that if the wind was pulling off roofs, he hoped everyone's boats survived.

He'd also reassured Katie that their property being on the east side of the island provided a great deal of protection. His family's old home place being on Moffat Cove gave them one of the best moorings around, second only to the ones in Rockhaven Harbor.

Katie tossed the bedding aside, and she searched with her feet for her slippers. The floor would be cold without them. With the electricity off, too, there wouldn't be any heat until she got a fire built in the fireplace.

Even their backup generator had failed to kick on, leaving them totally in the dark.

When she only found cold wood, she grumbled, "Generators need backup, too," remembering commercials for emergency units that worked seamlessly in all the television ads. And with the storm, Jeff couldn't go retrieve the one out on Carver Point. Three feet of snow told all there was to say about that.

She looked to the other side of the bed to where Jeff was lying, bundled for warmth. The bed could be empty for all she knew, it was so dark. Even her phone was dead, used up for lighting while Jeff struggled last night to get the generator online.

She sniffed, drawing in a long breath. She hadn't dreamed it. It was really there. Wood smoke. And turkey. In that she remembered what day it was. Thanksgiving, and all the plans that had been canceled, shattered by the unexpected change in the weather.

Standing and pulling her sensible—and very warm—flannel nightgown tighter at the neck, she became aware of a shimmer of light orange flickering underneath the bedroom door. Her heart thumped at that. Had the fire been dampened properly the night before? Surely the house was not on fire.

"Jeff," she whispered hoarsely, afraid that to say it was to make it true. When he didn't answer, she called again, louder. "Jeffrey."

That would get his attention. She never called him Jeffrey. He hated it for reminding him of being a boy, and how badly he'd wanted to grow and become a man. He laughed when he said that, but he also made sure everyone knew he was serious.

"Jeff, there's a fire in the other room. I think the house might be on fire." She worked to his side of the bed and felt for him beneath the covers. It was lumpy, and she poked farther and farther up the bed. Something beyond the door popped loudly, like green wood in a campfire, and she gasped in alarm.

"Jeff, where are you?" Her eyes had begun to burn with impending tears. He had to be here.

A knock on the bedroom door caused her to jump.

"Katie? You up?" Then the door was silent.

"Jeff?" She called louder, making one last broad sweep of the bed with her outstretched hand. "Is that you?"

"No, it's Roker, here on snowshoes. Of course, it's me. Who else would it be? Come in here where it's warm." There was laughter behind the invitation.

"Coming." She pulled her hair from her face, pushing it behind her ears. So. That was why she hadn't been able to find him in the bedding. He wasn't in the bedding. Opening the door, she was hit by a wave of smoky, turkey-laced warmth. A fire indeed crackled in the big stone fireplace. Jeff was at the front door, pulling thick gloves off. He was bundled in jeans—double layered by the look of them— with a thick turtleneck sweater in a pale merino wool. His hair was a giant, flyaway mane of outdoors abandon, and just the barest hint of a beard shadowed his jawline. Big boots on his feet completed the Maine outdoorsman effect.

"You've been busy this morning." One tell-tale sign was the damp ring at the bottom of his jeans. He had been outdoors, already, and probably more than once. With the fresh pile of wood, some still showing snow, outside maybe five or six times.

"Good morning, Katie." He smiled at her, and deep crevasses dimpled the slabs of his cheeks. "Be sure to pull the door to. No need to heat the bedroom."

"Oh, right. I didn't think." She turned to close it. When she clicked it shut, she backed up, only to find Jeff right there.

"Good morning, again, Katie." He wrapped his arms around her, and he buried his face in her hair, to nuzzle her along her neck. "I like telling you good morning. And don't worry about the door. Who can think after a night spent in a storm like this? You're becoming a true Mainer."

273

"Yeah," and she laughed, pushing him away to make it towards the warmth of the fire. "I leap in bed and sleep through it all. A true Mainer, right. I smell turkey, and it's not my imagination. It reminds me I need real food. Breakfast-type food. With no electricity, I suppose we're skipping that today."

"Turkey's the best. It's Thanksgiving. What can I say? Can't have Thanksgiving without turkey. And you don't have to skip breakfast." He looked amused as he took the poker and brushed aside some of the coals at the back of the fire. Buried inside was a large covered Dutch oven. He pulled out a smaller Dutch oven and brushed the coals off the top. He piled them back around the bigger one.

"The whole turkey?" It had been the biggest they could buy. Half the church membership had planned to share it. "We'll never eat all that."

"Someone will." He didn't seem concerned, still working with the smaller oven, and with the poker, lifting the lid. Off to the side was a stack of several paper napkins.

"How long do you need to leave it in there? And that smells good. What's in that?"

"I don't know how long to leave the turkey, but this is about ready. What do you think?" He dipped with a large spoon and worked out a steaming cinnamon roll. "Want to share?"

He wrapped the bottom half in one of the napkins and brought it to her. Wrapping his arms around her again, he tore off a portion and held it to her mouth, waiting as she pulled it from his fingers. His next words were soft in her ear. "Maybe we should leave the turkey all day, and we can snuggle on the sofa while it cooks. By tonight, it'll fall off the bone. Pulled turkey, how does that sound?"

"Like I'm freezing. I need to get dressed. Oh, and do we have any water?" Snuggling! The roll was good, but she was suddenly aware she had other needs. Morning ones. And no matter the fire, it was still cold. Jeff might be bundled up, but she was wearing her nightgown. Even flannel wasn't enough to ward off the chill of the worst winter storm she remembered in years, especially in a house with no power. Added to that, she hadn't found her slippers, and her toes were starting to hurt.

Jeff looked at her and shook his head, as if she should know the answer to that.

"No?"

"I drew up what I could before it froze. We can use what's in the tub to flush, as long as it doesn't freeze, and there's drinking water in the kitchen. Don't plan on a shower unless I can get the generator running. Welcome to Maine, Dame Carver."

"Dame Ragsdale." It had been less than two months, and Ragsdale still fit awkwardly against her first name, but she wasn't letting go of it. She might be Dame Carver to Jeff, but she wanted it very clear. Dame Ragsdale was here to stay.

"Ah, that's right. We did have a wedding, didn't we?" He chuckled softly. "Your clothes are on the stool by the fire. I thought you might enjoy wearing them preheated."

"Oh, I am so lucky to have you." Katie turned and embraced him, and with her hands on his face, she kissed him passionately.

"Maybe it's too early for you to get dressed." He smiled, but he chuckled suggestively, too, just enough that it was there.

"You fool. I'm freezing. I'm getting dressed, and now. Have some of that turkey waiting on me when I get back. I'm starving." She darted away, grabbed the clothes, and headed to the bathroom. When she closed the door, she was pleasantly surprised to see two pillar candles burning merrily away.

Jeff had thought of everything. He was so wonderful. Now if he could get that generator fixed, maybe they could have a proper Thanksgiving. It had to happen today, too, because tomorrow? Tomorrow was the first day of her upcoming Christmas schedule.

As Katie pulled on her long johns, she saw the card she'd slipped into the edge of the mirror the night before. It had been in her jeans pocket, and in the dark she'd been afraid she'd lose it. It had the upcoming month marked out by the day.

Looking at the card, she felt December coming apart in her head. It was Christmas in four weeks, and she had the biggest holiday of the year to plan. With a blizzard shutting down the entire island, her card filled with plans was now worthless for anything except a drink coaster.

Taking a deep breath, she laced her shoes and pulled on her double-lined sweatshirt. She might not look beautiful today, but she would be warm. Pulling the card from the mirror, she slipped it into her back pocket, determined not to let a month full of unraveling plans ruin her morning. It was Thanksgiving, her first one on the island ever, and she was spending it with Jeff. How wonderful was that?

When she stepped back into the warmth, Jeff was at the fire adding wood, and in the flickering shadows of the room, silhouetted against the flames, he was picture perfect.

"Perfect Christmas scene." Katie held her hands out, framing him in a box built of her fingers. "You should be on all our Christmas cards."

"Perfect Thanksgiving scene. Don't rush today away. Remember, we get to spend it together." He stood, and he walked to her. "You are so beautiful. I am the luckiest man in the world."

"Oh, you—" she started.

"Don't you 'oh, you' me. I waited on you half my life, and God brought you back to Rockhaven. He's done more for me than I ever deserved."

What could Katie say to that except agree? It was the way she felt every single day. Instead of answering, she pulled him to her and gave him a second Thanksgiving kiss, this one longer and more enjoyable than before.

It was the least she could do for the man who had completed her life, including building a fire and roasting her Thanksgiving turkey.

It would be her best Thanksgiving ever, bar none, and not even worrying over her plans for Christmas would get in the way.

"Jeff, I think that was a knock at the door." Katie rubbed the drowsiness from her eyes. She was snuggled next to him under a thick blanket, and the fire across the room crackled merrily. Jeff had piled it high with wood, and they'd moved the sofa close to maximize the warmth.

Now? She was very toasty, and she didn't want anything to disturb her cocoon of comfort.

"Nah," he replied, yawning. He shifted next to her, and his arm around her waist pulled her tighter. "The house is creaking. It does that in cold weather."

Katie moved the blanket enough that she could peer outside. Expansive windows wrapped the three walls facing the water. This might very well be a fisherman's abode, but someone in the past had remodeled it to take in the view of Moffat Cove. Once the dawn had peeked in around the blinds, Jeff had pulled them all up to allow as much light in as possible. With the omnipresent cloud cover, it was limited, but with all the glass, it was sufficient.

It was snowing again, and from time to time, Katie could see the smoke from the fireplace drift by in stained, cotton-candy puffs, all strung together like a giant cater-pillar with uneven sections. The ground was white down to the sea, and the dock and Jeff's boat were draped in wedding-cake bliss. Even the ocean seemed thick and creamy, as it churned against the remains of last night's storm.

The knock repeated itself.

"Jeff, there really is someone at the door." It was an impossible knock in this isolated world of snow and quiet. The only sounds came from the fire, and that knock, of course.

"Okay. I'll check." He threw back the blanket and disentangled himself from Katie. "Maybe it's a pumpkin pie."

"I wish." That was one thing Katie hadn't prepared for. She had promises from multiple cooks, all much better at pies than she. Now? She didn't guess many pies were making it across the island today.

"We'll see." He kissed her on the forehead and stood, making his way to the front door, a massive slab filled with the original beveled glass from when the house was built, and into the enclosed and unheated foyer. Good for this time of year, he'd said proudly when she'd asked why it was kept closed off. It was also where they stored their outdoor clothing to keep it out of the house as it dried.

Katie heard voices, and she shook her head, sitting up and running her fingers through her hair. She glanced that way to see another man with Jeff. Who? He was so bundled up that in the dim light she couldn't tell. It could be almost anyone. Maine islanders were tough people who would get out in anything. In Boston? They'd wait for the plows, and if, if they could get to their cars, they'd be out again. For a fact no plows had come down Jeff and Katie's drive, not on Thanksgiving, and certainly not at this fresh hour of the morning.

The door opened, and Jeff came in laughing, followed by Roker, a good friend of Jeff's that Katie had met back in July. It was only at the wedding that she'd learned his last name. Roker Robertson.

"Hi, Roker." Katie waved. "What brings you out?"

"This." It was Jeff, and he raised a five-gallon propane

tank.

"My fault." Roker had a sheepish look on his face. "Everyone wanted to top off their tanks before the storm, and I didn't make it here."

"But that size tank fits the grill. You want to have a cookout?" Katie sat all the way up on that one. The outside propane tank that fed the generator—and the cook stove—was the size of a refrigerator. She'd remarked on it to Jeff several times.

"I can tie it in to the generator. The hookups are exactly the same." Jeff grinned. "And if not, then sure, why not a cookout? I'll fire up the grill, and you guys can watch from inside."

"Sorry it's not more." Roker looked chagrined. "I couldn't get the propane truck out, but this will run your heater for a couple days." He looked at the oil heater sitting unused with the electricity off. "I'm guessing your water is off, too. The well pump, well, it doesn't pump very well without power."

"How did you get down the drive?" The town's propane truck was massive, and it would handle almost anything, but Roker's truck? It was in town at the city lot, and his car was an old Volvo wagon that hugged the ground.

"He's Rockhaven tough. Roker can get anywhere anytime of the year." The tank was now on the floor by the door, and Jeff had retrieved his outdoor gear from the foyer. He sat putting his heavy boots on.

"Snowshoes." Roker had his hands in his pockets.

"You didn't walk the entire way. Tell me that." She looked at Jeff hard. Roker lived two miles away. "Jeff, tell me Roker didn't walk all the way here."

"Okay. Roker didn't walk all the way here. But I bet his snowshoes did."

Roker let out a laugh, and he stifled it immediately. "Sorry, Katie."

"Oh, you people are crazy." She had moved to stand closer to the heat. "Since you're here, Roker, you two see if you can get us some power, and when you're finished, maybe we can pull the turkey from the fire."

"Yes, ma'am. I swore I smelled turkey, even from outside." Roker had a smile on his face. "That sounds pretty good to me."

"We can have pie, too." Jeff had his boots on, and he stood and stamped his feet. "Pumpkin pie."

"Don't make Roker promises. There are probably pies all over this island—" About five of them were supposed to show up that afternoon. "—but none of them are here. Sorry."

"I brought you one." Roker tilted his head sideways, rather like pointing, and he stepped to the door leading into the foyer. He returned with something wrapped in newspaper.

"How—" Katie was beside herself. Pleased, too, but totally flabbergasted. As far as she knew, the last time Roker had cooked anything, it was a wiener at the Rockhaven Town Cookout. On the end of a wire coat hanger. And he'd burned that. He was a microwave chef, not one to make pies.

"Here." He held it out to her.

"Thank you, but—"

"Roker didn't make it." Jeff interrupted her, stepping over and putting an arm around her. "Jess up on High Road did this, and when she saw Roker out, she made him bring it. It'll be good. Jess is the best pie cook on the island."

Katie's eyes teared up as she reached for the pie.

"I'm—" Roker released the wrapped pie, but he still held his hands under it. "You—not pumpkin? I didn't think, that maybe—"

"Katie?" Now Jeff was in the mix. "Are you okay?" He took the pie gently from her hands and handed it back to Roker, to give her a hug as the big man moved away, standing awkwardly with the pie still in his hands.

"I'm fine. Thank you, Roker." Katie smiled and waved him away with one hand. "Put it in the kitchen, and thank you for bringing the pie. We will all enjoy it very much."

He sauntered off, shaking his head, muttering about women and something or the other about how much easier

280

it had been when Jeff lived on his own.

"Don't worry about him. Roker's a card, and he'll do anything for you, but that doesn't mean you'll ever understand him."

"I understand one thing." Katie had separated herself from Jeff by then. "I'm going in there and telling that man that pumpkin pie is my favorite, and I'm having two slices."

"Ho, ho! Pumpkin? I was certain it was apple." Jeff's eyes twinkled when he said that, and he reached to pull a strand of hair from her temple.

"Apple's your favorite, and when I'm with you, that makes it my favorite. When a man brings me a pumpkin pie through three feet of snow, then pumpkin's my favorite. That means you need to get with the program, Jeff Ragsdale. Today, pumpkin pie is at the top of a very short list."

"And the rest of that list?" He chuckled, but so softly it was hardly there.

"Baked turkey and electricity. I want a shower." She popped him on the shoulder. "Now, go."

"And me? I don't make the list?" He held up both hands, palms out, with a hangdog look on his face.

"If you ever get my water on. Heat, too, I could use some of that."

"Roker?" Jeff called toward the kitchen.

"Yes?" Roker stepped into the room licking his fingers. "You ready?"

"How's the pie?" Katie slapped Roker on the shoulder as she stepped past him and into the kitchen.

"Good." He slurped one last finger. "You're not upset or nothing? About the pie, I mean?"

Katie turned to see him peering in the door. The pie was on the table, and about a fourth of it was gone. She heard Jeff in the other room, "Roker, not already. That was for lunch."

"Did I ever tell you, pumpkin is my favorite? With so much of this gone, it must indeed be the best on the island." Katie crossed her arms and leaned against the table right next to the pie. "What's your final opinion? Should I have a slice now, or wait?"

"Um—" Roker looked back at Jeff, and he turned to Katie as if not sure how to answer.

"Will you have a second slice if I have one, too?" Katie stepped to the cupboard and pulled out saucers and flatware. "Jeff, are you joining us?"

"Yes, ma'am, Dame Carver." He called it louder than absolutely necessary.

"That's settled, Roker. It's cold out there, and if you and Jeff are hooking up power, then I'm giving you food to warm you up."

Katie smiled at the big man's look of anticipation as she cut into the golden pie. She served up three slices, two large, and one that was half as big. It was Thanksgiving, the Christmas holidays were rolling in, and besides, her stomach hadn't been all it could be the last few days.

She dismissed the idea that it had been the last few mornings, thinking it would sort itself out in time. It was one of those things that came with new marriages, an attentive husband, and a perfect life.

To Katie it was about the pumpkin pie, the thick layer of snow covering the island, and the bathroom that was too cold to use. She carried her pie into the living room, and she curled up on the sofa she and Jeff had pulled up right before the fire, and she found out something.

Jess up on High Road did make the best pumpkin pies on the island. How did she know? She was holding a slice in her hand, and every single bite was even better than promised.

Either that or she was very hungry. One way or the other, Roker was the man of the hour.

She was equally pleased about ten minutes later when the lamp beside the chair came on, and the oil heater clicked three times and the fan began to run.

Then the muffled sound of running water came through the bathroom door.

"Yikes," she yelped, setting her half-finished pie aside. "The tub!"

She kicked off her blanket, and dashing in, twisted the

faucet to stop the flow. She also flushed the toilet to clear the bowl from earlier. As the hand-carved wood sign above the porcelain throne said, "Yellow Is Mellow; Brown Goes Down." Apparently, on the island, conservation was the rule, and Katie tried to abide by it, even if she did sometimes think it extreme. After all, how much water could two people use?

When she returned, Jeff and Roker were in the foyer peeling outerwear loose and stamping feet. She knocked on the glass door and waved, before moving back to the sofa. When the door opened, it was Roker who spoke first.

"Getcha warmer'n a bear cub snuggled with its momma." He grinned, pointing to the heater. "It come on?"

"When the lights did. We have water, too. Showers!" She rubbed her hands together excitedly.

"No showers." Jeff leaned over the sofa to kiss her on the cheek.

"Nope. No showers with just the generator." Roker shook his head. "Cept once."

"And that means?"

Roker laughed, and Jeff looked amused. It turned out the backup generator had been here several years. Three winters before, Jeff had been off island for an extended trip, and a storm had taken out the electricity, as it had today. Roker had no backup generator, and he'd come to stay at Jeff's until repairs were done to the power lines. The second day, he'd climbed in the shower and soaped up. Then, flipping the water on, he'd waited and waited for it to warm.

Jeff interrupted Roker's story, laughing so hard he could barely talk, to tell her that his friend didn't know the water heater circuits bypassed the generator. It just pulled too much power. Roker had to shower in water that must have been about forty degrees.

She could heat water for a bath, though. That worked pretty well.

"Thanks and no thanks. I'll wait for the power to come back." Katie pulled her blanket tighter under her chin, and she stared at the flames in the fireplace.

283

"Sure." Jeff found the cushion beside her. "Anything you want."

Roker wasn't finished, though. "That time I was here? It was nine days. Nine days. Think I can have another piece of pie, Katie?"

She waved her hand over her shoulder to tell him to go ahead, and she turned to Jeff, mouthing, "Nine days?"

He shrugged. "It's Rockhaven. What can I say?"

Katie knew. He could say hot water, as in Boston. However, when she had Boston without Jeff, she hadn't been happy, and now, even with no hot water, she was very happy, indeed. Was it worth it being here on this crazy, snow-bound island in the middle of a storm? Absolutely, even if it was still the middle of fall.

When she reached for the rest of her pie, she found it gone. She looked around to see her plate in Roker's hands, and the rest of the pie going into his mouth.

Ah, well, she thought. I didn't need it, anyway. Any more and she would kill her appetite for lunch.

She didn't want to do that. It was Thanksgiving Day, after all, and the turkey was still in the fire.

3

"A short service tomorrow morning, starting about eleven." As she replied to her caller's question, Katie held her phone to her ear and flipped through the church directory, looking for the N's. Nickerson, Nickerson . . . finding him, she checked Bryan Nickerson off on her list.

Katie had finally decided her Saturday morning would be easier if she stayed close to the phone. Bryan wasn't the first caller. That had been Tom Schutmaat and his wife Jackie up on 4th Street. It was their week to open the church—fire up the furnace, lights on, and such—and they didn't figure it made much sense if there wasn't to be a service. They lived just down the street, they reminded Katie, so getting there wasn't too much of a problem, but there were others that would have more trouble.

As Tom said that, Katie had looked out the window at the snow that still covered everything, in spite of the fact that it was now Saturday. Even the sun, blindingly bright through the uncovered windows, hadn't melted any of it. Yeah, she'd thought. We might have trouble getting to the church. She didn't say that, though. Instead, she'd agreed with the Schutmaats' assessment of the situation and thanked them for their foresight.

285

Katie had decided she might as well phone the entire church body when Jeff had intervened. Oh, no, he'd laughed, flipping to the final page in the directory. He pointed to the phone tree, with the Schutmaats at the top, and branching out from there. Tom and Jackie hadn't called because they were on the schedule to open the church, but rather because they were at the top of the tree. Two people called two people, and they called two people, and so on. Pretty soon, the entire island would know, and Jeff only had to speak to one person. Neat, huh, he'd asked her, with a twinkle in his eyes.

When she'd shown him the ones who had already called her, he'd grinned as she pointed to their names at the bottom of the list. "Eager beavers," he'd said with a chuckle, giving her the short message to read out to anyone else who called. "We like eager beavers. They're the ones who show no matter what the weather does."

"Katie, we're out of eggs." That was Roker. After polishing off the turkey on Thanksgiving night, Jeff had refused to send him home. There were extra bedrooms, he'd said, and Roker knew which one was his.

"There's oatmeal in the pantry." Roker had an appetite, and Katie wasn't surprised to be out of eggs after three days with extra company in the house.

He appeared in the door with a steaming pan of scrambled eggs, stirring with a spatula. "Nah, we've got eggs for breakfast. This is just all of 'em. Jeff said he was hungry, and my cinnamon buns were gone, so I decided to throw something together. You want sausage in yours?"

"Sausage is fine." The eggs were still runny, and Katie guessed Roker had the meat already prepped to go in. He'd taken over the cooking for the weekend, so she saw no use in trying to tweak a good thing, even if the pantry was growing barer by the meal. Roker ate a lot.

"Sounds right, there." He grinned, turning back to the kitchen.

"Where's Jeff?" She realized she hadn't seen him in a while.

"You didn't know?" His head reappeared, and then his

pan, and he pointed with the pan out the expanse of windows towards the water. "Down there." And he was gone again, the sound of the pan on the burner bright with his big man's heavy touch.

Sure enough. Tracks in the snow led around the house and towards the dock. There at the end, in the square box that perched high over the water, stood Jeff, attaching guy wires to the railings, one at each of the four corners of the box. In the middle was the most beautiful sight Katie thought she'd ever seen. It was a snow-covered tree, or somewhat snow covered, as it hadn't snowed since Thursday, but there it was, standing at the end of the dock, and Jeff was securing it against the upcoming season.

Christmas, the first sign it was really on the way.

The snow might have interrupted Katie's timeline for planning her holiday extravaganza, but it hadn't kept Jeff from his. He'd promised her a tree, but she didn't expect it there.

It was beautiful, though, and not just the tree. The whole scene, Jeff bundled in his heavy coat, his knit cap covering his head and ears, and the gloves on his hands. He held pliers, and he twisted wires running from the trunk of the tree to fittings at each corner of the box, tightening them repeatedly until he was satisfied.

She thought about her phone, and texting a picture to her good friend Winnie Catron back in Boston. Or New York, or wherever her latest fashion shoot was. That reminded her that her phone had to have a signal to text, and it had been dead all day. No town power; no phone signal. That was life on the island.

Then, of all things, Jeff pulled a plastic bin up beside the tree, and opening the top, he lifted enormous red bows and began to wire them to the branches. Katie felt her eyes water. That was her Jeff out there, bringing Christmas to the whole world, even though the world was snowed in, and no one would see.

"He does that every year, you know." Roker came up beside her, and he set a plate of steaming eggs on the table for her. He took his plate, mounded even higher, and he walked to the window and began to eat while watching Jeff with his red ribbons.

"Every year. That's nice." That meant it wasn't just for her. "It's pretty."

"It's more than pretty." Roker turned to her, speaking in between bites. "Those are his Katie bows. I call it his Katie tree."

Katie stood and walked to the window to stand beside Roker. Katie bows? Jeff had two of them in his hands, and he ducked under one of the guy wires, to disappear on the opposite side of the tree. It moved, telling that he was attaching the bows to branches on the opposite side.

"Katie bows," she murmured, reaching to put her fingers on the glass. "That might need some explaining."

"Oh, easy." Roker scraped the final eggs into his mouth and chewed once before swallowing them. He pointed out the window with his fork. "One for each Christmas. He said he didn't care how big a tree he had to get, he was adding another ribbon for you every year."

Katie laughed. "That might be a really big tree some-day."

"Oh, no." Roker was on the way back to the kitchen. "That's all the ribbons. He won't add any more."

"No more?" Easy to explain? Katie smiled. Roker had only confused her more.

"Yeah," he called from the kitchen. "Every year you weren't here he added a ribbon. The first year there was only one, and the tree was about two feet tall. He called them his Katie promises, and he wanted the whole island to know you were coming back some day." He could be heard laughing. "I'm glad you came back when you did. Pretty soon, we wouldn't be able to get the tree on the dock."

Katie felt her heart expand watching that man out there in the snow, doing something he always did, just because it was what he did, and the thing was, he'd been doing it all along for her, even when she hadn't been here to notice.

That meant one thing and one thing only. This Christmas had to be the best one ever. The biggest tree, the best decorations, and the finest gifts she had ever put together. She could get the whole church family involved, maybe even plan a bash at the Town Hall. Invite the whole island!

Gumdrops and candy canes swam in Katie's eyes as she pictured a flotilla of Christmas boats moored in the cove, all arriving in their holiday best, greeted by a fully garbed Santa out on the float.

"Roker," she called loudly. "How do you like the color red?"

"Red?"

"Yes, red." She turned and he was at the kitchen door, wiping his hands with a towel, his sleeves rolled up past his wrists. It looked like he'd been washing dishes.

"Don't know. Never thought about it."

"You need to start." Katie smiled. She'd not noticed before, but he was wearing red plaid flannel. For warmth, probably, but it certainly fit the season. "Lots of red, and white."

"Red and white," almost as if he'd never considered the two colors as compatible. He shrugged as he turned back to the kitchen, continuing, "Sure, I like red and white, though don't know why anyone would put the two together."

Santa Claus, Katie mused, looking back towards the dock, to see the tree finished and Jeff missing.

"Red and white?" Strong arms, warm with exertion, encircled her.

"I didn't notice you coming in." Katie pulled the arms tighter, smelling the remains of outside on her man.

"My boots were a mess, and I used the mudroom. What's this about red and white? Are we redecorating?"

"Roker, maybe." She smiled at that.

"Does he know?" He chuckled. "Visit his house, sometime. I'm not sure it's ever been decorated."

"Not his house, just Roker. The tree. It's pretty. Tell me about it."

Katie wanted to hear the story in Jeff's words. However, just then, a cardinal landed on a tree just up from the shore, disturbing the snow still mounded on one of the branches. The white powder dissipated into a cloud of haze,

289

creating a cascading effect as it tumbled earthward, the effect growing more pronounced as more branches shed their cotton candy bounty.

The red bird took to wing, startled by the sudden movement; and brilliant against the white background, it made its way to the Katie Tree, landing on a small branch at the top. It bobbed a few times as the branch absorbed its weight, but with Jeff having moved it that morning, the majority of the snow was gone, and the bird seemed content.

"Bird, go away," Jeff whispered in her ear.

"No. It's pretty." To Katie, it was like a living Katie bow, a red symbol of how much Jeff must have loved her all those years she was away, and how much that meant he loved her now. "Don't ever tell it to go away."

"Okay, Dame Carver. On one condition." His face rested next to hers, and he watched out the window. However, he didn't go on.

"I give." Katie started to look at Jeff, but his face was so close, she only brushed cheek to cheek. She smiled, instead. "Just name it."

"That you spend every Christmas with me for the rest of your life."

She laughed. She got it, what Jeff wasn't really saying. It was the ribbons, one for each Christmas they'd been apart. The cardinal—very much like one of the red decorations—meant a missed Christmas. Katie had seen only the beauty, but Jeff had seen something else. He'd seen the years he'd spent wishing for her to return.

"Thank you for the tree. It's beautiful. Is it beautiful to you?"

"Of course. Every bow is a reminder of the woman I adore."

Katie was so in love she thought she would cry.

"Hey, you two. You gonna stand there gaping at that tree all day?" It was Roker, and his voice was loud. It carried a measure of excitement, too.

"Might." Jeff didn't move, but continued to hold Katie tightly.

"Just that out front, thought I saw something that might interest you two. I told Katie, already. We're out of eggs."

"Out of eggs," Jeff whispered, snorting. He called louder, "And that means?"

"Certain it was the plow. Bet we could get out, now."

It was something they'd been expecting all weekend, the plow. Without it, no one would be at church the following morning. There was still the drive to consider, though. The town snowplow didn't do residential drives, and Jeff and Katie's was a winding twist through towering spruce. The snow was there until they cleared it themselves.

And Roker seeing the plow? He must have been keeping an eye out. The road was barely visible in winter, and not at all in summer.

"Driveway. Not plowed." Jeff called it, but not loudly.

"Jeep. If it'll mud bog, it'll plow snow." Katie disengaged Jeff's arms. "Roker's right. We're running low on food. We should get to town today."

"And take Roker home." Jeff put his hands in his pockets and nodded his head his friend's way. "Catch that, Roker?"

"Hadn't thought of that. My own bed sounds good." He frowned as if considering, then he nodded with a smile. "Have to visit the store, first. Then, maybe I can get the town truck down to refill your tank."

It was good he thought of that, because just then, the lights flickered, the oil heater went silent, and the only sound in the house was the crackling of the wood in the fireplace.

"Don't touch the oven," Roker called out, already back in the kitchen, with the sound of things rattling around. "Maybe my new batch of rolls will cook anyway. At least we still have water."

That enthusiasm ended about five minutes later with the sputtering of water from the pipes.

What had Roker said? Nine days? It seemed that if they had the plows clearing the street, surely they could get the power lines back in operation. Katie wanted her shower, and she wanted it now.

"Katie? Going with us?" It was Jeff, and he held the keys in his hand.

It was heading out the door when Katie knew everything would work out perfectly. There, sitting on the hood of the Jeep, brilliant against the mounded snow, was her Katie cardinal, a reminder to her that love had brought her to her island, and it was love that made everything okay.

Even Roker showering her with snow as he cleared the windows couldn't take that away. After all, it was almost Christmas!

Ring the bells, she wanted to sing, but when she climbed inside, she also wanted the heat on high, and she made sure both men knew just how cold the seat really was.

4

"I see you're stocking up, Mrs. Ragsdale."

"You know, with the snow . . ." Katie smiled, not finishing her sentence, and nodding at the thin, white-haired cashier, as she began to unload her cart at the checkout stand. Her battered nametag identified her as Ada Parkes, but Katie knew she was known about Rockhaven as Ada Simpers. Mr. Simpers had been here and gone, a late in life name-change for the cashier that had outlasted the man she married.

The grocery store was better stocked than Katie had expected despite the weather that had kept them penned in the house for two days. She hadn't thought it through, that while they were penned, maybe everyone wasn't. The town roads were perfectly clear—and dry—from the school down Main and past the ferry landing. It wasn't until she thought about it that she realized she hadn't heard the ferry all weekend, but only because she'd stayed inside the entire time.

That's cold weather, for you, she mused. Windows were for summer, and in summer, you heard everything. She would get used to the change, but now she was shopping, and Jeff was delivering Roker to his house. She

293

hoped he didn't get stuck there, and leave her here.

She pushed the last of her things forward, including eggs and a large can of pumpkin filling, as the cashier began totaling her bill, one item at a time.

"Ah, and you and the new man out there on the Cove. Moffat's never been easy in bad weather." The eggs went under the scanner, two cartons, eighteen in each. "When Mrs. Ragsdale—your man's mother—was alive, in weather like this, they came to town. Course, they heated with wood, then. Now you have a good oil stove, and you're toasty as a mouse. Wouldn't take for mine, not on a cold Rockhaven night."

"When it works." Katie pushed her bread forward, making it easier to reach. "Oh, and can I get you to add a tank of propane? I'll get it on the way out."

"Certainly. Two-and-a-half or five?" Gallons, she meant, but that went without saying, and Katie understood it as such.

"Five. Can I bring in the empty one tomorrow?" Katie thought the one Roker had supplied was a five. If not, then she'd settle that later.

"Not tomorrow." The cashier's eyes twinkled as she smiled, and she reached to touch Katie on the arm. "Not open on Sunday."

"Monday, then, unless you have to have it today."

"I've put the deposit here." She pulled the receipt from the register and spread it out for Katie, and she pointed. "You bring this back with your empty, and we'll get you a refund. I'm sorry I don't have anyone to help you to your car. The eldest Peavey was to come in for a few hours today, but there's just me."

"I've got Jeff here. He just ran down the street. Thank you, Mrs. Simpers."

"Don't you get chilled out there. The sun's pretty, but it's not warm by any measure."

"I'll wait just inside." Katie pointed to the vestibule of the store, separated by glass doors from the inside. It was where the carts were kept. "You have a really good day."

"Thank you, dear. I usually do." Mrs. Simpers smiled

and stepped into the store, disappearing among the shelves of merchandise.

The inside doors were automatic, and they slipped aside as Katie approached with her cart. It was colder in the vestibule, and she pulled her gloves from her bag and slipped them on. Glancing up, she looked at the vent and wondered if it was disconnected. About then, it began to whistle, settling to a gentle vibration as the heating system kicked on. She felt the warmth wash her face, and it felt good. However, after only a minute, it kicked off.

"So much for that," she muttered, pulling her collar higher against her neck.

A truck drove by just in front of the store, and it turned into the town lot across the street. A big man, bundled against the cold, got out and went into a wood-shingled building just to the side. Katie tried to remember what was in that building. A sign was beside the door, but at the angle she couldn't read it. After a few minutes he came out, carrying something flat, and climbed back in his truck, his lights flashing, and pulled into the street. He stopped in front of an empty building just past the Post Office, took the flat object inside, and in minutes, his lights flashed again, and he was gone. There was no one else.

The sun caught on the water in the harbor. It was greeting card perfect, with the houses built right up to the shore, the brightly colored doors and shutters, and the roofs mounded with snow. Several had smoke coming from chimneys, but even more were shuttered, closed up for the season. Water was drained, heaters were off, and furniture was covered to keep eight months of dust from invading the summer fabrics. It was nearly a ghost town, but what a beautiful ghost town! With the storm, Rockhaven had become a snow-covered wonderland paradise, as stunning a location to live as any in the world.

She caught the buzz of the glass, and reaching to crack one of the doors, she heard the faintest sound of a ferry horn. She smiled at that. Island ferries were like the Post Office. Neither rain, snow, nor sleet, except that in case of the ferry, high winds could indeed park the ship. After a

295

moment, she saw it come around the headland at the harbor entrance, and she laughed. There was one car on board. All that distance, over an hour of travel, and one car had come to the island. Probably none would return. Yet, the ferry would run anyway. What could she say? It was Rockhaven.

A horn honked, and Katie looked the other direction. It was Jeff, in his green Jeep, and he waved through his opened window. He was pulled up at the Post Office just next door. She waved back, not sure he could see her, and she pulled her hood around her face, ready to push her cart out the door. By the time she had begun to move forward, he was out and to the door, and pulling it open.

"Brr, Katie! Cold!" He pulled the door to behind him, and he rubbed his hands together, blowing on them. "Did they have everything you needed?"

"Eggs, in case Roker comes back." She laughed, lifting the bag with the two cartons inside. "Eighteens, two of them."

"Heard Kevie might be here. Thought we could offer him a way home if he is." He peered inside, waving. "I see Ada didn't let the weather keep her away. Let me check."

"Jeff—" He'd already started that direction, and Katie called to stop him. "—he's not here. Mrs. Simpers said he didn't show today."

"No? Blame the weather." The doors had already opened, and he called inside to Mrs. Simpers, "No, don't need a thing. How's business today?"

Katie didn't catch what was being said on the other side of the conversation, but it probably went much like hers had. She bumped Jeff with her cart, and when he looked, she motioned with her head that it was time to get moving. "It's cold out here."

"You stay warm, Mrs. Simpers," he called, as he stepped back to let the doors slide shut. "You roll, and I'll start the car. You can warm up while I load. How's that?"

He was already moving, and Katie pushed the cart forward. Outside, she realized the heat had been on in the vestibule. It was thirty degrees colder outside. Once inside the Jeep, she turned the heat on high and held her gloves in front of the vents.

When Jeff joined her, she grabbed his bare wrist with her hand. "Freezing out there. Did you get the propane? I paid for it, already."

"In the back. Roker should be finished by the time we're home, though. It'll be good to have a spare, just in case. Colder'n Boston?" He grinned like he already knew the answer to that.

"Let's just say Rudolph would be at home here."

"Wait until February. This is a walk in the park compared." He had his gloves off and his hands in front of the vents, too. "Notice the empty store? It's not going to be empty for long." He pointed to the large building just the other side of the Post Office. It had plate glass windows, and there was a big red SALE PENDING sign in the left-hand one.

"I saw the sign going in. New restaurant? Or clothes, maybe." She hadn't realized it was the sign, but it must have been what the man carried. She wouldn't mind that. And, it seemed to her it was a good location to catch the tourist season ferry traffic.

"Never can tell. They've got six months to remodel, just in time for the summer rush. Bet you were already thinking that." He grinned, and with one foot pushing in the clutch, he grabbed the wheel and the shift lever, and he eased it into gear and backed into the street.

"I heard your family used to winter in town." Katie hadn't paid Mrs Simpers' comment much attention, but here, in the car, and with no one around and no place, really, to go, it came to her.

"Ha!" He laughed a short and emphatic bark of a sound. "She can call it wintering. Where to? Lunch, if anything's open?"

"You skipped right off that question. And, do you think anything's open?" It had been several hours since her eggs, and the donuts in the back? She had a craving, already, and she needed to kill it with real food. She was distracted by the buzzing of a small airplane overhead. She watched it head west. There was a landing field out towards the back side of the island.

Jeff looked up at the noise. "Surprised someone's coming in on a day like this. Must be staying at one of the big houses, possibly until Christmas."

"How nice for them, but we're talking about food."

"Right, right. Harbor View, maybe. They never close, if they're home. Today, if you didn't see them get on the ferry, they're home. I can check, though." It was the other way, and he did a tight u-turn in the street.

"You're sure? Never?"

"They live above the store. How can they close? The restaurant kitchen is their kitchen." He gave the engine gas, safe on the dry street, and two seconds later, he hit the brakes, and pulled up parallel to Harbor View. The sign on the door said closed. "See? A light's on inside."

"It says they're closed. Can't you read?" Katie flipped the blind down on her side, and she twisted her back to the door. "You, though, I want to know where your family stayed in town. Mrs. Simpers was very clear. In bad weather, she said your mother came to town. Where did you stay?"

"Okay, if you must hear the story. My momma stayed in town, not my dad and me."

"You stayed . . . at the house? Why?"

"Look in the harbor."

"Sure." Katie glanced out, and it seemed very much like it had from the store windows.

"Where's Chipper's boat? And Rod's, and while you're at it, look for Al's and Winer's." He had a grin on his face as he spoke.

Katie shrugged. "At home?" She didn't know those men's boats well enough to recognize them, except maybe Al's, and that was if she saw Al on it at his dock. And it occurred to her that Al kept his boat in town, like most of the island fishermen. Jeff was lucky to have a permanent mooring in Moffat Cove, and she'd never thought of it that way.

"A day like this, they're out hauling pots."

"You're telling me you and your dad stayed at your

house and went fishing?" Fishing! Wrong word! "Sorry. Lobstering."

"You knew dad. He was a die-hard. That's why I don't lobster in weather like this." He looked to something behind Katie.

Katie jumped at the sound of knuckles rapping on the glass. Turning, she saw Nina Vinson, the proprietor at the shop. She rolled the window down, and she felt her skin cut by the sharpness of the cold. "Yes?"

"Saw you two out here, and I thought you might want lunch. You headed inside?" She was in a sweater, and she stamped her feet, rubbing her hands together and shaking her head. "Sorry, trying to warm up."

"If you're open—" Katie began, hesitantly.

"Girl, we're always open. Come on in." Nina patted Katie on the shoulder, and still rubbing her hands, she high-stepped back across the snow-covered sidewalk and into the building.

"Told you." Jeff had a broad smile on his face.

"But . . ." Katie laughed to herself. "It says closed. Why not turn the sign around?"

"No need. Everyone knows." Jeff was pulling his gloves on. "Ready?"

"How does everyone know?" She didn't, and she was someone.

"Just like everyone knows about my tree on my dock, and what those ribbons mean. It's Rockhaven. No secrets on the rock." He leaned forward and gave her a short kiss on the lips. "That's how they all knew you were coming back to the island."

"I wasn't here to tell them. They couldn't know that. I didn't even know, not for fourteen years." Katie shook her head, pulling her own gloves on.

"I knew it. Now, let's have lunch, just not lobster. I get that on my boat every day." He flipped his door open, and he climbed from the car.

Katie remembered what he'd told her that July day outside the church when she'd been so upset at the entire town knowing she was back, certain he had convinced them that she and Jeff might still be in love. *If I had said nothing about you, these people still would have known.*

Okay, she thought. I haven't started putting together Christmas yet, and I wonder who knows what I'm planning?

It was Kent Vinson, already at the grill, who called out to her, "I hear you're dressing Roker as Santa this year? Thought I'd never see the day!" And he burst into riotous laughter, standing there with breaded steak in his hand, waiting to toss it on the fire.

Katie put her hands on her hips, prepared to glare at Jeff, but when she turned to him, he had his hands up and a puzzled look on his face.

Katie started to laugh. She guessed Jeff was right, at least about this. Then, if Kent knew that, he certainly knew how much she loved Jeff, so she threw her arms around him and kissed him firmly on the mouth.

"Oh, get a room," Kent called, as the sizzle of the steak carried into the room.

Katie waved one hand at him and ignored him. They had a whole house, but it wasn't here, and Jeff was.

"Whew," he said, when she released him. "What was that for?"

"Some secrets I want the world to know. This way they don't have to guess."

"Then they'd better know my secrets, too," and he kissed her back, right in front of Nina and Kent and anyone who happened to be looking inside. The windows, fogged with the season's snows, told the true story. A fairy tale romance was happening just inside the door of this ordinary building, and if no one believed it, just look across the island. It was God's Christmas icing on the magical land of Rockhaven, where every kiss brought peace and goodwill into the hearts of men.

In this case, into Jeff and Katie's hearts, but in that kiss, theirs were the only ones that counted.

They were in love, and Christmas was only weeks away. What a lovely Christmas it would be!

5

The service that Sunday morning was sparsely attended. Katie felt a sense of disappointment that Jeff's preparations were only for a couple handfuls of people. It was Sunday, she thought, as she lifted her voice to recite the Lord's Prayer. What else do island people have to do when the whole place is snowed under?

Still, those that had braved the roads, ones that while plowed, weren't really completely clear, were bright and friendly, as if they had been apart for weeks, and were renewing old friendships. Bryan Nickerson was one of the first to show, and Kent and Nina, telling Katie that they were welcome to come by for lunch. They'd be open, and Nina had flashed her a quick grin. Al, Janine, and the boys had bustled in just as the service started.

Tom and Jackie were of course there before anyone else. Gracious people, they'd held the door for Jeff and Katie.

"Sorry we didn't get the walks," Tom had apologized. "Trying to get my own done, and the old ticker, it doesn't tick as strong as it used to. Getting up in years, you know." He'd tapped his chest and chuckled, but his cheeks were red, and it was clear he'd done enough.

Jackie had pulled him away, after giving Katie a hug, murmuring that Tom "should leave the minister alone to prepare for the morning."

The air in the auditorium was warm, although the walls emanated a chill that told of an unheated building over the course of the night. Even the benches had yet to warm. The mid-morning sun through the colored windows shimmered across the interior, and Katie was glad Jeff had decided to open the church even with the remains of the storm filling driveways and back roads; and the people who might choose to let those obstacles keep them away.

She remembered Jeff's "eager beavers," and she smiled. Even without looking, she was certain she could name everyone sitting in the benches this morning. As Jeff walked to the dais and spread his things before him, she pulled out her tablet and opened it. She had been pleased to learn church members were encouraged to use electronic devices for note taking and to access the most current online Bibles. She clicked hers on, prepared to take detailed notes over the service. As the minister's wife she made it her duty to send them to her list of missing parishioners, those either unable to attend due to weather or other circumstances, or the summer people who called the church their home just during the warm months of the year.

This one, of course, would go out before she left the church. She had a signal here on the building's Wi-Fi, but at home, with town power still off, there was nothing.

Scrolling her list of email addresses, one stood out to her. Ritchey Hickox, Jeff's good friend from all those years ago. Her friend, too, she guessed, although Ritchey had been an island boy, in contrast to Katie's summer status. Now it was reversed. Katie was the island girl, and Ritchey was nowhere to be found.

To be more specific, Ritchey was somewhere, just that Texas was pretty nowhere when you were on a Maine island in the middle of winter. In Texas, in November, they were probably still in shorts and Tees, unlike here with frozen pipes and water heaters that didn't work. Visiting the motel for a shower was sounding pretty good to Katie.

She'd heated water for a bath, one heavy lobster pot at a time, but it hadn't been all that warm, and it had cooled fast.

Something Jeff said caught her attention, and she looked to him and smiled. He was down front presenting the children's message, and the youngest three Peavey boys were among the handful of children whose parents had braved their snow-filled drives this weekend. One of them, Karlton, she thought, although their backs were to her, and she couldn't really see, laughed out loud at part of the story. The adults scattered throughout the audience laughed with him.

Jeff was so good with kids, to have none of his own. He would make a fine parent, someday.

Glancing back down, she clicked on Ritchey's name, and the replies he'd made over the past six weeks appeared. After moving onto the island, she'd found him on Facebook, and she'd brought him up to date on Jeff and their life on the island, and asked why she hadn't seen him at the wedding.

It seemed his third child had come at the end of September—three weeks early—and they'd had to cancel their plans. When she'd asked Jeff about it, he'd brushed it off as unimportant, telling Katie that Ritchey had let him know the situation, and he understood. Katie had known better. It was what Jeff hadn't said, and the look of resignation on his face, that told the real answer he couldn't say.

She'd also read between Ritchey's words in the email: his wife, and his kids, and how much trouble the trip would be for her. Not for Ritchey, but for her. And how she needed him at home. Even a weekend was too long for him to be gone.

Now Ritchey sent her a short reply each week, a thank you or something humorous about someone she'd mentioned in the week's sermon notes.

Christmas. Ritchey and Christmas. That would be something to pull together, if only she could figure out how.

Katie watched Jeff stand, and she idly tapped her tablet on the edge, ready to start her notes on the morning service, as the handful of children made their way back to their scattered parents. She would include Jeff's outline, of course, but her more personal narrative would make the people feel as if they were actually here.

She tapped the darkened screen to wake it, and she began her first line:

"Sunday morning, Thanksgiving weekend, Jeff Ragsdale speaking.

"Jeff calls children to the front; tells story of the Wise Men; Karlton Peavey laughs, and the church finds it humorous.

"Jeff sends the children to their parents and begins his message . . ."

All Katie had to do here was insert Jeff's sermon notes, and she clicked and pasted them in. Now she had a break until he began to wind things down. It was visiting speakers that kept her fingers busy the entire service. She had to take down the core points in everything they said.

As she set the tablet on the bench at her side, it softly dinged. Looking at it, she noted a new email from Winnie. In her preview window, it showed, "Hey, Sweetie, I'm not at church this morning . . ."

Katie growled beneath her breath, and she picked up the device and tapped a hurried and somewhat irritated reply. "I'm ashamed of you. Get to church!" and she hit Send.

The reply was almost immediate. "I can't. I'm babysitting. And the baby is so cute . . ."

The emails were still in preview mode, and Katie clicked to bring them up. The full text didn't give her much more information. The messages were very short. That meant Winnie was leading her on. Besides, who did her friend know that had kids she could babysit? No one that Katie was aware of.

"Whose baby?" She typed it and hit Send. Then, immediately, she sent another email, "Where are you?"

The reply was one word. "Texas."

"And?" Katie hit Send again. Texas was a big state. It could be almost anywhere. She remembered Winnie's Colorado photo shoot, and refrained from rolling her eyes.

Maybe she had been called back out West, the ideal cowgirl. She sent, "Modeling?"

It was two minutes this time before she saw her reply. "Sorry. The baby. To answer you, not today, Sweetie. Babies are so cute. You need one. I've got a feeding, so I'll talk to you later. Don't forget you've got a phone, and it accepts text messages. Turn it on sometime."

This time Katie did roll her eyes, and when she heard Jeff stumble over a Greek phrase he was pronouncing with some difficulty, she looked to see him with a puzzled expression on his face. His eyes were on her. She smiled and waved to let him know all was fine. She pulled her phone from her purse, and held it just above the bench to show him what the problem was.

He nodded and began the difficult-to-pronounce phrase again.

Katie let the series of emails scroll through her thoughts. Winnie, Texas, and a baby. Somehow, she couldn't put the three together. There was no common cord there at all.

Her phone vibrated in her hand, and she glanced down to see the text message icon. It had the number fourteen on it.

Fourteen text messages? Good heavens! What was that about? She unlocked the phone and tapped the icon. The last one pulled up first.

"Now, Sweetie, does it all make sense?"

Katie scrolled up. All fourteen were from Winnie. She'd been sending all weekend, and only now that her phone had synced with the church Wi-Fi was it catching up.

After reading through them, she sent one in reply. "How do you know Ritchey Hickox?"

It seemed Winnie was at his house in Houston. Ritchey now owned a sporting goods store with locations in Colorado Springs, Houston, and soon to come to North Carolina, just outside Raleigh. His had been the photo shoot in Colorado Winnie had attended just before Katie's and Jeff's wedding at the first of October. Of course, Winnie hadn't known that, but he'd wanted her back for a second

305

session, this time to do a live promotion in his Houston store. He said she was perfect, she'd typed with exclamation points. They were about to expand, and he wanted Winnie to be the face of his new product line.

Still. How in the world could her friend have made this connection, and be babysitting for the very man who'd missed hers and Jeff's wedding?

The answer popped up. "Facebook." After a moment, another message appeared. "After the wedding, I looked up all Jeff's old friend, and I friended 'im. That's why Ritchey called me back, because I'm Jeff's friend, too. How 'bout that?" There was a smiley face at the end.

Katie smiled. She'd find out more of the story later, but now at least her quest from earlier didn't seem quite so impossible. Ritchey and Christmas. She might have to twist Winnie's arm to get Ritchey here, but Katie thought she now had a plan.

6

"Where did the snow go?"

Katie asked the question of no one as she stood high on the Point and pulled her sweater tighter around her neck. She had hoped to find the Point covered in Christmas icing, something she had never seen. It was still December, after all. Yet, here she stood in a sweater, so she should have expected it. Indian Summer, she believed they called it down in Massachusetts, although here in Maine, they were lucky to get one day.

Now? It was the midday sun that felt good, not the breeze blowing in off the water. Still, with much of the previous week's storm quickly disappearing, they'd been able to drive out for a picnic.

What had Katie told Janine? I need a break, and your boys need to stretch their legs. It had surprised her how fast her friend had agreed, and now they were having a picnic on the Point, and everyone was soaking up the warmth.

The day was not quite perfect, though. The road out had been a mess, with shaded areas still thick with snow, and the places that had melted? They were a muddy mess. And now, the boys were out along the shore path. Little of the snow had melted there, and Katie could just see them

307

having a snowball fight. At least they were giving their mother some peace, and with all the boats locked in the boathouse, they couldn't get on the water.

She turned her attention from them, relieved about one thing. Being on an island, even if you ignored them, they couldn't get lost, could they? After all, it was an island.

Katie smiled.

They'd set up the picnic near the foundations of her grandmother's old summer home. It was sunny here. However, they'd brought fuel for the generator at the cabin down on the water, and even from here, Katie could hear it humming just at the edge of perception. Someone else might think it a distant boat or a plane, but she had slept a week last summer with it just outside her window, and the sound had become Jeff, or rather, his concern for her welfare. It was a good memory.

Now, it was running a small heater, and Janine was taking a well-deserved nap. Ten minutes, she had asked Katie. Give me ten minutes of peace, and I can make it until spring. It had been forty-five, and Katie had no intention of waking her yet.

It was Christmas that kept Katie wound up, or her thwarted plans for Christmas, anyway. She'd imagined lights down Jeff's drive, and two trees in the house. One at the church, of course, and manger scenes. Plural. One had to be live, in the gazebo at the Town Park. She was the minister's wife, and she could call on all the townspeople to "step up to the plate" to do this for Jeff.

She hadn't considered Rockhaven. Maine. An island fifteen miles out to sea. Storms. Ordinary island stuff like that. Unlike Boston where storms happened, the sidewalks were cleared, and life went on as usual, in Maine, a storm happened, and life shut down for three days. The Thanksgiving blizzard was proof of that.

Even the Thanksgiving dinner she had organized with her church members had been swallowed in a barrage of snow, buried three feet deep. Their only guest had been Roker, and he'd stayed the entire weekend.

Still, giant balls on the evergreen in the park. Plastic,

not glass, not after the storm over the weekend. And tinsel, wired on with pliers. She'd gotten that from watching Jeff at the house. You wire stuff on, because otherwise, the wind takes it off. She could get Kevie and some of his friends to help with that.

The banquet at the Town Hall? That was proving more difficult. Corrine at the bakery said she was swamped with orders at the school. She did the treats for every class party, and of course they had them on the same day. After school was out for the holidays, thirty-four pies were already ordered, two birthday cakes always came the third week in December, and her daily cinnamon buns? She just couldn't find the time, with her daughter heading to Florida for the holiday with her grandparents from off-island.

Jess Tambour up on High Road had promised several pumpkin pies, if Katie'd clean the pumpkins—fresh, the only way to make pies—and while grateful, Katie considered it another mess she'd unwarily gotten herself into. She couldn't back out after asking, could she? Jess was a member of the church.

It crossed her mind that her friends from ALDMass would be drawing for Secret Santa about now. Gifts would start to show up on desks, and the Christmas party would line up on the 20th or the 21st, close to Christmas, but early enough for those traveling out of town to be able to attend. Last year it had been at Deuxave. Too elegant, they'd all exclaimed, but they'd had a great time nonetheless. This year, who knew?

Her desk. Who would receive their daily Christmas surprises there? Or was it empty, still? That was a bit of an emotional hollow spot, still, this being her first Christmas gone. Once she got past this one, though, she'd be fine. Surely she'd be fine.

Katie pushed that aside, moving on. Ritchey Hickox. He was proving to be a booger. Still, she was working on it. Winnie's help? Not as empowering as Katie had hoped. Come to find out, the children's nanny was babysitting, and Winnie was doing no more than pretending to give them a bit of her time. She was waiting on Ritchey to drop her off at the airport. Flights had been cancelled at Hobby Airport, closer to the Hickox's home, and she'd had to wait to be rescheduled into Houston's larger Bush Intercontinental.

Katie had told Winnie that the two weeks of the holidays were hers. She expected her friend to be on the island the entire time. If any modeling gigs came up, she had to tell them no.

"Even Hawaii?" Winnie had teased over the phone.

"You'd better not," Katie snapped back.

"Just as well," Winnie had returned, her voice light and bright, as if there was more she wasn't saying, and Katie had played into her hands.

"Why do you say that?" Katie had been on the verge of apologizing, recognizing her inconsiderate response even as she spoke it. Being here with Jeff was the end-all dream she'd known it would be, but there was more to life than just Jeff. Getting married wasn't like doing your nails. Just clip off the old parts, and flush them down the drain. No, the life Katie had lived for twenty-eight years had to be filed gently, pampered, and polished into something that was new and comfortable. At times, she missed what she'd left behind. She missed Winnie, and she wanted to see her again.

"Oh," and Winnie was silent for a moment, with just the tapping of a pen on a desk, or so it sounded. "I already turned three down. Did you know they don't celebrate Christmas in the Maldives? How sad is that? It's just another day, shooting pictures on the beach."

"You—" and Katie heard her voice stumble. "You turned down the Maldives in December?"

"Sweetie, I'm spending Christmas with you." Then she'd giggled. "And Jeffie, of course. How fun is this going to be? You do have an extra room, I hope. Not the sofa, please." She'd giggled again.

Ritchey, though. She had to find a connection that would be strong enough to get him here.

Connection! Katie pulled out her phone and opened the voicemail app. She tapped the microphone icon and said, "Remember to call Cousin Nikki. She might want to see

310

Rockhaven in the dead of winter."

On second thought, really? Katie considered the plausibility of her cousin actually coming all the way to the island, but she might. With Francois to drive her, she might be willing to travel almost anywhere. Then, Katie could find out what her sole-surviving and very wealthy European relation had been up to, living in Katie's old apartment back in Boston.

Katie turned to see Janine on the deck outside the cabin. She had her jacket in her hand, and she yawned. When she saw Katie she waved.

"Where are the boys?"

"Out." Katie waved one hand toward the water. "How was your nap?"

"How long—?" She looked at her wrist and shook it. "You let me sleep an hour?"

Katie smiled and held up a finger. It was a good ways to the cabin, and she headed that direction. Yelling at each other—and they'd been pretty close to doing that—didn't make for much of a conversation. Closer, she started again.

"I thought you deserved a few minutes with someone else watching the boys. They've been fine." Katie's last comment was to forestall the frown on her friend's face at the words *someone else watching the boys*. She understood, though remembering Kevie stealing . . . no, borrowing Katie's little dinghy back in the summer, then Konnar being tossed in the ocean—twice!—by his brothers on a chilly September night. "They've been down on the shore path tossing snowballs at each other."

"Oh, my heavens!" Janine's hand went to her mouth. "Did you see Kevie putting rocks in any of them? Kevie always puts rocks in his snowballs. Kevie!" She yelled, already striding up the hill.

Getting a live nativity going in the town gazebo? A Christmas banquet for the entire town? How about getting Winnie, Nikki, and Ritchey here for the holidays? How hard could it be? If Janine could survive her four boys, Katie could do anything she dreamed up.

"Austie?" Katie called out another of hers and Jeff's

summer friends from so long ago, turning and speaking to the trees as she did so, talking to no one, with Janine already gone over the rise. "Apple? Bennie and Bobby? Maybe Babes would like to come, with her new baby, even if it would be fifteen by now."

Katie got pulled away from her fanciful and carefree rhetoric with the sound of Janine's voice coming down the rise.

"Katie? Do you have the keys? We have to get to the hospital now!"

"It's Christmas, God," Katie said, although not too loudly, as she started to run up the slope. "Can't you be here just for Christmas, taking care of things?"

And when you show up, bring Ritchey for Jeff, and make everything else work out, too. That was all she had time to pray, because by then, they were in the car, and speeding down the driveway as fast as the rutted mud would allow.

Three stitches. The rock-infused snowball had hit Konnar, the nine-year-old, just on the temple, and the blood had been worse than the cut. Katie was glad for that. She hadn't been to the hospital since arriving back on the island, but in Boston it would be called an emergency clinic. There wasn't even a doctor on call. They were all in Wells or Camden or on Deer Isle. The medical technicians had been skilled, though, and the cut was repaired and bandaged, quick as a spring snowstorm melts under the warmth of the midday sun.

She wondered how it was done delivering babies on such a remote island. The thought had never occurred to her before. She might have to deal with that question someday. She made a mental note to check to see if midwifery was still a legitimate occupation.

She had called Jeff on the way to the hospital, but he was out on his boat for the day, and voicemail had picked up her call. When Janine had rung up Al, it was the same. On the island, Katie was learning, you did for yourself, because there was no one else to do for you.

The hardest part of the drive in from the Point? The youngest Peavey, Keithie, at only four, had screamed the entire way in, with tears running down his face, convinced that his brother was going to die. Kevie, who had done the deed, had sat in the rear seat and sulked.

Maybe she didn't need to worry about midwifery services on the island, not with Janine's examples of why kids weren't a good idea. Katie was pretty sure she wasn't having one before she was forty, if then.

Now, Janine was at home with her three youngest, and Katie had Kevie riding in the car with her.

"Why do I have to go back?" Kevie had one elbow on the armrest, and his chin in his hand. His eyes were glued to the window at his side, and they narrowed at the passing scenery.

"Because I need your help." Katie said the words brightly. The real reason was Janine had been at her wit's end with the three youngest. This one had been torturing Keithie by the time Katie had driven up to their home, that Konnar was probably going to die and come back to haunt him. When Janine started to cry, Katie had stepped in and told Kevie to get in the car. They had stuff to collect at the Point.

"I've already been out there once, today. It's boring."

Katie ignored that, glad they were in Jeff's Jeep. How had she ever thought she could get Kevie to help out with her Christmas tree? He was a monster. He'd just as soon cut all the branches off, just to create trouble for someone else.

"It's Christmas in three weeks." Okay, Katie thought to herself. Where am I going with that?

"What's special about that?" Kevie threw himself back into the seat, crossing his arms across his chest.

"Kevie, how can you say that?" Katie downshifted the transmission going up an incline, and she glanced at him. He wasn't a bad-looking kid, stocky, with even features. Just to see him you wouldn't think him anything but adorable. It was when he moved or spoke that the real boy came out. But to not like Christmas?

"It's not real. None of it."

That was too much for Katie, and she pulled the car to the side of the road and set the parking brake. She reached and turned the key, killing the engine.

"What? Am I in trouble for telling the truth?" Kevie snorted and refused to look at her. He had his knuckles at the glass, and he rapped it repeatedly.

"Nobody's in trouble." Katie kept her voice even, trying to picture Jeff with the boy. She had no practice at this, but she did know that to get angry was to lose him. "Tell me, what's not real about Christmas?"

She almost said it was her favorite time of the year, but he wouldn't appreciate that. It would be like proselytizing, her knowing he hated it and trying to convince him otherwise.

"There's not a Santa Claus." He tapped again, but stopped after three times, as if waiting on a response.

"No. Not a real person Santa." Whew. What do you say to that? Katie waited on him, unsure where he was going.

"Konnar's so stupid. That's why I hit him with the snowball. How can he still believe in something that's just a lie?" He looked through the windshield for a moment before looking down.

His eyes were red, and that told Katie something was coming out. Something important. What, she wasn't practiced enough to figure out, but it was there. And important to the boy.

"Karlton and Keithie. Do they believe?"

"Yeah, but they're just kids. Who can blame 'em? They want it to be true." He hit the palm of his hand against the side of his face, sliding it, and it left a damp smear along his cheek.

"You know better, though." She saw a quick nod of his head. "What about the Jesus part? How do you feel about that?"

"They lied about Santa." He brushed at his face again, then balled his fist in his lap. "Why not that?"

"They?" Katie was pretty sure she knew, though.

"Everybody. Even Jeff." He spit out the man's name, as if that hurt worse than all the rest.

Oh, Kevie, Katie thought. "So, are you going to tell Karlton and Keithie? About Santa?"

"No." He frowned at her. "Why would I do that?"

"You did whack Konnar with a rock." She shrugged. "I thought maybe you planned to break the news to everyone."

"Shows what you know. Konnar's nine. He's not a baby, anymore."

"Then, what's the plan this year?" Okay, Katie. What would Jeff do? What was that old acronym? W. W. J. D. What Would Jesus Do? Here it was What Would Jeff Do? She'd seen him in action with the boys. Now she got to leap into the fray.

"Plan?" He said it with a snort.

"Sure. Christmas. You don't believe, because it's all a lie. Your brothers do, and you're not going to tell them. In that case, what's the plan? Are you skipping it all together this year?" This was what Jeff did, called their bluff. She wondered if it would work.

"I can't do that." Not a real answer, just a pronouncement, as if it was an obvious fact, and she should be able to see it.

"Sure you can. You're eleven. You know they don't have Christmas in the Maldives." Thank you, Winnie! "Everyone goes to work. They don't do the holidays or Christmas vacation. No presents. Nothing."

"They're stupid. Everybody wants presents."

"They don't. No Jesus, no Santa. None of it." She shrugged. "Tell your brothers you're going to the Maldives for Christmas, and people would laugh at you there if you had Christmas."

"I can't go wherever that is. That's the stupidest thing I've ever heard." He didn't sound angry anymore, and when he glanced at her, he smiled a bit before he forced it off his face.

"I've got a friend who was going to the Maldives. They were going to pay her a lot of money if she would go there and skip Christmas, but she said she liked spending Christmas with me, and she turned them down." When he looked at her, Katie nodded at him. "She's coming here for two weeks."

"Does she believe in Santa?" He looked impressed that

someone would turn down money just to have Christmas.

"Maybe. I don't know. She acts like she does." And being Winnie, maybe she really did. "When she's around, I pretend like I believe, just for her, because it makes her happy. I think maybe that's why she didn't go to the Maldives."

"Oh." He took a deep breath, like he'd figured out something.

"Does that mean you've got a plan? You know, for Christmas?"

"I might be eleven, but I'm not stupid. We can go, now."

"Okay, as long as you have a plan." Katie started the engine of the Jeep, and shifting it into gear, she released the clutch, and eased it back onto the road. She tried not to smile as she asked, "Is it a secret plan, or is it safe to tell me?"

"I have to have Christmas." It came out heavy, like he was rolling his eyes with his words.

"Like me and my friend. You pretend, and they have a good time. That's a good start. Now, what are you going to do first? Buy them presents?"

"You have to have money to buy presents." He wasn't tapping the window, and that was progress.

"How about decorating a tree? I have one that needs decorating. You could invite all your friends, and it could be like a pretend Christmas party. I'd bring the treats." She smiled at him. Maybe this would work after all.

"Like what treats?" He actually sounded interested.

"Cupcakes?" She shrugged. "Pizza, maybe. Your choice. You choose."

"You'd really do that?"

"Sure. It's Christmas."

"Cool. I want pizza."

"Done deal." She held her hand out, and when he saw it, he grinned and shook.

Two points, Katie crowed inside. One Peavey won over, at least to decorate one tree. She might get something checked off her Christmas list after all.

Ready or not, Christmas, here we come!

8

"Winnie! I'm glad you called." Katie held her phone to her ear with her shoulder, as she ran a stitch of wire through the plastic hook on one of her giant Christmas ornaments. She had one hand gloveless, the better to answer her phone, and her fingers were growing stiff. "We're outside, and it's cold today. If you hear the wind, that's what it is. Still, if I drop my phone, it might sound even worse."

She laughed, but holding a cell phone this way was difficult, that and attempting to manage seven preteen boys decorating the tree by the town gazebo. At least one— Brookie George—was tall enough to reach the top of the tree without a ladder, and that was fortunate, because Katie hadn't thought to bring one.

"We're outside? Sweetie, if you're with Jeffie, of course you're outside." Winnie laughed, and it sounded like she was talking to someone in the background for a moment. "Oh, sorry. That was Ramon. He's waiting our table today."

"Ramon, at No. 9? Honey, you better hop out the door. You know you can't afford anything there." No. 9 Park was one of Katie's and Winnie's favorites, specializing in French and Italian dishes, but it wasn't cheap. They often chose one option, tasting and sharing, more for the fun of the experience than a filling meal. That was the way of high-end dining, though. Lots of little bites to fill you up, rather than one big dish to load up.

"Oh, no. We're covered. Hold a second." Winnie's voice was muffled, but she was clearly discussing something about the menu. "That was Nikki. She's insisting Francois join us for lunch. He's out in the car, and we had to send Ramon for him."

"They haven't griped at you, yet?" That wasn't Katie's real question, although it was a real question. At No. 9, chatting away on a phone during lunch wasn't the best of manners. However, her real question involved Winnie being at No. 9, and Katie being here with three half-emptied pizza boxes on the tailgate of Jeff's Jeep. It didn't seem fair.

"Nobody knows I'm talking to you, except Nikki, and she doesn't care. I have one of those ear things on, and my hair covers it. I'm having salmon, with pine nuts, I think. Nikki's paying." She whispered her last two words, and she giggled. "So, what are you and Jeffie doing out today? Fishing?"

"We are not fishing." Katie huffed. "What makes you think I'm with Jeff, anyway? He's on his boat."

"Oh, we, and you're outside. Oh, oh! I said yes in French, and I didn't mean to. How funny!" The phone scratched for a second, and Winnie said, "Hold on, Sweetie. Don't hang up."

Katie had finished wiring her ornament, plus two more, and at one of the boys' complaints—Jeremy? She thought so, Jeremy Boggs, possibly, if she had the last name matched up—she was restringing longer wire through one she'd done at the very beginning. It had fallen twice, and it needed to be firmly fixed to a branch. Rockhaven storms! It would have to survive at least one, she'd been warned. Thanks, she'd thought. I presumed that's what Thanksgiving was all about.

Redoing the ornament, she heard the sounds of her friend back in Boston making room for the chauffeur slash housekeeper that her second cousin had brought with her from France. It seemed a new place setting had to be sorted out, with apologies, and a quickly spoken string of French flew between her cousin and the driver.

"Sorry. Whew, but that's settled. I know a little French, but when they talk fast, I'm lost. Bon appetite! I know that one. And oui! That's what I said a moment ago, but just by accident."

"Honey, you enjoy your lunch. I've got seven boys here, and this tree will be a mess if I don't give them some pointers." Katie took an ornament from the tall boy, Brookie, and she traded it with a different color, showing him she wanted it on top.

"Seven boys! You do work fast. See you in a week?"

From over the phone, it sounded like their drinks were being served, but Christmas wasn't for three weeks. Katie started to clarify that, and about then, she dropped the ball she was holding, and it began to roll away from her.

"I'll call you later. Eat something for me."

"Sure, Sweetie. Bye, bye!" Winnie could be heard oohing over something being set on the table as she hung up.

Katie slipped her phone into a pocket; and pulling her missing glove from her back pocket, she slipped it on, calling, "Kern, Matt, reds don't go together. You have to keep the colors separated."

The first one, Kern Pearsons, thin and angular in his oversized coat, giggled, and he poked the second one with his elbow.

The boy Katie had called Matt pointed to a dark-skinned boy across the park who had given up on the tree and was clumping what loose snow he could find under the bushes and tossing it at yet another boy. It wasn't holding together in flight, but rather disintegrating into a miniature blizzard on the way. Only about every third one remained clumped together enough to reach its target. "That's Matt. I'm Paulo."

Ahh. Paulo was light-skinned and blue-eyed. Blond, too, if she remembered correctly. She guessed Rivera as a last name didn't mean much when it came to ethnic appearance.

"Then, Paulo, bring me a blue ball from the box. I've got wire right here." She didn't, but she would by the time he returned.

Snow hit her in the back of her neck, and when Katie ducked her head forward, she felt some of it slip down inside her jacket. She grabbed the chunk of snow that was left and pulled it off her neck, and held it in her hand. She turned to see Matt looking at her wide-eyed.

"Matt. Leaf, isn't it?" He was the dark-eyed boy she'd thought must be Paulo Rivera. "Who was that for?"

"Kevie." That's all he said, but his eyes jumped to the side for a moment, and then back to her face.

"Kevie?" Katie turned to see him just behind her. "That was meant for you?"

"Yes." He stood wide-eyed, unlike the boy who would have run to kick someone a week before. He looked in her hand and back to her face.

"This snowball was meant for you, but wound up down my neck?"

"Um, I'm sorry?" The other boys had stopped to watch, and he looked to them, only finding Katie's face again when she didn't say anything else. "Um, I'm really sorry?"

"You're going to think sorry." She pointed a finger at him, making sure to keep her face stern. Marching forward, she grabbed him around the neck with one arm, just like she'd seen Jeff do, and before he could react, she stuffed the snow down the back of his jacket, making sure to shake the fabric so it would go all the way down.

"Hey," he cried, grabbing at the neck of his coat.

"Are you sorry, yet?" Katie had given up on the stern act, and she was laughing. "Boys, more snow!"

"No!" Kevie cried. "You guys better not!"

"You guys had better! I bought the pizza, and it's me taking you home." Katie yelled to them, holding to Kevie with both arms. "Hurry!"

She got as much snow down her coat as Kevie did, because the rest of the pretend Christmas party did just as she asked, except there were too many hands to get all the snow down Kevie's coat. They were eleven, or within a year either way, after all, and boys that age don't have a clear and present off switch. That snow had to go somewhere, and any collar was game.

Katie was on the ground, and the snow was going everywhere when a horn honked, getting her attention. She looked up to see Al's truck alongside the curb. Al called out, waving his hand.

"Never saw a tree decorated like that, before. Wish I was eleven again." He grinned. "Kevie under there somewhere?"

"Hey, boys, let me get up." Katie pushed one of the youngsters off, and she stood, pulling her hair back from her face and waving. "On the bottom."

"Good for you. Keep him there." Al laughed.

It was Jeff's voice that made her realize that Kevie's father wasn't alone.

"You want to decorate our tree at home later?"

"You did, already." She laughed at him, brushing his question away with a wave of her hand. "On the dock, remember?"

"I can undecorate it, if you'll do that with me." He could be seen in the truck, nodding his head towards the boys.

"Katie, can I trade Jeff for Kevie? I can take Tim, too, if he's done enough damage." That was Tim Swisher, and he lived out near the Peaveys, but that was understood, and Al didn't say it.

"Sure. I've got extra pizza. You want some?" When he motioned for her to bring it on, she left the boys—the commotion was wearing down, with all the snow used up—and headed to Jeff's car. She sorted through the boxes to give him at least one slice of each kind, and she emptied one of the boxes to load it up for Al. Then she called, "Kevie, your dad wants this," and she held it out for him to take.

"Sure." He ran to her, and he grabbed the box, only pausing when she didn't let go.

"So, how's our plan working? Think your brothers will

be fooled?" She noticed Jeff walk up, and he seemed puzzled at her question. She ignored him and kept her attention on the boy.

"Not fooled." He grinned. "Convinced. Bye!" He took the box and was gone.

"Did I hear a little deception going on there?" Jeff leaned and kissed her, putting his arms around her and drawing her in. "What's the plan?"

"Oh, something between me and Kevie." She snuggled in, enjoying the sea-smell of his coat, the smell that told of Rockhaven and boats and winter in a land that wasn't Boston. And she had envied Winnie. Winnie wasn't here. Winnie didn't have Jeff.

"So, how's the plan working?" He murmured to her, repeating her words to the boy.

"Is the tree decorated?"

"Mostly." He chuckled. "That's your plan?"

"Does it look like Christmas?"

"Pretty much the way I want Christmas to look. No Katie bows, but that's okay. It's the town's tree. Something's missing, though."

"Oh!" Katie pulled away from Jeff. "I let Kevie get away, and we didn't put up the tinsel. He put wires all down it, too."

Sure enough, it was in a pile on the floor of the gazebo.

"Okay. Get these boys to do it."

"It's time for them to go home. Oh, Jeff. What will I do?" She fell against him again. "It was all going so perfectly, too."

"I could do it. You know, a little Santa magic. How would that be?"

"Oh, Jeff!" Katie threw her arms around him, giving him a broad smile. "That's perfect! Santa magic! But it's got to be a secret. You can't tell anyone you did it."

"It's Santa magic. Santa magic is always secret. Otherwise, it's not Santa, is it?"

"Jeff, you are so perfect. Do you know that?" She turned to look at the boys, now tossing sticks at each other. "I couldn't have Christmas without you."

323

"Without who?" He fought a grin as he said it, and he kept his eyes on the boys as they played.

"You heard me. Without you." She pushed on his chest with two fingers.

"Ho, ho, ho. Without who?" He was fully grinning, and clearly digging for a specific response.

"Oh, you. Without Santa. I get it."

"You do, huh? I'll tell you, Dame Carver, I really am Santa, every year, for all the little kiddos. That means if I string the tinsel, you can really say Santa did it, and every word will be the truth. How does that fit into yours and Kevie's little plan?"

"Perfect, Mr. Claus. Absolutely perfect." She reached to give him a kiss.

"Thank you, Mrs. Claus. Now, you need to get that sleigh started, and get all the little children home. You can start a list on your phone, too, so Santa can know who all the good boys are. Tell 'em you're planning on texting it directly to the North Pole, because you know Santa really, really well. Now, go." He released her and turned, "Boys! In the car, now! Be good. It's almost Christmas!"

Katie thought she would explode with love! No. 9 had nothing on Rockhaven. Nothing at all.

9

"Jingle bells, coconut shells." Katie sang the nonsense words softly as she hummed the familiar tune under her breath. Jeff was in the other room playing with the fire, rather, building a fire in the fireplace, and she could hear the torn paper, the logs clunking, and the occasional snort of irritation when something didn't go exactly right.

"Bryan's coming, you said?" Jeff called to her. Nickerson, he meant, but Bryan could only mean Bryan, one of the "eager beavers" from the snowstorm.

"And Jerry," she called back.

"Little J and Debsy, too?" He yelped, and something fell. "I'm all right," he called out.

"That's good to hear." Katie was in the kitchen wrapping presents, and she'd told Jeff to keep on the other side of the wall. What she was putting under the tree was none of his business.

Her list, not actually that long, was mostly marked off, but the big one was the same unresolved present as before. Ritchey. How was she going to give Ritchey to Jeff for a Christmas present? She laughed to herself, picturing her husband's friend as a jack-in-the-box, wrapped tightly, and springing out at the turn of a handle.

325

"Jeff, what toys did you play with as a kid?" She was doodling, and it was turning into a box. Above it she drew in an oval with eyes and a nose. "Jeff?"

At no answer, she flipped her pad over—just in case he wandered in—and stepped to the living room. There was the start of a fire, but no real flames. Some singed paper curled off to the side, and one smaller fag of scorched wood had fallen onto the hearth, still smoking.

"Jeff?" Katie pulled on an oversized, fire-resistant glove from atop the woodpile, and stacked the partially burned log back on top of Jeff's carefully constructed stack inside the firebox. Tossing the glove back, she began looking, first leaning into the bedroom to call out, "Jeff? The rapture hasn't come, has it? I expected to go up, too."

She caught sight of him outside hefting a cloth carrier heavy with wood. Seeing the back door partially open, she pulled it wider to allow her husband to step through.

"Thanks, my love." He leaned to kiss her on the cheek as he passed. "Thought I better do this before the fire gets too big."

"Too big?" She nodded that direction with a smile. It was doing nothing at all, except smoking a bit from a fragment of paper that was about to go out.

"I just had it going." His words told his dismay. "Where's Roker when I need him? Do we have more newspaper? I used what I could find."

"That reminds me. I added Roker for tonight, also. Jess, too. When she heard Roker might be here, she practically pleaded."

"I told you that pumpkin pie wasn't just for us."

"The Thanksgiving pie?" A small picture snapped into place for Katie. Roker with his snowshoes walking to their house, and Jess watching outside to catch him just at that exact time. How much bother had it been to bundle up and chase Roker down? Not anyone would have done that.

"Roker loves Jess' pies." Jeff transferred the wood from his carrier to the pile as he spoke. "Newspaper?"

"In the kitchen," she said absently, "but you don't go in. I'll get it, and you never said anything about that pie being for Roker."

"Sorry." He shrugged. "Thought you knew. It's sort of like an open secret, waiting for Roker to figure it out."

"Does that mean there's romance in the air?" She smiled, liking the sound of that. Christmas was for romance, lovers and all that. It was hers and Jeff's first, and she knew it would be special for them. She wanted it to be special for Roker and Jess, too.

"In Jess' air, but Roker's slow on the take. The newspaper? I can go get it myself, if you'd like." He knelt at the hearth, holding a lighter wand in his hand, and his eyes twinkled as he said it. "I'm good at keeping my eyes closed."

"No, you don't, nosy. Still." She wandered in the kitchen and returned with the day's paper. They hadn't read it, but it wouldn't tell anything new, not about Rockhaven, anyway. It was the Globe, and it was all about Boston. Jeff had subscribed, for her, he'd said. She handed it to him. "I think I'll do assigned seats tonight."

"Katie." He held the paper, now rolled in his hand, and looked at her, shaking his head. "It's just a party. Nachos and dip. Assigned seats?"

"Sure. You and me in that chair, everyone else on the sofa, and Roker and Jess in the kitchen." She smiled brightly. "That can be their privacy spot."

"I'm ignoring that. Al and Janine? Heard from them?" He was wadding paper and stuffing it in between logs, but his question said more than just his words. The four boys were normally relegated to the kitchen in cold weather, and the temps were expected to plummet after dark. It was December, and dark meant about four, so it would get cold.

"They can drop off Karlton to play with the Watson-Stryker kids, if he can stay till morning. The rest want to go to movie night."

The Schutmaats had a large garage, and once a month this time of year they moved their cars out and set up a makeshift theater. Children, if their parents accompanied them, were encouraged to attend. It was B-Y-O-Popcorn, but the kids looked forward to it every month.

An unintentional conflict had come up between the movie night and Katie's party. The movie had been scheduled for the Saturday after Thanksgiving, but with the storm, it had been bumped forward to tonight.

The Schutmaats were showing a Godzilla movie, and the Peavey boys had been ecstatic. Al and Janine had given in, apologizing to Katie they couldn't make the evening, but Katie didn't mind. She didn't have the boys' presents wrapped, yet, and she could put it off another day or two.

The phone began to ring. Katie picked it up to see Winnie's number displayed, and she raised her eyebrows, looking at Jeff. "It's Winnie, on the land line."

"Not on your cell." He chuckled and pumped the lighter, and flame shot out. "That's a first."

Katie clicked the talk button. "Hey, Honey! How's your Saturday?" As she spoke, a car door slammed outside. She covered the phone. "Jeff, we have company."

"I'll check." He set the lighter aside and stood. The fire was still dark.

"Sorry, Honey. We have company at the door."

"I know, and I'll be better once you move your car." Winnie bubbled over the line. "Don't you keep your cell on, anymore?"

"My cell? Of course—" Then it dawned on her, it had been low the night before, and she hadn't plugged it in. Here on the island it searched for signal constantly, and that ate her battery life.

"Katie?" Jeff called from the front entry.

"Yes, Jeff?"

"You'd better come see." His words were insistent.

"Hold on, Honey. Jeff needs me. Oh, first, what do you mean once I move my car? It's in my drive."

"I know, and it's in my way. Okay, Sweetie, in our way. Cousin Nikki insisted I come with her."

"Katie?" That was Jeff again, with a certain manic quality in his voice. "We have company, and they're early."

Winnie was here? She'd told her two weeks, but she hadn't thought it would be the two weeks before Christmas. She'd meant the two weeks after Christmas, when she could

328

have her friend all to herself.

Nikki, though? Cousin Nikki from France, via Katie's Boston apartment? She tried to remember if she'd invited her yet, and she couldn't recall actually doing so. Surely she wasn't here, too!

Then the front door opened, and Katie heard Winnie's voice.

"Jeffie! You're so beautiful. Let me give you a hug. Now, enough of you. Where's my Katie?"

Katie was still processing, but when she saw her friend through the beveled glass doors, she felt the smile on her face. She couldn't help it, and when Winnie bounded into the living room, Katie called out, "Winnie, Winnie, Winnie!"

She got exactly the answer she expected when her friend called back to her: "Katie, Katie, Katie!"

It was a huggy kind of moment, even if Katie was still a bit confused. When they quit dancing in each other's arms, Katie looked Winnie in the face, and she asked, "You said Nikki's here?"

"Oui, ma chère. May I sit? It is a very long walk from the car. Francois?" Nicolette held a gloved hand out, and she nodded her head in thanks when he took it to help her across the floor.

Oh, my, Katie thought, her mind racing. She had to come up with three beds, and Nikki could not sleep upstairs. Hers and Jeff's bedroom was the only one on the ground floor, and she had been fighting a slight case of the flu. She couldn't give up her bathroom.

And Nikki? She was used to the best. How would Katie ever satisfy that, and here on Rockhaven, and two weeks before Christmas?

"Winnie," she said, very softly. "I need to move my car?" That was the best Katie could do just then.

"Sweetie, the limo just wouldn't go around. Since it's rented, Francois couldn't risk any scratches. Now, tell me everything that's going on in your life. But before you do, hold that thought. Where's Jeffie?"

"I think . . ." Actually, she didn't know, until she heard

her car starting. "I think he's moving my car."

"Good. I need a fire, and I see one right there, ready to go. It's cold up here. Did you know that? I'm glad I brought my long johns." She giggled and said to Nikki, "Cousin Nikki, how do you say long johns in French?"

"Um, caleçon long, perhaps." Nikki shrugged.

"See? Caleçon. I'm learning French." Winnie grinned.

"Non, my dear. Not caleçon. Caleçon long. One is the, how do we say, boxer shorts, and the other is the, um, warm leggings."

"Oops," Winnie giggled again. "My mistake."

"I'm so glad to see you." Katie grabbed her friend's hand in hers, and she squeezed it. She'd forgotten how much she enjoyed Winnie's light-heartedness and enthusiasm for life. She needed this. It would help her get through all the plans she had yet to finalize for Christmas.

"Me, too, Katie, Katie, Katie." Winnie shivered her shoulders, and her hair bobbed up and down.

"Winnie, Winnie, Winnie!" Katie shook her shoulders in turn.

"Ah, d'être jeune. To be young. How lucky you are, my dears." That was from Cousin Nikki.

She had a smile on her face when she said it, and Katie was glad they'd both come. Releasing Winnie, Katie stepped to her cousin to give her a kiss. Although not a real one, the greeting was just as heartfelt. "Welcome, Cousin Nikki. I'm so glad to see you again."

Nikki returned her kiss and shooed her away with the fingers of one hand. She had a smile on her face as she did.

"Is there anything I can get for you?"

"Non. I see Francois returns from the car. He will be my right-hand man." She smiled and waved him her direction. He stepped to Nicolette and stood her collapsed walker at the arm of her chair before he began laying out several medications.

Katie turned back to Winnie, and she grabbed her arms, and they jumped up and down in excitement. This was going to be a better Christmas than she'd ever thought possible. All the problems in the way? They'd work out.

They always did.

10

"I have a Christmas surprise for you." Winnie teased with Katie, and her eyes twinkled with fun. "You'll never guess what it is."

"And you cannot go in the kitchen." For Katie, Christmas gifts were for Christmas, not for two weeks out. She changed the subject, instead. "How are things at Trinity? Cristina and Alf? Has the baby grown much? I miss Noah. He taught such profound biblical lessons."

"You don't want to guess?" Winnie looked aghast. "Nikki? I come all the way here, and my very best friend doesn't care. What did you say that was? Gross?"

"Grossier, ma chère." Nicolette laughed, repeating the French term fluidly and beautifully. "Gross is your American word for a very large number. You do not wish to say little Katie is a many-numbered person, but a rude person, if you so intend." Her pronunciation of the English version came out more like grass.

"Gross will do fine, because it means something else, too. But since you won't guess, I won't tell you, and you'll have to find out when Christmas gets here. Besides, it's for Jeffie, not you." Winnie didn't look all that offended, rather like it was a game, and she was pleased to still own her secret.

"Sure. We'll let Jeff guess later. Luggage. What about that?" Katie looked brightly from Winnie to her cousin. She remembered the luggage from Boston when Nicolette had shown up in her massively long limousine, and she dreaded how much there might be on this trip. Winnie didn't exactly pack light, and this was the winter season. Cold-weather clothes took a lot of room.

"We brought lots of special stuff. We filled the car. Guess with what?" Winnie cocked her head sideways, with her expression bright.

"A case of broomsticks, and you're late. Halloween was two months ago." Katie grinned, pleased to get in a dig.

"Ahh! I do believe you just called me a witch." Winnie waved one hand at Nicolette. "Katie's being a frump-frump, so she can wait to hear about all the stuff we brought. Now, Noah. Poor, poor Noah." Winnie shook her head and tutted.

"What about him?" Katie poked Winnie on the leg. "That's not fair to say that and not tell me the rest."

"He's in England." Winnie nodded her head at Nikki. "Queen and country, and whatever else goes with that. Isn't that right, Nikki?"

"Okay. Explain." This was apparently something Katie was unaware of.

"You have to remember that Angolan mission trip he took."

"Did I hear Angola?" The door closed behind Jeff, as he stepped into the room and dropped the car keys on a side table. "Has someone been there?" Without waiting for an answer, he disappeared into the kitchen.

"Noah, one of the lay teachers at Trinity," Katie called to him. "Don't you dare look at those presents. I haven't wrapped them all yet."

"Your church in Boston. I remember him. Tall, soccer type. Isn't he on the church team?" Jeff reappeared with two cups of coffee, handing one to Francois, and grinning at Katie. "And no, I didn't peek."

"Yes, that's him." Winnie let out a dreamy sigh with her eyes closed.

"He went to Angola?" Jeff seemed very interested, and he walked over to sit on the arm next to Katie. "Was it on that trip two, no, three years ago, where that ship was boarded by pirates?"

"You know about that?" Katie was impressed.

"The Anglican Church does keep in touch with its American counterparts." Jeff chuckled. "I was supposed to be on that trip, but your Noah beat me out for the honors, and now he's being received by the Queen."

"No." Noah Bainbridge? Trinity's Noah Bainbridge? "I knew they ran into some pirates, but what's with the Queen?"

"Oh," Winnie said, with a toss of her head, and a flip of her hand, "just a grandson who happened to be on board, there as a representation of the Church of England," and she reached to poke on Katie's arm, "and he was practically saved by our Noah."

"Oh." Katie had no idea.

"That means you can touch someone who has connections with royalty." Winnie held her hand out for Katie to touch.

Katie slapped it, instead. Not too hard, but it was a slap.

"Ow! What was that for?" Winnie kissed the offended spot.

"You're about as close to royalty as I am." Katie laughed. "Get over yourself."

Jeff was looking out the windows at the water, and he fought a smile.

"Ma chère, Katie, do not be too quick to be amused." Nikki held up one finger. "Many Frenchmen make claims to a royal connection, even if our royalty is long gone. Louis XIV had many children, all of which he, um, made legitimate. You have one of these, possibly, in your blood."

"Katie!" Winnie squealed. "You're a royal."

"Not exactly." Katie stood and moved to the fireplace, shaking her head. "French royalty all got their heads cut off, remember? It's called the French Revolution."

"In that case, you can't be my princess?" Jeff teased her. "I always thought of you as my little princess, and now you deny it."

Katie snorted. "Tell me about Cristina's baby. Does it really look just like Alf?"

That brought a chuckle. The truth was that Winnie was coming off a very busy schedule, and she'd only been to Trinity three times in the past two months, and other than her visits to Rockhaven Town Church at the time of the wedding, nowhere else. She'd heard of Noah through Nicolette, who'd become close friends with Mrs. Annie Rosenbaum, Katie's neighbor from her apartment in Boston. Everyone else Katie asked about? Winnie's stash of information was sketchy.

Winnie did drop a hint to Jeff that he had a surprise waiting, but Katie diverted her before she said too much, pointing out the Katie tree out on the dock.

"How pretty! Those are really big bows. Did you put that up?" Winnie patted Katie's knee, smiling brightly.

Katie told her the story, inciting a bit of clapping from her friend by the time she finished, but it was the sleeping arrangements that were on her mind, even with the stories and teasing. Nicolette was the one who cleared that up.

"Ma chère, Katie," Nicolette inserted into a lull. "Francois and I must go before much time is escaped from the clock. Francois can remove your friend's bags, if you wish her to stay. I will have very much room at my bien locatif, if you do not have so much bedrooms."

"Your—" Katie paused to pull her thoughts together, not very quickly, she had to admit. "You have a place? On the island?"

"Oui, ma chère. I should be clear. Bien locatif, um, perhaps, property rental. I would not ride the big boat back and forth unless very necessary, non? There is, Francois? Round Road, you say?"

"Non, mademoiselle." He continued in a short speech of fluid and very beautifully spoken French.

"Oui, oui. Merci." She smiled at Katie, tapping her temple with her fingertips. "It is Round the Island Road. How should I forget? Eagle's Roost. You may know of it."

Katie shrugged, but Jeff chuckled. "What?" Katie asked

him.

"The big place? The shingled gateposts?" He spread his hands to indicate how wide each one was.

"The De Groot house?" Katie had been there once. It was out towards her family's property on Carver Point. She'd wondered what the De Groot heirs had done with it since the grandparents were gone.

Jeff shook his head. "Bigger. Three miles this side."

"Oh." Katie pictured the home he was talking about. It wasn't ocean front, although she was certain the acreage across the road that fronted the shore was part of the property. The appeal about Eagle's Roost was its location on one of the highest points on the island. From Lookout Ledge near Carver Point, the Eagle's Roost could be seen rising from the trees. It was the island's most exclusive estate, behind gates triggered by electric eyes and powered by private generators.

It offered unparalleled 360 degree views, and had been featured in numerous architectural magazines over the years. No one Katie knew had ever been inside. Now she wondered just why her cousin had bothered with her little apartment. It must have seemed a shoebox compared to her home in France.

"Sweetie, do you have room for me?" Winnie smiled brightly. "I just need a little space, and a bathroom, of course. No outpotties."

"Outhouses," Katie automatically corrected. "Are you sure? Cousin Nikki's place . . . I suspect you would love Eagle's Nest."

"Oh, Sweetie, I came to stay with you. Fancy houses don't make Christmas. Best friends do." She held out her arms for a hug.

"That is so sweet." Katie grabbed her and hugged her back.

"Inside bath?" Winnie whispered it in her ear.

"Inside bath." Katie found that funny. She remembered last July and the seal that blocked their path to the outhouse. Winnie had been a trooper, and they'd had a great time. Now, though, she required a bathroom. Duh! It was

335

freezing outside. This time Katie couldn't blame her.

"Good. Then I'm staying here." Winnie ran a hand down Katie's smooth hair, and she let out a very satisfied sigh. "Now, presents. We brought presents. Jeffie, Francois, follow me."

"We've already got a Santa." Katie called to her. "Jeff."

"That's what I said. Jeffie, Francois, come be Santa. We came loaded down."

Jeff looked at Katie and rolled his eyes, shaking his head. Katie shrugged, and with a laugh, she shooed him after her strawberry-blonde friend.

Cousin Nikki sat tapping her finger against the arm of the chair. She hadn't said much during the biggest part of the conversation, and that was when Katie noticed the earbuds in her ears. A music player lay on the arm of the chair, and Nikki was gazing out at the scenery, tapping in time to her private musical fantasy.

Nikki, Katie thought. My only real family, come all the way to Rockhaven just to see me. How much better could this get? She had her new husband, her best friend, and her only blood-relative here for Christmas.

Now if she could just get Ritchey sorted out for Jeff. Ritchey, get yourself up here. Katie didn't know if she could do it, though. In the past week, he'd become a very difficult man to attach a message to.

He wasn't replying to a single one.

11

Jess arrived first, of course with a pumpkin pie in tow. By then Jeff had the fire roaring, and Winnie and Katie had bags of chips opened and ready to dump into several big bowls. The afternoon's family gifts and all those from Nikki's car had been delegated to an upstairs bedroom, and a very special decoration had been added over the kitchen table. A twig of mistletoe was tied to the kitchen light.

"This is beautiful," Winnie exclaimed over the pie.

"We call it Roker pie." Katie reached over and took it from her and moved it to the side cabinet.

"Roker . . . isn't that Jeffie's friend? Did he make it?"

Katie saw the red around Jess' neck, and she pulled her into a quick hug. "Love you, Jess, and your pie, too. Thanksgiving? He ate a quarter of it just putting it in the kitchen. I got three bites."

"I should have made two." Jess was very soft-spoken, and she studied her hands. "Will Roker be here soon?"

"Roker, you, are you two a couple?" Winnie smiled, pointing to Jess and to the pie.

"Stop it, Winnie." Katie pushed her hand down. "Roker doesn't know."

"Oh. You want to be a couple. I know some guys like

that, too. They don't know I exist."

"Oh, they know." Katie laughed, as she pulled the dip from the fridge. "They just know better."

"Oh, you can be so mean. Come on, Jess. You and me, let's go where we're wanted, like in any other room. Katie can join us when she gets her polite on." Winnie said it all with a smile, and she waved over her shoulder as she dragged Jess away.

At a knock on the front door, Katie heard Jeff inviting Roker in, with the big man's buoyant voice carrying throughout the entire house. He called to Winnie and Jess, telling them he was heading in the kitchen. Katie overheard Winnie telling him he was not, and that made her smile. He was going to sit down in front of the fire and keep an eye on it with Jess.

With small plates and napkins on the counter, and bottles of water and soda lined neatly up, Katie stood back and admired her preparations for the Christmas party. It looked pretty festive, if she did have to say so herself, and the invitees were arriving right on time.

"Chips," she said to no one in particular. Pulling out the chip bowls, she turned two bags over, filling them, and stood back, pleased. She crumpled the packages into a sack off to the side and set it on the floor. The only thing left was to heat the cheese. She set it in the microwave and started the timer.

Earlier she'd taken time to welcome Bryan and Jerry, and of course Jerry's kids. She had heard others coming in, since, and had accepted deliveries of baked goods for their after-nachos snacks, but only Nina Vinson had stayed in the kitchen to help.

"I live in a kitchen, and I'd be lost in there without a spoon in my hands." Nina laughed. "Besides, I'm not frying, and that's nice."

Nina had brought makings for home-cooked eggnog, and she stirred away at the stove. Two gallons of milk and a carton of eggs were in the pot. The empties were off to the side, and she tapped her spoon on the rim and slipped it in the sink.

She had dropped in a bowl of spices, telling Katie that it was her grandmother's recipe, and she'd promised never to divulge the secret mixture. Katie would enjoy it, though. Customers at Harbor View did every year.

Nina had brought something else. Off to the side nestled a bowl of powered cocoa. Add it to the eggnog, and it was hot chocolate to die for. The rest would go in the ice bath in the plastic cooler Nina had brought. Hot cocoa, but chilled eggnog. It would be perfect either way.

Katie's stomach growled. She looked forward to it.

"Hungry guests." Jeff leaned in, his shorthand reference coming with a wink and a grin. "If we don't want them to start gnawing the walls, we might need to get the nachos out."

"Have Al and Janine dropped off Karlton, yet?" Katie pulled the melting cheese from the microwave, and she tested it with one chip. "Almost perfect, even without the dip mix. Jeff?"

When she held the bowl out, he took a chip from the table and dug in, smiling in satisfaction. "Thanks. I was going for the front door trim in about a minute." He scratched at the door frame to emphasize his reference to a hungry beaver.

"My restaurant door has a few gnaw marks on it." Nina patted Katie's arm with a knowing smile. "Can't feed a man too fast or too often. Get that dip mixed in, and he won't be able to resist."

The front door slammed, rattling the glass. It opened again, the second time closing much more gently. Something fell over in the living room, and the talking got louder.

"Katie?" Janine appeared in the doorway. "Hi, Jeff, Nina. Are you sure Karlie's okay with you all night? We can stop by after the movie, but it'll be late. Al said several families are going, and Tom might do a double." A double feature, she meant, but her listeners got that.

"You have a good time. He's fine." Katie put her bowl down and took Janine's hand. "Jeff's a good enforcer. We've got extra lobster traps out back if we can't control him. You brought clothes for church?"

"By the front door, and thank you. You're the best. Karlie's been a pill tonight, and I was afraid he'd disturb the movie if we had to drag him along. You guys have fun with the party." She grabbed a chip with a laugh, and dipping into the cheese, she put it into her mouth as she headed out. She could be heard greeting several people in the other room, and wishing them a fun evening.

"How long until I send in the crowd?" Jeff returned, and at his side was a five-year-old pounding on his waist with clenched fists. He pulled him up, and held down his arms, asking him, "Hey, and that's for?"

"They won't let me play in the fire." The boy's face was screwed up as if he was about to cry.

"And quite right. I won't either." He smiled as the boy wrapped his arms around Jeff and laid his head on his shoulder, sniffling. "Katie?"

"Five minutes. I need to mix the dip in the cheese. Just five, okay?" She held up her opened hand, showing her outstretched fingers.

"Five. Then here they come." He winked again, and leaving, he leaned into the boy's ear, "And how long was your nap this afternoon?"

"I didn't have one."

"Oh. Maybe that's part of the problem . . ." His voice disappeared into the general hubbub in the other room.

"He's going to make a good father, that one is." Nina had poured the bigger portion of the eggnog into metal ice cream canisters buried in the ice filling her plastic chest. She placed the plastic lids on and covered them with more ice. Then she dumped coarse salt over them. "There. I don't make ice cream, but I make good use of my ice cream tubs, anyway. Now, hot chocolate, and we're good to go."

Cups of steaming cocoa, complete with sticks of cinnamon, soon spread across the unused half of the counter. Katie called for Jeff, and he made the formal announcement that it was time to eat. After a short prayer, those gathered at the Ragsdale household for an evening of fellowship and good times began to fill the kitchen.

"Where's Karlton?" Katie stood with Jeff in front of the fire, and she had his arm wrapped with hers. The diners were drifting back in to find anyplace they could to sit and enjoy their food. A couple had made it to the deck, but it was long since dark, and she didn't expect they would remain long.

Later, there was a gift exchange planned, but it was meant to be comical, and there was no real rush. The wrapped boxes and gift bags were on a table in the foyer, festive and bright, but now was for food.

"Out. He was gone before I could get him to the bedroom. I put him on our bed for now."

"Ahh." That made Katie smile. "We'll leave him until everyone's gone."

"My thoughts exactly." Jeff chuckled.

When the hubbub settled to the crunching of food and subtle conversation, Winnie stepped beside Katie, holding a steaming cup of cocoa. "Have you tried this? It's good. Like chocolate eggnog."

"It is chocolate eggnog. I'm ready to go for my food."

"Don't you dare!" Winnie held out one finger, pointing firmly. "Privacy, first!"

"Privacy?" That was Jeff. "It's a kitchen, and the door's open."

"No, Jeffie, it's mistletoe land." Winnie scrunched her shoulders and giggled. She pulled out her phone and clicked it on.

"You didn't!" Katie grabbed the phone. She tapped the camera icon and pulled up the latest picture. There were Roker and Jess, in Jeff and Katie's kitchen, their arms wrapped around one another, almost directly under the mistletoe.

"Roker?" Jeff pulled the phone from Katie's hand. "And Jess?" A smile spread across his face.

"If that's the way it is, I need something." Katie took Winnie's cup from her, and she took a long draught of cocoa. When she was finished, she smiled appreciatively. "That's good."

"Told ya'. Winnie knows best. And, you're welcome."

Winnie smiled, but she took the cup back, anyway.

Love was truly in the air, and that was the best news in the world for Katie. She wanted everyone to share in how much she loved Jeff, of course with their own partners, but to share, anyway. If Winnie had a hand in that for Roker and Jess, then she'd accept it. Winnie did know best, and she was glad she'd come to the island two weeks early. It had been the perfect thing to do.

"Can we try it out next?" Jeff leaned down to kiss Katie on the nose.

"Try out what?" Katie frowned.

"Silly." Winnie poked her on the shoulder. "The mistletoe, of course."

"The mistletoe, of course," Jeff repeated, kissing her this time on the cheek.

"Just do it." The gruff words were from Kent, Nina's husband.

And Jeff did, and Katie knew one thing for sure. She couldn't be happier if she had all the money in the world. And since she didn't, that was okay. She had Jeff, and he held her in his arms, and that was the most anyone could ask for.

12

"Don't forget." Katie tiptoed just a fraction, to give her husband a quick kiss on the lips. "Al and Janine need us this afternoon."

"The ferry ride?" They were outside the church door, greeting arriving parishioners, and he glanced at the late-morning sun and squinted. "Least the weather's pretty."

The ferry ride was about Janine's father. He'd died several months earlier, and he'd wanted his ashes poured into the sea. Off the ferry into the sea, to be exact, and returning from the mainland, not the other direction. Jeff and Katie were on the support team.

"I think everyone's here. I'm heading inside." Katie released Jeff's hand and pulled her hair back from her face. "It's chilly today." She missed Winnie being at services on this special Sunday, but her Cousin Nicolette was having a slow morning, and they were having "church on the hill." Katie had told her to look for her email after service. There would be a quiz that evening.

"Did you see the tree?" Jeff took her elbow before she could get away and nodded the direction of the Town Park. They could see the gazebo from the church steps, and the decorated tree was just to the side. It was now wrapped in glittering tinsel. "I think Santa's been busy."

"Oh, Mr. Claus. Has Kevie noticed it?" Katie hadn't seen it, and she was thrilled. It was beautiful, filled with the magic of Christmas. It was proof the holiday spirit even applied to eleven-year-olds.

"I think so. Perfect timing, especially if we're doing the ferry thing today. Anyway, it's cold, and you need to get indoors." He kissed her on the cheek and nudged her inside.

During the service, Katie gave up her normal seat at the front of the church, and she joined Janine and the kids. Al was with the communion team, and he was sitting in a special section closer to the front of the building. Karlton was next to Katie, with crayons and a Jesus coloring sheet. He worked on the back of a hardcover hymnal, intent on his own private version of crayon perfection. The other boys were the other side of Janine, not perfectly behaved, as they were scribbling notes or passing pictures to one another, but they weren't disrupting the service, either.

The message was about Joseph, and the forgiveness he gave his brothers, even after they sold him into slavery. Jeff tied it into Jesus, who would one day come in a manger, to be sold into slavery. In the children's story, Jeff had told of Moses, and how he was kept safe in a straw basket, and how that was almost like a manger, and invited the children to bring their parents to view the live nativity scene the following weekend beside the gazebo. Did they know Roker? Of course they did, and several of them turned to point to him on the communion bench. He would be Joseph. Come see him in a white beard.

Jeff's story reminded Katie of the previous summer, and how angry she'd been at God for taking her life from her, and how, when she'd opened back up to God, he'd given it all back. Jeff had been here on the island waiting, even when Katie had railed against God for stealing him away. She hoped she could make the connection with Janine that afternoon that what God takes away with one hand comes back to us in the other.

After service, Jeff and Katie joined their friends at the Peavey's home for Sunday lunch.

"It's just cold shepherd's pie." Janine set the casserole dish on the table along with a serving spoon. "With this afternoon, I—I've been too frazzled to think about any real cooking."

"The movie last night is partly to blame. Godzilla II ran past midnight. No cooking happened after that." Al grinned, and he took Janine's hand, looking in her eyes. "We love shepherd's pie, honey, cold or hot. Sit and eat. There's nothing else you need to do."

Katie knew all about the Godzilla movies. Three of the boys had ridden out with them, and the two youngest had brought Godzilla figurines, reenacting the movies, line-by-misremembered line, on the way over.

Katie stood behind her chair. She had done the drinks, ice and tea, and milk for the two youngest boys, even taking it on herself to refuse to serve soda to Kevie and Konnar. Then, Al had popped a soda to pour into a glass of ice, and Konnar's face had darkened. It wasn't Katie's house, however, and she had shrugged it off.

Kevie, though, glanced at his father and back to Katie, trying to fight a grin. He seemed to find it funny. Maybe he was growing up after all.

Leaving the church, Kevie had made sure to point out the tree and the tinsel as they drove by, asking Katie who had done that. The ornaments? She made sure her question sounded perfectly innocent. It was somebody special, she was certain. No, Kevie had demanded. The tinsel, he'd whispered to her.

Katie had replied that she'd last seen the tinsel inside the gazebo. It had been Kevie's job. Hadn't he? Once his dad had come by, she'd left to take the rest of the boys home. Jeff? she'd asked. You?

Wasn't my tree, Jeff had replied. Must be magic. Santa magic.

Kevie hadn't looked entirely convinced, but he hadn't called them on it, either. In Katie's book? She was certain he wanted to believe, and if he couldn't, he wanted his brothers to.

She was certain she heard him whisper to Keithie, his

youngest sibling, that Santa had decorated the tree.

"Katie?" Jeff reached to her chair and scooted it out a bit, jarring her back to the moment. "Ready?"

"May I give the prayer?" Katie took in Al's quick glance at Janine, and Janine's face filled with gratitude.

"Thank you, Katie." Al nodded. "Boys, bow for the minister's wife."

"Minister's wife." That was Kevie, and he snickered the words in a whisper. "It's Katie, Dad."

"Shush." Janine reached and poked him on the arm. "Bow your head and show respect."

"Anytime, Dame." Jeff had a grin on his face as he cut his eyes her direction.

"Heavenly Father, these are my friends, and they make up my life. Kevie, Konnar, Karlton, Keithie, and Al and Janine. What would I do without them—"

"What would we do without you and Jeff?" That was Al's mumbled comment.

"Anyway, God, today is special, and we ask you to be there for us, for everyone, and let us feel your love. And Lord, thank you for the food and the hands that prepared it. Amen."

"Hands off, Konnar. I'm first." Kevie grabbed the serving spoon out of his brother's hand.

"I guess they're hungry." Katie looked at Jeff and chuckled. "That tells me cold shepherd's pie must be very good."

"Janine's is the best. However, do I fall into the friend category, or somewhere else? I didn't hear my name in there." He had a laugh in his voice as he spoke.

"Don't know. Where do you want to be?" Katie caught Janine's eyes, and she was attempting to keep from laughing.

"Ouch," Jeff said, as he dished up a spoonful of pie. "Should I have asked?"

"Silly." Katie nudged him with her arm. "You're the minister. How's that verse go? The two shall become one?"

"You can't win, Jeff. Give it up." Al said that.

Katie laughed. Al was right. She had already won, over

346

two months before, when she and Jeff had held hands and said I do.

Katie shifted the conversation a new direction, quietly asking Janine, "Are you taking your car on the ferry this afternoon?"

"Ferry? We taking a ferry ride?" Keithie, four, overheard that just fine. His face brightened with excitement.

"Dad," Kevie began. "It's Avengers on TV. It starts at four."

The two middle boys had their Godzilla figurines out on the edges of the table, and they were having a mock battle.

"Janine, you told them, right?" Al looked at her questioningly.

"Oh, Katie, Jeff!" Janine's eyes filled up, and she fled the table.

"I guess she didn't. Sorry, you guys. Enjoy lunch." Al stood and went after her.

"Oops," Katie said. She had no idea she would set off the waterworks. It had been months, after all.

"Okay, Konnar. More pie?" Jeff stood and held the spoon. It was an undisguised distraction.

"Pie?" His plastic figurine stopped, and he looked up, finally interested. "What kind?"

Some days are better than others, thought Katie. This one? It looked like it was going downhill quickly. Still, the sun was shining, there was good food on the table, and Al and Janine had their best friends to prop them up.

She just hoped they had their sea legs on. She suspected the ferry ride back from the mainland would be an hour and a quarter of messy waterworks.

"Kevie?" Katie waved her hand to get his attention. He was pouting. When his eyes turned to her, she said, "Four, you said? If we get away from here early, we can set our machine to record it. How's that?"

"Can we?" His eyes found the clock on the wall. "What time—" he snuffled "—do we have to leave?"

Katie looked at Jeff. "Your guess?"

"Ten minutes. Take the Jeep." He shrugged. "Have

347

fun."

"You are a hoot, if I ever saw one. You should give me more warning next time." She nudged him again with her elbow, and she wasn't easy about it.

"I do what I can." He smiled. He was spooning more pie onto Karlton's plate.

"Kevie . . ." Katie turned to the boy, to see him already shoveling food into his mouth.

"I guess that means you need to get busy. Eat, woman." Jeff kissed her on the cheek before digging into his own plate of pie.

Katie dug in, too. It was over three hours plus the stop by the house. She'd be hungry by the time she returned. What was she thinking? Who cared about three hours in the future? She was hungry now.

She shoveled a bite in, and she began to chew.

 *13*

Katie and Jeff stood alongside the ferry railing overlooking the sea. Jeff's Jeep was beside them, with Al's truck just behind, the only two vehicles making the trip. They were on their way back to the island, and in spite of the bright sun, it was cold, being December and all. Janine and her bunch were inside out of the wind.

Jeff wore a loose coat, and Katie was snuggled inside with him as best she could. His arms cut much of the wind, but her face was cold.

"Look!" She nodded alongside the boat to a gray form swimming just below the surface.

"Your seal," Jeff said softly. "That means you're home."

"You softie. Earlier, that was very touching, the kids each dropping in ashes." Katie still had the picture in her mind, and she supposed she always would. Janine had a plastic bag partially filled, and one at a time she'd poured a small amount into each boy's hand and let him fling it off the side of the boat. Then, together, she and Al had emptied the bag. Janine had pulled Al tight and whispered, "Go, Dad, the oceans are yours forever."

"Thank you for supporting them. Al and the kids have

been important to me. Janine, our friend from all those years ago. We have to stick together." He had his head next to hers, and he rubbed her hair with his cheek.

"Or we have nothing." She murmured the words.

They were passing between Settler's and Rockhaven, and the tide was high. All the rock ledges were covered, and the sea had eaten the shoreline to the base of the trees. Then, Settler's Island disappeared behind the ferry, and more and smaller islands filtered by. Soon, they would pass the headland leading into Rockhaven Harbor, and they would be home.

As the town came into view, Katie looked for the church steeple. It had always been special. Now? It was hers.

"Look, Jeff, a cookout." Sure enough, a thin column of gray smoke twisted skyward not far from the church.

"I see." There was something else in his voice, though.

"What? Are cookouts not allowed?" She wanted to laugh at him, except that he wasn't laughing with her. "People do have cookouts on Sundays."

"That's from the park."

"The park?" There were no facilities for outdoor cooking at the park, just the gazebo, the tree the boys had helped her decorate, several granite benches, and a grassy expanse of lawn, now winter brown. "Who would be—"

"Hang on, Katie." Jeff had his phone out, and he put it to his ear. "Al, get up here. I think we have a fire in town." He listened a minute and replied, "Near the park. Do you want to call it in, or should I?" Then he said, "We're up front. Come decide for yourself."

"You think it's . . . serious?" Oh, Katie hoped not, not this close to Christmas. How horrible that would be, to lose your house right before the holidays truly got into swing! And there were houses right next to the park.

"It's not black." Jeff took a deep breath, pulling away from her when Al walked up to look at the rising smoke.

Katie understood. Wood burned clean. Fabrics and petroleum-based products didn't. If it was a house, it would burn black.

Al turned from the view, and he had a phone to his ear. One hand was in his hair, and he looked down. Someone must have picked up, because he raised his head and looked back toward town, pointing, as if whoever it was could see.

"Jeff?" She took his arm. "If it is a fire, what then?"

They were arriving at the landing, and Jeff exhaled loudly. "You go with Janine. Al and I'll take the Jeep. Better get in the truck before we finish docking." He kissed her and pulled out his keys, and he disappeared into the car.

Katie caught that he hadn't really answered her.

"Katie, is it anything?" Janine was just coming out of the passenger area. The boys were running for the truck, calling out claims on various seats.

"I'm riding with you." She shrugged. "Al's going with Jeff."

"Oh, not a fire now." Janine had her hand on the door handle, and she looked across the town. In front of her, the Jeep was already running. "Might as well climb in. We'll know when we know."

Across the water, a siren started up, and they could just catch sight of the town fire truck speeding down Main, with all lights flashing. A couple of trucks flew past after it, with one small and rusted station wagon bringing up the end.

"Al's a volunteer, right?" Volunteer fireman, Katie meant.

"Everyone is out here." Janine started the truck, and as Jeff's brake lights flashed, they watched him tear past the ramp—nearly level with the high tide—and across the empty lot. "Al's lead, though. I don't have a good feeling about this."

"Not the church, I hope. Can we drive by?"

"No choice." They had to drive by the church, unless they circled the entire island, but her words told that. Janine put the truck in gear and followed much more slowly than Jeff had exited.

"Mom," Kevie urged, "faster. I want to see the fire." He pointed over the seat to a rusted four-wheel-drive speeding by. "There's Chipper. He'll probably get tangled in the fire hose."

"Will not!" That was Konnar, and he yanked his brother back and began pummeling him.

"Boys." Janine shook her head and turned right towards town. The smoke was thicker, and it was lighter in color. "That's good. Look at that, boys. White smoke."

"Ah," came their disappointment from the back seat. "They'll have it out before we get there."

"Why is white good? Thicker smoke means the fire's bigger, doesn't it?"

"Not white. That's steam from the fire hose." Janine downshifted, and they turned the corner towards the Town Park down from the church.

The big red truck was there, with lights still flashing, and three men wore regulation fire-fighting equipment. Jeff, Al, and several other men were around, moving equipment and talking to concerned citizens. Cars lined the streets on both sides of the park, and half the gazebo was blackened.

"Cool!" That sounded like Karlton. "Look at that, Keithie. It almost burned down."

"What did?" It was a little boy's voice, meaning it was Keithie's.

"Goon, look!" That was Kevie. Something smacked, and Keithie yelped in response.

"Boys!" Janine said that sharply, and the noise quieted. "There's your father. Let me go find out what happened. Katie, do you mind waiting?"

Katie motioned her on. She watched Jeff, so much in control of the situation. As if people deferred to him, just because he was Jeff. Being minister might have something to do with that, or maybe people just liked him, and they knew he would step in and help out in whatever situation came about.

Kent from Harbor View crossed the street just in front, and Katie waved back when he lifted one arm to her.

As Jeff walked to the truck, he waved at her with a smile, and she rolled the window down.

"Hey, is it out?" She reached to take his hand, and she smiled when he squeezed it back.

He nodded and leaned into the truck, calling to the kids,

352

"Glad Santa got that garland up. It would have been toast left in the gazebo. Yea, Christmas." He shot the boys a thumbs-up sign.

"Could you tell what happened?" Katie could now see that one of the suited firemen was Roker. He'd removed his helmet, and he was talking with Chipper, she thought.

"Roker thinks electrical. There's an old plug around the back, but I'm thinking early fireworks. Dry leaves and a bottle rocket. It doesn't take much." He grinned. "I remember a few times I nearly started a fire or two."

"Oh, you do, do you?" Then it hit Katie. "That's where we planned the nativity. Jeff, it's next weekend."

"We'll find a place, but it's not as bad as it looks." He pulled her hand up to kiss it. "Only this side's burned. Maybe we could rename the holiday this year, call it Fired Up For Jesus."

"Ooh, kissy, kissy!" Keithie called it from the back seat.

"You'll think kissy, kissy." Jeff released Katie and pulled the back door open. He leaned in and pulled the four-year-old forward and planted very noisy raspberries all over his arms.

"Yuck!" he screamed, but all the boys were trying to push Jeff away, and it was more fun than anything else.

"Boys!" Janine climbed back inside, shaking her head at the scene in the back. "Al's heading to the firehouse to help clean up the truck. Jeff," she called over the seat, "Al said you can pick up Katie at our place. He'll catch a ride with you."

"Sure thing. You, boys, are lucky your mom's driving away. You, Karlton, were next in line." They squealed, and he laughed. "Bye, Katie. See ya'." He leaned over the seat and kissed her on the neck.

As they drove off, Janine thumbed the direction of the boys, and she said, "You know, Jeff can take any of these home anytime he wants. Al and I don't mind at all."

Katie laughed, but she would rather wait for one of their own. If it looked like Jeff, it would be the most beautiful child on the island.

353

She pressed on her stomach, feeling just a twinge of nausea. That fire, and at the gazebo. She guessed the success of the nativity worried her more than she thought. Oh, well, come Christmas, things would settle down, and she'd feel right as rain.

She felt something wet hit her neck, and pulling it off, she saw that it was a spitball. She turned, and narrowing her eyes, she said, in as stern a voice as she could muster, "Whose is this?"

Three of the boys pointed to Kevie. He shook his head, but he didn't point at anyone else, and with a wicked grin, Katie unsnapped her seatbelt, twisted around, reached over the seat, and grabbed Kevie's knee. Then she squeezed it, laughing when he began to beg for mercy.

When she sat back in her seat, she noticed Janine watching her. "What?"

"The ones Jeff doesn't want, you're welcome to." Janine grinned and turned her attention back to the road.

As much as she wouldn't have thought in July, Katie actually liked the boys. In small doses. Take them? No. To live with them would make them a pain in the neck. She wanted to be able to enjoy them instead.

"Thank you, Janine. They're good kids."

"Not really." Janine looked at her, and she laughed.

"Some of the time, maybe." Katie laughed with her.

"Like when they're asleep."

It was a good day, even with the burning of the gazebo, and Katie looked out the window, enjoying the sun shining on her face through the glass, and thanked God for friends like Al and Janine, and for her wonderful life on Rockhaven Island.

It was everything she'd hoped it would be.

14

Katie was bundled, and it was a good thing. She stood on the town wharf, and the wind whistled past her hood, doing its best to reach chilled fingers inside to nip at her ears.

The week since the fire had been a nightmare of mishaps, and she pushed them aside. Today? They had awakened to a brisk north wind, and the men in the church had decided it was perfect for racing sailing skiffs in the harbor.

Katie's take? They were crazy, and now, because they were crazy, she was frozen. Her nose, anyway. Even the knitted scarf she had around her face didn't cut out every bit of the wind.

"Look at that." Nina nudged Katie's arm. "Kent's been in the water three times, and he's still trying to win. If he gets himself sick, we may have to shut the restaurant down for a week."

"Maybe he should. You could use a vacation." Katie twisted to look at Nina, peering at her from her knitted cave. "Stay inside where it's warm. Now, that's a good vacation."

"You're right, there." Nina laughed. "Where's Winnie?

I thought you two were joined at the hip." Before Katie could respond, Nina grabbed her elbow and pointed to the water. "In red, that's Ada. She's beating all the men."

Sure enough, someone in a red waterproof suit sat astride a small craft with a tightly trimmed sail, and it flew across the waves, almost hidden in a blur of scattered spray.

"Ada Simpers?" Katie pulled her scarf down a bit to make sure she was heard. "From the market?"

"The same. She's a competitor, I tell you that. Often wins, too."

"I'm impressed." Katie was, and that was a fact.

"Thought you might be out there. I see Jeff. He couldn't talk you into it?" Nina had an impish look on her face, what could be seen of it.

"Haven't felt well." Katie touched her stomach. "Indigestion or something. It comes and goes." It had, too, and she had begun to suspect it was a long-term type of indigestion, the sort that comes from loving a man too much, and perhaps from not being careful enough.

"Ah," Nina said, in a knowing way. "Kent's and my children are long gone, but I've felt that way before. Have you been to the clinic?"

Katie noticed she didn't call it a hospital, and she smiled at that, but she didn't want suspicions to get out. If it wasn't what she suspected, well, this was a very small community, and she'd be fending off inquiries by the hour. They would all mean well, but she didn't want to go there.

"Shush." Katie put her finger to her lips. "We've got company—" half the town standing on the wharf watching "—and I'm not sure, so . . ." She left the rest unsaid.

"Speaking of company, there's some on the way." Nina pointed to Katie's side. "My lips are sealed. And, we're still on for Monday."

"Thanks, Nina." Katie gave her a quick hug. Monday was the Town Hall Banquet, and it hadn't come together yet for Katie. In fact, not at all. Winnie—globe-traveling fashion model—had poo-pooed her difficulties and said she knew what a good banquet needed. Katie should leave it in her very beautiful and capable hands. Then, somehow, Nina had offered hers and Kent's help, and Katie had felt just unwell enough that she'd had to let it go.

She was glad she did, too. She'd learned a Christmas Sunday children's musical was expected from the minister's wife, and even with parents volunteering to help, she'd struggled to keep ahead of that.

"I'm off to cheer on my husband. I'll be at the nativity tonight. Bye!" Nina waved and wandered off.

"Hey, Kevie." Katie put her gloved hand on his beanie-covered head. "Why are you not out there?" His three brothers were picking up small pieces of gravel and chucking them in the water, totally preoccupied in their own little worlds.

"Tonight. Mom said I might get sick." He shrugged, as if that was an excuse he didn't really mind.

"Tonight. You're still one of my wise men, then." She pulled her scarf down to speak, so he could see her smile.

"Yeah. You know, part of the plan." He shrugged again, but he grinned.

"Sunday, too? Lighting up the Christmas miracle?" She had given him a special job in Sunday's musical. A scary one, but a job she was sure he'd enjoy. It involved fireworks.

"Of course." His face lit up with a smile.

"Is the plan working?" It seemed so to Katie, her part of it, anyway. She had Kevie involved, and that's what she'd intended.

"Think so. Dad said he's never seen us be so good."

"Which one's your dad?" She pointed to the water. The boats were all over the place. Sometimes it seemed less a race than a mad cacophony of exuberant enthusiasm, but they all managed to round the turn markers and generally head in the same direction.

"See the Ninja Turtle? That's mine, and Dad's using it." He pointed, grinning broadly, clearly having fun with his father fighting for the prize underneath a Ninja Turtle banner.

"Oh, that's too good. I'll make sure Jeff never lets him forget it."

Katie looked up to see Nina back, with Jess from up on High Road. Jess carried a cup of steaming cocoa, and Nina had two.

"Thought you might like one." Nina held a cup out. "They've got more, Kevie. See Matt's mom. She's serving with Mrs. Boggs and Mrs. Swisher."

"Cool," he said, calling to his mother in a folding chair down the wharf, "Can I have hot chocolate?" He was running her direction as he said the words.

"Boys," Nina said, shaking her head. "Too much energy. Jess is here to cheer on Roker. I told her she needs to do more than cheer him on."

"Oh?" Katie had the drink in her hand, and she drew in the aroma. She wasn't sure drinking it would sit well, though, and she hesitated. "What should Jess do?" She pulled her scarf down, beginning to regret wearing it, as it wasn't really that warm, not with pulling it down so often, and she took a sip of the cocoa. She enjoyed the heat more than the flavor, and she kept her hands wrapped around it.

"Snag that man. He's been single too long." Nina grinned mischievously. Jess looked down and shook her head, but she smiled, too. "Back to your friend, Winnie. I got distracted by Ada a few minutes ago, and I apologize. Did she make it down today? I'd hate for her to miss the fun."

"There." Katie pointed down the town lot to where the front of Cousin Nikki's limousine could be seen just the other side of Jeff's Jeep. "She's keeping my cousin company. Staying warm, too." Katie grinned, but she was envious.

"Nikki? She's better?"

"Some." Word had been passed the previous weekend that she was having trouble getting around, and while she had Francois, Winnie and several of the townies had been spending time giving her attention and help when needed. Katie had run out with a casserole from Nina and a pie from Jess one afternoon, but with her stomach, she'd barely made it back home. After that, she'd given Winnie the keys to her car, and told her to make good use of it.

"Think sharp, ladies. They're heading in." Nina called it out, and the crowd's attention shifted to the water. Janine was standing, and all four of her boys were at the railing, cheering for their father.

The pending finale trumped all other discussion, and the entire wharf was riveted to the small boats jumping over the ragged whitecaps. Undulating tides of animated support burst forth when the occasional sail dipped into the churned froth.

Jeff was out there, but Katie hadn't tracked him well. He was in light gray, with a blue slash across his chest. It was a borrowed suit, and the boats were similar, generally with white sails and light-colored hulls. In the cacophony of motion, with the continual spray misting the scene, the boats sometimes disappeared from view.

Jeff had been lost to her most of the race.

"Roker!" Jess clapped excitedly. "There he is, in second!" She began to cheer him on to go faster.

"Daddy, Daddy," the youngest two Peaveys yelled, jumping up and down.

As the skiffs passed the finish line to the cheers of their respective supporters, one at a time they made their way to the town float at the end of the ramp. Neither Al nor Kent came in first, and Jeff didn't seem to be in the running. Ada Simpers took third. It was Roland Heyniger that claimed the blue ribbon, and on his arrival, his teenage daughter and two of her friends jumped up and down, hanging on his arms, squealing, and almost pulling him off balance.

What Katie didn't see was what began to worry her.

"Roker?" She pushed through and caught him on the arm. His face was flushed, but he glowed with excitement. Jess had an arm wrapped in his on the other side. "I can't find Jeff."

"Ah, not to worry." He laughed. "Jess and I are headed to pick him up. I was just telling Jess here, he went over at the far turn marker—"

"And he broke his rudder." Jess finished for him. She looked brighter and happier than she had since Katie had been on the island.

"The boat, I'm sure he tied it up at the Zwecker's. It's why I didn't finish first." Roker grinned and shrugged. "But you notice I didn't stay to help. I still wanted to win."

"That's Aidan's house, right?" It was at the end of a built-up jetty. Aidan and his wife Tatiana were summer residents that were at the wedding but gone two weeks later. The Zwecker's float was in, but their wharf would allow Jeff to moor the boat to a piling and make his way up the rock ledge that formed the original foundation for the jetty.

"Want to ride along? We'd haul the boat and bring it back, but in this weather, it'd be best to motor out and tow it in."

Even to Katie that made sense. The wind was whipping the waves into ice cream froth. Much stronger, and the race wouldn't have taken place at all.

It took longer to walk to Roker's truck than to drive to Aidan's. Jeff had hiked the 300 yards from the wharf to the drive beside the house, and he was huddled out of the wind on their porch, waiting. He waved when he saw Roker's truck making its way down the narrow street.

"Hey!" He threw himself into the seat and slammed the door after him. "Katie, nice." He took her hand and held it to his face. His suit was wet, although he would be dry on the inside, or mostly dry, as going in the drink would allow some water to penetrate even the tightest of seams.

"Second!" Roker held up two thumbs over the seat.

"You'd have been first if you hadn't slowed for me." Jeff clapped him on the shoulder. He began to peel his gray outer suit off. "I was okay. You should have gone on."

"He had Katie to think of." That was from Jess, and she glowed, with her eyes twinkling. "What would he say if you drowned, and he hadn't at least slowed down?"

"Aha, good friends, aren't we all? Slow down to watch the minister drown." Jeff grinned at Katie. "See what they think of me?"

"Just a jumpstart to the great sailboat race in the sky, that's all." Roker was turning his truck around, but it had four doors and a very long bed, and the road was very narrow. He'd already backed it up and pulled forward three times, and he called to Katie, "Mailbox, starboard side. Be my lookout."

They made it with Katie's precise instructions, and with Roker's careful driving, they were on their way back to the party. It would be a party, too. Most attendees at the race were gathering at Harbor View for cocoa, if they had other plans and couldn't stay long; and a late lunch, if they were hungry. Regardless, it would be warm inside, and after enduring the wind, warmth was what they needed.

For Katie it was more. She had asked the members of her nativity scene to stick around. They had the final plans to pull together, and a few costume details to stitch up. Also, with the wind, there had to be room under each costume for long johns, coats, and gloves. No one was catching pneumonia on her watch.

In addition, Katie wanted to see how the banquet was pulling together. It had been her baby, with decorations, a tree, and special music. She had planned to shine, bringing Boston glamour to the island year-rounders. With feeling ill, and Winnie "practicing her French" with Nicolette, she had no idea how things were coming along.

There was the limo, though, just down from Harbor View, and Katie was relieved. She missed Nikki, too, and she hoped to catch up with her. Roker let them out at the door.

"Save me a seat," he called with a wave as Katie shut her door.

It was indeed warm inside. Race attendees were sitting around in various-sized groups, four here, one long table with over a dozen, and in the back by the windows were Cousin Nikki, Winnie, and Francois. The chauffeur stood to the side, and at one point, he helped Nicolette adjust her chair.

"Ah, ma chère," Nicolette called out, when she saw Katie and Jeff walking up to the table. She held a hand to Katie and called again, "Ma chère, my little Katie. Come, a kiss."

"It's good to see you, Cousin Nikki. Has Winnie kept you good company in that big house?" Katie gave her the expected "air" kiss and hugged her by gently resting her hands on her shoulders.

"And so many others. I did not remember that I still know people who live here. It has been magnifique. How do you say, magnificent. I am sorry we do not see so much of each other, but, what shall we do? It is the way it is." She motioned Katie closer, and she reached a hand to touch her cheek. "You, I do think, must be very happy. You say unwell a few days past; I say very happy."

Katie was surprised at that. In English, unwell did not mean happy, and at this moment, she was feeling the qeasies quite strongly.

"She is. You know, happy." Jeff put his arm around her, and he chuckled. "Even if I didn't win."

"Last place." Roker was coming in, and he called it loudly. "Jeff didn't finish, and that's worse than last. She picked a loser." He grinned and pulled up a chair from an unoccupied table, then a second one for Jess.

"Says the loser who left me out there." Jeff laughed to those seated at the table when he said it. "A broken boat, and he sailed right on by."

"My, my!" Winnie's eyes were wide. "I thought you men were good friends. When did that change?"

"Ho, ho," Roker chortled. "Don't you worry about that. Rockhaven men change friends about as often as they change underwear. Jeff's stuck with me as long as he's on the island."

Katie had just pulled her chair up, and she dropped her forehead to the edge of the table. She was laughing so hard she thought she might cry.

"Roker! TMI. Now, look what you've done." Winnie patted Katie on the head. "He doesn't mean it, Sweetie."

Katie raised her head, still laughing, and she wiped her eyes. "No, it's picturing the stuck together part. It adds a whole new meaning to a man not changing his, um, well, you know."

Roker looked mystified. "TMI? What does TMI mean?"

Jess was bright red, and Cousin Nikki? She had her lips

pursed, and if anything, Katie would have said she was fighting a smile of her own. However, she couldn't stay to find out, because her stomach did a flip-flop, and she had to run straight for the ladies' room.

"Katie?" Winnie went after her, calling, "Katie? I promise, Roker didn't really mean it."

Katie did make it, if barely, her queasy tummy spoiling what could have been a very nice lunch. At least, there was one good thing. One sip of cocoa wasn't much, so there wasn't much to come up, and for that, she was truly grateful.

15

"Roker, you are the most handsome Joseph I've ever seen." He was, too. Being a bit rough and burly fit perfectly with the shepherd persona he was to portray. Katie thoroughly approved.

"Thank you. I never expected to find myself in a dress, though." He growled the words, shaking his head. "Wearing an Arab hat, too."

Roker had a striped, loose-sleeved costume on over his heavy winter gear, and a contrasting cloth on his head, secured with an elastic rope. He was perfectly in character, and Katie wouldn't listen otherwise.

"Have you seen Jackie?" Jackie Schutmaat was scheduled in for the role of Mary, and Katie hadn't seen her. At lunch earlier, she hadn't given any indication she'd be late. Off to one side, Jeff knelt, adjusting Konnar's shepherd robe. She called to him, "Jeff, have you seen Jackie?"

Before he could answer, someone else called to Katie.

"Me! Me! I'm Jackie for the night." It was Jess, running up in a snowsuit, with mittens on her hands. She carried her costume, one in three blocked colors: an inner robe, an outer one, and a headpiece similar to Roker's. "Tom's under the weather, and Jackie asked me to trade. I had to stop by and pick it up."

"You two get baby Jesus and wrap him up for the manger. Make sure only his face shows. We don't want him to get frostbite." Baby Jesus was a life-sized doll, and it was in a sack next to the gazebo.

"How's it coming?" Jeff came up behind her and put his arms around her. "I see your angel's ready to go. The gazebo's not too bad, is it?"

Winnie was the angel. With her halo hair, she was perfect, as if she did indeed have an angelic aura surrounding her head. Her complaints before Katie convinced her to take the job? Not so angelic.

The gazebo, with its half-burned structure, was unrecognizable. It was now draped with fabric, in undulating swathes, much as a Middle-Eastern tent might look. One section was pulled back, revealing steps leading into the unburned section, and the inside was illuminated. The entire structure glowed.

There was activity all over the park, and the areas where people were working were lighted by gas-powered lanterns or car lights. The Swishers had goats, and three of theirs were staked on the grass. Babbitt George, Brookie's father, owned a horse he rented out in the summer, and it was in a blanket near the curb, hobbled to keep it from wandering off. Babbitt was off moving the trailer out of view, so as not to ruin the effect. Brookie had a curry comb out, and he brushed at the animal's flanks.

Katie heard a generator start up, and numerous floodlights winked on, shining where the individual characters would be standing. She had called on Kevie to help her stake out everyone's position that afternoon, and Al had come up to position the lights. He disappeared into the gazebo and came out with a portable lantern, turning a dial and extinguishing the flame. The tented structure still glowed, so Katie knew a light had been installed in there, also.

She had some concerns about the weather. During the sailboat races, the sky had been clear, with full sun. The wind had brought in clouds that afternoon, and the sky had turned murky. The air was still, but it was bitter. If it rained, they would have to move everything to the Town Hall, and the night was specially planned as a drive-through nativity. No one had to get out of their cars; just drive by and enjoy the experience. The Town Hall was a viable option, but only if they wanted half the attendees.

"Please, God." Katie looked skyward, even though it was dark, and she couldn't see anything. "No rain. Please, no rain."

"And if it does, Tinka's brought a basket of ponchos and umbrellas. We'll be fine." Jeff's voice whispered his assurances in her ear. Tinka was Rod DiLalla's wife. Rod ran a lobster boat—as did Jeff—as well as attended Rockhaven Town Church.

"You eternal optimist." Katie patted one side of his face with her hand.

"The eternal optimist needs to check on the camel. We'll see if it works." He kissed her cheek and moved off towards the horse.

Katie knew the story behind the camel. It was the George's horse. A special saddle had been rigged with a foam topper, and a brightly colored sheet would be its disguise. It wasn't exactly a camel, but as close as they could come on a murky and cold Saturday evening in December Maine.

She actually thought it was funny. The goats? Those were a good substitution. They'd considered a cow to stand in for the ox, but good sense had taken hold, and that was the reason for the goats. Cows tended to leave gifts, and cleanup afterward had to be considered.

Jeff clapped his hands loudly, and he called, "Attention, everyone. It's about to start. Fifteen minutes."

Sure enough, just where Main turned into Round the Island Road, two cars waited behind a sawhorse barricade, their parking lights on and their engines running. The night's presentation already had guests, and everyone wasn't in place.

Katie searched out Winnie. "Honey, is there anything

you need before we start?"

"A hot tub?" She smiled, but it was a pleading smile, not a happy one. "It's cold out here."

"You did wear your gloves?" Katie lifted the sleeve of the angel costume to see that her friend did indeed have substantial gloves on her hands. "Long johns? You remembered those?"

"Two pair." Winnie bounced up and down. "Maybe I can warm up like this. Look out. Incoming."

"Keithie!" Katie turned just in time to catch him. The small boy grabbed Katie's leg and hid behind her. "Hey, say hello to our angel. Who do you think this is, Michael or Gabriel?"

"Don't care. Keep Karlie away."

The other brother came running up, and tried to grab at Keithie's arm. Katie held up her hand. "No, he's with me. You know Kevie and Konnar are shepherds, tonight."

"Want a real Jesus." That was Keithie, and it was muffled into Katie's leg.

"But Jesus is here." Katie knelt and tapped on the boy's chest. "We can't take him out of here and put him there. That's why we use the doll, instead."

"Don't care. Want baby Jesus."

"Karl, would you want to sleep in your crib, again?" Katie had a tactic in mind, one that hopefully would answer the smaller boy's concerns as well as alleviate whatever they were fighting over.

"That's stupid. That's for babies." He snorted in disgust.

"So, Keithie, do you think Jesus feels the same? He was a baby, and he grew up. He doesn't want to be a baby again."

"Okay," he mumbled. "You're it." He tore off after his brother, leaving Katie wobbling.

"Winnie?" She held out her hand. "Help me up?"

"Okay, Sweetie. It's time to get me in place. Help me with my ladder?" Winnie smiled. She pointed down the street to where more parking lights glowed, and they watched, another car pulled up and dowsed its driving lights. "We've got more tourists, and I want my angel to be real."

It was simple to do. The two pulled a stepladder from the gazebo and opened it, setting it up just behind the manger. The baby Jesus was already inside, and his smiling face was their point of reference. When they were sure the baby would be looking at Winnie, they tossed a sequined cloth over the ladder, and spread the extra fabric out over the ground, giving it the effect of a snow-covered mountain.

"Let me help you up." Katie held a hand out to steady her friend.

"Coming down might be the problem." Winnie hiked her white angel robes up to reveal jeans and heavy outdoor boots. "Unless I fall, then you can put me back together again."

"You're not Humpty Dumpty, so quit whining. Just sit still once you're up there, and it'll be fine. Is Nikki coming?" That was to distract Winnie. "She looked tired at lunch."

"I hope so. She's my ride home." Winnie was to the top, and she'd let go of Katie's hand. "Make my skirts pretty."

"If I can take your shoes off. Here, let me pull this down." Katie yanked at the bottom edge of the costume to get it to cover the boots, causing the ladder to wobble in the process.

"Careful." Winnie slapped her hand away. She reached in a pocket and handed Katie her phone. She smiled brightly. "I need to post a picture. Take a pretty one of me as an angel."

"Not really possible." Katie backed up, turning the phone on and pulling up the camera icon. "Does this phone have an angel app?"

"Angel app? Sweetie, just take the picture."

"No, I've seen them. You take a picture of someone, and the app adds a background, like Santa or a scuba diver. You said you wanted an angel picture, and that's the only way I can think to do it."

"Oh, you. I am an angel. Already. Now take it and give

it back. I want to post this before the train starts." She put her hands on the top of the seat and smiled prettily.

"Smile." Katie held the phone up.

"I am. Take it." Winnie's words sounded forced.

"Bigger!"

"Katie!"

A hand reached over her shoulder and tapped the icon to take the picture. "Done. Five minutes. I'm moving in the camel now."

"Thanks, Jeffie. Phone, Katie." Winnie held out her hand.

As the characters moved into place, the spotlights making them seem more than just townies wearing hokey costumes, Katie was filled with satisfaction. One thing. Just this one thing had finally come together, and if she could get this to work successfully, surely Christmas would happen right on key.

"Hey, how's the tummy?" It was Nina, and she reached to pat Katie's stomach. "Any more incidents?"

"Not since lunch, and thank you for not saying anything." Katie smiled. "This is pretty. The whole town's come together to do this, and just wow!"

"You've pulled us together to do this." Nina took her hand and patted it. "Thank you. Oh, there's Kent, about to move the barricade. Looks like Roland's got the other one. It's showtime."

The spouses and others who had helped set up were gathered across the street from the park. Nina had provided more of her eggnog cocoa, and it steamed in several hands The remaining lanterns still burning were extinguished, leaving little more than glowing eyes where their mantles still cooled. The only lights were on the nativity characters and baby Jesus, with the glowing, tented gazebo in the background.

"Oh, Nina. I had no idea it would be so beautiful." Katie felt tears come to her eyes. "Do you really think everyone will love it?"

Darting across the road, the two youngest Peaveys ran into the park, yelling, "It's really Christmas. Yea!" Al chased after them, pulling them back across the street, as they yelled, "Hi, Kevie! Look at you, Konnar!"

"Somebody does. Before I forget, I picked up something for you at the market. Here." Nina pulled a fist-sized box from her coat pocket, and she slipped it in one of Katie's pockets. She patted Katie's stomach again. "Just so you know for sure. I'm headed off to stand by Kent. Congratulations for this. It's all due to you, and don't think we don't appreciate it."

Katie watched her walk away. She had intended to grill her on what was happening with the Town Hall Banquet, but it had gotten away, and now she was gone. Somehow, she didn't trust Winnie to pull this off.

She pulled out the box enough to recognize what it was before slipping it back inside. She closed her eyes and shook her head. This was what she didn't want to happen. Still, Nina had been very discreet, and as she said, this way she would know for sure.

Jeff walked to her as the first cars began to pull by, their parking lights on and their headlights off. He wrapped one arm around her. "You did it."

"Not by myself." She pulled his arm tighter. "Look," she pointed. "I think it's snowing." Small flakes were starting to fall, and already, several cars had wipers undulating across their windshields.

"For you. That's God's way of saying Merry Christmas."

"It is, is it?" She smiled, wondering what made him say that. It was sweet of him, no matter.

It was only minutes before the wind began to pick up, and the snow increased by a power of ten. The dead grass was soon crusted with white, and the fabric on the gazebo flapped with enthusiasm. The participants in the nativity were holding their robes around them, and the goats bleated incessantly. Katie thought the sound effects, if anything, were on the money, but the snow? Maybe it had snowed in long-ago Bethlehem. If so, this was the most accurate nativity she'd ever seen.

They actually held it together for forty-five minutes.

Anyway, by that time, there were no more cars, and the road had disappeared under the snow. Katie fought the wind as she helped Winnie to the ground, only to have the ladder blow down and tumble against the gazebo as soon as it was vacated.

Securing all the nativity equipment was a nightmare, and by the time they had things in place, Katie was almost in tears.

Not even the nativity had gone right, and it had started out perfectly. Would Christmas fall apart, too? What else could go wrong?

Even Winnie ran off and left her, headed back to the big house on the hill with her Cousin Nikki.

It was riding home with Jeff when she went to put her gloves in her pocket and remembered the box from Nina. She was glad it was dark, because all it did was make her want to cry.

Pregnant, and at Christmas? How would she get everything done?

16

Sunday morning, and the wind whistled off the water. Snow still whipped the landscape just outside the window. Katie hadn't felt like eating, and she was cold even with the oil heater running full tilt.

"Jeff, you're sure we'll have services in this?" She turned to him, both wanting to stay inside and watch the storm from the protection of her window-filled room, and knowing the importance of the children's program that was the entire morning service.

"No one's called in and bailed. Islanders are a tough bunch." He leaned in from the bedroom, his shirt undone, and two layers of long johns showing underneath. "Besides, it's supposed to clear. Weatherman's promised."

"You are a Mainer through and through." She smiled. She supposed her words could be interpreted to mean his pragmatic attitude, but she had noticed the long johns.

"Oh, what gives you that idea?" His words came through with a laugh.

"You know how to stay warm." Even so, she was bundled up in about as many clothes. Her legs would be exposed during the service, but she had heavy leg socks with open feet ready to pull over them for the ride to

372

church.

She should give in to pants and insulated outerwear, but she hadn't bridged that gap, yet. Sunday mornings were for fine clothes, dressing up in the best one owned, and showing God's glory to the world. At least that had been her world in Boston. Services at Trinity had sparkled with diamonds, gold chains, and designer boutique finds across the auditorium.

Today was all about mufflers and scarves, and trying to stay warm.

"I like it when it does this." Jeff stepped up behind her, wrapping her in his arms, and kissing her on the temple. The wintry scene beyond the warmth of the glass looked out across Moffat Cove, and past the dock extending into the water. The tree filled with Katie bows shivered in the wind. Jeff's boat moored farther out rocked, pulling against its mooring, fighting the thick, gray water. It was barely visible in the sideways-driven snow. "As long as I don't have to take my boat out."

"Tonight? Will you cancel?" She didn't have to explain her question. Out in the boat, she meant. Jeff would get that, as this was the biggest, most important boating event of the year. For Jeff, at least, even if no one else was out.

"Hardly." He kissed her again, before withdrawing to continue dressing for the morning services.

Katie sighed. She wanted tonight to happen, and she wanted to go along, as Mrs. Claus. It was Jeff's yearly Santa tour. He put a lighted tree on the boat, filled it with candy and gifts donated and wrapped by diligent church members, and motored around the island to all the docks that were lighted and had waiting carolers singing. He pulled the small gifts from the tree to hand to the carolers.

Last year he'd finished after midnight, Ada Simpers had warned. She had a summer cabin on Otter's Reach, and she'd been one of the last. She hoped he got to her earlier this year.

Her phone rang, and she stepped to her purse to pull it out. "Katie, here."

"Hi, Sweetie. It's snowing! How exciting! I can see the

whole island from here."

"I can see my tree from here. So, you like the snow. Stay through February, and I'm told you'll get all you want for a lifetime." Katie smiled. She pictured Winnie jumping up and down with excitement, and it lifted her spirits.

"Are the kiddies still doing their thing at church? You see, I kinda promised Nikki, and she's been in there all morning with Francois choosing her most Christmassy ensemble." She whispered, "I suggested a Rudolph sweater we found under the stairs, but I don't thinks Nikki's into sweaters."

"I wouldn't think so. As far as the musical, Jeff says yes. We're about to leave. Do you have my quiz questions from last Sunday?"

"I didn't think you were serious." Winnie giggled. "Besides, I've been doing Christmas stuff, so who's worried about an old quiz? Oh, there's Nikki." She sounded like she covered the phone and called out, "That's beautiful. Everyone loves candy canes." She whispered back to Katie, "Rudolph would be more fun, but I think she's wearing a Sorbier. I've always wanted to model a Sorbier. Nikki's so lucky."

"Rich is the word. What's Sorbier?" It sounded like an ice cream drink.

"Oh, you poor girl. You really need to come on a fashion shoot with me. He's French haute couture with a capital H. Oh, look, Francois has on real clothes. I think he's coming, too. Isn't that exciting? Nikki says she used to attend services at your church, and she wants to check out your honey. That's Jeffie, if you didn't know. What do you want to do this afternoon?"

"Who's that?" Jeff stepped from the bedroom, pulling a tie around his neck. With the morning's musical, he was excused from his ecumenical robes this week, and it was his chance to show he did own a tie. Normally, it was casual wear under the robes.

"Winnie." Katie covered the mouthpiece. "She won't slow down. I did get one thing from her. Do we have plans this afternoon? She wants to do something."

"I have to deliver my gifts. I am Santa, after all." He grinned, adding, "Mrs. Claus."

"What time do you start?" She uncovered the phone. "Hold a minute, Honey. We're discussing this. We're working around Jeff's Christmas plans."

"Three-ish, but I have to have time to get dressed and the boat loaded. That means I should be back here by half past one. Lunch, then?" Jeff was pushing the knot of his tie to his neck. He nodded the direction of the phone, indicating Winnie. "Ask her if she wants to be an elf."

He laughed at that.

"Do you speak elf?" Katie grinned, speaking into the phone. "Santa and Mrs. Claus need a helper to deliver presents."

"Another Christmas party? How exciting! Where's it at?"

"On Jeff's boat, and on every dock that has carolers out waiting."

"Oh." Winnie sounded disappointed. "We don't have a dock, or a boat. I don't guess we can come." Cousin Nicolette didn't have a dock or boat was what Winnie meant.

"No, you ride on Jeff's boat, and we deliver presents to other people's docks. It'll be fun!" Katie made sure not to mention the blowing snow and overcast skies. While the snow was beautiful outside, and it might give them a white Christmas, without the sun, the wind would carry a bite. She tried to sound bright and encouraging. "You could hand out the gifts."

"You could have it here. There's plenty of room." Winnie's lack of enthusiasm for being a Christmas elf on a Maine lobster boat was apparent.

"Okay, Honey. Wimp out, if you want. But you'll be at church to see the musical?" Katie got the message.

"Time, Katie." Jeff interrupted as he pointed to his watch, and he draped his overcoat across one arm.

"We have to go. Be there. Promise?" Katie moved away from the window, snatching her thick leg socks from the chair on her way to the door.

"Both of us. Miss you, Sweetie. I'm so excited about lunch!" And she clicked off the phone.

"Where are we going?" Jeff lifted Katie's long coat and held it for her to put on.

"Oh! I didn't ask." Katie looked at her purse, and the phone she'd just dropped inside. "I could call her back . . ."

"We only have about three choices, anyway." Jeff smiled, twisting his shoulders in a shrug.

"Harbor View, I know." Katie laughed. "The others?"

By then, she had her coat on, and she turned to Jeff and rested her forearms on his shoulders, looking into his face. He was so handsome, and in his suit, who'd ever picture him out on a lobster boat, trolling for traps, and hauling lobsters from the depths of the ocean?

"Here." He pulled her to him, and he kissed the end of her nose. "However, if we're coming back here, no one else is invited." He kissed her nose again. "I want you all to myself."

"I already promised." She enjoyed his attentions, though. "Besides, I don't have anything prepared."

"If we're here, you don't need anything prepared. We won't have time to eat, anyway."

"Oh, you!" She slapped one shoulder. "What else do men think about? We'd better head out, lover boy, if we want to be on time. If we don't go now, we'll be late for meet-and-greet."

"They'll understand." He kissed her this time on the corner of her mouth.

"Not." She did kiss him back, though, and she didn't miss.

17

"Debsy, you hold this, and when Joseph says, It's a boy, you wave it high in the air."

Katie was presenting the children's musical *The Bethlehem Star*, and Debsy was the star. Rather, she would be holding the star. She was dressed in a silvery angel costume, with a tinsel halo, and all she had to do was walk behind the manger and hold her glittered foam star on a stick.

However, the girl just didn't seem to understand what Katie wanted her to do.

The rest of the cast was on the other side of the makeshift curtains stretched across the front of the church, already acting out their performance before the church members. Katie and Debsy were still hidden from view, and the musical was winding down. Katie could hear the events she couldn't see. Little J and the two youngest Peaveys formed the rest of the star brigade already standing around the manger, but Debsy was the piece de résistance. Her star was five times the size of the others, and it would lead the shepherds and the wise men to the baby Jesus.

Debsy had to get this right.

"I need to potty, Miss Katie." Debsy put her hands over

herself and began to jump up and down. She called it out rather loudly, and scattered laughter could be heard from the audience on the other side of the curtain. Most of them had seen at least one rehearsal, and they had a pretty good idea of what was coming next, as well as who was playing the part. Debsy didn't have a quiet voice, or a subtle presentation, not at three.

"Now?" Katie held the child's face and whispered her question. "It's your time to go on."

"I can't hold it. I can't wait." She continued to dance.

Katie glanced up to see Kaylene Watson-Striker, Debsy's mother, peering around the end of the curtain.

"Miss Katie, I'll take her." She motioned to the girl with her hand, and Debsy took off running, her silver angel costume billowing around her legs.

Now Katie was in a pickle. The music was building again, and it was to the part where the lights would fade, and the sparkler team—incidentally made up of her tree-decorating boys, led by Kevie—would run in waving sparklers over the manger to simulate the miraculous power of God come to earth, and not so incidentally, to disguise the moment of the birth of Christ. It was a kids' musical, after all. Then, Debsy's part was to march to the back of the manger, raising her star for everyone to see. Without it, the wise men wouldn't know to start their march.

The lights dimmed, and Katie cringed. This was the critical part of the morning, the one thing she'd included that would be a blinding success, or her total downfall. The sparklers had been her idea, and she had no idea how they would play out. It was Kevie, after all, leading the festivities.

The room brightened, flickering, and at the laughter of the crowd, Katie knew the fireworks were on the way. She waited for Debsy, wondering if she would be brave enough to make it backstage in the onslaught of darkness. Probably not, Katie surmised, preparing to stand in for her part. That's what a director was for, and the kids wouldn't think it too odd. She'd filled in as the Star of the East in most of the rehearsals.

The fireworks burned themselves out, and as the lights came back on, Katie stepped through the curtain holding her star high. There was scattered applause, and one, "Where's Debsy?" from the auditorium, but the shepherds, two of them carrying stuffed animals, and the third dragging his by a plastic leash, came up one side of the church. On the opposite aisle, the Wise Men trudged along in ten-year-old pomp and glory.

As the final members of the cast gathered around the manger, Katie felt a tug on her dress. She looked down to see Debsy holding her hands up for her glitter star. Off to the side, Kaylene waved with a smile and headed back to her seat. Gratefully, Katie passed on the star, and moved the curtain aside to disappear backstage.

She was relieved when the announcer read, "And the Bethlehem Star leads the faithful, even today, unto Christ." The lights went down, and applause started, with one or two call-outs from the crowd.

Katie was glad it was over.

When the lights came up, she worked her way back through the curtain to announce that as soon as the cast members were out of their costumes, they were free to go, and to thank all the parents for coming out in such blustery weather.

"I think I liked the first angel better." Jeff stepped to her, still in his suit.

"You did?" Katie knew just what he meant, and she smiled. There would be no enduring kisses offered or taken in church, but his smile told his feelings.

"Go," Jeff told her. "Bryan's promised to help for a few minutes, and we'll look after this. Your friend's in the back chatting up Roker. Go save him." He grinned, pointing. Sure enough, Winnie and her strawberry halo obscured part of Roker's face.

"He's a big boy. Is Jess helping out at the restaurant?" If she was, that's where they were going, and they were making sure Roker was with them. After Winnie's matchmaking at their house, those two weren't going to be allowed to go their separate ways.

Bryan stepped up with a canvas bag, and he held it out to Jeff and Katie, sort of like a peace offering. "Can we start? The wife wants to get home to lunch before long."

"Katie, we'll be just a minute. I'm sorry." Jeff leaned in and gave her a quick kiss, and he turned back to the stage and began working the curtains to the side.

Katie wasn't sorry. She had worked with the church women to put it all together. She was happy to have someone else pull it apart. Kern, one of her sparkler boys, was sitting on the third row, probably waiting on his mother, and he had a small ball he bounced continually on the floor.

"Kern, how'd the sparklers go? I was behind the, um—" She pointed behind her, to the men taking the curtains down. "—and I didn't have a very good view."

His face lit up. "It was cool, Miss Katie. Nobody's ever let us have fireworks in the church before. Paulo and Kevie and Jeremy and me want to do a Fourth of July show, too."

"You do?" Katie laughed. She bet they would. "I'm glad you had fun. You boys have been the best, with the tree, and everything. Are you planning on caroling for Santa tonight?"

Not everyone on the island lived on the water, and Kern was one who didn't. His parents lived on a hill up on Second, with a greenhouse they maintained year round. However, just like everyone on the island, people who didn't live on the water invariably knew someone who did.

Those who didn't, or more likely, who were on the outs with those who did, could show up at the town float on Main. That was available to everyone, no matter how well they got along with their neighbors, and if they were singing, it would be one of Jeff's stops.

"Brookie's dad said me and him could stay the night with Kevie." He grinned as if that were a big deal. "Mom said thank goodness."

"Kern?" His mother called from the back. Unlike her slender son, she was stout, a true Mainer. From Down East, she liked to brag, as if the hardiest Mainers came from there.

Katie supposed they did. She understood the weather was more brutal there than here, but it seemed to Katie she was still a Flatlander, and those in the interior could better lay claim to be called the toughest residents in the state. Still, Kern jumped when she called, waving to Katie, and with a "Bye," he was gone.

It was Nicolette in the foyer who seemed to be the Grand Dame of the morning.

"Merveilleux, my little Katie." Nikki held her hands out for a kiss from her only niece.

"You are so kind, Nikki." Katie reached to her and gave her the perfunctory pseudo kiss. She touched the very puffy sleeve of her dress in admiration. It was flamboyant in a crisp and festive red and white. Katie understood the candy cane reference from earlier. "You are beautiful this morning. I understand this is a Sorbier. Do you know the designer?"

"Oui." Nikki smiled, looking very pleased. "C'est un très bon ami."

"Help me out, Cousin." Katie laughed. "I didn't catch that."

"I know!" Winnie had her hand up, and she came running to join in the conversation. Her interjection caused Nicolette to smile.

"Sure, Honey. You can barely say bon appétit. No cheating, either." Katie looked to her cousin, to see her with her hand held just in front of her lips.

"She said he's a good friend. See? I am smart." Winnie beamed.

"Nikki?" Katie couldn't believe this.

"Oui, ma chère. Franck and I, we have known the other for a very long time." Nikki waved one hand dismissively, as if it were a matter of no real interest.

When Katie and Winnie got to themselves, Katie pulled on her sleeve and demanded an explanation. "You, Honey, do not know French. How did you know what Nikki said?"

"And you, Sweetie, do not know designers. How did you know that was a Sorbier?" She tossed her head flippantly, and she had a superior smirk on her face.

"Um, I asked . . . you."

"Sorry. I'd forgotten. Besides, what do you think Nikki and I talked about all the way to the church? Clothes, Sweetie. I wear them, and she buys them, all the best designs. So, there. Who's smart, now?"

Katie had a pretty good idea. She had open-footed knitted socks for her legs, and Winnie sported bare ankles. Winnie might shout fashion, but Katie wouldn't get frostbite.

Before she could point that out, Jeff and Bryan appeared from the auditorium, Bryan carrying the bag, now stuffed with the curtains, and Jeff holding the wooden manger, now folded flat. As they exited, the auditorium lights went dark, leaving the interior of the main building shimmering in the muted glow filtering through the stained glass windows.

Bryan set his bag in the corner, and pulling a heavy coat on, he said his farewells and was gone out the door. Jeff leaned the manger against the bag, and he adjusted the thermostat to its lowest setting.

"Ready for lunch?" He clapped his hands together with a smile. "Make sure you have everything. I'm locking up until next Sunday."

Katie was ready for lunch. When she stepped outside, she was pleased that the wind had died down. Except for the tracks left by the cars pulling in and out of the lot, and hard, compressed snow covering the street, everything was coated with white. Even the damage to the gazebo was hidden in the falling snow's sifted-flour wonderland.

"Apportez la voiture." Nicolette spoke the words quietly to Francois, who was in a plain suit rather than his uniform. He nodded and made his way outside.

Katie got that one. Francois was the chauffeur, and they were leaving. She expected her cousin had sent her driver to bring the car to the door.

It was only moments until tires could be heard crunching through the parking lot snow. Katie whispered to Winnie, "She told him to bring the car."

"Silly. I already knew that. It's what she says every

382

time we go anywhere."

Katie huffed, but she wasn't angry. She was very pleased. Her best friend and her only blood relation had found a connection, and they were getting along like chums. Now if she could get Roker and Jess to wrap things up, life on the island would be cheery indeed.

And to think, three months before, she'd been stressed about leaving her Boston life behind. It didn't seem she was missing it much. Instead, it seemed Rockhaven life was exactly what Katie had been born for.

Katie was convinced as she had never been before. Rockhaven was her home, right where she wanted to be.

18

It was the sun breaking through the clouds that decided Katie she would play the part of Mrs. Claus with Jeff on the boat.

Being at Harbor View had helped.

Leaving the church, the sky had been thick, and the snow had blanketed the car all the way to lunch. Katie had ridden with her cousin and her friend, enjoying the unusual comfort of a pre-warmed vehicle, and the space that only a limousine could provide. As Francois moved out and onto the street, the big vehicle hushed the world outside, and Katie could have believed they were back in big-city Boston once more.

The landscape outside the windows told the difference. Spruce branches loaded with snow hugged the ground, and the houses along the way hunkered down, with great, thick roofs of cottony white. You didn't see that in Boston.

"Nikki? Are you feeling well?" Katie took her hand and squeezed it gently.

Once in the car, Cousin Nikki seemed to wilt. Although giving her a glamorous and poised appearance at the church, now her haute couture Sorbier served to highlight the contrast between the cutting-edge magnificence of the outfit and the elderly woman who wore it.

"Ah, ma chère." With her free hand, Nicolette patted the top of Katie's. "We feel so well as we choose to feel, is not it so? To answer, non. Cousin Nikki seems to have exhausted her day."

She smiled wanly and looked out the window, releasing Katie to place her hands in her lap.

Katie looked at Winnie to see her mouth, "She tires easily." Then Winnie pulled out her phone, and indicated Katie should do the same.

"Sweetie, it's been like this all week." The words appeared on Katie's screen when she tapped the text message icon. Then a sad-face icon appeared. "I haven't told you because I know how busy you are, and you haven't felt so well yourself." Winnie looked up and grinned impishly at Katie, patting her tummy twice.

"I've felt just fine today." Katie typed her reply text hard onto her screen, annoyed at the suggestion. However, even as she did, she was aware of why little Debsy had irritated her so much. She had felt just what Winnie suggested, and she hadn't yet used Nina's gift. She wasn't sure she wanted to know. Not for certain. Not with Christmas coming in two days.

She tossed her phone back into her purse and turned to the window. The harbor appeared, and she realized the snow had stopped, and out across the ocean, lighter breaks in the clouds suggested the weatherman might be right for at least once this season. Wouldn't it be wonderful to have Jeff's Santa jaunt to come off perfectly this year? Especially if she intended to be aboard.

Nicolette didn't stay for lunch, with Francois explaining in fractured English that he must get Miss Nikki to rest, as the weather had absorbed her fuel. He only used three words, and Katie thought he meant the weather had sapped her energy, but the message was clear. She and Jeff would be taking Winnie either home with them or out to Nicolette's place. And it would be in the Jeep, because Katie's car was out there.

The Jeep had two doors, and Winnie could be the one to

crawl over the seat and ride in the back. That was how Katie felt about that, and she had told Winnie so during lunch, only afterward realizing she had been irritated about her friend's insinuation in her text, and she had apologized for being curt.

Now Katie looked out into Moffat Cove to see her Katie tree firmly mounted to Jeff's boat, and he and Roker were attaching lights to the branches with plastic zipper ties. A box of small gifts was at their feet to hang on the tree. The cove was like glass, and all around, the snow on the shore made everything taller, thicker, puffier. Whiter, too, just like on a Christmas card. It was the perfect winter wonderland. It also made the red on the Katie ribbons stand out like a jolt of electricity, a series of glowing firebrands punching through the cotton candy to draw one's attention to the brightly wrapped presents that would soon adorn the tree.

Katie turned from the view and perused her clothing on the foot of the bed. She had every set of long underwear in her chest out, plus three pairs of socks, and an insulated jumper. She smiled at the array. Mrs. Claus would be a plump Mrs. Claus tonight. Her dress, a long, heavy, red affair borrowed from the Town Hall storage room, would have fit a person three times Katie's build. It was, she thought, literally, one size fits all. It came with a wide black belt to resolve that, and anyway, she would be hiding behind the tree most of the time.

It was Winnie's green elf outfit that was the humorous one. It came complete with oversized, green-striped shoes with long, curved tips, to slip over her own more cold-weather-appropriate footwear. Winnie had ranted, but Katie had been very matter-of-fact. Her friend didn't have a car, as she had left Katie's out at Nikki's, and Jeff had to be home by half past one. Oh, and we're stopping by the Town Hall to get my Mrs. Claus costume, and when I was in last week, I just happened to see a green elf suit hanging next to it.

The elf costume had an equal amount of room inside, as it was usually worn by Roker, who needed ample space for his ample waistline.

The sound of the living room door that opened to the deck brought her back to the moment.

"Katie, we're about ready." The door closed with a firm thud, and the sound of feet on the wood floor said Jeff was inside.

"You don't know how much I appreciate this, Katie." That was Roker's voice, and it said he was also inside.

Jeff appeared in the doorway, and he glanced back into the other room with a grin before turning back to her. "I told him he owes us big time. I think we might get about two cords of firewood for this."

"You had better thank Winnie." Katie called it loudly, to make sure Roker heard. She walked to Jeff, running her hands inside his coat where he was especially warm, and hugging him. "He'd better, too. Otherwise, I might lose her for a friend."

"She'll have fun. By the time we get back, she'll be glad she went, and no way could we ask for better weather. No wind, plenty of sun, and lots of people looking forward to our visit." He chuckled and rubbed his hands over her back. "I love you, my Dame Katie. To find a woman who would enjoy this as much as I do, well, that took God, and I'm glad he brought you to me."

"Hey," she said, pushing away from him. "I get you out of the deal. I think we're pretty even."

"Oh, no," and he pulled her back. "We're not done here, yet."

"Oh?" She looked up at him, gazing into his eyes.

"Come on. Say it." He grinned.

Katie knew what he meant. His Dame Katie? He was teasing her in the most endearing way, and he liked to be teased in return. She tapped him with her knuckle on the forehead just between his eyes, and she said, "I love you, too, Preacher Jeff. Now, though, Mrs. Claus has to get insulated, or she'll be in the hospital tomorrow with a bad case of frostbite."

She pushed away, and she stepped into the living room, calling loudly, knowing it would carry up the stairs,

"Winnie? Are you dressed yet?"

"Katie!" The irritation was plain in the sound of Winnie's voice. "I can't believe you're making me do this!"

"Be a grown-up. And be sure to put on every bit of those underthings. You hear me?" She was still loud.

"The orange thing, too?" That was an old ski bib, again from town.

"Yes, the orange thing, too. It'll be under your green thing, and no one will see it." Katie saw Roker coming out of the kitchen with a piece of pie in his hands, and she looked hard at him. He was dropping crust on the floor. He disappeared back through the door.

"If I have to." That was Winnie, again, and then all was quiet from upstairs.

A timer dinged from the bedroom, either Jeff's or Katie's phone, telling them they had thirty minutes until launch. It was now two-thirty, and the sun would begin to sink below the mainland in an hour and a half. It would be very dark when they returned.

Thirty minutes was plenty of time, though, and as they gathered in the living room, they made quite a team. Winnie, beautiful as always in her green and white, and her striped shoes, rolled her eyes as she handed Roker her phone, showing him which icon snapped pictures for her photo album.

"If I'm doing this, I want it on Facebook. Winnie, the Christmas Elf. Who knows, I might get a Christmas gig out of it this summer." She smiled brightly.

"You mean next Christmas." Roker looked at Katie, making a face and nodding his head towards Winnie, as if she wasn't quite all there.

"She means summer. They shoot half-a-year out. I also want Jeff and me in a shot. Let me get mine." Katie's phone was in the bedroom, though, and before she could go after it, Winnie intervened.

"No, Sweetie. You come over here, and you, too, Jeff." He was just coming out of the bedroom, fully dressed except for his cap and beard. Winnie pointed to Roker, "You can take a bunch. Me, Katie, and Jeff, alone, and then all together. I want lots."

Katie sighed. She remembered a few she'd rather not have had put out there for the world to see. "Promise not to post mine?"

"Sweetie, I make no such promises. You hoodwinked me into this, so it's my right. Now, come here, and let's be beautiful together." She held out one arm, motioning Katie in.

"Yeah, let's be beautiful." Jeff was adjusting his beard, and he grinned at Katie. "Don't forget your hat, Mrs. Claus." He pulled a heavy, knit cap over his head, and he fitted his red and white Santa hat over it.

Roker snapped over a dozen, finally sorting out the flash, and doing a few of those, also. Once she had her camera back, Winnie tapped away, finally declaring she had posted every one on her wall.

"That'll be a sight to see." Katie shook her head. "Now, to the float. We have presents to deliver."

"Can I take my camera?" Winnie held up her phone, giving a charming smile.

"You may not have any signal." That was from Jeff.

"That's all right. I can post tomorrow." Winnie seemed very pleased, as if posting what she did made everything right with the world.

Katie supposed it did. What had she said one time? When you store your memories in a photograph, that becomes your memory. Take a happy picture, and you always remember being happy at that time in your life. To judge by that, Winnie was having a very good day, even if she was dressed like an elf, and in a costume many sizes too large.

To tell the truth, she hoped her friend took lots of pictures, because she wanted to remember this, her first time out as Mrs. Claus, as the best time in her life.

Why? Because it was, absolutely, without question, the best Christmas that anyone could ever have.

 **19**

They finally made it to the town float, where there were lanterns lighted, and about a dozen people waiting with their voices ready. They were dressed in bright, Christmassy colors, and against the powered-sugar icing covering the float and decorating the ramp, they were bright ornaments illustrating the joy of the holiday season.

Overhead the sky had dimmed into an orangey-red haze on the back side of the island, one that deepened into a deep cerulean blue overhead. A nearly full moon hovered on the horizon, as if given a special dispensation by the Good Lord above to light Jeff's and Katie's and Winnie's way along the shore tonight, rather like good will and peace on earth shining down from heaven above.

It helped that Jeff had full GPS navigation, and every dock and underwater ledge was fully marked out. Even in complete blackness, there was no danger of running aground.

Kern had indeed been at the Peavey's, along with Brookie and Al and Janine's four. That had been one of Jeff's first stops. There were special presents to deliver, ones that crowded the boat more than was comfortable. They were from Al and Janine to their boys, direct from

Santa, and the younger three had jumped up and down, their eyes shining with excitement.

"How's the plan working?" Katie had called to Kevie, giving him a big wave. He just grinned as he tore into his own gifts, ripping the paper away as fast as he could.

Pulling into the town harbor, Jeff remarked, "Finally, it's getting dark," as he throttled down the engine and eased the boat past the buoys marking the various ledges that might scrape the bottom of his boat. "I can see my way."

"See your way?" Winnie was getting into the elf thing, and she had her phone out snapping shots of everything she passed. "I can barely see in my camera anymore." As she said that, the flash went off, and she looked at the screen. "Oh, that one turned out okay."

It was a shot of one of the Katie bows that decorated the tree now set up and anchored on Jeff's boat. With the flash, the string of Christmas lights formed little more than bright fireflies against the tree.

"Oh, oh, I have signal. I can post!" She began frantically tapping at her phone, nudging Katie and whispering, "Why does Jeff want it to be dark? It seems he could see the rocks better in the light." To keep from sinking was also clear in her question.

"I can hear you, Winnie. I don't mind telling you." Jeff looked at her and grinned, as they approached the town float. "It's not seeing the rocks, it's finding the docks I need to stop at. I look for lights and head that way, and I can skip the rest. I don't exactly get notifications of who's going to be on which dock."

"He does have an idea, though." Katie made a point to whisper in a loud stage voice, just to tease Jeff. "There are seventeen stops on the list, plus anyone else who just happens to make it down to a dock."

One they hadn't visited yet was the De Groot dock. It was a massive granite monstrosity out near Katie's place on Carver Point, and some of the original family had come out to spend the holidays. That was the airplane she and Jeff had heard. Katie had wondered if the family still owned it, and she was very pleased to find it still controlled by the family she'd met when she was still a "summer" girl all those years ago. It gave her back a sense of permanence, as if people who settled on Rockhaven stayed on the island, and homes lived in and loved in continued to be filled with that love forever and ever.

Katie needed that, with the empty foundations at her place on the Point.

Yes, they had an idea of which docks they would visit, and those on the docks had a rough idea of when Jeff might be by. The Santa voyage took hours, and it wouldn't do for people to be forced to stand and wait in the growing darkness and the bitter cold that would settle across the island once they were in full dark. If that was the case, there would be no participants at all. They would all be huddled inside, warm and cozy, leaving Santa to fly overhead, and purchasing their gifts online for Dyer's Delivery to bring to their door.

Kent and Nina were two of those on the town float, brightly festooned in their seasonal best, and festive when contrasted against the softening backdrop of the fresh snowfall. Jess was there, too, and Roker, who'd driven in to spend the evening with the woman he'd finally begun to notice. Babbitt George was there with his wife, together with Mara, their teenage daughter, in tow. The adults got boxes of chocolate candy, or canning jars filled with cocoa mix, if they preferred, but Winnie pulled gifts from the tree for the children.

Katie didn't know all the people, as her church family were the ones she recognized. However, no matter who had gathered, they did have to sing for their gifts, a Christmas song of one sort or another, either religious or secular. This group sang as a choir, a rousing rendition of *Jingle Bells*, albeit with many mistakes, and several breaking into laughter and pushing at the shoulders of yet others.

The song was what Katie expected. Even from the entrance to the harbor, they could be heard practicing, their voices starting and stopping, as whoever was leading them tried to correct misremembered verses and melody lines, ones that never did quite fall into place.

All in all, the evening went wonderfully. The De Groots down at the dock were unfamiliar to Katie, but she welcomed them, anyway, and the house was fully lighted. In that, Katie knew someone had brought electricity out. Running the lines was expensive, and that meant they could afford to keep the place up. Ada Parkes-Simpers? Once again, someone had to be last in line. She was out waiting, though, and she sang a very emotional *Away in a Manger*, a solo for the Santa team, and Mrs. Claus cried by the end. It was beautiful, a single caroler, wrapped in her winter warmth, standing on her pristine, snow-fluffed dock, and singing a capella under the light of a Christmas moon.

Even Winnie said she'd never seen anything so beautiful, and she'd taken a picture to post to Facebook as soon as she got signal back again.

She did complain about taking Ada's cocoa mix up the ramp, but that was to be expected. Winnie loved the glamor and glitz. It was the legwork that poked a hole in her holiday enjoyment. However, Katie reassured her as she stepped from the boat onto the float, there were never seals out at this time of the year. They only ate little green elves in the middle of the summer.

Winnie had laughed lightly, as if she discounted Katie's reassurances, but Katie was fairly certain she heard her friend humming *Rock-a-bye Baby* as she stepped back onto the boat.

It was as could be expected: And fun was had by all.

20

Monday, Christmas Eve, dawned late, because it was the end of December, and cold, again because it was the end of December. It was also beautiful outside, once more because it was the end of December.

Who would not want to live on a Maine island on Christmas Eve?

Francois arrived in the limousine to retrieve Winnie. "Mademoiselle Nicolette, um, need your presence, s'il vous plait." He was in his driver's livery once more, all formal and officious, even in his roughly phrased English.

This morning Katie didn't care one whit whether Winnie stayed or went. She just wanted to survive. It was the night of the Town Hall Banquet, catered, if she understood it correctly, by Kent and Nina. The Town Park displays belonged to everyone. The Christmas musical rested firmly in the arms of the church members. This? She had claimed this as her own. and she wanted it, her first real Christmas bash on the island, to come off perfectly.

If she didn't throw up, first.

"Go, go." She was curled on the sofa, wrapped in a throw, and trying to make it to lunch. "Sorry!" She leaped to her feet and ran for the bathroom, slamming the door

394

after her.

"Sweetie? Are you sure?" Winnie knocked on the door. "I can't leave with you sick."

"Jeff's here. He'll be inside in a bit. He can look after me." He and Roker were undoing what they'd done the day before to Jeff's boat. The Katie tree was returning to the dock, and the boat was being readied to haul lobster pots once again when Christmas wound down. Having an income was important, and Rockhaven Town Church? It was a small town, and that told how well that paid.

Katie didn't want to open the door and face Winnie. Instead, she looked at herself in the mirror. How could she feel so bad? She opened a drawer and pulled out the box Nina had slipped into her coat pocket the day of the sailboat races. It stared her in the face. Pink or blue, she didn't know, but if she saw the line, dear God, that would explain a lot. She looked ceilingward. Please, God, know what you're doing.

Another knock startled her.

"Sweetie? What should I do?"

"I'm fine. It's just indigestion. Don't forget about the banquet tonight, and give Nikki my love." She tried for a bright sound to her voice.

"I won't, and I will. Bye-bye, and I'll see you tonight. It's a busy day." Winnie finished brightly, thrumming her fingernails on the door; and it went silent. It was hardly any time at all before there was another knock on the door.

"Katie?" It was Jeff.

"I'll be out in a minute. I'm just finishing." She made sure her voice was bright this time.

"Winnie said you didn't feel well. Are you certain we don't need to call the doctor? Maybe we should cancel tonight."

"Ha, ha." She said it as two separate words, not as a real laugh. "That's Winnie, always thinking everyone's sick. She's not getting out of the banquet that easily. She promised, and I'll be there to make sure she comes through."

"If you're sure."

"I am. How'd the boat go?"

"It's all taken care of. If you're really all right, I might run with Roker out to Neil Foote's place. Roker got word his generator went out during the night, and that's his only power source for his heater. Are you okay with that?"

"Go. I'm fine." Or she would be, in about six months, if this was what she thought it was. Besides, she knew Neil. He barely got around anymore, an old island landmark who'd been old when Katie was a girl. If she remembered correctly, his generator ran only the blower on his oil heater, one similar to theirs. He probably had a wood stove, and propane, but his heater would be oil. Without electricity, it was dead in the water.

"The Jeep's here if you need it, and the keys are on the table. Bye. I love you, Katie."

"I love you, too. Enjoy your day."

Katie was relieved to have the house to herself for a while. She felt somewhat better after her recent bout of nausea, but it would be easier to deal with this box alone. She thought Jeff would be pleased, but they hadn't discussed it, not seriously. It was more looks when Al and Janine's kids were going crazy, and the looks said, not now, not ever!

The test was as simple as the box said, and once it was over, Katie sat on her bed and looked out across the water. Their lives were going to change. Big time. Al and Janine big time, and she wasn't sure that was a good thing. Would life be a Debsy life, little more than unplanned trips to the potty, or a Matt, huddled under a tree to chuck rotten snowballs at passersby? Oh, dear God, she thought. Why are you doing this to me?

Distraction, she thought. She needed distraction, not to sit here and think about this all day. She stood, relieved to be feeling passably well, and she headed for the kitchen and the car keys. She would make her way to the Town Hall and see how the banquet was coming along.

Her car would have been a better choice. Katie knew that as soon as she began to move down the drive. Jeff's off-road beast sat high, and the big tires, while great for traction in the snow, did nothing for stability in the cockpit. She was glad to reach the paved road to where the surface was relatively level.

The road was an empty ribbon of white, with little more than tire tracks and curbs of sugar-iced greenery to indicate the asphalt underneath. She pulled out and headed toward town. In Boston, this would be one of the busiest shopping days of the year. Here? There were no malls or big boxes on the island, so if it wasn't already bought now, it wasn't going to be. Island people were at home, enjoying their holiday, except for Winnie, she hoped. Her friend had promised to be at the Town Hall preparing the banquet for the evening. A special Christmas surprise, she'd said to Katie the day she and Cousin Nikki arrived.

If Winnie came through, this would be the best surprise her friend could give her, to take this day off her shoulders and make it a grand success. Katie wanted to see what Winnie and Nina had dreamed up.

Pulling up to the Town Hall was the first suggestion that something wasn't quite right. There was no one there, not one car, and not one light on that she could tell. The snow was as fresh and new as yesterday's snowfall, with only one set of tracks from their quick stop the day before to pick up last night's costumes, telling her no one had entered or exited the building at all today.

She parked and got out, stepping gingerly through the thick snow. She tried the door, with no success, and stepped to the window to find the blinds drawn. Pulling her phone from her pocket, she tapped Winnie's number and listened to it ring. It immediately sent her to voicemail, and in that, Katie knew her friend was out of range. She left a message anyway, telling her to call, because she was at the Town Hall, and there had better be a banquet tonight. She would have slammed the phone down, except she couldn't. All she could do was press her finger against the end call icon.

She wiped at one eye. The box, and now this. Sniffling, she touched Jeff's number, only to have the same thing happen again. She said she loved him, and she hoped Neil's heater was working fine.

397

Driving through town, Harbor View was closed, but Katie expected that. Who was out on Christmas Eve, except the frustrated minister's wife? Tire tracks told her someone had been there, but even Kent and Nina's car was gone.

Katie pulled to the side of the road and rubbed her forehead with one hand. Her nausea was rolling again, and she didn't feel like driving out to Nikki's to look for Winnie there. The night before was so perfect. It was the way Christmas was supposed to be. How could Winnie let her down in this? Katie had invited everyone who wanted to come, and now?

Now, all Katie wanted to do was cry.

21

"Katie Carver here." Katie laughed, holding the phone away from her face for a second. "My apologies. Katie Ragsdale, here."

She had laughed, but she didn't feel happy at heart. Nervous? Silly? Maybe even stupid? All those fit. Happy? Not by a long shot.

And Jeff hadn't come home. Even the sun outside her windows hadn't cheered her. It was a relief when she heard his voice.

"I always knew you were still my Dame Carver."

"Jeff, where have you been? I left you a message, and I haven't heard back." After the first surge of relief, she felt irritation rise. Why hadn't he called back before this?

"I apologize. After finishing at Neil's, Roker and I had another errand to run. Have you been out today?"

"Once." Now she was even more irritated. It was Christmas Eve, he should be here with her, and he was out running errands for everyone else on the island. He hadn't married them. He'd married her. It was self-pity. She knew that. She also knew she deserved her self-pity. She had been abandoned, and Boston was looking pretty good to her right then.

Anyway, he didn't sound very sorry, and out? Why had he asked her that? He'd left her the keys.

"Where'd you go, Katie?"

"What's this?" Her irritation was developing claws. "Is there someplace I'm not supposed to go?" Like, to town, maybe to the Town Hall, maybe to see that Winnie really is a flake, and she's going to make a promise, then decide she likes fashionista Nikki better than me, her best friend?

"I thought you might like Janine to come by to keep you company while I finish my errands."

"Janine!" Katie melted at the mention of her name. Her boys, and all Katie could see was having four just like them, and all at one time. Quadruplets! In the wintertime! Throwing snowballs with rocks, and how high would their doctor bills be then?

"Not Janine?" For the first time, Jeff sounded concerned. "Um, I need Jess, but, how about Jackie? I think Tom can take over for Jackie for the rest of the afternoon. Do you want Jackie to come over?"

"Oh, I don't know. It's just that it's Christmas Eve, and I miss you—" The front door rattled with the sound of a repeated pounding fist. "Someone's at the door."

"Ahh, too late. That's probably Janine. Honey, you two have a good time. I'll see you tonight. Bye, bye. Love you." And he was gone.

Katie groaned, standing, and she looked through the glass doors. Sure enough, there stood the diminutive mother of four, and she waved and smiled when Katie stepped into view.

"Katie! Look what I brought!" Janine bustled in when Katie opened the door, and she had a foil-covered pan in her hand. "This is my grandmother's favorite recipe, and I want your opinion on it."

"We'll sit in the kitchen." Katie couldn't work up any enthusiasm for food. She wanted Jeff.

"Look at you." Janine stopped and looked carefully at Katie's face. "You look beautiful. Al told me that once, when I got pregnant with Kevie. Before he even knew, he told me one night I was beautiful. The other three, pah!

400

They were just muffins in a pan. Come on. I need your help."

Katie had to take a deep breath. Oh, Janine. If only you knew. She put it aside, though. She had to. When she said something, Jeff would be the first to know. Not Janine, although telling this friend seemed the best choice if she did have to spill the beans, so to speak. She would understand.

By then Janine was rooting through Katie's cabinets, and Katie was trying to keep up.

"A stool. I can't reach your top cupboards. Jeff has this serving platter, footed, like a rectangular cake stand. It was his mother's. Do you know it?'

"Pink glass?"

"I would have said rose, but pink will do. Sort of iridescent. You know where it's at?"

"Here." Katie reached over the fridge, and she pulled it down. "We've not used it since I've been here." She hadn't even known it was special in any way, just old. And it had one chip out of the foot. It needed to be kept turned to the back to hide it.

"Sit that down." Janine motioned, and she set the covered dish right in the middle of the table. "This is to die for. Does that phrase date me? Ha. Now, this, though, is the best thing you've tasted in your life. Baklava."

With a flourish, she whipped off the foil, and there, in one of the Harbor View's pans, was a gleaming pastry cut in a diamond pattern. Katie knew it was Harbor View's, because it was embossed on the handle. Harbor View. Rockhaven Maine. Not for Sale.

"This is your grandmother's dish?" Katie tapped the words on the handle. "And my stomach's been, well, I don't think I could eat any right now."

"Oh, the pan?" Janine laughed, as if making light of the pan and Harbor View's name. "My oven's out. Sorry. And it's not really baklava, but that's the closest thing I know. It's good, though. I need you to help me arrange it."

By the time they were finished, Katie wondered how many ways there were to arrange little diamond pastries on a pink iridescent footed serving platter with a chipped foot.

401

Apparently more than she'd ever dreamed possible.

"I have to take this to a get-together." Janine dug in the drawers and found some plastic wrap. She whipped out a long piece, and she tucked it in and over the diamond sort-of-baklava artfully displayed on Jeff's mother's platter. "Come on. You can ride along. No kids." She chuckled.

What else did Katie have to do? She shrugged and pulled on her coat, not the least enthused, and she didn't try to hide it.

"Now, don't be a grump. This is for an elderly lady, and she can't come to pick it up." Janine smiled cheerfully and pulled Katie out the front door. "In my car, and we won't be gone long."

Long was subjective, Katie decided, sitting in the seat of Al's truck, and holding the serving dish with the almost-baklava in her lap, as they drove through town, and headed towards the north side of the island. Town Hall? Still deserted, and that depressed her. Heading past Harbor View, she saw her blue Volkswagen, and she frowned at that, irritated. What was Winnie doing there? She reached for her phone, only to realize her purse was at the house. Janine had said not long, so she didn't say anything. Even so, she planned to bite when she got close enough to Winnie to leave good teeth imprints.

Finally, Janine turned on her blinker, and Katie had to say something.

"This is my Cousin Nikki's place. I mean, she's only rented it for two weeks, but why are we here?"

"Oh, I need to drop off something." Janine smiled, waved her hand dismissively, and tugged at the steering wheel of the big truck to swing it into the drive. "It's bumpy, so hold on to that dessert."

It was towards the end of the drive that Katie grew suspicious. Cars lined the roadway, Corrine's and Roker's. Jess'. There was Tom and Jackie's in the trees and out of the way. Jerry Watson's and Kayline Stryker's was blocked in by Bobbitt George's. And more. They were everywhere.

Inside was where it became real. When Katie stepped through the door, holding her almost-baklava, a good portion of the town and the entire church membership stood in front of the massive glass wall that made up the back of the home, and they yelled with all the gusto they could muster, "Merry Christmas, Katie! We love you!"

"Merry Christmas, Sweetie!" Winnie yelled from the far side of the room, where she stood by Cousin Nikki, next to the most massive Christmas tree Katie thought she'd ever seen inside a private home.

Jeff handed the baklava off to someone else as the people dispersed into smaller groups and began talking, and he wrapped Katie in his arms. "My Christmas gift to you. Everyone's pulled this together for you, as a surprise. And it's catered by Harbor View, so we know it's going to be good."

"I thought—" Katie was choked, and she didn't know what to say. "Then, Neil—"

"Really needed his heater repaired. Did Janine keep you busy?"

Katie shook her head. He had no idea. "I drove to the Town Hall, and I thought Winnie had forgotten. Then you didn't come home, and it was Christmas Eve." She felt her eyes tear up, and she refused to cry. People might think her unappreciative, and it was Christmas Eve. She had to be bright and festive!

"I had no idea! Katie, Katie. Winnie cares about you. She would never let you down, and neither would I. Promise."

Katie laughed, more to disguise her embarrassment than anything else. A voice across the room distracted her.

"Joyeux Noël!" The voice was cracked, but it was strong, and across the room, Cousin Nikki stood with Winnie's and Francois's help.

"Everybody!" That was Winnie. "Everybody listen up!"

When the talking quieted, Nikki continued. "My only surviving relation, ma chère Katie, has brought me to your wonderful America, and I welcome everyone to my home. Please, please have a merveilleux and Joyeux Noël."

"Forgive me?" Jeff had her wrapped in his arms once more.

"Of course, and always." Katie took a deep breath, and she knew she meant it. What could be better than this, a Christmas Eve spent with family and friends, and held in the arms of the man she loved?

It was indeed the most wonderful present anyone could have planned. It showed Jeff's love to her in every possible way it could, especially when he kissed her, long and hard, right there in front of Cousin Nikki's massive Christmas tree.

22

Katie opened her eyes. The room was darkened, with small slivers of early morning light coming in around the blinds. She knew what day it was, and she buzzed with anticipation. Christmas Day on Rockhaven. Her first one ever.

Jeff lay at her side, his shoulder touching hers, the warmth of his body bleeding through his pajamas. His face, the morning stubble she adored, and his eyes, closed in sleep. Christmas sleep. The best sort, the kind that happened only one morning a year. The kind that could only happen one morning a year.

She slipped sideways from underneath the bedding, and she made her way to the living room, gently closing the door behind her. On one side were the gifts brought by Nikki and Winnie, all the way from Boston, still waiting to be unwrapped. Katie was sure they had brought enough for everyone on the island to have at least one. The other direction, the blinds on the windows were all raised, and just at the horizon, the sky was a rosy-pink band of color, lifting the ceiling of the earth as the day peeked at the world to see if it was time to wake.

"It's Christmas!" the sky seemed to say. "Wake, World,

and celebrate the birth of the King!"

Katie shivered with the unfulfilled expectations of the day. Christmas! Life couldn't get any better.

She pulled out her phone, and she tapped a number. It picked up, and a sleepy voice spoke to her.

"Hello?"

"It's Christmas!"

"So it is. The sun's barely up. Let me sleep till nine."

"Honey, it is almost nine. Well, eight. It's Christmas!"

"The sun comes up at four."

"In the summer. It's Christmas!"

"Call me when it's time for lunch. Merry Christmas." The phone went dead.

Katie smiled, but she wasn't letting Winnie's lack of enthusiasm put a crimp in her Christmas plans. Last night had been for the entire island, but today was for her family and closest friends. Plus, she had a special gift to share with Jeff today, and she wanted everyone here when she did.

It was the kitchen that took up the next few hours. Her most prized concoction? Her pumpkin pies, fresh from the real thing, following Jess' instructions. Add to that a chocolate cream, something new and untried, just for Janine's boys. The turkey came prepped for the oven, directly from Nina's kitchen. Everything else would arrive with her guests, enough to feed everyone, and probably plenty left over. Like the Bible story of the loaves and the fishes, bring a little, take home a lot.

Putting on the coffee finally pulled Jeff from the bed, and he wandered in, giving Katie a sleepy kiss, and wandering back in the living room to wake up a while. He called out a belated, "Merry Christmas," as he began to rumble around, making a fire.

Winnie had demanded a two o'clock lunch, saying she would never make it before then, but Katie's guests began arriving by ten. Roker, first, and Jess at the same time. Their addition to the feast? Another pumpkin pie. When Katie showed her two already prepared, Jess said she remembered the story of the pie on the day of the storm, and she wanted to ensure that Roker had plenty. Then she pulled out some of Nina's eggnog, already chilled and ready to drink.

Janine had the four boys with her, coming in about noon, and telling her Al would come later. Even on Christmas, there were errands to run, and loose ends to tie up. Something for Jeff, she whispered, pulling Katie aside. I'm not supposed to say anything, so don't mention it.

Katie shook her head, thinking it must be good if Janine couldn't keep it inside. She'd done pretty well the day before. Katie hadn't even guessed, not until they were halfway up the drive.

She didn't expect Cousin Nikki until Winnie arrived. Katie let Jess and Janine take over her kitchen, and she joined Roker, Jeff, and the boys in the living room. The men were stoking the fire, although to Katie, it looked as though they were playing to see how high they could get the flames to leap. Occasionally the wood sparked, and one of them would stamp the ember or kick it back on the hearth to let it die out.

Even the windows got into the festive spirit, steamed up with the joy of a houseful of Christmas guests, that and pies, turkey, and all the other things being prepared in the kitchen.

The boys were preoccupied with their hand-held gaming systems. Katie watched them for a time before realizing they were playing each other. When she asked Kevie about it, he told her, without removing his eyes from the screen, "Bluetooth, and we can't talk," and he continued his game.

"Bluetooth," Katie said to herself. She understood Bluetooth. It was a way of connecting without connecting, although that wasn't really right. It was a way of connecting when there was no connection system available, when there was no Wi-Fi set up. It was a local connection, and it only worked when the devices were close together. If one of the boys carried his game too far away, the connection was lost, and he was no longer part of the action.

Like Babes and Ritchey and Austie. Apple. The Reynolds twins, Bennie and Bobby. The island pack she and

407

Jeff had run with as children. They had been Bluetoothed, then they'd spread too far from one another, and the connection had been lost. She'd wanted to return some of that connection for Jeff, to reunite him with his best friend from childhood, but that was the one thing that hadn't come together for her. Why, even Kevie, no longer believing in Christmas, had leaped in with both feet and made it real for his younger brothers. Everything else had fallen in place, except for the Bluetooth.

Still, it was a pretty good Christmas all around, and perfection? Sometimes good enough was the best life offered.

Roker was bringing in more wood when he pointed out the first sign of something unusual.

"Jeff, you know of anyone flying in today?"

"Not that I'm aware."

"Come see." Roker stepped outside, closing the door when Jeff joined him.

Katie walked to the window, and wiping a spot clear, sure enough, there was a small plane, and it seemed to be looking for something. The one she and Jeff had seen before hadn't come to this end of the island. It was too far out of the way. At one point, the craft flew close enough to the house to read the lettering on the wings. It dipped one of its wings and flew off the direction of the airport.

"Was it important?" Katie quizzed them when they came back in, stomping their feet.

"It was odd, I'll say that." Jeff peered through the glass where the craft could be seen in the distance. "Why would it fly over here? Hey, Roker, who do you think's unlocked the airport?"

He shrugged, as if it wasn't important. However, to Katie, it did seem important if someone was landing there. She understood the question. The "airport" was little more than a level field, and it had a locked gate so the local teens didn't tear up the field by doing donuts in the middle of the night. Anyone landing there would need someone to get a car in and out.

It was nearly two by then, and the boys were getting

restless. Katie was about ready to eat, too, and those pumpkin pies? Katie was certain her guests needed something to tide them over before they attacked those.

"Hey, everyone, it's Christmas day. Jess brought over some of Nina's specialty eggnog. Thank you, Jess." Katie pulled her from the kitchen and gave her a one-armed hug. A round of applause echoed in the room. "To begin, let's start off with that. Jess, do you mind pouring?"

They were still on the eggnog, serving the final cups, when someone banged on the front door. The windows that direction were equally misted with all the people and the cooking going on, but the door wasn't locked. Anyone knocking knew they were to join the festivities.

"Ah, we can eat!" Katie called to her guests, expecting their new additions to invite themselves in. After all, Winnie and Al? They were as much family as friends. "The rest of the Christmas feast has arrived. I'm not sure what they brought, but I'm certain we'll enjoy it very much."

Janine came out of the kitchen at Katie's speech, and she fought a smile. Roker was doing the same. Even the four Peavey boys had ready-to-burst secrets written all over their faces. Katie saw, and she looked to Jeff to see if he knew what was going on.

Jeff shrugged, and he turned to Roker. However, before he could question him, the door banged again.

"You gonna get that?" It was Roker. "You, Jeff, with Katie, why don't you head to the door?"

Katie hesitated, looking to Janine's boys, but each one in turn shook his head and sank back in his seat, smiling all the while. She looked to Jeff and held out a hand. "Preacher Jeff? Shall we answer the door?"

"Sure, Dame Katie. Everyone else is too lazy." He chuckled, and he led his wife through the first glass door and through to the second. Opening the door was when they understood, from Winnie's suggestion of a Christmas surprise, to Janine's whispered secret, to the mystery plane in the sky. Even Al's absence fell into place when Jeff opened that door.

A man Jeff hadn't seen in nearly ten years stood there,

and he held out his hand. He grinned with just a bit of an embarrassed smile, and he said, "Hey, Jeff. I've missed you wicked bad."

"Ritchey? Hey, man, what are you doing here?" Jeff looked like he couldn't get his head around the man's sudden manifestation on his front step.

When Jeff reached to grab the hand, the man laughed, and he grabbed Jeff in a bear hug. He slapped him hard on the back, this time saying, "Oh, man, I've missed being here more than you can know."

"Ritchey?" Katie looked to him, then to Winnie and Al helping Nicolette out of her atrociously long limousine. As she watched, its lights flashed, and it began to turn, moving away from the house.

"And you, I would know you anywhere, Katie Carver. Winnie showed me pictures of you, but I had no idea you'd become so beautiful. Maybe I should have stayed around." Ritchey laughed and gave her an equally big bear hug.

That wasn't all, though, for about then, another man stepped around Al and slapped his hand on Ritchey's shoulder, and he wore a cap festooned with embroidered pilot's wings. He pulled Ritchey out of the way, and grinned a broad and winning smile.

"Don't forget about me. This turkey wouldn't be here if I hadn't come along. Did you notice that wing dip? Just letting you know we saw you."

"Austie! Man, you were willing to fly this guy? In the same plane with you? You are a sucker for an ugly face." Jeff grabbed Austie William's hand, and he threw an arm across his neck. "Welcome back."

It was Ritchey he couldn't keep his eyes off of. Katie noticed that. And Ritchey was focused on his old friend, just like old times, like two handfuls of years had melted away, and all it had taken was one simple hug.

"Do we get to come in?" That was Austie's question. He still had his arm across Jeff's shoulders, and he gave him a mock punch to the stomach. "I remember being king of the world with you. I should at least get to come into your house. Besides, you've got more company coming."

He pulled Jeff in and said that right in his ear before leaning around and pointing to Katie. "And you. I thought you were beautiful at fourteen. Hubba, but look at you now."

"Yeah, yeah. Come on in." Jeff elbowed Austie as he shook his head and looked away from Ritchey's face. Except for one brief glance when Austie walked up, Jeff broke eye contact with Ritchey for the first time. He had a smile on his face that wouldn't go away.

The four of them crowded the foyer, making room for Winnie, Nicolette, and Al. As they passed, Winnie said, "See, I can keep a secret. Merry Christmas, Sweetie." Nikki said a simple "Joyeux Noël." Al? He handed Jeff a set of keys, and he said, "Thanks, pal. I locked the airport back up. You get to keep these."

When everyone was past, Jeff grabbed Katie in a full hug, and he whispered to her, "Thank you, Katie. This means more to me than anything. I love you so much. I knew you weren't telling me something, and now I know what it was." He kissed her several times on different parts of her face.

"Jeff," Katie cautioned, beginning to laugh. "Jeff, I had nothing to do with this. I'm as surprised as you are."

"Then?" He stepped back and looked in the living room. "Not Winnie?"

Katie shrugged. However, she thought so. She just didn't know how.

23

"Attention." Nicolette tapped the side of her glass with a knife, and the sharp sound quieted the room. Francois had been playing the role of butler, and he was unobtrusively clearing dinnerware away. Nicolette waited until he was out of the room, and she motioned for Jeff to help her stand. "Is magnifique to spend this day with family." She lifted her glass, and she motioned to those around the room. "And friends who come as family. We spoke in the car, and of my friend, Winnie, I know more, but I would that everyone hear. Please. Stories!" She raised her glass to clapping and cheers, before gingerly returning to her chair.

"Yeah, Ritchey. You first. Your wife? You? I'm at a loss how you can be here." Jeff shook his head, and while he may have been at a loss, the look on his face didn't include disappointment. "Bare your soul to everyone here."

The two men had been telling old stories, with embarrassing ones about Austie, including the story of the rotting clams that they'd had to dump in the harbor when they couldn't sell them. Austie had turned red with embarrassment. However, that had been the simple renewal of old friendships. Now with Nicolette's demand, it was time for the real stories to be laid bare.

"My wife, my wife." Ritchey ducked his head and ran his hand through his hair before he looked up. "You've met Tricia, but not Allie and Mark. They're five and three now. Of course, we have the new one, why I couldn't make the wedding."

"So you'd said." Jeff seemed to find relief in Ritchey's casual reference, as if it had bothered him, even having known, and now he could let it all evaporate undiscussed.

"You know from before why Trish isn't here. Boats!"

"I remember." Jeff laughed, glancing at the ceiling for a moment. "But you are. Not to stay, I'm sure, though I'd be happy if you didn't leave too soon."

"Trish is at her mother's until the first, so I have a week. The wife rules the life." He shrugged, even as he kept his eyes on his friend's face.

"You just what, decided, and on Christmas? Spill, dude, spill."

"You know Katie and I have been keeping in touch." He nodded Katie's direction.

"Katie?" Jeff looked to her. "How, and when?"

She shrugged, and she smiled. It was the sermons, but Jeff hadn't wanted her to bring up Ritchey, so she hadn't. Now was not the time to go into that.

"The real reason I'm here? It's that girl." Ritchey pointed to Winnie. "Stuff happened, now she's up to be the face of my stores. You'll soon see her in all my adverts. Since she has a connection here—" He pointed to Katie and Jeff. "—I got to thinking, and I decided to buy that old place on Main, you know, just down from the Harbor View. Expansion is the name of the game. I'll be right next to the Post Office. Perfect location, and it wouldn't have occurred to me without these women. Hey, Kent and Nina still run Harbor View, right?" He looked around to judge people's responses.

"You just ate their turkey." Katie said that with a smile. She was remembering why Jeff had bonded so tightly with Ritchey. He was charming everyone in the room.

"Ah. That's why it was so good, not to impugn your cooking, my good Katie." He smiled at her. "That's my story. Austie? He's my man. You want to tell it?" He held his hand out as an invitation.

"I'm good listening to your version." Austie gave it back to him with a laugh.

"My man there flies the skies for what, American?" When Austie shook his head, Ritchey shrugged and went on. "Anyway, I offered him a free weekend up here just for flying me, and here we are. Two old buddies, catching up on old times on the way up. Now, three, four, five old buddies." He pointed to each of the old pack that was in Jeff's house.

"I can't stay, though." Austie rapped the table a couple times in an unconscious motion. "Tomorrow I have to be in Bangor to catch a flight to St. Petersburg. Off to the Sunshine State. I'm not really a snow person."

"So you're stuck with me." Ritchey pointed to Jeff. "And I want my old room. Remember how we used to stay in that little room with the bunk beds and sneak out at night?"

"I still have those bunk beds." Jeff's grin was back. "They're yours anytime I can convince you to visit."

Katie couldn't contain herself any longer. She stood and wrapped one of Jeff's arms in hers, and she waited until everyone looked at her.

"Katie?" Jeff lifted her hand and kissed it. "Yes?"

"I have a present I would like to announce." There were call-outs and clapping, and Katie felt her face warm. "Jeff thought I was keeping a secret from him, and that it was Ritchey. Ritchey, you I didn't know about, but that bunk bed is yours anytime you want to come visit. I'll stand behind Jeff's invitation. Never think it's not open, with or without advance warning. However, I have been keeping a secret. I'm pretty sure Nina guessed, but I asked her to keep it quiet, and it seems like she did. Jeff, this is for everybody, but it's really a present for you. In about six months, as close as I can judge, you're going to be a daddy."

"That's why you've been sick?" He looked like he was in shock. She nodded, and he threw his arms around her and hooted. "Oh, that's the best news I could ever hear."

414

The room broke into several minutes of animated conversation and high-handed slaps of congratulations. Winnie threw her arms around Katie, saying, "Oh, you girl, you can always top everything I do. This one's the best one of all. I get to be Auntie Winnie. You have to promise!"

Cousin Nikki began tapping her glass once again. When the room quieted, she got Jeff to help her stand once more, and her voice shook with emotion as she began to speak. "For years my sister and I were separated by an ocean. She was stolen from me, and I wish to give my family back what was lost. Katie, ma chère, will you accept a gift from me?" She held out her hands, and Katie reached and took them, to have Nikki draw her into an embrace, a real one. When they separated, her cousin had tears running down her cheeks.

Katie looked into Nikki's face as she said, "You coming to Rockhaven for the holidays has been gift enough. You being here has given me back much of what I lost. I couldn't ask anything more." She meant it, too.

"I wish to give you back your home. Will you accept such a gift from an old woman?"

"I'm confused, Nikki. I have a home. Right here." Katie glanced at Jeff to see him shrug.

"Non, I wish to give you back your grandmamma's home. Then, your new little one can make the memories you know so well."

"I don't understand." Katie knew what she thought Nikki was saying, but the funds to rebuild the old place? The cost would be staggering.

"Just say thank you." Jeff wrapped her in his arms. "It's Christmas, Katie. It's the season for giving, and today, everyone gets exactly what they want. Everyone. Everything."

Katie looked across the room, and she knew Jeff was right. Here, on this isolated island in the middle of the ocean, in this one room, she had everything she had ever wanted. God had given her Jeff and their baby, and Winnie, and all her friends here. Roker, Jess. Al, Janine and the boys. Then God decided it wasn't enough, and He opened

His hands, and in stepped Nikki and Ritchey and Austie. Now, she was being given her childhood home back again.

All this, and they still had a mound of gifts to unwrap. It would be fun, but the best one had already been offered and received.

Katie took Nikki's hands, and she leaned in to give her a kiss, telling her that having her grandmother's house back again was the best gift anyone could have given her, ever.

"Non," Nikki replied. "Your gift to your Jeff is a gift to me, also. You give me back life. It is the best gift of all."

"Your Cousin Nikki is right." Jeff pulled Katie in, and he gazed into her eyes. "Your gift is the best Christmas gift of all.

Then he topped it off with a Christmas kiss, one that was cheered on with gusto by everyone, both large and small, young and old, in the room.

As they finished, the boys cried out, not quite in unison, but certainly in chorus, "It's time for Christmas gifts! Can we open ours now?"

It was, just as Katie had hoped, the best Rockhaven Christmas ever.

Rockhaven
Spring

1

"Look. Another Wyeth."

Katie Ragsdale and her friend Winnie Catron had said those words to each other a dozen times in the thirty minutes they'd been in the small gallery along the Maine coast.

Jeff, Katie's husband, had been more specific, wrapping his arms around his wife and whispering, "There, on that beach. I'd live there with you forever and ever and never miss the rest of the world." Once, he'd pulled her hair back on one side and kissed her on the neck, murmuring, "Andrew should have chosen you to sit for him. Then the paintings would have been worth twice as much."

"Thank you, Jeff. You might pay thousands of dollars for a painting of me, but no one else would." Katie had laughed.

"They're fools, then." Jeff, a minister at Rockhaven Town Church, chuckled. He was dressed in a warm overcoat, but he looked more lobsterman than preacher. He'd joined his wife to wish her best friend bon voyage after her extended visit over the Christmas holidays.

Just outside the plate glass windows fronting the gallery was the small mainland town that connected Rockhaven Island to the rest of the world, and it was filled with galleries and restaurants and wonderful storefront shops to entertain the casual visitor. This was their third gallery, and Jeff had said similar things to her in each one.

The women had moved on to a new painting, and Jeff leaned between them, pointing to a picture of a woman prominently displayed on one canvas. "You know, I delivered a mess of lobster to Betsy Wyeth on her island just south of here once."

"Betsy?" Winnie ran her finger along a postcard she'd picked up showing a group of Wyeth paintings all displayed on one wall. Each individual image was very small. She looked up with a smile, tilting her head to the side, and asked, "Who's Betsy?"

"Tell her, Jeff. Who's Betsy?" Katie wanted to hear this.

"If I must." He took a deep breath, running a hand through his flyaway hair, pulling it into place only until he released it. Jeff was indeed a lobsterman, and the sea kept his thick mop terminally unruly. "Andrew was one of the Wyeths, N.C., Andrew, and Jamie, three generations of a local family that are considered the First Family of American Art."

"And Betsy?" Winnie, still smiling brightly, fanned herself with yet a different one of the postcards.

"Yes, Jeff. Tell us about Betsy." Katie fought a laugh as she grabbed Winnie's arm. The postcard was creating a breeze.

"Betsy is, well, was Andrew's wife." Jeff grinned. "But everyone knows them around here. Ladies, we need to make sure we keep an eye on the time." He pulled his sleeve up to glance at his watch, rubbing his thumb across the face and frowning at it.

"They're divorced?" Winnie looked confused.

"He's being silly. I think she's his widow, right Jeff?" Katie reassured her friend. Then she turned to Jeff, placing two fingers on his chest. "And don't you worry, Preacher

420

Man. My phone alarm's set."

Winnie was headed back to her home in Boston. Jeff's lobster boat was moored at the city wharf, but Katie had brought her car over on the ferry. The trip to the airport was only about ten minutes, so they were doing okay on time, but Katie was willing to admit that they might need to start thinking about heading that direction. They could not afford to be late.

"If you want that, you have to pay for it." Katie tapped the card in Winnie's fingers. "Which painting does it show?"

"Oh, I don't know." Winnie flipped it to the back and squinted. "Monhegan, I think. What's Monhegan?"

"Jeff?" Katie took the card and held it for him to see. It showed a house on a windswept island.

"One of the Wyeths owns that house. Monhegan is the name of the island. Buy this, and you'll own a piece of it." He chuckled.

"You'll own a postcard." Katie held it back out to Winnie.

"I like it. Thank you, Jeffie. I can't believe that family painted all these. They should have used a phone, like me. It would be so much easier."

"They didn't have phones when most of these were painted. Not cell phones, anyway." Katie wrapped an arm in her friend's, as she picked out one of the postcards for herself. "Look, for Cousin Nikki. This one's pretty. I can just send it to my old Boston apartment. I'm glad she's living there."

"I am, too, but I don't know about that picture, Sweetie. My phone does better pictures that that." She had her phone out, and she scrolled through to show a number of pictures she'd taken while on the island.

"Your phone's not a painting, and pictures you've taken aren't worth half-a-million dollars."

"Oh . . . they're worth how much?" Winnie's eyes were round, and she giggled. "If I had that for every picture I've posted on Facebook, I'd have a lot of money." She checked the time on her phone. "Forty minutes until my flight."

"I'll have you there. You put that phone away. Trust Katie. Katie is your friend. Katie is good. Katie is wise." She said it like a hypnotist, and she laughed.

"How small did you say the plane would be?" That was something that had concerned Winnie when Katie scheduled the flight. There was an issue with the amount of luggage returning to Boston with her. She'd ridden up with Cousin Nikki in a massively long limousine. Weight hadn't counted, then.

"Six seats. Quit worrying about it and enjoy the Wyeths. You won't find a collection like this just anywhere. The Wyeth family is local for three generations, so this is their home." Within fifty miles of Rockhaven was what she meant, but anyone homegrown would already know that. "You know Grandmamma had a Wyeth, once. It would have been worth a lot, now."

"Oh, Sweetie!" Winnie dropped her phone back into her bag and hugged Katie with one arm. "The fire. I'm so sorry."

A late-season fire had consumed Katie's childhood summer home on Rockhaven many years earlier. Katie's grandmother hadn't survived, and an empty foundation was all that was left.

"I don't remember a Wyeth at your grandmother's place." Jeff had spent much of his summers there as well when they were kids, in and out of the house with Katie and all their friends.

"No, no. I wasn't clear." Katie laughed. "It was at her place in Boston. No one knew what it was, and it went in a tag sale when my parents liquidated her estate."

"You poor baby. Are you still sad?" Winnie patted Katie's face with one hand.

"I barely remember it. Let me see if they have it here." Katie scanned the display and pulled a postcard out of the rack. It was the one showing the series of paintings on a wall, and she pointed to the smallest image. "There it is. That one. I might buy this. Just think, I'll own a Wyeth again." She chuckled.

"You'll own a postcard. Let me see." Jeff looked it

over, flipping it to the back. "This would have been worth tons. Shame."

They paid for their postcards and braced for the stiff breeze that had driven them into the galleries in the first place. Once outside, the sky was a brilliant blue laced with wind-softened doilies, and a seabird with wide, white wings squawked at them before landing across the street to pick at something along the curb. Small strips of snow tried to hide in the shadowy areas along the foundations of buildings, reminding pedestrians and drivers alike that winter had a lot of oomph left in it, and not to trust the sun. Elsewhere, the sidewalks and roads were clear. Katie and Winnie wore borrowed hooded coats, with faux fur around the face. The coats had been left by Katie's Cousin Nikki when she departed for Boston two weeks earlier. For a bone-chilling winter day? They were perfect. For style? They screamed over-the-top Nikki.

"How are you holding up?" Jeff had his arm around Katie, his own rugged coat bulky against the cold breeze.

"Okay." She knew what he was asking. Three-and-a-half months along, and she'd lain in bed with her fair share of morning sickness. "Today's been good so far, and I wouldn't miss seeing Winnie off for anything."

"The cold. How's that working?"

"It settles my stomach." It did, too. It was the ferry ride that had given her more problems. Hopefully, the return trip would be better. Eating? Until she got home, food was not an option.

A horn sounded. In the direction of the ocean, the ferry plowed through the harbor, leaving whitewater boas in its wake, heading out to sea. The car deck was mostly empty, with the bulk of the boat being swallowed by a gravel truck.

"Someone's getting a new driveway," Katie commented.

"Sweetie, look at this." Winnie tugged Katie's arm, and she pointed across the street.

"At what?" Katie followed the finger. It led to an antiques shop with an old-fashioned footed child's crib in the shop's window. She looked at Jeff and rolled her eyes.

Jeff shrugged and grinned, whispering, "She's your friend."

"Honey, not baby stuff." This was what Katie didn't want, people to fawn over her just because she'd announced on Christmas Day she had a little one on the way. She also didn't need reminded of the ferry ride back with her stomach. Not today. And anything baby would do just that.

"It's too cute. Can I go inside and get it for you?" Winnie clapped her hands in excitement as she stepped off the curb and started across the street. "Then I can post pictures of my little nephew in it and see how many likes I get."

"Having a baby's more than a Facebook photo op. I will have to raise this kid, and she might be a girl." The crib was cute, but practical? Not by modern safety standards.

"Or it might be a boy. I like the word nephew." Jeff chuckled, calling out, "He'll be your nephew, Winnie. Keep your fingers crossed."

"Oh, you two." Katie knew it was hopeless, and she gave in. "We have a few minutes if you want to go inside."

"Thanks, Sweetie." Winnie beamed, and she pulled the door wide, laughing when an old-fashioned cow bell jangled to announce their entrance.

It was warm inside, and it smelled good, too, pine needles or perhaps a hint of eucalyptus. Old wood and the faint smell of decay suggested age. Weathered buoys, rush-bottomed chairs, and paintings—probably prints, Katie surmised—lined the walls. Winnie drew her directly to the old crib in the window.

"Ladies? May I help you?" An elderly man, nattily dressed, pushed through a curtain from a back room.

"My friend's catching a flight to Boston. She wanted to stop in and look at your crib." Katie pointed to it. Jeff had abandoned them when they passed the wall filled with old lobster buoys.

"Ah, the crib. Beautiful workmanship from the forties. Hand built. It would make a wonderful decorative piece." He stepped to the window and rocked it gently. "I'm Quincy Sorensen, proprietor. Do you collect dolls?"

"We're having a baby." Winnie's eyes followed the movement of the crib. She laughed, her strawberry blonde hair bouncing with the back and forth movement of her head. When the crib slowed, she laughed again and grasped Katie by the shoulders, calling out, "My friend is, anyway. I'm going to be an aunt."

"Ah, I'm afraid I can't help you there. This is a decorative piece only, nothing more. I can't sell it for use as an actual crib. I do have some old baby things over here that would be wonderful as display accessories, excellent in a baby's room." He smiled engagingly, indicating an alcove off the back wall of the room.

"Thank you, but no thanks." Katie smiled at him as she squeezed her friend's arm. She whispered to Winnie, "It was a good idea. Thanks, Honey. Maybe Jeff can build us one."

Something dinged, and Katie reached in her purse. Her phone glowed, and she dropped it back in. "Jeff, we have to go. Thank you, Mr. Sorensen. My friend's flight calls."

"Ah, come back again, anytime." He reached a hand to shake.

"This was fun. Thank you, Quincy." Winnie grabbed his hand with both of hers and pumped it vigorously. "Bye, bye!"

Jeff joined them underneath the dangling bell as they exited the store.

The car ride to the airport was barely five minutes, but unloading Winnie's luggage took three times that. The terminal was little more than a white building with a stretch of tarmac behind it, so Jeff served as the skycap to help them check in.

Before Winnie boarded, she hugged Jeff and thanked him for taking such good care of Katie. When she hugged Katie, she said more.

"I love you so much, Sweetie. I'll miss you forever, but I promise to come back and see you."

"Be sure to visit Nikki. And you behave on all those shoots. I want to see you in my new catalogs." Katie felt her eyes burn. It was suddenly very real to her just how much she enjoyed her friend's exuberant lifestyle and her funny stories about the modeling gigs she attended all over the world. She already looked forward to her visiting again.

"I will, Sweetie. I'll keep you posted on Nikki, and I'll take you with me on every shoot I do. Now, a second hug for little Jeffie." She giggled at that and patted Katie's tummy, before hugging her again.

Jeff laughed and shook his head.

Giving Katie an extra hug, Winnie whispered, "Don't you worry about all that bad stuff they said about your grandmother's place out there on the Point. They built Venice on muddy islands. You've got solid rock. You can build whatever you want." Winnie waved and headed out the doors to climb into the aircraft.

"You heard that, Dame Carver. You can build whatever you want." Jeff had his arms around her, and they watched Winnie disappear inside with a wave.

Katie laughed his words off, but they had read the report that the existing foundations of her grandmother's old house were unstable. It had certainly put a kink into their plans to rebuild. The old design was grandfathered in, as long as Katie rebuilt on the same footprint. To have an architect draw up something completely new? Well, that was more difficult.

As the small plane taxied down the runway and lifted into the air, Katie and Jeff stepped to her car, and they climbed in. "Lunch, maybe, if you feel like eating?" Jeff took her hand.

"I want to, but I'm wearing down. I'm sorry."

"You're not sick, are you? I can call someone. A doctor. Do you need a doctor?" He pressed one of her hands to his face.

"Silly, of course I don't need a doctor. I need to stay off my feet for a while. The ferry ride will give me a chance to do just that." That wasn't how she'd felt earlier, but maybe it would be true this time. Reaching to the dash, she pulled down Winnie's postcard of Monhegan. "That Winnie," she said. "She couldn't even remember to take her postcard with her."

"Look on the back. I suspect she meant to leave it." Jeff touched it with one finger to peer at the underside.

Katie flipped it over to see a message in her friend's elaborate handwriting.

"Au revoir. (I got that from Nikki. It means good-bye for now.) I will miss you so much, Sweetie. All my love forever, Winnie."

Katie wiped the tears from her eyes, and she put the postcard back on the dash. As Jeff started the engine and headed the direction of the ferry, she was certain of one thing. Winnie, in spite of her many flaws, knew how to make her feel loved, and that was why she was the dearest friend she'd ever known.

"Was it a good message?" Jeff looked at her as he turned the corner towards the ferry. "I'm headed back out on my boat, and I don't want you riding the ferry alone and miserable." He grinned and tapped her chin with his fingertips.

"The best, Jeff. I've enjoyed her visit very much."

"More than you enjoy me?"

"Hey, now, you are a funny man." She laughed, but she especially enjoyed the feel of his hand in hers all the way to town.

2

"Nina!" Katie rolled the glass down, calling to the heavily bundled form looking across the water from the car deck. It was the coat she recognized more than the person. Outside, in winter, on the ferry? The clothes made up half of who the person was. You learned to recognize people by fabrics and the cut of their clothing, or you didn't know them at all.

This was a coat worn by Nina Vinson, the proprietor of Harbor View restaurant, one of the few and the best on Rockhaven.

The coat turned, and Nina's face appeared. She lifted an arm, and pulling her hood tighter, she moved toward the car. "Katie! How are you doing, girl? Thank goodness the ferry hasn't pulled out, yet. I'd have been inside trying to warm up. Jeff told me you were bringing Winnie over today and to look for you on the way back."

Nina had leaned over, and she was speaking through about a three-inch gap in her hood opening.

"It's warm in here if you want to join me." Katie looked forward to visiting with Nina on the 75 minute ferry ride, but as importantly, she needed her friend inside. Katie could only run the engine until the ferry took off, and she needed

428

the window up, or the car would be unbearable by the time they were to the island.

Nina glanced at the back of the ferry, and she laughed. "Sure. I have some things in the car, but they're as safe without me as with. Thank you. Doors unlocked, please." She tapped the locking button on the top of Katie's door, and ran towards the opposite side.

Katie tapped the unlock switch just as Nina's hand hit the handle.

"Ah," Nina breathed, as she pulled the door to. "I keep recommending electrical outlets on the car deck. It'd be worth it to me to have an electric heater wired into my car. Then I could run it on days like this."

"You look warm enough." Katie wrapped her hand around Nina's wrist—still in the coat—and squeezed. She couldn't find her friend's arm inside.

"Window dressing. This is January, in Maine, and all the bundling in the world can't keep a body completely warm. Now, you. I hear there's been an engineer out to your place on the Point. Have you received the results, yet?" Nina threw her hood back, and she began to unbutton the front of her coat. Her gloves remained on her hands.

"Let me show it to you." Katie reached into the back seat just as the ferry horn blew. The boat began to move, and the car shifted, sliding a large flat envelope out of Katie's grasp.

"Key, girl." Nina tapped the key in the ignition. "We're moving."

"Right." Katie chuckled and reached to kill the car. She leaned into the back seat again, this time barely touching the envelope with her fingertips. Pulling it forward, she slipped out a letter, and held it out. "Read this."

"Here, so," and Nina scanned down, keeping track with a finger, and occasionally stopping to read in detail. She flipped through several attached pages, one that showed the existing foundations, and another that showed buildable parameters that cut off one end of the old house. At the last page, she looked up. "All that money only to find the fire weakened the foundation walls, and they won't hold a new structure up? That I understand, but there was a house there before. Why can't it be reconstructed in the same spot, even if you replace the existing foundation?"

"A flaw in the bedrock. That isn't in the paperwork, but it seems Grandmamma was fortunate the original house never fell down. The old foundation walls are already pulling apart right where that line's drawn. It would seem the engineers actually know what they're talking about."

"For once." Nina chuckled. "What are your plans, now?"

"We feel stuck. It's a little disappointing, but at least we have the sleeping cabin." Katie shrugged as she slipped the engineering report back into its envelope. It was more than a little disappointing. Jeff had seemed as devastated as she felt, but there was nothing to be done about it, not in the middle of January. "It's not like the Point is five hours away. We can run out there in thirty minutes anytime we want. Who needs a real bathroom?"

The cabin didn't have one.

"You do know Kent and I bought a little place on Settler's Island about three years ago. Nothing much, little more than a primitive camp, with one room downstairs, and a loft that holds a bed." Nina smiled expectantly, as if that changed everything.

"You?" Katie laughed. "You live on an island, Rockhaven, and you have a vacation spot on an island, Settler's, that you can see just across the channel. What happened to Key West, or Hawaii?"

"Settler's Island is convenient. It's not the distance, it's the change of pace. And on Settler's, we can go every weekend, if we want."

"Where . . . I mean, where on Settler's? I might know it." Katie had sailed around Settler's numerous times as a girl. She hadn't been a girl for years, but still, she remembered every house that had been along the coast.

"No, you wouldn't have seen this one. It was empty land when we found it, all we could afford. Kent and I hauled the supplies ourselves and put it up. It's basic, but it's like magic to be there." Nina took a deep breath and smiled, as if enjoying the memory of it very much.

"You really love it, don't you?"

"Yes. You and Jeff? You need that place on the Point. Your baby needs it. So, what's the plan?"

Katie looked out her window and laughed. There was no plan, not with the engineer's report dashing dreams of her family home being rebuilt. Her generous Cousin Nikki had offered to provide the funds, but since replacing her grandmother's home was out the window, perhaps she'd change her mind. That was the real issue, and Katie and Jeff didn't know if the original design from a century earlier could be approved even in another location without the existing foundations as part of the grandfather clause. Building requirements had changed a lot over the past century.

So, what's the plan? Katie smiled. That question was one she'd asked an island boy from her church before Christmas. He had younger brothers who still believed in Santa, but he no longer did. Katie had convinced him not to spoil the moment for his brothers by coming up with a plan for Christmas, and things had gone every bit as smoothly as she'd hoped.

For her own problems, she had no plan at all. She turned when Nina cleared her throat.

"So, is there a plan?" Nina looked at her expectantly.

"Not yet. We're still working out this engineering report." She held the envelope up and laughed.

"I'll tell you, girl, what I'd do if I owned that property. I'd toss that report—" She took it from Katie and flipped it into the back seat. "—and I'd get me an architect on the phone. Send in the engineer's report, and find out what you can build. You might be surprised."

"It wouldn't be my grandmother's house." Katie sighed. She had long ago resigned herself—and quite happily—to using the property without the house being there. She and Jeff could be content with the sleeping cabin as a daytime getaway. It was her second cousin's unexpected offer to rebuild it that had stirred up the old longings again.

The ferry hit a rough patch in the water, and Katie felt her stomach churn. No, she thought. It's afternoon. I cannot be having morning sickness here. Behave, baby!

"Two things." Nina took Katie's hand in her gloved one. "One, never ride the ferry when you're pregnant. I saw that look. Second, this new house, if you rebuild, will be yours and Jeff's. The memories you make for your little one out there? The style of the house doesn't matter. Only the love that fills it is important. Now, you sit quietly, and you'll feel better by the time we get to the landing. Me, I've got to get ready to change cars." Nina pulled her coat around her, and she occupied herself with buttoning it.

"You're sweet, Nina." Katie smiled.

"Practical. Kent says it's the same thing, but thank you." She didn't look up.

Katie smiled again and turned to her window. However, Nina's reassuring words hadn't stopped her stomach from churning, and she didn't want to leave frozen stomach waste on the ferry deck for the entire island to see. Everyone would know. She tried to distract herself by imagining what a different style house on Carver Point might look like. Two stories or one? Lots of glass, or did she want clerestory windows and imaginative openings in interesting locations? A garage. Her grandmother had always wished for a garage. A full basement for rainy weather, a place to hang sheets and towels to dry. And, would she rent it? Many people on the island did, to cover expenses such as utilities and taxes. If so, that would need to be considered in the design.

Then it hit her. Taxes! Katie rubbed one temple with the tip of a finger. Cousin Nikki hadn't thought of that. If Carver House were replaced, taxes on the property would skyrocket. With the car payment Katie had brought from Boston, and no job on the island, money was not exactly flowing from the kitchen taps.

As they rounded the headland into Rockhaven Harbor, catching a swell much harder than normal, Katie's little Beetle jerked. Her stomach jerked, too, and she knew she couldn't hold this one back. She grabbed for the handle and

432

opened the door; and leaning out as far as she could, she lost what little she had inside.

Nina tapped her arm when she was finished. "You pay no mind. They have cleaner for that. I've got to get to my car, though. I've enjoyed my visit. Think about that house, and let me know what you and Jeff decide. It might be fun." Then she was out the door and gone.

As Katie wiped her mouth, she saw Nina pointing out the mess to one of the ferry attendants, and before the ship hit the landing, he already had an absorbent covering the spill.

Baby, come quickly, Katie moaned, as she pulled forward and off the ferry. She had no idea it would be like this. Carver House? Who cared, when little Ragsdale was at war with her insides.

3

The beveled glass in the front door clattered as it closed, bringing Katie awake. The room swam when she tried to sit.

"Katie, honey?" Jeff called to her.

"On the sofa." She let her head drop and raised a hand like a periscope. "It's not a good day."

"Will this make it better?" He sat on the coffee table and took her hand. With a smile, he lifted it to his lips and kissed it. "Any improvement?"

"It's my stomach, not my hand that hurts. Baby exhaustion. I should trademark that phrase." She laughed, enjoying the attention. Jeff smelled good. Ocean good. He'd been out on his boat, and he still wore his weatherproof gear. "If I write a book about baby exhaustion and how to get through it, then I'll never have to work again, and we'll have plenty of money."

"I have you. I don't care about the money. What can I do for you?" He pressed her hand against the side of his face.

"Have this baby. All I did was run Winnie to the airport, and I'm wiped out. How could a baby sap so much of my energy?"

434

It was more than that, though. It was the house she couldn't get clean, the car she'd kept that Jeff didn't really have the money to pay for, and his talk of selling his Jeep. He loved that Jeep, with its ragtop and four giant tires, and she didn't want him to be forced to give it up.

She'd never considered how the year-rounders survived on Rockhaven. As a girl, being a summer person, she'd just assumed they did. However, besides lobstering, how many jobs were there on the island? Not many, she was finding.

ALDMass, take me away! She laughed to herself as she looked into Jeff's eyes, and enjoyed the touch of his skin against hers. She'd gone so far as to send an email to Connie Rivera, her old boss, asking information about doing piecework for the company. If she could work from home . . . but she'd received no answer back, yet.

"If I get us something to eat, will you have energy to listen to the latest news?" Jeff fought a smile. It was clear he had something big to tell.

"I can listen. Just tell me." She wanted to smile back, but that took energy. The baby had all of hers.

"No. Food first." He stood and went to the window and looked out over Moffat Cove. "The boat's running well. That cough from last week hasn't come back. See? A little prayer goes a long way. Now, though. Food. What'll you have? Yesterday's chicken soup, or a fresh BLT?" He turned from the window and smiled.

"Bring me what you like. It'll probably come back up, anyway." Thinking back, she'd felt fine before the ferry ride back from the mainland, and no, she hadn't eaten since losing everything. Being hungry might be part of the problem. She struggled to a sitting position and put her feet on the coffee table. "Beans, do we have any of those? Chili and beans, and a Coke. The real thing, with caffeine and sugar."

"Real chili? From scratch?" Jeff didn't sound sure about that.

"Yes, from scratch. Out-of-the-can scratch. There should be one left on the shelf beside the fridge."

"Yes, ma'am, Dame Carver." He grinned and saluted,

and headed into the kitchen.

That made Katie smile, like everything would work out fine. It was a private endearment that no one else understood, a connection to her return from the island the summer before after a fourteen-year hiatus, and finding Jeff still in love with her, still waiting on her, and giving her the opportunity to discover she was still in love with him. He had teased her with those words, and she had bristled; now they had become part of a bond that linked them as surely as life on Rockhaven was linked to the sea.

"What's the latest news?" She called it loudly to get over the noise in the kitchen.

"Oh, it's Ritchey." The words came to her, filtered through the doorway. "Work's moving ahead on the shop."

"The empty storefront? The one on Main?" That surprised her. Not that Ritchey, Jeff's friend from their teen years, had anything to do with the shop, but that it was happening now. The sun might have been out all day, but winter still had Maine firmly bundled up and wishing for spring.

"You didn't see when you were in town today?" Jeff stood in the doorway with a pan in his hand, and he scraped the sides with a large spoon. "A truck came in on the 1:00. Isn't that the one you were on?"

"I didn't notice. Sorry. Nina was there, and she joined me in the car for a visit. I never got out." She remembered how the wind had cut her skin when she had the window down. Then she'd begun to feel ill, and she hadn't cared who else was on the boat.

"Ah. It was a box truck, anyway, so you wouldn't have been able to tell. It was unloading at the new store when I was dropping off today's catch at Orren's wharf." Orren Swears handled Jeff's daily catch for a percentage. "They were taping brown paper over the insides of the windows. The delivery truck had the street blocked, so I'll bet Archie Coombs raises a complaint at the next town meeting. If we want to eat, I'd better get this on the stove." He raised the pan to show Katie, then he laughed and turned back into the kitchen.

436

"I like Archie." Katie didn't know him well, but he seemed nice enough. He'd been to services at Rockhaven Town Church once, and he'd smiled when he greeted her. She'd asked if he had an email address so she could send him her weekly sermon notes, and he'd guffawed, telling her that email was for city folks. He'd put in a phone line forty years before, and no one called him on that. Why would they send him an email? He'd chuckled as he walked away, getting into an old van that looked more rust than rusty, and started it up in a cloud of blue smoke.

"So, Archie has a fan." Jeff's amusement could be heard in his words. "Good for you, Katie. More people should be like you, able to find the good in people."

"Is that so?" She leaned her head back and closed her eyes, sinking into the building drowsiness that seemed ready to consume her day. It wasn't worth fighting any longer. She heard the oil heater click three times, and the fan began to blow. Pulling a throw from the end of the sofa, she covered herself and tucked it under her chin. She smiled at the touch of a kiss on her cheek.

"You look comfy. Can I join you?" Jeff whispered the words to her.

"You can bring me food." She took a deep breath, and she smiled again, filled up with her love for this man who treated her so well. She smelled food, too, and her stomach grumbled. Real grumbles, not nausea flip-flops, and for that, she was grateful.

"Said and done. Open your peepers."

Katie looked to see a steaming bowl of chili in front of her, seated in a second bowl lined with a paper towel. They were on a plate with four crackers to the side. When she took it, Jeff produced a Coke in a bright red can, and he set it on the table at the end of the sofa.

"Oh, Jeff, I think I can survive the day." She spooned up a bite of the chili, and she bit into a chunk of meat. The flavor exploded into her mouth. "This is the best thing I've ever tasted. Hand me that drink, please."

"Better than Thanksgiving turkey?" He teased with a twinkle in his eye.

"Even better than pumpkin pie, but don't tell Roker that." Roker was Jeff's friend on the island, although he had quickly become a good friend of Katie's, also. Roker's favorite pie was pumpkin, especially when prepared by Jess up on High Road.

"My lips are sealed." Jeff drew a conspiratorial finger across his mouth, "zipping" his lips together. "You, my beautiful woman, enjoy your chili and beans, because I want you to get to feeling better. We need to head out to the Point later."

"The Point? Today?"

"Today. I have something very special to show you." His expression said that's all he was going to say.

"It'll be closing in on night by the time we get there." She was feeling better, though. Beans, chili, and caffeine were proving just the thing. As her doctor had instructed her when she told him that she didn't feel like eating when she was nauseous, whatever gets food and water into her system was better than dehydration and starving the baby.

"I remember a time when I would have looked forward to it being dark." Jeff's eyes crinkled in barely controlled laughter.

"Not anymore?" She was teasing, and that told her she was definitely feeling more like her old self. She dipped up the last of the chili and held out the bowl to him.

This time Jeff laughed aloud. "Now, you never heard me say that. I'm always happy to be in the dark with you."

Katie watched him walk away, and she felt of her belly, thinking, And look where it's got us now. She didn't mind, though, at least not most days. However, for the next six months, she was staying off the ferry, unless someone was dying. Puking was not fun, and that's where Katie drew the line.

She did let Jeff help her stand and put on her coat. She was grateful it still fit around her waist, and maybe spring would come before the baby got too big. She couldn't afford a new one, not unless she heard from ALDMass with some very good news.

Having a baby on a Maine island. In the winter. What an experience this was turning out to be!

438

4

"Jeff, is that Kevie?" A boy trudged beside the road about a quarter mile in front of them, headed the same direction. "I know that walk. It is. Stop up here, and let's see what he's doing."

Kevie was Al and Janine Peavey's eldest of four. He was the boy Katie had convinced to go along with Christmas for his younger brothers a month back. He held something oddly shaped in one hand.

Jeff chuckled, glancing in his mirror. "We've got company coming up, but I think we're good." Good to stop beside Kevie, he meant. The "company" was a car a good distance behind them. "You can tell it's Kevie from his walk?"

He had a point. The boy had on a thick coat, a hood pulled over his head, and mittens on his hands. As they grew closer, he turned to wave, and his face was wrapped with a muffler. They could barely see his eyes.

"Don't you watch people? Of course I can tell." Katie pointed. "Pull over here."

"Sure, I watch people, but usually their faces." He teased her. "I don't recognize anyone's backside."

He forced the four-wheel-drive machine into a lower

gear, and the engine roared as they slowed to a crawl. He applied the brakes as he eased two wheels off the road. The car coming up gave a warning honk, then pulled to the opposite lane and sped up to go around.

"Kevie? Do you need a ride?" Katie had the window cracked, and she called out through the opening as Jeff rolled to a stop.

"Hi, Miss Katie. Hey, Jeff." He waved with his free hand. His voice was muffled through all the fabric. "Nah. I'm fine. Besides, I've got this, and I need to carry it outside." His eyes crinkled, and it was clear he was smiling.

"How was school today?"

"Fine. Konnar had to sit in the corner." His eyes were crinkled again. Konnar was one of his brothers.

"I'll bet he was embarrassed." Katie expected Kevie had done his best to make sure of it, and she was certain Konnar would do the same at the first opportunity.

"He wasn't embarrassed. He was just stupid. Everyone kept asking me why he was in the corner. I told them it was the stupid corner, and Konnar has to sit there for the rest of the year."

"Kevie!" Katie fought to keep from laughing. "Come on and get inside." She motioned with her hand.

"I would, but—" He held up the package.

"We don't mind. What is it?" Katie rolled the window down more, noticing that the heater fan had turned up a notch. She rolled the window down farther. "We have plenty of room."

"Nah. Mom said I can't let anyone pick me up. I better get on. I've got a long way to go. Bye!" He waved again, and turning his back to them, he started down the side of the road.

"What was that about?" Katie rolled her window up. "Janine is making him walk outside in this?"

"He's thoroughly insulated. I don't think you have to worry that an eleven-year-old will freeze on Rockhaven. Kids here know better." Jeff worked the transmission into first, and he pulled back onto the road. As they passed the boy, he honked twice. "Once for each of us."

"In Boston, they'd chase you down and shoot a gun at you for that."

"For what? Stopping to offer a ride to a good friend's kid?" Laughter was twisted in Jeff's question, telling how absurd he found that. He picked up her hand and kissed it. "What about if it's a pretty girl? One I'm married to? Can I stop and give her a ride?"

"You are so silly. I'm glad I married you." Katie refused to let go of his hand, even when he pushed the lever into a new gear. She liked touching him, any part of him. It filled her with satisfaction in a way that nothing else could.

"Tell me, why is someone planning on shooting out my back window?"

"The honking thing. Up here, people pass and they honk. That's strange." She shivered.

"Only if you're not a Rockhavener. And all of us aren't strange, you know. Only those with broken horns. We think they're the strange ones, because they don't honk at us." He laughed. They were passing the Town Park, where the gazebo that had caught fire just before Christmas still showed damage on one side. It wouldn't get repaired until warmer weather, though. As Jeff had told Katie when she asked about it, nothing outdoors got repaired in winter in Maine, not unless it was urgent. It was too much trouble arguing with Mother Nature, because Mother Nature almost always won.

"The truck's gone." They had reached Main, with Rockhaven Harbor to the left, and Ritchey Hickox's empty and very raw storefront to the right. "Slow down. I want to look."

Vast sheets of brown paper covered the windows of the old building, just as Jeff had said. It, as did everything on Main Street, dated from the heyday of Rockhaven over a hundred years before. The double-glazed glass walls fronting the road were newer, and the piers holding the backside up over the saltwater pond that flooded under Main street at the turn of every tide had been replaced more than once, but a casual visitor would only see age and character.

It was why Katie knew it was a perfect location for Ritchey to branch out with his sporting goods chain of stores. It was as exciting as it was surprising to see progress already happening in the middle of January. No one had expected to see anything going on inside the building until March, at the earliest.

"Okay, Starry-Eyes, what are you seeing?" Jeff pointed to the roof. "Ritchey must be doing well. There. The heat's on." Above the building steam rose from a vent. "Either that or they've already turned the water on. If so, they'll have to run the heat from here on out. I'd hate to pay his heating bill."

"Yeah," she said. She was thinking, though. ALDMass. Ritchey's store, whatever he decided to call it. Ideas flashed through her head, and she tried to catalog them away. She was distracted by Jeff.

"Are you ready to head out?" Jeff squeezed her hand.

"Sure." She glanced at a sign in the window. Construction Permit Approved. There was more underneath, but the words were too small to read.

"Then we're off." Jeff took the shifter and pushed it into neutral, rocking it back and forth, and he looked behind them. Then, with the clutch depressed, he slipped it easily into first. Before he could pull forward, Katie put her hand on his.

"Not too fast, Jeff. I'm feeling better, but I won't be well for another five and a half months. Speed is not what I need."

"Okay, my little turtle. I'll creep along at your side. Can I do a fast creep? I'd like to get there in daylight."

He had a point, and Katie took her hand from his. He pulled forward, whistling a familiar Christmas tune, *Oh, Christmas Tree*. He told her it reminded him of his Katie tree. He'd probably wear it out in early May. Roker razzed him about it, but it was all about love, so Jeff laughed and ignored Roker. The man was single. What did he know?

Katie thought Jess up on High Road might have an opinion on that. She still had a question about Kevie, though.

"Jeff, what do you think Kevie had that he couldn't put in a car with someone else?"

"There's no telling. Remember those clams we dug up when we were kids? We carried them to town from out at your grandmother's. I don't think anyone would have let us inside their car." He chuckled. "It didn't help that we were covered with mud."

"A ride would have been nice, though. How did we carry them? Wasn't it in the Lil' Dude?" The Dude was Katie's twelve-foot sailing skiff. That summer Jeff, Katie, and all their friends had sailed around the islands in it. It seemed there wasn't a day they weren't out on the water.

"Ha!" Jeff laughed. "I do remember that. We had so many clams we nearly capsized. Twice. We finally made Bennie and Bobby get out and swim. Do you remember? We towed them with a rope."

"And their feet and hands were blue by the time we pulled them out of the water at the town float." Katie was laughing, too, and she wished she wasn't. It wasn't doing her stomach any favors.

"Don't you think a few people saw us in that boat and felt sorry for us? Oh, those poor kids. Why doesn't one of those lobstermen stop and help them out?" Jeff's eyes twinkled. "We'd have refused if they did. Wouldn't we?"

"I get it. Kevie's doing fine, even though I'm freezing, even in here. I still want to know what he was carrying."

"If people had checked on the Dude that summer, they'd have regretted it. Sometimes it's best not to know."

"Then, let's change the subject. What's at the Point? It'll be dark when we get there." And cold. Katie wanted her fire, well, Jeff's fire, built with his hands, and her warming in front of it on the sofa. She wanted him, next to her in bed, the heat of his skin against hers. The Point? That was for summer and sunshine and languid starry nights, even if Maine evenings did require a blanket in the middle of July.

"What do you want more than anything in this world?" Jeff downshifted as the grade of the road increased. That meant they were coming up to the hawk's nest. This time of the year it would be unoccupied.

Katie considered Jeff's question as she looked at the empty nest high in the trees. At Christmas, it had been a snowy mound. Jeff told her a number of years back, an old bird had wintered over three years in a row. Then it was gone, and the nest had once again become a summer residence, just like most of the waterfront homes across the island. Now, with the sun of the past week, it showed bare woven sticks teetering at the top of a tree, a fantastic display of the birds' ingenuity, but lifeless, nonetheless.

Once she would have answered Jeff's question with, "My grandmother's house," and she wouldn't have had to think about it. Now, Nina's words haunted her. The style of the house doesn't matter. Only the love that fills it is important. Carver House, rebuilt and new again? It wouldn't give Katie her grandmother back, or Nikki's gift of a ring, lost with everything else in the fire that took it all. The pies and the nights in front of her grandmother's old Franklin stove, they were in Katie's head, but they could never fill a new house, even if it was exactly the same. Smiling, Katie made her decision.

"You." She laid her arm atop Jeff's, and she rubbed the skin just where his thumb crooked against his palm.

"Me, what?" He chuckled. He pushed in the clutch, and pulling his hand free, he changed the gears once more, taking her hand in his when he was finished.

"I choose you. You asked, what do I want more than anything else in the world, and I choose you."

"Okay, you scamp. After me. What do you choose after me?" He sounded pleased, but he laughed it off. "Be serious about this. It's important."

"I am being serious. If I can't have you—"

"Not so fast, Dame Carver. I didn't say that. I said after me. You're not being serious, yet. I want adult serious." He slowed for Round Pond. It held the town water supply. A sign said No Swimming or Boating Allowed. After crossing over the small earthen dam holding back the water, Jeff speeded up again.

"Adult serious, Girl Scout's honor." Katie held up three

fingers. "I choose Jeffie." She patted her stomach. There was just enough of a baby that she could feel the difference.

"Pregnant women." Jeff said it with dismay, but his face showed his amusement. "We'll be there in ten minutes. What do you want?"

"Winnie here." Jeff's question was bringing up all sorts of emotions, and Katie knew it must be the baby. This wasn't like her at all. Yet, she missed her friend immensely, and her eyes burned. She wiped at them carefully, hoping Jeff wasn't watching.

"Oh, honey, I know you miss her." He took her hand and kissed the back of it. "No tears allowed. I'll have to kiss them all away, and I'll have a wreck if I do." The cutoff from the main road was coming up, and he slowed to turn, releasing her hand once again to shift a series of gears to make the corner.

This part of the road was dirt and gravel all the way to the house. Katie knew the going would be slow, and Jeff's hands would be busy, especially when navigating past Lookout Ledge, the highest point on the island. It came at the end of a sharp incline, then the road immediately twisted and climbed twice as steeply.

She smiled at Jeff's words, and she did feel better. Hormonal pregnant women! And she was one of them! Jeff's hands worked the gears, and he turned the wheel to avoid rocks and depressions in the road. He was so busy, and as he hummed his little tune, he occasionally laughed, calling out, "That one's gotta be fixed before long." Then he steered around whatever obstacle was in his way.

This was real life, Katie decided. This ride to the Point was life boiled down to its bare essence. You held hands when you could, released them for a moment when you had to change gears, and when the road got really rough, sometimes you were doing completely different things, one person navigating the treacherous terrain, and the other person watching it all happen. It wasn't like all the sugary sentiments that said, "Love is both people having their hands on the wheel at the same time," or, "Love is like kindergarten: Never let go of the other person's hand."

445

No, if you held on all the time, you caused a crash. Two people couldn't continually be in control. Sometimes you had to let go and let trust come into the picture. Sure, ask for directions, or change out drivers when the trip was tiring, and when possible, hold hands as you traveled down the road. If you held on too tightly, people suffocated. Jeeps wrecked. Friendships faltered. Katie thought of Carver House's old Franklin stove, lost with everything else in that long-ago fire. It had metal doors to close up the firebox, containing the flames and restricting the air to make it burn brighter and hotter, so that you got the most heat possible out of the wood. A relationship was like that. Marriage, especially. Your vows were the doors. You closed up the firebox, and love burned ever hotter. Close it up all the way, and you choked the fire. A flame needed air, or it would smolder and eventually die. Just like Jeff driving with Katie at his side, there were always careful adjustments to make. Work at it long enough, and the adjustments became as natural as living and breathing. Refuse to make them, though, and you had no relationship. All you had was control.

She had discovered she had no control over the Point half a lifetime ago. The fire had taken all that away. Now it was like the hawk's nest. It was the living each day to its fullest that filled it up. She'd once wanted her grandmother's house back more than anything, and then Nikki had offered it to her. Yet, it was Jeff's house, now hers and Jeff's, on Moffat Cove that had become her home. Carver Point was the memory of her grandmother and the good times Katie had enjoyed while growing up there with all her friends.

Jeff slowed to spiral past Lookout Ledge, and with the engine growling in protest, he nudged her with his elbow. "So, have you decided, yet?"

"I may be stubborn, but I'm not stupid." She laughed her comment off. "Your question is about the Point, or else we wouldn't be out here. So, I'll bite. To be able to rebuild Grandmamma's house. Since that's impossible, now we can move on."

"Oh, no, we can't." He glanced at her, fighting a smile.

"We have the report, Jeff. You know where that leaves us. Nina on the ferry said to call up an architect and come up with an all-new plan, but I need to see where Nikki stands first. It is her money." Katie gritted her teeth. The pull up the steep incline was doing a number on her. It seemed the baby didn't like going uphill.

"I get it. Everything hinges on your cousin, right?" Before he could continue, he topped the rise and cut left to follow the road, immediately hitting his brakes and coming to a full stop. A large branch lay across the road.

"That's the last straw, Jeff. Don't move." Katie began to fumble her seatbelt off.

"The last straw? You're the one who said it, but I guess you're right. She really does have all the money." He looked straight ahead, one hand on the steering wheel, and the other on the gear lever, his eyes evaluating the blockage.

"I don't care about money. Baby says move." With that, she threw the door open, and leaned outside for the second time in one day. She barely had the wither all to think, and her mouth was occupied, but if she could have barked out her feelings, she knew what she would say. Jeff, you did this to me. Why can't you be the one to lose your stomach twice in one day?

She wouldn't mean it, of course. It was the thinking it that make the moment almost acceptable. A baby in winter. On an island. With gravel roads. What had she been thinking?

Of course, that was the entire problem. She hadn't been thinking, or this wouldn't be happening.

"Katie, are you all right?" Jeff touched her on the arm, holding out the box of tissues from the console.

"In a minute." She spat and sat up, taking the tissues, and looking straight ahead. At least she felt better with her stomach emptied. Maybe the chili hadn't been a good idea. "Whatever you're showing me, it had better be good."

"It will be. Trust me. I'll be right back after I get the road cleared."

Katie watched him dragging the branch out of the way, the ends of his unmanageable hair loose under his knit cap, and his strong legs barely contained in his jeans. She did love that man, and he'd better be glad for it. If she didn't, the next six months wouldn't be worth it. Losing your stomach on a daily basis? Baby Jeffie, she thought, you'd better be beautiful, because you might be the last of your line.

By the time Jeff returned, she was over her moment of self-imposed pity, and she was able to smile. It helped that he looked perfectly contrite, as if he wished he hadn't forced her to come. Good, she thought. I feel exactly the same. They were almost there, though, so she would see what they'd come to see. After all, the ride home from here was only a couple thousand feet shorter than the ride from the Point. This, she could do. For Jeff, this she could do.

It was Jeff picking up her hand and giving it a kiss that really salved her spirit. Her preacher man Jeff, always coming to her rescue. In spite of this baby testing her limits, she loved Jeff, and if the Point fell off the island, she would still live out the happiest existence anyone had ever known.

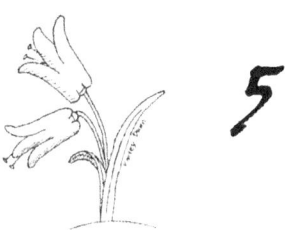

5

"What is that, Jeff?" Katie frowned. The question was rhetorical, because it was unmistakable. It was an aluminum-sided trailer house. Still, Carver Point was private property, and that trailer shouldn't be on Carver land.

"What?" He parked the Jeep across the grassy expanse that fronted the wood gate leading into the yard proper, looking very smug.

"Stop it. Someone's squatting on our property. It's against the law." Katie pushed against his arm. She remembered what he had told her the summer before. For the fourteen years she'd been away, he'd come out and checked on the property regularly to prevent this very thing from happening.

That was when she realized this was exactly the reason he'd insisted they come out today. He'd heard about this, and he knew she'd want to know. He was right. She certainly did.

"I see a sign on the side. I think it has a phone number. Where's paper and a pen? I intend to get that number down and call someone to get this removed." She was already digging in the glove box as she fumed. That episode with

449

her stomach back on the road? Fiddlesticks. It meant nothing to her against this.

"Do you want your gloves?" Jeff held them out to her.

"Thank you. Hold this." She took the gloves with one hand and slapped a small pad and a clicker ballpoint pen onto his palm. She tugged the gloves on, and she glared out the window. "Just because there's no house here, and it's winter, they think they can move in, and no one's going to notice. A decade ago they might have gotten away with that—"

"No, they wouldn't." Jeff still wore his smug expression.

"Right. But if you hadn't been here, they might've. Well, I'm back, or haven't people noticed that?" She had her coat buttoned, and she tugged a knit cap over her head, preparing for the wind. It was nearly always windy at the Point. That's what a point of land on an island meant: exposed, and therefore, windy.

"Oh, I think they've noticed." Jeff nodded his head and looked out his window. There was nothing for him to see, except a wall of greenery. The real views were past the wood gate, where the ever-prevalent spruce and its accompanying undergrowth were cleared. His face, reflected in the glass, grinned.

"You sit right here, and then we've got some phone calls to make." Katie pointed a finger at him, and realizing how condescending that appeared, she made her hand into a loose fist. "Sorry, Jeff."

"No offense taken. Go. Get your numbers. We'll get this all sorted out." He held the paper and pen out to her. "Don't forget this."

"Thank you." She took it and pulled the door handle, releasing the door and stepping outside. "It's cold out here. And to think, when Grandmamma's house was built, people lived here year round. Crazy."

"Crazy." Jeff chuckled.

Katie marched over, her feet walking across last summer's grass, and she clicked the pen out, ready to scribble down the number and get back into the car. Only after she pressed the pen to the pad ten times, writing all ten numbers—as well as scribbling in one corner when the ink wouldn't come out—did she notice the words above the number. Chetwynde Architectural Design and Construction. To the side, it added in a cursive script, Almon Chetwynde, Owner.

She turned to look at Jeff, to see him waving cheerily through the window. Slipping her pad into her breast pocket and forcing her hands into pockets of their own, she headed towards the car, not exactly happy.

"You knew what this was." She pulled herself inside and closed the door hard after her. "So explain it."

Her concern had to do with the engineer's report, the fact—and it was a very real fact—that the original house couldn't be restored, and it was only that exact house her cousin had agreed to fund. Not a post-and-beam glass-infused structure, or a low-slung cottage, but an 1892 manse filled with porches and family history. They couldn't do this on their own.

"It's simple. I'll tell you about it on the way in. I want back on a paved road by dark." Into town, he meant. On the island, everything was either in—towards town—or out—any other place on Rockhaven. His comment about the dark was obvious, too. Past the end of the driveway, the dirt and gravel road was easily navigable in the light. At night? The potholes and frost-heaved rocks all looked the same. He shifted into gear and turned the vehicle around.

"Chetwynde." Katie pulled the pad out and looked at the name. "Didn't we know a Chetwynde growing up?"

"You're making the connection. John. His dad's Almon." Jeff smiled. "John lived up on the Reach. They were summer people like you, but he spent his summers at camps off island. Tennis, usually."

"His father's an architect. Hmm."

"No, John's the architect. His dad has the money."

"And you invited him to do what?" That worried Katie, and especially that Jeff would do it without consulting her first.

"You need the rest of the story. John's firm is finishing

up a new build out on Smalley's Point." It was an isolated area overlooking Rockhaven's sister island, East Haven. "I met him in town, and he'd heard the old place on the Point might be going back up. He has another project coming together, a remodel in town, and he'd be interested in bidding on ours. He could cut out some of the costs, since his crews would already be on site."

"They'll be on the island, anyway. The Point isn't a building site, yet." Katie took a deep breath, holding on as Jeff navigated the turn to head back towards Lookout Ledge. At least the baby didn't seem to mind going downhill as much as he had uphill. "I think he doesn't want to move the trailer out until winter's over, and parking at Carver Point is convenient storage."

"Maybe, but he said he'll be glad to look at the reports and evaluate it, maybe even come up with some tentative options. All I need to do is shoot him some parameters so he'll know what we need."

Katie thought on that. If they had something on paper, then when they talked to Nikki, she'd have concrete examples to weigh over in her mind. That might be a very good thing.

"Okay, Jeff. You keep track of this—" She put the pad with the number on the console. "—and I'll think over what I'd like out there. It has to respect the house my grandmother lived in all her life."

"Of course." He took her hand and squeezed it, then released it to downshift to navigate a pothole.

"And a downstairs bathroom. Grandmamma hated having to climb the stairs every time she had to go."

"Downstairs. Got it." He smiled.

"A garage. Do you want a garage?"

"A garage would be nice." He chuckled. "Any porches?"

"Oh, Jeff. Porches everywhere! That was my favorite thing about Carver House. It had porches everywhere, with a porch swing. I would love to have a porch swing."

"Write it down." He picked up the pad and held it in the air. "Porch swing, number one priority. We can't leave that out."

Katie laughed, taking the pad and putting it back on the console. "Will he charge us for this?"

"Oh, I'm certain, if we decide to build. He did say he'd offer us a good deal, though."

"It's just that it's not our money we're spending. Maybe we should leave off the garage. One porch, maybe. Surely Nikki wouldn't mind paying for that." She smiled as she said it, but it wasn't what she really wanted.

"That's not what John said. We're to shoot him ideas. Let your cousin knock them down." He pulled onto the main road. His headlights were on, and with the tarmac, he picked up speed.

"It's getting my hopes up that worries me." She'd lost everything a long time ago, and it had been hard. But she'd done it, forging ahead to a new life in Boston. To have it offered back to her stirred up longings that she didn't want to have to squelch once again.

"You let me worry about that. Oh, I bet you don't know something else." His face lighted up in an impish grin. He held her hand full time by then.

Katie laughed. "Apparently not, or you wouldn't be saying that."

"The remodel on Ritchey's store is John's other project. How about that?"

"Good for John." Katie nodded, finding it oddly satisfying. The old pack was coming back together, all connected in one way or another, with a new man or two to fill in the gaps. Who else would she see before her first year as an adult in Rockhaven was over? Apple Dumpling? Babes Baker? Maybe even Bennie and Bobby Reynolds? How great would that be, to have everyone together once again on Rockhaven Island?

She put that aside, though. She had to get the house completed first. Otherwise, where would everyone stay?

453

6

"Janine! Al! I'm glad you could make it this morning."

Katie was in the church foyer, welcoming Jeff's flock to the Sunday morning services. It was rare for Janine and Al to miss, although it was almost equally rare for them to be on time. With four boys, who could blame them? Janine had once confided to Katie that it was sometimes the only hour of the week she got with just Al. Someone else got to enjoy her boys for a while. Janine had chuckled as she'd stressed the word enjoy.

"Kevie, the man with a plan!" Katie raised her fist and gave him a fist bump. He grinned and returned it. The youngest two, Karlton and Keithie, were in an ongoing tussle as they came through the door. Janine groaned and told them in a tightly-controlled voice to find their Sunday school room now. Konnar didn't come in at all, but as the door closed, Katie could see him standing just outside.

"He wanted to ride up front." Al laughed, like it was no big deal. "Keithie got the honor. It was a bit of divide and conquer. It worked until we got out of the truck." He snapped his fingers at the two youngest, still arguing, calling out, "Now, boys. Off to your rooms."

"I'll check on him." Katie smiled. She was learning to

enjoy being the minister's wife, because it gave her an open door to step into all sorts of problematic situations. People let her attempt to resolve issues that other islanders wouldn't be allowed near.

"Thank you. Janine knew you'd be glad to talk to him. She's already inside, so I'm heading in. Send someone for me if you have any problems." He looked relieved and disappeared into the auditorium, where the adult class was about to begin.

Jeff was involved in welcoming Archie Coombs to the service. It was his second visit, and Katie was convinced her pleasantries his first time with them was the reason for his return. Jeff held one of the man's hands in both of his, and he laughed at something Archie said. Katie touched her husband on the elbow and said, "Door." He nodded to her, and she stepped outside.

"Konnar, it's cold this morning." Especially as Katie didn't have her coat on. It was on the rack, and she hadn't thought before deciding to do this.

"I'm mad." As if that told the entire story, and even perhaps that Katie was intruding on his private misery.

"One of those days. I have them sometimes." Katie shivered, but at least she had long sleeves. If it were windy, she wouldn't have made it this long. "Sometimes telling someone helps."

"I called front. I called it, and it was mine. Then Dad made Keithie sit there." He wiped at one eye with his hand.

"Did he say why?" Al had explained to her, but had he told the boys? Or maybe it was like telling them to go to their Sunday school classes. He got tired of their behavior, so he told them to just do it.

"Yeah. The little twerpies were fighting again." He coughed—the cold, probably—and he stuffed both his hands in his jacket pockets. "I don't like little brothers."

"Did it work?"

"Did what work?" He looked at her. That was progress.

"Did your brothers stop fighting?" She smiled at him encouragingly. Maybe he would smile back.

"Until we got here." He almost grinned. "I hit Keithie

on the knee all the way to church."

"And he didn't say anything?" Katie smiled, this time because it was funny. Paybacks, the boys would probably call it.

"I would've hit him harder." Konnar snickered, as if it were a good joke. "I'm cold. Can we go in, now?"

"Absolutely. I'm cold, too." Katie pulled the door open and followed him inside. He heaved his coat off, tossed it to land underneath the others on the rack, and tore off to his classroom. Jeff was already in the auditorium, moving among the pews to greet people she had welcomed, but who had bypassed him. He was good at that, searching out people, and making them feel as if they were the most important people on the island. It was why crowds showed up even in the worst of weather. It was because they felt like Jeff really cared.

On the right she found Roker. She smiled at who was next to him. Since Thanksgiving, Roker and Jess from up on High Road had become a common sight together across Rockhaven. Katie searched, hoping to see Neil Foote. He didn't often get out in the coldest of weather, and she wasn't overly surprised not to find him.

It was more surprising not to see Babbitt George. Katie had seen Brookie and Mara, his children, come in early. And Libby, Babbitt's wife, was on the second row. Shrugging, Katie let her eyes move on. There were a dozen places he could be, from the usher's box to filling in for a Sunday school teacher who hadn't made it in. She smiled at the Schutmaats. They were the most faithful in the entire congregation. It helped that they lived on 4th Street, just blocks from the church. Ada Simpers had made it in, in spite of living the other side of town. And Bryan Nickerson, one of Jeff's eager beavers, those trusted church members that always went overboard to see that they were involved in every activity, no matter how much it got on other people's nerves. Katie didn't mind. She liked eager beavers.

It was the Watson-Strykers that reminded her of Debsy, their daughter, in the Christmas pageant. The girl had abandoned her part to take off for the restroom, leaving

456

Katie to assume her role. And the girl had been the adorable star of the production, carrying the final Christmas star to hold it over the baby Jesus. What spoke well of the Rockhaven Town Church flock was that the congregation found the child charming in spite of it, and that had endeared them to Katie.

Katie hadn't seen them since Christmas, and she made her way to Kayline, Debsy's mother. She touched her on the shoulder to get her attention.

"Katie! Good morning!" Kayline set her Bible and gloves to the side and stood, grabbing Katie in a quick hug. "I'm so sorry we haven't made it to services the past few weeks. Jerry's father, and then Little J took the flu. We can't seem to get ahead for falling behind." She laughed. "Are you doing okay, with the baby, I mean?"

"Most days. When I remember not to ride the ferry. It's good to see you here today." Katie made to move on, only to have Kayline grab her wrist.

"If you've just a minute, I have something for you."

"Of course." Katie had no idea what it could be, and she'd only meant to connect with the family, not intrude into their morning. However, Kayline was already opening her Bible, and she pulled out a folded sheet of tablet paper, the sort pulled from a wire binding.

"This is from Debsy, and she's only three, so take that into account. She really wanted you to have this." She pressed the paper into Katie's hand. "Jerry and I, well, we want you to know how much we appreciate you stepping in as minister's wife here. You are so good with our little ones. Thank you." She took Katie's hand in hers and squeezed it.

After a brief smile, Kayline sat, cutting off the conversation, but Katie was pretty sure that was because of the impending tears she'd seen. Now she felt bad about being irritated at Debsy during the play. She was three, and three-year-olds did three-year-old things. Katie guessed she would understand some day. Maybe this was her first lesson.

The organ started up as the signal for people to finish

their visitation and move to their seats. After two or three more handshakes, and two whispered good mornings, Katie settled into her seat. She opened the folded paper, and on it, in bright and erratic crayon, was a sunflower, a sun, and a big red heart. At the bottom was Debsy's name, painstakingly written, although with a backwards "b."

Katie felt her eyes water, and there was a knot in her throat. What a sweet thing for the child to do, and she had clearly put a great deal of effort into it. The oversized heart got Katie to thinking, even as she pulled out her tablet to take notes on the morning service. Valentine's Day was only a month away. She would have to plan something special for all the children. Especially Kevie. He was turning twelve in March, but he wasn't too old for a little valentine fun.

Katie clicked her tablet on. Not all churches would approve of their members—especially the minister's wife—having their personal devices out during services, but even before Katie had come to live full time on the island, Jeff had been very proactive in embracing the future. The building was set up with a Wi-Fi system everyone could connect to, and using online Bibles was encouraged. The congregation's favorite was one that allowed them to insert comments about certain verses, and the other church members could view them on their own devices. Once a month, Jeff coordinated the comments and published them in the church's weekly email. Katie's job was to provide a weekly email of the entire service for those who were stuck at home for the morning, and of course it went to all the summer people who attended, if they'd provided their email address to the church.

Katie had a few more people she'd put on her list. Winnie Catron, her best friend. Ritchey Hickox, Jeff's closest boyhood friend. Recently she had added Austie William's name to her list.

She was still searching for Babes and Apple. They had to be out there somewhere, and email? Surely everyone had email. It was the 21st century, after all. Then there were the Reynolds twins. Where were they hiding? It was as if they'd fallen off the ends of the earth. People can't just disappear. They have to be somewhere.

She would find them. Just give her time. The old gang would get back together one way or another. Katie had mentioned them in her private prayers enough, and she was convinced of one thing. God always came through, and she had no doubts this time. After all, she was back on Rockhaven, married to the childhood sweetheart of her dreams. If that wasn't the hand of God, what was?

God could do anything. This? It was a piece of cake. With God, everything was a piece of cake. Katie smiled at that. She also knew you had to wait for the cake to come out of the oven to enjoy it. Jeff? He'd baked for fourteen years. Now, God, Katie mentally sent up as she typed in the title for the morning's notes. Turn up the heat. It's time for the latest cake to come out of the oven.

Then, she set her tablet aside and stood for the first song of the morning. She began to sing, "How great thou art . . ."

She meant it, too, every single word that came out of her mouth.

7

"Jeff, I was finally able to reach Connie. She got back with me, thank goodness, and she said she'd see what the company could put together. She sounded hopeful." It was about going back to work, although it had to be something she could do from home. Traveling to Boston for employment was not an option.

Katie held a cup of steaming cocoa in her hands, and she looked out the broad expanse of windows that gave the living room a sweeping view of Moffat Cove. It was beautiful, even if the warmth of the past few days had melted the snows, leaving the winter-browned grass in sharp contrast to the vivid green of the surrounding spruce trees.

However, there was one particular part of the scene that wasn't beautiful at all.

"Sweetheart, that's not the solution." Jeff came up behind her and wrapped his arms around her. He pulled her hair back and kissed her on the neck. "The island takes care of its own. See?" He pointed out past the dock to his boat. Roker was bundled up, and he was working on the engine. They'd see him disappear for a few minutes, then he would reappear, occasionally scratch his head, and then vanish once more. He didn't look as if he were making all that much progress.

"The island doesn't make the car payment." That, and Jeff's four-wheel-drive, and now the medical bills involved with an upcoming baby. Even with insurance, their share had dropped Katie's jaw.

"Neither does my wife working a part-time job. We'll be okay. After all, we have the house. See? We're fine." He leaned in and began kissing her neck again.

The house had been from Jeff's father, a family legacy bequeathed to him in his will. Katie was certainly grateful for that. Still, she studied the boat, seeing Roker reappearing once more, fully aware the problem had deeper roots still. And if Cousin Nikki did rebuild Carver House, they would have to assume the increased taxes, but how could Katie say no to her cousin's offer? She'd never have another chance to see Carver Point reborn without her cousin's generosity.

"Look, Roker's waving. I think he wants you." Katie jabbed her husband in the ribs. "Enough, Jeff. You'll wear a hole in my skin. Go help him get your boat back on the water. You've got lobster out there waiting in your traps. You can't leave them to starve to death."

"I don't think pulling pots compares to spending time with you, but I'm at your command. I go, and I'll do all I can to meet Roker's demands of me." Jeff chuckled and bowed to her, looping his hand in a circle.

"You're too silly. I've got a valentine activity to put together, so you get out there and leave me in peace. Just because I'm home all day doesn't mean I sit around and twiddle my thumbs."

"Of course not." He was putting on his coat. "I can't imagine you twiddling anyone's thumbs, ever. My boat repairman and I will need something to eat when we get wrapped up. Can you find enough time to twiddle that together?" His eyes twinkled.

"Go!" She held up her cup. It still steamed. "Remember the thermos on the table. It has more of this inside. Roker will worship you for bringing it out."

461

"He'll worship you, but then, I think he already does." He vanished into the kitchen and emerged with it in his hands. He had his gloves on, and he pulled a knit cap over his head, making sure his ears were covered.

"I love you, Jeff." Katie waggled her fingers at him.

"Eh?" He tapped one ear, showing her it was covered.

"I love you," she called louder.

"What's that?" He pulled the cap from over his ear. "Say that once more?" He was grinning by then, though.

"Oh, you. I should kick you." She laughed. "You could hear me the entire time."

"You can't blame me. I like hearing you say you love me. I love you, too, Katie." He twisted the door knob, and he stepped into the sun, the faint sound of *Oh, Christmas Tree* trailing after him.

Katie shivered, watching him walk across the yard and out on the dock. Sunshine in Maine didn't equate to warmth. This time of year, it provided light, but that was it. Still, it caught on Jeff, light and shadow, showing him for the lobsterman he was. Broad shoulders. Long legs. His clothes fitting and not fitting at the same time. It wasn't that they didn't fit, just that they weren't loose, and neither were they tight. Rather, they were loose when he relaxed a limb or a muscle, and tight when he stepped forward or bent to pick up something. It was the look of a lean, muscled man, one who worked for a living, not someone who simply thought for his life's work. There was a difference, and seeing Jeff there, moving in the sun, the sharp shadows in vivid contrast told her how lucky she was to have found him once again.

Taking a deep breath, she turned away from the window. She had to jump into her valentine thing, or she'd never get it planned. With less than two weeks to go, it had to be something simple. Taking out a paper pad and pencil, she titled the blank sheet Love Spectacular. Then Katie was hit with what she considered a brilliant idea. Her Love Spectacular needed to be all about the children. Have the parents make cards for their little ones, do cakes, cookies, and special presents all around. Then bring them all together for a banquet, with streamers and red punch and more. Parents could dress in red and white, and they could be the waiters and waitresses. They could have a father-daughter, mother-son dance, and finish with a fun, kid-friendly movie. It would be a family night to end all family nights. And if the kids didn't know it was coming, that would be even better, a surprise to top any Valentine's Day they had ever had.

Now enthused, she began to make a list of the children at the church, and it occurred to her that every other child on the island could join them. And families without children? Yes, invite them, too. Katie felt giddy with excitement. Connie Rivera and ALDMass could wait, at least until after Valentine's. Katie was going to be very busy until then.

8

"Nina, I have a proposition for you." Katie was having lunch at Harbor View restaurant. She'd decided to call it lunch, in spite of it being well after two, but her late lunch was purposeful. She needed Nina to have some free time to talk.

"Certainly. Does it involve money?" Nina winked, just a barely visible movement of one eyelid, as she rolled her damp towel into a compact cylinder. She pulled up at Katie's table, taking an uneaten hush puppy from her plate and munching on it. "Kent does make good puppies. We should eat here sometime."

"They are good." Katie pushed a half-eaten one to the back edge of her plate, and she laughed. She was pretty sure it was Nina who could take credit for the hush puppies, but that was what made it funny.

Nina smiled at Katie's response. "You didn't eat very many, so I have to ask. The morning sickness? Are you completely over it?" She wiped her hands on her cloth, destroying her perfect cylinder, and clumped it in front of her. She watched Katie expectantly.

"Except on the ferry, but you saw that." Katie warmed with embarrassment at the memory and shook her head.

Having someone see that still bothered her. "Jeff's off-roader sets it going if he drives too fast, but otherwise, I'm okay. Okay enough to enjoy these." She broke off a fresh end of one of the puppies and popped it into her mouth, chewing with a smile.

"Good. That wasn't your proposition, though. So, what can I do for you?" Nina sat back and smiled.

"It's almost Valentine's, and I've been thinking. I have what I think is a really good idea, but I need your opinion on whether it's practical." Katie pulled out a sheet of paper and a pen. She unfolded it to reveal a series of squares with a heading in each one. She chuckled. "Look at this. It's called my Love Extravaganza." The word Spectacular was blacked out, and Extravaganza printed neatly above it.

"For you and Jeff? Maybe you'd better plan this at home." Nina's eyes sparkled, and she turned the paper to look at it. As she skimmed the sheet, she rested a finger on each heading before going on. When she finished, she looked up. "I gather this isn't just for you and Jeff."

"It's for the island's children." Katie's enthusiasm burst out. "After the Christmas play, I saw how the people loved little Debsy, even as she abandoned her part to head off to the restroom right in the middle of the crucial final scene. Rockhaven's young people are the best thing the island's got, and their parents love them. Immensely. We need to let them know in the most extreme way possible."

"How extreme?" Nina's eyebrows were raised, and she looked ready to pull Katie back inside reasonable bounds, if necessary.

Katie reached to touch one of the sections of the paper. "I want it to be all about the kids. Like a surprise. It'll be like a Valentine's party at school, except the parents will give the cards. I've listed some of the children from the church, but I don't know everyone who winters over." She moved her finger to touch Little J's name, and the Peavey boys in their various blocks. There were Debsy, Brookie, Kern, Matt, and all the rest she'd been able to think of on the spur of the moment.

"And I'm to fill in the blanks?" Nina had begun to

465

smile.

"For a start. I'd like parents to come in red and white, serving and entertaining the children."

"I'm following you. It's a kids' night out, one all about them." Nina had moved on to pursing her lips, like she was thinking.

"Yes. Exactly. Everyone involved." Katie knew Nina was the one to come to. She was a get-'er-done type character, and she'd be able to see Katie's vision.

"We need to think bigger, though. Not everyone will show up just for this."

"It's for their children. Surely, Nina—"

"Islanders around here love their little tykes, but it's winter, and they get tired of them. So, let's up the ante. Let's make it about the school. That way we can plan it, even tell the children, and they won't suspect a thing." Nina winked again, one conspirator to another, and she grinned impishly.

"You'll have to explain that to me." Katie had pictured something similar to a school party, with the parents acting as room mothers, but that was her imaginative limit of school connection.

"We'll do an auction, or a raffle. The money we bring in can be used to do something schoolish, maybe playground equipment or books for the library. Or both! I've got a quilt I made during a March blizzard that shut the entire island down for a week about a decade ago. I thought my daughter might like it, but she's in South Africa. She has yet to express an interest in the quilt. There's our first item in the pot."

"I see." Katie did, too. "The kiddos can sell the tickets, and when their parents bring them up for the drawing, we have a banquet planned."

"Girl!" Nina laughed. "You and I are on the same page one hundred percent. Now, Kent collects sports equipment and model cars. I'm pretty sure I can talk him out of one or two. We have to have something to appeal to the younger set."

"Snowshoes. Jeff has a pair he's never worn, and my

466

good friend Winnie gets free makeup and clothes at her fashion shoots. She always tries to get me to take some. I can have her ship me a box."

"Now we're riding the train right out of the tunnel. Let me think, who do I know not on your list? There's Lavern's daughter, Spice. She's thirteen, so she goes in this box. And Ken and Ellen Amiro have three you've probably never met. They live up on Black Seal Cove out the other side of Smalley's Point. They homeschool." Nina put in their names, Ken Jr, Lane, and Sadie, with Ken in one box, and Lane and Sadie together. Twins, Nina said when she saw Katie watching. She also said the family tended to live off the land, so don't expect much cash to come from them. However, Ken and Ellen would work like draft horses if they thought it would benefit their kids. They'd be a good family for selling tickets.

Katie saw it all coming together. This could be better than she'd imagined. There was one caveat. The extravaganza was two weeks away, and that meant all this had to happen quickly.

Very quickly.

Thinking about it made her dizzy, and it wasn't morning sickness making her head spin. The whole island? What had she been thinking? Maybe it was like her wedding night. She hadn't been thinking at all, and now look what she carried around with her. At least any babies that appeared at the extravaganza already had parents to take them home. Whew!

Nina assigned her the job of heading out to the Amiro's. Nina said she'd like to just call, but it was remote, and out that direction the Thanksgiving blizzard had taken the phone lines down. The Amiros hadn't had good service before, and now? They needed a face-to-face meeting, and Katie was just the one to do it.

About then the door slammed, and the two women looked up to see Archie Coombs removing his coat. Nina placed her hand on Katie's wrist, whispering, "See? Just when I have a moment, in comes a customer. Don't want Archie riled up. I'd better take care of him. I'll get back with you."

Katie watched Nina shift gears, calling out to Archie, and teasing him into laughing with her. What a wonderful woman to have for a friend, she thought. What a wonderful place this was to live. Now, she had to find Black Seal Cove. If she headed west, she thought, towards the Point, then cut right at Upper Island Road, it would take her past John Chetwynde's new build on Smalley's Point and on to the Amiro's. It wasn't in close sailing proximity to Carver Point, which make it unfamiliar to her. Still, she couldn't get very lost. She was on an island. Every road had to eventually wind back to town, didn't it? Katie laughed at that, imagining driving around and around the island, all the roads dropping off into the sea, and never finding her way back again. It would be like an adventure. How had she seen it written? Today was a good day to have herself a good day. With that in mind, she also felt today was a good day to learn a new part of the island. By the time she was Ada Simpers' age, she might know the better part of it. Maybe.

Katie waved to Nina as she exited the building. She pulled her coat tighter around her throat, and she patted baby, whispering, "I love you, Baby. Be good and stay warm." With a beep, she unlocked her car door and slipped inside. She set aside the troublesome thought that before little Jeffie showed up, they might very well lose Jeff's four-wheel-drive toy or her wonderful blue Bug. Yet, that wasn't happening today, and probably not tomorrow, and for that she was grateful. It was up to Connie now. If ALDMass would get on the ball, then everything would work out fine.

As she pulled out, the sun caught her eye, and she flipped the visor down. Two things fell in her lap. One was Winnie's postcard of Monhegan with her warm sentiments on the back, and the other was a folded paper Katie hadn't seen. It had a man's name and phone number on it, and in Jeff's writing it said, "Willing to offer $22K for Jeep. Will call back next week."

Katie pulled to the side of the road and stopped, looking

468

at the words with dismay. She knew . . . Jeff had told her . . . but this made it real. Too real. God, she sent up in a silent prayer, you cannot let this happen. You have to work this out. Jeff gives everything to you. This one thing. You can work out this one thing and let him keep his car.

That done, she pulled out on the road, and an online devotional she'd read that morning popped into her head. It had compared God to a sunrise. At times He makes His presence known in a blaze of glory, but He knows that if all we do is watch Him in worshipful adoration, no one would farm the fields, put roofs over their children's heads, or reach out to the lost. So, He lets the colors of the sunrise fade so humanity can get on with the business of life. Yet, like the sun, even though the brilliance of His beauty has faded in our eyes, He is still shining over us, bringing us life every minute of the day.

It was the getting on with the business of life that had Katie thinking. Maybe that's what God expected her to do. God had blazed through her life in July, bringing her and Jeff together, and now He was standing back and watching, and it was His way of telling her, "Get busy, Katie. I love you, but this life is yours. You get to live it. I'm not through with all the sunrises I'll bring you, but this day? That's up to you. Don't let me down, girl."

Katie knew what that meant. She planned to be back on the phone to Connie, just as soon as she left the Amiro's. If God expected Katie to be the one to live her life, then that's what she'd do, and by that, she intended to do whatever it took so that Jeff could keep his car. $22K? Not on that man's life were they taking $22K for that big green off-road machine. It was Jeff's, and that's all there was to it.

It hit home with her that she also had her Love Extravaganza on the burner. She steeled her backbone. There were no two ways about it. She would have to handle both. She wasn't about to let God down, or Jeff, either.

Any good minister's wife would feel the same, she was sure, even if she didn't quite know how she would manage to get it done.

9

"Good morning, Jeff!" Katie wrapped her arms around her husband. She'd said nothing about the Jeep, but she now checked each morning to see that it was still in the drive. If it was muddy with winter's grime, so much the better. It meant no one was headed up to look at it that day.

"Katie, sweetheart." He pulled her down to sit in his lap. Putting his hands on either side of her face, he kissed her on the lips twice, then once on each cheek.

"Hey, what's that for?" She laughed. "You have coffee breath."

"You didn't mind coffee breath last night." He chuckled. "I thought it might put you in the mood. Is that how they say it, in the mood?"

"Not since 1954. I'm meeting John in an hour, and I believe you have Roker waiting on you in town. So, that means you need to let me up, and good-man-Roker gets to appreciate your coffee breath for a while."

"He won't care. I've got a jug made up for him. That's John Chetwynde, with the plans, right?" He let her go and reached for his cup, with a chuckle and a wink. "Did he promise a garage?"

"He promised something buildable, and that means

470

Nikki will probably nix the whole thing. My hopes are not up."

"What about the Love Extravaganza? I understand you've been out to the Amiros. How was that?"

"Wonderful! Did you know they built their house from trees felled on their own property? Ken cut them himself with an ax, and he and Ellen hand-sawed the boards for the house. That's impressive."

"Don't know about that." Jeff downed the contents of his cup and set it in the sink. "Seems to me hauling lobsters twelve months a year's pretty impressive."

"Jealous?" Katie was loving this. Jeff? Feeling like he needed to compete?

"You do know Ken and I were on the football team together at university. He has a degree in environmental science." He looked at her, his arms crossed, and he leaned against the countertop. "He's quite brilliant. Turned down a job with the EPA to move back here."

"No." Katie had been surprised to find their place out on Black Seal Cove to be tidy, well-designed, and perfectly pleasant. She guessed, with hearing that they home-schooled their children and tried to live off the land, she'd assumed they were hippies. "So, he could work anywhere."

"That's right. He loves here, though. Ellen teaches university classes for that online school in Arizona. It's how they make ends meet. She has a Masters in, um, foreign language, Latin, or something like that."

"I am impressed." And she was. Brilliant people choosing to live in the woods because they wanted to, not because they had to.

"Just don't tell them I told you. They like the homespun version better. They're good people. I'd love to have them part of the church, but they do their own religious instruction. Who can argue with that?"

"They're on board for the extravaganza, and I'm glad you told me about them. Two thumbs up for their family. Oh, and I got your message about Winnie calling. She didn't pick up when I returned the call. Did she say what it was about?"

He shook his head. "No, just for you to call, and now, I've got to go. I'll be away the entire day. If the shop on the mainland needs to keep the boat overnight, Roker and I'll ride back on the ferry. I'll call if I need you to pick us up at the landing."

"One phone, ready to go!" Katie pulled it from her back pocket to hold it up to him.

"I'm so lucky to have you." He leaned in and kissed her on the neck before moving up to her face, and kissing her again on the lips. "It's cold out, and they're saying snow before the weekend. Don't stay out after dark if you can help it."

"You be careful on the water. I don't want any body parts frozen. I like you in one piece."

"Yes, ma'am, Dame Carver."

"Ragsdale, you silly man. Go!" she said, laughing.

"You're always Dame Carver to me." He pulled her up and kissed her once more, before releasing her to begin pulling on his heavy weather gear. On the boat, and with temperatures in the thirties? It would be very cold on the water today.

Then he was gone, heading down to the dock and onto the float. He waved once as he rowed out to his boat. Starting it up took three tries, and even Katie could hear the knock that had him worried. Fix it now, he'd said, before he had to really fix it later. He'd expressed that with a deep breath before and a deflating sigh afterwards. Then he'd laughed, but it wasn't a real laugh, not the fun sort.

Katie pulled her things together. She and John were meeting at Ritchey's new store in town. She'd found that exciting, to get to see on the other side of the brown paper, but he'd laughed, telling her they were still in the tear-apart stage. Don't expect anything impressive.

As she headed out the door, her phone began to ring. Digging it out of her pocket, she saw it was Winnie, and she smiled, tapping the answer icon to bring her up.

"Winnie! I've been trying to get back with you. What's going on, Honey?"

"Sweetie, thank goodness you're finally at your phone.

I have the most awful news! Hold on a sec." She spoke to someone not on the line, calling to them to hold the lemon. Just plain water was all she wanted. Birds could be heard in the background, and it faintly sounded like kids playing. Winnie laughed. "I'm sorry, Sweetie. There's so much stuff happening. I can barely keep up."

"I can tell. What's the awful news?"

"Oh, that. You know Francois, your cousin Nikki's little man?" She stopped as if waiting on Katie to answer.

"Yes, I know Francois." How many men named Francois did her friend think she knew?

"Oh, right. Francois called, and he doesn't communicate very well, unless you're there, because then he can point, but on the phone, I have no idea. Bourgeois, and merci, but the rest? I say, oui, oui, oui, and he keeps talking. Hôpital. Do you think he meant hospital? Katie, Sweetie, are you there?" She spoke to someone else again, whispering loudly, "Don't worry. I can drink it with lemon."

"Did he mention Nikki's name?" Her cousin hadn't seemed all that peppy when she'd left at Christmas, but Katie hadn't considered she might actually be ill, seriously ill.

"Sweetie, when Francois calls, it's always about Nikki. We're not an item, you know. Grow up!"

"Did he say what's wrong?" Katie tried to push aside a sinking feeling.

"Cassé la jambe. He said that four times. I would have said a dance step, but nope. Not in this case. Sweetie, I have to be on the runway in two, so I'll try you again later. Give a hug to Jeffie and baby Jeffie. Bye, now."

"Talk to you then, Honey." Katie pulled up her translation app, and she said, "French to English." When it showed her it was ready, she said, "Cassé la jambe."

Her phone spoke back to her, "Broken her leg."

"Oh, my word," Katie breathed out loud. Then her phone rang again. She answered, "Katie here."

"It's Jeff. We've been ashore, and we're heading out again. We have to run the boat to a shop in Bath. Guess who I just saw at the ferry landing?" His boat roared in the background, and Roker called out hello.

"Who, Jeff?" All she could think about was her poor cousin Nikki. How bad must it have been to put her in the hospital?

"Ritchey's headed out to the island. But you'll see him when you meet up with John. I'm about to lose signal. Love you, Katie. Bye!"

"Bye, Jeff." Yet, he was already gone, and she was slipping the phone in her back pocket as she spoke. Poor Nikki. Then she thought of John Chetwynde. If Nikki was ill, was there any point in going in to meet with him? She might as well call him and say the whole thing was off.

Still, she did want to see Ritchey's new store, and if Ritchey was here, then she wanted to meet up with him, too. Sorry, John, she thought. All your plans for nothing. Katie breathed deeply, realizing she had hoped, in spite of what she'd told Jeff. She simply hadn't been brave enough to admit it. Now that she saw it falling through? It hurt, all over again. It really, really hurt all over again.

10

"It's certainly beautiful. Who wouldn't want to live there?" Katie felt a rush of . . . not envy. Missed opportunity. John hadn't simply put together some ideas. He had an entire floorplan designed, with full exterior elevations. One was in color, with the ocean in the background.

"I overlaid the virtual mockup onto images of the Point. It looks stunning, doesn't it?" John sat on the opposite side of the rugged work table, and he occasionally leaned over and tapped the keyboard to change the image. "If I drag this, you can see it in full 360 degrees."

True enough, Katie watched the image rotate, and there was Carver Cove down the hill. She looked closer to the dock and laughed. "That's me with Jeff. How'd you do that?"

John spun the computer around and looked closely, and he grinned. "I'm just good. No, really—" He chuckled. "—Jeff uploaded some photos from an event out there last summer. This is a photomontage of all of them. The program is designed to edit out people when possible, but it missed you two. I can't say I'm sorry, because this is absolutely perfect. You and Jeff, at your new home on the Point. By the way, that's the most beautiful location on the island, and that's God's truth. I envy you."

Katie wondered if he'd feel the same way when he learned their money seemed to be drying up even as they sat there.

"I felt a separate building for the garage would maximize your views, so I kept that on the outside of the yard proper. See, here is where I intend to cut back into the hillside . . ."

John had the floor plans up, and he pointed to the building that would tuck just off where his trailer was now. Then he moved to the house, showing her wide porches under cantilevered overhangs. The upper floor was ringed with clerestory windows, with larger ones on the south and the west to maximize solar gain. At the very top was a third-floor glass-enclosed rotunda, with a sharply-canted roof. The rotunda was for the views. The big windows tucked under the overhangs? Free heat, he assured her, can extend the season by an easy three weeks on either side, and she and Jeff would appreciate that in Maine's cool summers. But then, he didn't have to tell her about that, did he? And he laughed.

Katie saw more in the plans he worked through, the bedrooms with massive windows, and open decks and covered porches for whatever weather the island threw at them. She saw a little boy or a little girl running around, jumping off the dock, and begging to sleep alone in the cabin by the shore; and at the same time begging, Mommy, please come with me and stay until I fall asleep.

"John," she interrupted, "This is exactly what I pictured. The funds are from my cousin, so I have to run everything through her. I want this, everything, but—" and she laughed, looking towards the door, wondering where Ritchey was. Her escape. Her chance to pretend these plans were nothing, and to remind herself she had all she wanted in Jeff and the baby and the life she had been given on Rockhaven.

"If you wish, there are several scaled down options we can consider. The garage, of course. That can go, and if you stay with three bedrooms, or even two, the rest of the home

476

remains perfectly functional. It's the views you're there for, in any case. As long as we have the glass, you'll never feel closed in at any time." He smiled, shifting the scene to a smaller floorplan of the house. "I don't have the exterior on this one, but imagine a smaller version of the one I showed you."

"If you can email me both—" Rapping on the glass door startled Katie, and she turned to see it opening, the knob held by a black-gloved hand.

"Hey, in here. I see cars out front." It was indeed Ritchey, bundled up and in a black overcoat. His head was bare, and his ears were red with the cold. "Katie, John." He called with a wave, as he worked the coat off.

"Ritchey!" Katie stood and went to him. "Jeff can't be here—"

"I saw him in town. Look at you, pregnant mom! Give me a hug, you beautiful mother-to-be!"

"You fool! You think without Jeff around, you can get away with whatever you want. Well, don't forget. We have a chaperone." Katie laughed and let him hug her.

"John." Ritchey leaned across the table and shook his hand. "So, did you two decide on a house?"

Katie laughed. "John decided, and I fell in love. Now we have to get approval."

"From the town?" Ritchey frowned. "I can't see John's designs not passing muster. He's the best."

John chuckled. "Thank you, Ritchey. Keep saying that, because we're still disassembling this building, and you'll not see anything resembling progress today. No, Katie needs to get with her cousin, who is part of the entire process. We'll move on when that's settled."

"Good. Katie? Come tour my new store. I don't know that this one will make me rich, but it gives me a good excuse to come back home from time to time, and my wife can't complain. And because it's business, she doesn't feel obligated to tag along."

"Did you get to visit with Jeff?" Ritchey had her arm in his, and John walked at their side. "He'd hate not spending time with you if you can't stay long."

"Just a shake and a greet. The ferry was loading, and my car was next to go on. He made me promise to stay one night. I'll have to explain that to my wife, though." He grinned impishly.

"Well, I'm glad you're here, even for one night. Jeff will be back this evening, and you two can do whatever you men do together when you've got free time. Now, tell me all about how this is progressing." The store, she meant, but that's where they were, so she knew he understood.

"The building is all John's, so that I don't know about. I've got a team back in Houston putting together a product line specific to the island." He stopped and smiled at her. "I could ask you to do something for me."

"Sure. I don't know how I can help, but if there's anything, I'm glad to pitch in."

"I grew up here, and I don't think things have changed that much. Still, it's been ten years. I need to know who might be interested in working in the store. More specifically, who'd be good at working in the store. Can you do that, come up with some prospective employees?"

"I can do that." Me, was Katie's first thought, but with a baby on the way, she knew working in a store wasn't realistic.

"One other thing. I've got construction insurance through my provider in Texas, but they don't provide long-term coverage in Maine. Can I get some recommendations?"

Katie smiled at that. Could she ever? ALDMass was affiliated with New England Home, residential and business insurers. She now had a foot in the door with Connie Rivera. If she could bring a new business prospect to Connie's table, how could they not let her back in?

"I just might. Are you familiar with ALDMass?"

"Insurance? It sounds local. I don't think I am."

"The biggest auto insurer in New England. My employer." She laughed. "Well, my employer before moving here, but I'm in contract negotiations to get my job reinstated, and we have a subsidiary that handles residential and business policies. If you're interested, I could get your information and approach them for a quote."

"Katie Ragsdale, you're a lifesaver. I would love to have you handle this. Here. My card. My secretary will have all the information you need." He pulled a card out of his wallet and handed it to her.

Ritchey began asking John about the upcoming changes to the building, and Katie followed along, enjoying the conversation. Ritchey's offer wasn't exactly a new home on the Point, but perhaps it meant saving the Jeep. She breathed, "Thank you, God," as she slipped the card in her pocket. God did care. He really, really cared, providing the answer to something very important at just the right time.

Check off one box, she thought. Only about a dozen to go. Yet, she couldn't help the sense of satisfaction that filled her in knowing that God was on her side.

11

"Jeff, I've been thinking about Cousin Nikki. We have to get down to see her." Katie looked out the kitchen window. She and Jeff were having an early breakfast. Ritchey was still asleep in the guest room upstairs.

"I've been expecting you to say that." He munched into a slice of toast lathered with purple jelly. "The boat's out of circulation for at least a week. Now might be a good time."

The boat hadn't been good news. The engine needed a complete overhaul, which was not cheap by any measure. Yet, their choices were limited. Katie and Jeff had prayed about it and decided to let the Lord have control in the situation. Maybe there was a reason they had a week free. Jeff had taught on Blind Bartimaeus the previous Sunday, telling the congregation how it was Bartimaeus' lack of sight that allowed him to hear Jesus coming. Yet, it was his faith that allowed him to call to the Master, in spite of the crowds that tried to silence him.

Perhaps, Jeff had whispered to Katie as they lay in bed afterwards, the Lord was removing one thing so they could sense something else, perhaps His hand guiding them another direction. They had to trust that He knew best in their lives.

Katie had agreed, but she'd seen Ritchey's insurance opportunity as saving Jeff's Jeep. Now she suspected it might be what saved Jeff's boat and his livelihood. The Jeep haunted her. She had trusted God, and she no longer felt she was on firm ground.

"Ritchey's heading out early. We could follow him, spend that hour on the ferry catching up, and head to Boston afterwards. What do you say?" He was behind her, whispering in her ear, and she hadn't heard him approach.

"Winnie's on St. Simons Island in Georgia. She won't be there." It was an empty place Katie couldn't fill at the moment.

"Nikki will be. That's who we're going to see. Since you met with John yesterday, it'll be a good time to show her the plans for the Point. What do you say? We can take your car. It'll be like a mini-vacation." He kissed her on the side of the neck, moving up to her jawline in a series of small kisses.

"Stop that." Katie felt the tears building.

"Stop?" He chuckled. "Why would I want to do that?"

She turned and put her arms around him. "I'm sorry. I feel lost today. Yes, absolutely. Let's spend the day together, you and me, all the way to Boston. With Nikki in the hospital, we might stay at the apartment. Francois surely won't mind. We have to plan for Sunday if we're staying over."

"I already have." He kept his arms wrapped around her.

"Who?"

"Al stepped up when I asked him. Guest speaker. What do you think about that?" Jeff chuckled. "Never thought of Al as a minister, but he tells great stories. I suspect the story of Jesus will involve a lot of boats and lobster pots."

"Jeff, you are such a good man. Al is so fortunate to have you for a friend, and you, him."

"Good morning. I see what I'm missing out on." That was from Ritchey, and he was still in his flannel pajamas and an old pair of Katie's furry house slippers. His hair was on end, a wild tangle that showed its losing fight against the pillow. "Do I get a hug, too?"

"Good lands, man, check the mirror before you come

481

downstairs." Jeff laughed. "Don't forget you've got a ferry to catch."

"Yeah." Ritchey yawned. "Ten-thirty, something like that. Is there anything for breakfast?"

"Toast is done. I can throw in a few eggs, if you want." Katie pushed away from Jeff, letting her hand rest on his chest for a moment before turning to the fridge.

"Sounds good. Snow's starting up. Did you two see that?" Ritchey turned to the window, yawning again, with one arm in the air, and his hand in his hair, attempting to pull it flat.

"It's beautiful!" Katie hadn't noticed. It must have just begun. "I hope it's coming down while we're on the ferry. I would love to see that."

"I've had snow up to my chin. I'm thinking Boston sounds like a really good idea." Jeff had moved beside Ritchey, the both of them looking out over the cove.

"They're expecting snow there, too. I'm connecting at Logan, and I got an update about possible delays. I'm remembering why I like Texas so much." Ritchey looked at Jeff with a grin.

"Cause you're a wimp." Jeff hit him on the shoulder with the back of his hand. "Real men stick it out, turning into Mainers."

"Real men know when to turn tail and run." Ritchey pushed on Jeff's shoulder in repayment.

"Real men? Ha! Remember this?" Jeff threw one arm around Ritchey's neck and began to rub his knuckles back and forth across the man's scalp.

"Hey! Surprise attack! Katie, call him off!" Ritchey's arms were swinging, but Jeff had him.

"I'm preparing breakfast. Sorry!" She wasn't really, as the eggs were still in the carton, but to watch two men behaving like teenage boys? It was too good, and more importantly, it was separation from her money worries. A day off the island would be good for her and Jeff. Boston. Her cousin, and if she had time, maybe she could look up one of her old friends. Perhaps a visit to Montecristo for a chimichanga. It'd been six months since being home, and she missed it. The taste of a well-made chimichanga could very well improve her outlook on life for a good many months to come.

Ritchey pulled away from Jeff, his hair worse than ever. He tugged his pajama top back into place, and he pushed his hair away from his face, laughing. "You got me there, Jeff. I get it. I did that to you all the time growing up."

"I've missed you being around, Ritchey." Jeff was red-faced and grinning. He bent his hands backwards and cracked his knuckles. "Texas is a long way aways."

"Yeah. You know, we never get snow in Houston. I do miss this, just not as often as you might think. Weekends at our beach house in Galveston, even in February—" He chuckled. "There's a lot to be said for Texas in winter."

"I'm sure." Jeff didn't sound so certain.

"Anyway, I'm taking back a place here on the island, so we won't be strangers any longer." Ritchey smiled brightly, and he looked like he was waking up. "I'll pull some clothes on, and I'll be back for breakfast."

"Oh, right." Katie was still holding the carton of eggs and watching the two men. "Sorry. I got distracted. It'll be ready when you get down."

He gave a casual wave to show her it was nothing, and he grabbed Jeff around the neck and pulled him into the living room, saying something about getting supplies to the island, and good heavens, did it have to cost $200 to bring a load of building supplies across?

Katie was glad for Jeff, having Ritchey stop over for the night. She was gladder for herself. She was getting a vacation, to Boston! She'd never thought of Boston as vacationland. After all, it was Maine that claimed vacationland on their license plates, but where you lived was never a vacation. It was the getting away that made a place special. She remembered Nina's words. A special place doesn't have to be on a tropical beach. It just has to be away. Different. Special.

There was still the Love Extravaganza in the works, but Katie had people working on that. Island people were responsible and willing to step up to the plate. This weekend, Katie wasn't accepting any responsibility at all.

She intended to have fun.

12

Katie caught herself falling back into her Boston surroundings like she'd never left. Yet, it wasn't the same, either.

After leaving Ritchey at the airport on the mainland, she and Jeff had followed Route 1 to the Interstate, and sped along through light snow at 70 all the way to New Hampshire and beyond. Seeing the familiar Massachusetts welcome sign had filled her with a giddiness she hadn't expected. She felt she was in a different world. A different century, almost, with the traffic, overpasses, and business-filled side roads.

Everything she saw in Boston she felt she could touch as if no time had passed at all. It was more like visiting a museum than a hometown, though, a place where every-thing was on display, and it had little to do with her. She remembered summer and standing overlooking the town harbor on Rockhaven. A man on the ferry had been snap-ping photographs, memorizing the beauty of the town, and she'd known he'd always remember Rockhaven exactly that way when he pulled out his pictures. It wouldn't be the winter storms or the spring gales that he'd see. This was the same. She was catching a glimpse outside of time. The

484

people here, they fought with snowstorms, and shoveled walks to exhaustion. They had to shop in crowded stores on the way home from work. Traffic probably drove them to despair. Yet, what Katie saw was the reminiscence of good times that she'd stored away in her memory book of snapshots, totally independent of the reality of the world.

She knew that, and still, Boston tugged at her heart.

"What are you thinking, beautiful?" Jeff reached to her and took her hand.

"Nothing much." She gave a quick laugh to show it was no big deal.

"Is that a glum face?"

"I'm letting the city soak in. Everything here triggers a memory. I grew up in this place." She chuckled at that. She'd grown up here, yes, but not really, either. She'd grown more on Rockhaven each summer, at least in her own thoughts. Each June, the nine months in Boston slipped away from her like shedding an old layer of dead skin. She'd come alive in Rockhaven, new and glorious. It was a kid thing, she supposed. Summer. Friends. Freedom. Still, it had felt very real to her, and that made it real.

"You're not wanting to come back?" Jeff squeezed her hand, and his voice smiled at her. She looked up, and his eyes twinkled.

"To visit. How about we attend Trinity Church tomorrow?"

"Trinity?" He laughed. "So I can return guilt ridden that our services aren't better?"

"No! So I can show you off to all my friends. If it weren't Saturday, I'd love to stop in at ALDMass and talk to Connie, but that's not possible."

"To show me off to her, too?" He released her hand to brush the backs of his fingers down her jawline. "Anyway, aren't you in job negotiations with her?"

"We're hashing it out." She hadn't mentioned Ritchey's offer, and Jeff hadn't asked her about it. That meant Ritchey was leaving it all to her. It was the businessman in him, she supposed. Once you delegate, it's hands off. Responsible employees pull their own weight, or they're

485

not worth their pay and need to move on to somewhere else. Katie was determined to pull her own weight on this. She wasn't a moaner, and she had wanted to surprise Jeff when his Jeep didn't have to be sold. Now she hoped she could mark his boat off the list of debts to be paid. However, false hopes weren't better than no hopes. She would tell him when she knew for sure.

"Hospital sign." Jeff pointed. Mass General, Right Lane. He tapped the blinker wand and moved over. "Would you like to stop for food before we visit your cousin?"

Katie didn't get to answer. A horn blared somewhere, then from a distance came the thudding sound of metal on metal, loud, tearing, and silence followed for a moment. Then another thud happened, with the shattering sound of glass. On the turnoff just ahead, brake lights became a string of bright red dots, and Jeff hit his brakes to slow down. A car cut behind them just as he slowed, and it stood on its horn for a long moment.

"Hey," Jeff called, looking in the rearview mirror. "I can't go anywhere, dude."

"Be patient." Katie patted him on the arm. "They'll figure it out. I wonder what happened."

"Sounded pretty obvious." Jeff was checking his mirrors, looking for traffic. "Is there another way to get there?"

"It's best to wait. It'll be like this anywhere. Boston traffic." She laughed it off, but this part was bringing back memories, too. How many times had she scheduled her errands around Boston's overtaxed roadways? She never had to consider that on Rockhaven. There, if you wanted to go, go. There were never cars on the roads. The worst thing she might encounter was someone in her favorite parking spot, and then, she just moved over two or three places. "This I don't miss."

"What?" They were inching forward, and Jeff was very focused on the brake lights just in front.

"Boston traffic. I don't remember noticing it all that much before. Now?" She chuckled. "How do these people stand it?"

"So you're not wanting to come back." He smiled, then pressed the brakes hard, as the car in front of him came to a complete stop. "If they'd stop riding their brakes, I could tell when they're slowing down."

"Jeff, Jeff." Katie cautioned him, taking a deep breath, and she pressed against her abdomen. "Little Jeffie doesn't like that. Easy on the brakes."

"Tell these dudes." A siren started in the distance, quickly growing louder. He looked at Katie, and he shook his head. "I'm sorry. I shouldn't blame them. Are you going to be all right?"

"If you stay off the brakes."

"Done. It sounds as though this might be something serious." They began to move forward again, and he remarked, "Finally."

They were well off the main road by then, and they could see flashing lights. There were police cars, one fire truck, and an ambulance. Orange-marked cones directed the traffic into a separate lane, and officers stood with arms outstretched, motioning to motorists to give the First Responders plenty of room. When they got close enough, they could see a small car wedged underneath a city bus. Both ends of the small car were crumpled. A larger SUV was behind both of them with its front bumper pushed underneath. A ragdoll of a woman was being laid out on a stretcher.

"How terrible." Katie felt her heart go out. "That car is crushed. How could that have happened?"

"We heard two impacts. I bet the SUV hitting the car was the second crash. We need to remember that poor driver in our prayers. At least they're close to the hospital. If you have to be in a crash, here's the place for it." The traffic was clearing, and Jeff had his blinker on to turn. "There's the park. We're here."

Red Sox field. He would recognize that. It was a man thing, to navigate by the means of sports venues. Katie had been watching for familiar restaurants, like Little Lamb and Harvard Gardens. Jeff had asked about food. Her answer? Yes, yes, and yes.

Even so, that woman on the stretcher wasn't far from Katie's thoughts. She would hold her up in prayer, but she hadn't looked very alive. How easy it was to lose someone you loved. You said good bye in the morning, and they never came home for supper.

"Nikki," she prayed, "be safe and healthy. Good Lord above, keep your hand on my cousin."

"Amen," Jeff repeated.

"I love you, Jeff." Katie rubbed his forearm tenderly.

"And I love you, too, Katie. We're here." He triggered the blinker once more, and he pulled into the parking garage.

13

"Jeff, I hate this." They were in the elevator, thankfully alone, and she glanced at the bag he held. It was their laptop computer with John Chetwynde's house plans for the Point. She touched it with the end of her index finger. "This embarrasses me."

"Sweetheart, your cousin did offer, and we'll never know if we don't ask." He lifted her chin and kissed her on the lips, and he smiled. "Remember, all she can do is say no."

"She can laugh at us." It wasn't the asking about the house so much as doing it while Cousin Nikki was in the hospital. They should be here for no other reason than to support her emotionally. Bringing the plans in like this? It felt like they were opportunists, here to take advantage.

"Then let me walk in first. I can pull the computer out, she can laugh at me, and when I collapse in mortification, you can come in and scold me for bringing the house up while your cousin is in her current situation."

That got a laugh from Katie. "I can't do that. It would be a lie, like we were dishonest."

"Then let's be honest, ask her if she feels well enough to look at a really good plan an architect has put together,

489

and if she doesn't? We won't need to open the computer at all. Is that a plan?" He smiled brightly, like a teenager who had just presented an audacious adventure as something ordinary and practical.

Yet, when he put it that way, it sounded perfectly logical.

"Have I ever told you how lucky I am to have married you?" She tiptoed and kissed him on the cheek.

"Today, or in the past week?" He fought a grin as he asked it. "I don't mind hearing it again, as often as you want to say it."

"You!" She slapped him on the shoulder as the elevator reached their floor and dinged. The door disappeared into the walls, and the pale colors of the hospital corridor opened before them.

"My lady." Jeff motioned with one hand, like a servant from two centuries before.

"It's Dame Carver to you, buster." She laughed, stepping outside. "This is a beautiful building. All this glass. I guess I expected lots of concrete and florescent lighting."

There had been some of that, but not here. Even in the depths of an early February, sunshine flooded the space through walls that were more glass than solid substance.

"There. Reception. Hold on, Katie." Jeff stepped to ask the final directions to Nikki's room. He looked every part a Mainer out of his element in his heavy coat, his hair teased by a knit cap and much static electricity, and his wide lobsterman's shoulders.

That was what Katie loved about him. On Rockhaven he was in his element. Completely. Even in the church, he fit like a glass doorknob in a Victorian house. It works because it's the only way it can be. Here, with all the svelte and inner-city décor, and the people who matched it so well, she truly saw Boston as she never had before. Jeff fit the island, and the people on the island fit Jeff, because they were of a kind. Alike. Attuned to the same needs, wants, and desires. They loved island life, and in that love, they became the island. Then, Rockhaven loved them back.

It made her wonder how Ritchey saw Rockhaven after being gone so many years. Did he fall back into a comfortable pattern, or did it fit roughly on his shoulders, the place and the people lacking the polish he'd grown accustomed to in Houston?

Katie couldn't help but smile at that, picturing Ritchey in his flannels and her old house slippers, with his hair sticking up on end. When he and Jeff had stood next to each other at the window, they could have been brothers, for all the difference in them. Nah, she thought. You can take the boy off the island, but you can't remove the island from the boy. These polished city people had never been to Rockhaven, not to live. They didn't look like Rockhaven, because they'd never lived Rockhaven.

"Mademoiselle Katie?"

She turned to see Francois at her elbow. "Francois! Jeff, my husband, and I are here to see Nikki." She pointed to Jeff still at the desk, looking over a pamphlet with the attendant.

"Ah, Monsieur Jeffrey. This way. I take you." He touched Katie's elbow gently, giving an almost imperceptible bow of his upper body.

"Jeff, we have a guide," she called, waving when he looked up. "Francois's here."

"Francois!" Jeff waved back before turning to disengage from the attendant and walking their way.

"Monsieur. This way." Francois nodded to Jeff in the same half bow, more a slight movement of his head, really, and leading off down the corridor.

"Winnie was wrong." Katie whispered her announcement to Jeff. "Francois speaks very nice English. I didn't have any trouble understanding him, and his accent is very engaging."

Francois had stopped at a door, and he knocked before stepping partially through. He spoke in a quick and fluid French before turning back to Jeff and Katie with a smile, his head going down again, saying, "Monsieur, Mademoiselle, I take you. This way."

"Thank you, Francois." Katie paused to put her hand on

his forearm and smile at him.

"Mademoiselle." He smiled back.

"I think you've maxed out his English," Jeff whispered to Katie as they entered the room. However, he also looked the man in the eyes and recited his thanks for his help.

Inside, Cousin Nikki was covered with a brown houndstooth comforter, and her hair was heaped high on her head, with a vibrant scarf tied around it for a flamboyant touch. She was finishing up a jab of brilliant lipstick and closing the case. Her hand shook as she searched for a place to put it and finally dropped it beside her onto the bed.

"Your things. You must put them there." Nikki pointed to a brown leather sofa stretched beneath a wall of windows flooding the room with light. Beside it was a cream recliner, also in leather. It held a man's overcoat draped across the back. She took several shallow breaths when finished, and she looked like she struggled.

"How are you, Nikki?" Katie stepped forward to give her a kiss. She leaned in, only to have Nikki grasp her hand in both of hers as she stood back up.

"Non, my little Katie. We talk about you. I am so glad you are here. I have something for you. Francois. Francois!" She covered her mouth and coughed, before pulling several tissues from a small box, and patting the corner of her mouth. "My apologies. Francois!"

Nikki's eyes were reddened, and Katie noticed how pale and frail she looked. It had been less than six months since her cousin had arrived at her Boston apartment. She had used a walker even then, and her balance hadn't been great, but she had exuded fire and energy. Now Katie was truly worried.

After a short exchange between the two in their beautiful and flowing French, with Nikki's words roughened at the edges, and Francois in a tone barely more than a whisper, Francois pulled several file folders from a bedside drawer. He held them out, fanned, and Nikki looked in two before selecting one. Francois placed the others back in the drawer and nodded before exiting the room.

Jeff had taken one of Nikki's hands, squeezed it, and moved to the sofa, where he sat with his coat on the arm, and his elbow resting atop it. The laptop bag hunkered on the floor at his feet.

Nikki laid the folder on the bedding in front of her and opened it. She smoothed the top paper. It had an official look to it. "Pardon Francois. His English is only a few words. He is a good man, though. His father was my driver many years in the past. He is in Lyons. He no longer drives, and Francois is anxious to return to him. Il ne sera pas longtemps maintenant." Nikki sighed broadly, once again running her hand over the paper.

"What was that you just said, Nikki?" Her cousin still held one of Katie's hands, and her question caused her to release it.

"Ah, ah, the thoughts of an old woman. You do not see it, I am sure, but I am very old, my little Katie. Very old. Your American doctors agree with me, although those in France did not." She laughed brightly, but it was filled with more resignation than amusement. "I think they humored me."

"Will you tell me what you said?" Katie sat on the bed, and she placed her hand on Nikki's.

"A saying for a very old person who has received unwanted reports. I would mean the words to say, ah, it won't be long now." Nikki nodded as if she'd taken care of something she didn't really want to reveal, and she patted the corner of her mouth with the tissues once again.

"So, you're getting out, soon?"

"Katie." Jeff stepped up beside her. "I think I understand. Nikki, has the staff here given you bad news?"

"Ah, what is bad news to an old woman?" She smiled, waving his question away with her hand. "Bad news is an old friend that turns against you, or a storm that strands you without fine wine or good food. My news? It is what a woman of my age should expect."

"You will be well, though. You'll be okay." Katie felt Jeff's hand on her shoulder and reached for it, wrapping her fingers under his.

493

"Everything will be, as you say, okay. Now, though, this I wish to discuss." She patted the papers twice with a splayed hand. "I wish you to start my house now."

"Your house?" Katie felt herself floundering. It seemed all she could do was ask empty questions. Jeff squeezed her hand, and she tried to relax.

"Pardon, my dear. I will claim it for a time, but it will be yours. If we do not start now, I may never see the end. I do so want to see it as it stands completed. Look, this." She pushed the papers Katie's direction. "It is all signed and ready. I need you to look over this and see if you approve. Then sign, and we are ready to go."

"Nikki, do you mind?" Jeff held out his hand, and he took the papers from her when she nodded. He flipped through the sheaf and frowned. "This is—" He paused and faced the windows, and flipped back a page, before turning to the women again. "Katie, your cousin is being very generous. This is an open line of credit for construction of the new house on the Point. I think you'll be able to keep your garage."

He handed Katie the paperwork, and she flipped through it, only to have Jeff stop her at one point to show her a figure. Katie dropped the papers to her lap to look at her cousin.

"Nikki . . ." Katie's eyes welled up, and she couldn't say anything else.

"Non, non. I have more than enough, and you, my little Katie, are my only living relation. How can I not gift this to you? For your little one I will do this. You will let me, oui?"

"Oh, Nikki. You are so sweet. The architect just emailed us sample designs for the Point. They're tentative, but they're something we can show you. They can't rebuild the exact house, so he wanted to try something completely new. He sent me two different plans. Would you like to see them?"

"Oui! I had so hoped, but I did not want to ask. It has been so busy for you, with the baby, I am sure, and I was afraid you would find it difficult to make the plans so quickly. Now, where are they?"

Jeff had the computer out, and he opened it and pulled the plans up. Nikki oohed, and she aahed, exclaiming the windows were pictures to be seen from the inside, and it reminded her of her chalet in St. Moritz. Oui, oui, she exclaimed over and over.

"You will stay at the apartment, oui?" Nikki made sure to ask that, telling Katie that Francois had a room at the Wyndham right beside the hospital. The apartment was empty for the foreseeable future, and she simply must use it if they were staying over.

Later, leaving the room, with Nikki pleased but wan, although noticeably hoarser, and a hospital aide settling her for an afternoon rest, Jeff located a staff member to find out more about what Nikki had meant when she said it wouldn't be long. They soon discovered there was ongoing complications from advanced osteoporosis and several medications Nikki had taken for years. They were unsure whether the hip would ever heal, and worse, her spine had been fractured in the fall. Because of the extreme weather, they were also fighting the possibility of pneumonia. She didn't have it at this time, but with her lack of mobility? It was a concern.

The news brought home the reality of what Katie's cousin was facing.

After a warm good bye to Francois, Katie quizzed Jeff in the elevator. "If Nikki is truly that ill, what happens to Francois? He seems very devoted to her."

"I'll have to find out, I'm sure he'll return to France to be near his father."

"I would, if mine were alive. Now, though, to change the subject, I know a really good restaurant about two blocks from here. We're already parked, so, do you want to have a very late lunch with me?" Katie thought of Harvard Gardens. Glazed salmon sounded good to her right then.

"Or an early dinner. How about that?" The door opened, and Jeff hoisted his computer bag to his shoulder. "Should we put this in the car?"

"In Boston?" Katie pushed on Jeff's arm and chortled.

"Only if you have it insured. You keep that strap firmly wrapped around your neck until we head off to the apartment. It's got my house plans inside."

"Nikki's house plans. See? I was listening." Jeff's eyes twinkled. "Now, which way to Harvard Gardens?"

Katie pointed to the restaurant just across Cambridge, in dark brick, with a gold-lettered sign. They held hands as they made their way to a crosswalk and waited patiently for the light to change.

"Not quite like Rockhaven." Jeff rolled up on the balls of his feet, with a poorly concealed grin.

"It's not supposed to be like Rockhaven." Katie squeezed his hand and shook her head. She knew what he meant, though. However, you weren't going to get Harvard Gardens on the island. Sure, Harbor View was good, and the proprietors were warm and friendly, but the Gardens served up masterpieces, and at reasonable prices. Katie intended to enjoy this opportunity to the very last bite.

"Good," Jeff said, as the light changed, and they started across the street.

"Why good? I thought you'd want the rest of the world to be like Rockhaven."

"Ha!" he said, laughing out loud. "Then we'd be like them, and what would be the fun in that?"

"Come on." Katie tugged his arm, chuckling, as she opened the door to the restaurant. "Let's get something to eat."

"Hey, momma-to-be. Let me get the door." He leaned forward to take it from her.

"So you can get your food first? You have no idea how hungry I am." She let the door go, though.

"No, because I love you very much." He took her arm and insisted she enter first, whispering as she went by, "But I might give the waitress my order first."

"I don't think so, Jeff Ragsdale. Not on my time. This is my home turf. And for you, no lobster. You cannot order lobster."

He stopped, his hand on the door, holding it open. "And why not? I happen to like lobster."

496

"Because then you'd be like every other Bostonian on the street. Besides, I don't think you can get lobster here. Steak, yes, if you want steak."

"Then steak it is, my good woman. For you."

Katie, however, had her heart set on salmon. Jeff could have all the steak he wanted. Her stomach growled, and she didn't consider that the baby might be hungry, too.

This meal was all about her.

14

"Jeff, that was so much fun!" Katie closed her car door and looked up at Trinity Church, glad they'd found time to attend at least one of the Sunday services, albeit an early one.

"What's your friend going to say when she hears that all her secrets didn't stay secret while she was gone?" His eyes crinkled, and he fought to keep the laughter off his face.

"Oh, oh, Mary Allen's story about the foam reindeer berries, and to think Winnie tried to eat one—" Katie hooted with laughter and couldn't go on, because she was crying so hard.

"I don't think Rockhaven Church will ever live up to this. I might as well resign now." Jeff finally let his grin spill over.

"Resign now—" Katie roared. "Resign now, and you can have—"

"—a position at Trinity Church!"

Jeff repeated the final five words with her, and by then, they had their arms wrapped up together, and it seemed they'd never be able to see well enough to drive away.

"Okay, that's enough." Katie straightened her back, and

she wiped her eyes. "We really don't have time to waste."

"Because everything goes to waist!" Jeff shadowboxed her arm, grabbing his stomach through his shirt as he pooched it out in a parody of a running joke that had consumed the Sunday school class they'd attended.

"No, I'm not going to laugh at that." Katie held a serious face for a moment before letting out a burst of laughter, then working hard to get it back under control. "Do we have time to stop by and see Nikki before we head out?"

They had, indeed, stayed at Katie's old apartment overnight, but it had been eerily uncomfortable. It was the same, and it wasn't the same. Then, Katie's old bed, and having Jeff there. It was odd, she'd told him as they snuggled under the covers. Not wrong, exactly, but out of step with life as they'd grown to know it. That morning they'd locked up, knowing there'd be no time to get back to the apartment. They intended to make the last ferry to the island, which meant getting on the road before noon to have a comfortable margin for possible traffic complications.

Nikki? That was a different matter. To see her, Katie had been willing to sacrifice lunch at another of her favorite restaurants. Nikki was paramount, she'd told Jeff the night before, suggesting the early service to give them plenty of time.

"I didn't want to spoil your time at Trinity this morning. Between services, I phoned the hospital about a possible visit, and they said she had a rough night. They've given her a tranquilizer. I think seeing Nikki is out for today."

"I did so want to get back by." Katie felt the last of the laughter fading away. This was true disappointment. It wasn't easy to get to Boston from Rockhaven when you were tied to the ferry schedule. She had understood Jeff's infrequent visits before they were married. Now she appreciated the visits he did make. It was work.

"The good news is that Al called. The boat's not as bad as they thought, and it'll be ready on Wednesday. He said he'd run in with me to pick it up. How's that?"

Was that an answer to prayer? And how much was "not as bad as they thought"?

He took her chin in the crook of one finger. "I'm trying to cheer you up. How about this? I did see another restaurant I might want to visit. Since we can't spend time with your cousin, I think we can squeeze in a lunch date."

"Good. I'm starving. What did you see?" Something not too expensive, she hoped. His mention of the boat depressed her, reminding her of the job at ALD-Mass that hadn't materialized yet.

"Little Lamb. What's that, Eastern?"

"Asian barbecue, I think. Winnie brought home take-out from there once, if I remember correctly. They included a menu in the packaging. They have seafood, too." It pleased her that Jeff had suggested someplace, and the prices would be reasonable. She wanted him to enjoy Boston. It had been her home for the first three decades of her life. Of course she wanted him involved in that part of her, also. To make this dining connection, and at his suggestion? It was one more thing to bond them together in a life that Katie planned to enjoy for decades in the future.

"Do you think we can train Little Jeffie to love Asian barbecue if we eat there every time we're in Boston?" He started up the car, only to jump when someone knocked on the window. He rolled it down to greet Kambri Green, one of Katie's old chums from ALDMass. Katie had called her after they'd left Harvard Gardens the night before. She'd already had plans for the evening, but she'd agreed to attend services at Trinity with them.

"Jeff, Katie, what are you guys planning for lunch?" She had a long coat on, and fake fur around the hood rippled in the wind.

Katie called across the car, "Do you know Little Lamb?"

"Cambridge?" Street, she meant, but any Bostonian would understand that.

"You're welcome to join us." That was Jeff, with a smile.

"I'll have Harry. Is that okay? My sister's meeting me

500

in about five minutes to drop him off for the day."

Katie laughed. "Yes, of course. Harry will have fun. We'll save you a spot."

Kambri waved and took off, fighting the wind. Jeff chuckled.

"What's that for?"

"The place looked really small last night. I hope they have room for four. Who's Harry?"

"Kambri's nephew. He's three, well, three back in the summer. Just watch what you say. He has a photographic memory. He repeats everything."

"Oh, this should be good. Like, I can train him to say 'Polly wants a cracker' just by saying it once?" He shifted into gear, and with a look for traffic, pulled into a lane.

"Don't you dare. Remember, you're a minister of the Faith." Katie held her fingers loosely covering her smile. It was funny to think about the little boy as a parrot in a cage, blithely repeating whatever Jeff thought up for him to say.

"And you're a minister's wife. You shouldn't be smiling about it."

That made Katie smile wider. It seemed indeed they were made for each other. She remembered an old rhyme one of her coworkers had called out during a very unusual shower they'd thrown for her back in September. Two little love birds sitting in a tree. Yes, that was Katie and Jeff, she had to admit, and she'd found the ditty fit like a glove. Perfectly, comfortably, and as if they were indeed made for each other.

"What are you thinking?" Jeff touched her with his elbow as he turned on the blinker into a parking space.

"God makes people perfectly, doesn't he? Perfectly for each other."

"I suppose so." He killed the engine and removed the key. "At least I feel that way about us." He tapped her on the nose with his knuckles and grinned.

"Good answer, Preacher Ragsdale."

"I love you, Dame Carver."

"Dame Ragsdale, now, you silly."

"Always Dame Carver to me." He hefted the keys, and

he leaned in to give her a kiss on the cheek.

"For that, I'll let it pass, Otherwise, I'd have pushed you overboard."

"Ha! We're not on a boat. That says all there is to say about that." He opened his door, but Katie grabbed his arm, and he looked back.

"Then I guess I'd have to catch you before you hit the pavement."

"After we eat. I think I see your friend arriving." He pointed to a car pulling up across the street. The door opened, and Kambri waved.

"You get to sit by Harry." Katie let go and opened her door. "I get dibs on Kambri."

"Hey, I like kids."

Katie knew better with Harry. She was pretty sure Jeff would wish she'd pushed him overboard by the time they left the restaurant, but that was the way of things. She, for the next hour, intended to let Jeff babysit, and she and Kambri were catching up on all the latest news.

This was Katie's last lunch out for a very long time, and she planned to enjoy it very much.

15

"Archie's complaining about what?" Katie was preparing for the Love Extravaganza. It was that afternoon, and she was one of the servers. She'd pictured herself as an emcee, holding a microphone, and everyone else serving their children all their valentine goodies. It hadn't worked out as she planned.

Now she wore a white blouse and red pants, with long underwear next to her skin. Rockhaven was cold in February.

"The trucks coming in with the construction." Jeff was also donning his red and white. He'd agreed to join Katie as a "supporting cast member." Besides, he'd said, it's for an island cause. One for all, and all for one, or something like that.

"What trucks?" She knew what construction he referred to. The Point. With Nikki's funds, John hadn't wasted any time in putting his crews to work. It was only preparation work, though. Underlayment for the new foundation, she understood. How could that be a problem?

"Archie's a good man, but he has his days. It seems the trucks take up too much space on the ferry. He's had to wait twice, and I think it's gotten his gizzard."

"His gizzard?" Katie stopped and looked at Jeff, holding one long, white sock in her hand. She already had socks on both feet, but she intended to be warm. This was set number three. "Did I hear that correctly?"

"You heard me. His gizzard. It's that thing inside that grows thorny spikes when someone doesn't get his way. I think Archie forgot to have his removed when he was a boy."

Katie patted her stomach where it now protruded so that she could no longer hide it, saying, "You'd better not be growing a gizzard in there, Little Jeffie. No gizzards allowed in your mommy's tummy." Then she looked at Jeff. "You'd better not let anyone besides me hear you say that about Archie."

"Scout's honor." He held up two fingers.

"I'll have to get up to his place and see if I can smooth things out." Katie didn't want anything about her life here on Rockhaven to disgruntle the old-time residents.

"I've already talked to him. He, um, doesn't want smoothing out. He wants the trucks off the ferry. He claims there's a regulation he can pull up, and so on. I'll work through it with him. Tonight? You get to enjoy your extravaganza." Jeff was dressed, and he picked up her shoes and carried them to her. "And I get to spend the evening with the most beautiful woman on the island."

Katie smiled. She enjoyed his compliment, but she didn't intend to let Archie go. In the next few days, she planned to search him out. He'd always been polite to her. Sometimes a woman's touch was better than the best argument in the world.

Before she could tell Jeff that, a huge racket erupted at the front door, as if someone were trying to break in. Faintly, they could hear Jeff's name being called repeatedly.

"I guess I need to check on that." Jeff set Katie's shoes down and headed out.

"Tell them we're not home." She followed him into the living room, stopping to slip one shoe on, then in a few more steps, the second.

Roker burst inside when Jeff opened the door. He was grinning from ear to ear. "Hey, all! Happy Valentine's Day!" He threw a handful of pink and white confetti into the air, and it showered over the living room furniture.

"Hello, Roker." Katie looked at the damage and shook her head. "I thought we bought that for the extravaganza."

"You don't understand." Roker pushed past Jeff and lifted Katie off her feet. He swung her around, while Jeff laughed, wide-eyed and incredulous. "It's Valentine's Day, the best day ever!"

"Enough. Don't forget the baby." Katie's feet hit the floor, and she grabbed the back of the sofa to steady herself. She didn't want to be sick, not tonight.

"Why's it the best day ever?" That was Jeff. "What's happened to you?"

"Everything's happened to me! Jess has happened to me!"

"You're engaged!" Katie knew that had to be it. Since the first pumpkin pie Jess had sent for Roker, she'd known they'd get together. It just took time for them to figure it out.

"Almost." Roker's eyes were alight with energy.

"How are you almost engaged?" Jeff slapped his hands on his friend's shoulders, and he looked him in the face. "You are, or you're not."

"Okay, well, I'm not because I haven't asked Jess yet— "

"Well, man, why not?" Jeff shook his head.

"She said I couldn't, not until tonight." Roker moved his head back and forth in an aw, shucks, sort of way, and he laughed as if embarrassed to have to admit it.

"So you did ask her." Jeff was grinning.

"No, Jeff, I'm seeing this. Jess asked you, didn't she?" This was clear to Katie. Jess was a smart woman, and she knew Roker liked her, but he'd never cross that bridge without some encouragement. She must have asked him, just to prod him over the jump.

"Is it obvious?" Roker's words tumbled on without waiting for a reply. "She said I couldn't say yes then, but if

505

my answer was yes, I had to ask her tonight in front of everybody. With a ring. Do you have a ring I can borrow?" He looked at Katie with his question.

How could she say no to that? She asked him Jess' ring size, and he shrugged, but she said she'd take care of it. Now, he had to get home and get dressed, because he was handling the cookies, and the cookies went to the children; and by the way, congratulations, Roker. Jess is a lucky woman.

Roker's proposal that night took down the house, even outshining the auction and the prizes the parents passed out to their unsuspecting children. Well, maybe not in the eyes of Rockhaven's children, but to two long-term islanders, that one moment took the prize.

Just as Chipper Murchison moved in on the microphone as auctioneer, Roker jumped on the platform and pulled it from his hand. Jess was at the back with a pile of dirty plates she had collected from the tables. Roker cleared his throat, and when everyone got quiet, he called to her. When she turned to look at him, he said, "I got the ring, Jess."

That was all it took. Jess dropped the plates right where she stood, and she ran to the platform yelling, "Yes, yes, yes," all the way. It was her final leap that took down the house. She jumped into Roker's arms, and she kissed him until Chipper tapped her on the shoulder and suggested that it was time for the auction to begin.

Katie watched it all, and she wasn't a bit sorry to give up one of her rings to ensure Roker's and Jess' happiness. If they were half as happy as she and Jeff, it was worth every diamond and ruby in the world.

It was all about the love. Nothing mattered more than that.

16

Katie's eyes were closed against the warmth of the March sun. It was one of those rare island years when spring rolled in easy and warm. Two days before they'd had snow on the ground. Now? She was in shirt sleeves.

She hoped the baby was warming up inside. He was out there enough to get frostbite when the nights grew really chilly. How could a child be so big at almost six months? To look at herself in a mirror, she'd think she was ready to domino right there and then.

A car door slammed, and she turned to see Janine's truck. Her friend must be on the opposite side. Being very short, Katie wouldn't see her until she walked around. The doors facing Katie opened, and boys started scrambling out. When Katie got to seven, she stopped counting and looked back to the workmen scrambling over the Point, preparing to pour the foundation for the new house, with the sounds of hammers and power saws singing in the sunshine. With the boys off for Spring Break, and the concrete work coming at the same time, Katie had suggested that Janine's boys might like to see the trucks in action.

There were a lot of concrete trucks lined up, but then it was a very large house. Katie thought of Archie Coombs and his thwarted ferry access. She hadn't yet been to see him, although she had made several attempts. He didn't seem to be available to her under any circumstances, and that disappointed her.

And now, seeing all this, she could understand his point. She also imagined he was especially irritated at the current crop of trucks that had filled the ferry today.

Out of the tide of yelling voices from the boys, Katie caught Janine's voice calling to her. Katie found her at the back of the pack, and she raised one arm high and waved.

"The old cellar." Kevie was first to get to her, and he stopped up short. "It's gone."

"What old cellar?" Tim Swisher, the boy who lived closest to the Peaveys, had a well-worn basketball, and he thumped it on the ground. Without waiting on an answer, he tossed the ball to Kern Pearsons, a thin, angular youth, whose white legs protruded from over-sized shorts. He wore black socks and white sneakers.

"Turkey!" shouted Kern. He bounced the ball once, calling, "Tee," and, "Paulo!" before making a wild pass to Paulo Rivera, a blond, blue-eyed youngster who barely looked up in time to dodge the incoming torpedo.

With them were Matt Leaf, Jeremy Boggs, and Brookie George, the tallest of the bunch. Janine's three youngest pulled a remote control off-road vehicle from the bed of the truck, and the motor sent up whining cries of protest as they forced it all around the parking area.

"Space!" Janine reached Katie, and she spread her hands toward the expansive Point, indicating the unobstructed stretch of lawn. "Room to let the wild ones of winter roam."

Kevie hadn't received his answer, though, and he asked again, "The old cellar was too cool. What happened to it?" It was a smooth expanse of soil now, right next to the forms for the new foundation.

"They moved it over. See?" Janine motioned vaguely with one hand. "Go up there and look inside. That hole goes way down."

He did, and apparently satisfied, he gave a contented

508

grunt, and he was off after the other boys.

"I guess you're the Spring Break babysitter?" Katie gave Janine a quick hug, and she laughed.

"Only today. I'd be out of my mind if I had these boys all week. Tomorrow it's the George's day. You want the other three?"

"One's all I can handle." Katie rubbed her stomach. Her back had started hurting, and at not even six months. She hated to think of how it would be at nine. She also held her sweater in her hand, because she could no longer tie it around her waist. She'd never considered the trouble of such little inconveniences when she'd started this process. Now, she was barely buttoning her coat. At least the warm weather was a reminder that it wouldn't be winter always.

Thank God for that.

"I expected the foundation to look bigger. At least the new location will give you better views out to sea." Janine had her arms crossed, and at a noise from the parking area, she turned to check on her three youngest, and she yelled, "No, you don't, Konnar! If you don't share, it goes back in the truck!"

"Mom!"

"Don't you 'Mom' me! I'm coming over there if I have to!" She turned to Katie. "I hope you get a girl. Boys? Oh, my heavens, who wants them?"

"If you think your race car drivers will be all right, let's head to the cabin. John can't be here today, but he said they'd begin to pour the concrete about eleven. I need to get off my feet for a few minutes. I also want to ask you about Kevie's birthday. It's in what, ten days?"

"The 30th. He's so excited to be a teenager. Al teases him that twelve will still be tweener. Poor Kevie." She didn't look like she felt too sorry for him, with the smile on her face and the twinkle in her eyes.

"What have you planned?" Some parents might consider her question noisy, but Kate knew Janine wouldn't care.

"A day off the island. Roker's promised to watch the three youngest, so it'll be just the three of us. I don't expect it'll be much except a lunch, although we hope to get to Bean's and let him pick out whatever he wants, within reason." L. L. Bean's, she meant, the outfitting superstore. Their main outlet was a couple hours south, just close enough if they took the first ferry out.

"Bigger question, although probably a silly one." Katie had the cabin open, and she pulled two deck chairs out. The sun kissed one side of the wooden structure, and it would be warmer there.

"Shoot."

"Jeff and I saw Kevie walking to town a couple months back. He was carrying something, and he wouldn't let us give him a ride. What was that about?"

Before Katie had finished the question, Janine was laughing. "That, my friend, was a dead raccoon."

"No!" Katie's nose wrinkled as her stomach turned. To think, they'd invited him to carry it in their car. "Why a dead raccoon? What did he want with that?"

"Oh, he didn't. He just wanted the tail, but it was frozen, and he couldn't cut it off without taking the chance of damaging it. Keithie is a big fan of Daniel Boone. Al got him the old series with Fess Parker on DVD, and he watches it nonstop. Kevie's idea is to get his brother a hat like Daniel Boone's."

"A real raccoon hat." Katie chuckled. This was the best thing she'd ever heard, and from a real, dead raccoon she'd seen him carrying down the street. Only on Rockhaven, she thought. "When's the birthday?"

"June 1. He turns five. Kevie was lucky we had that snowfall, although he didn't think so at the time. It takes more than a tail to build a coonskin cap. Ken's doing the tanning, and he's using the rest of the skin for a full hat."

"Amiro? On Black Seal Cove?"

"Yes, the ones who helped with the auction back in February. Wonderful people. Private but wonderful, anytime someone needs a hand."

"Or a hat." Katie chuckled. The sounds of the cement trucks' engines revving up let her know it was time. "If we want to watch, we need to round up the crew. I'm told the basement walls will be first. Then they'll pour the floors. John hopes to take advantage of the warm weather and get it all done today. He makes no guarantee the break in the cold will last."

"Can't he insulate the pour?"

Katie looked at Janine askance, curious how she knew to ask that. She'd only found out it was possible after quizzing John about putting the foundation down in winter.

Janine shrugged. "Al likes home remodeling shows, and I do pick up a few things."

Sure enough, when they got close, they could see the forms lined with sheets of foam, labeled Polystyrene Insulation Board, on the outside parameters. The wall forms were filled with rebar, and looking inside, they were sunk far deeper than the ten-foot height that would make up the basement walls. Dotting the prepped basement floor were numerous holes that dropped into the ground out of sight.

"What are the holes for?" Janine pointed, as one of the trucks began approaching the foundation. "I've never seen that on the shows Al watches. Drainage?"

"Footings, I think they're called. They go an extra twelve feet, or to bedrock, whichever John found first. He promised me the house will never crack." Katie laughed at that. "It'll be an extension of the island, like a piece of the granite itself. Look. The trucks have caught the attention of the wild bunch."

The boys were running up from the shore, screaming to high heaven. Katie could hear them over the roar of the trucks. Kern had the basketball, and every few steps, he bounced it on the ground.

"Wild bunch! You're not kidding. Keep an eye on them. I don't want to go home and find I left one behind buried in the foundation. Unless he's mine, of course." Janine whistled loudly with her fingers at her mouth, pointing for them to go around, and five of the boys turned to veer toward where they were standing. On the opposite side of the pour, one worker could be seen backing two of them to a safer distance.

"Guess who I heard from?"

Katie raised her eyebrows. "On island or off island?" The machines were roaring, and they had to raise their voices to talk.

"From when we were kids. Guess. She was the beautiful one."

"Babes?" Katie couldn't think of anyone else who fit "beautiful" from when they were growing up.

However, Janine pointed to one of the trucks. It had extended a long pipe out over the construction site, and it ended in an open trough. Gray, wet cement was just starting to slide out. "We don't see that very often here on the island."

"Concrete trucks, you mean?" Katie pulled out her phone and took a picture of the mixture. Jeff would be interested in seeing it later. "Or new foundations going in?"

Her mind, though, was on Babes. She had existed in a world of her own, always wanting to be gone from Rockhaven. Katie had never understood that, hating the end of summer, knowing that she would be leaving it all behind for nine months.

Janine laughed. "Either one, trucks like this or foundations being poured. Babes, though, she's in Vermont. She and her husband run a bed and breakfast. She's Babes Fifield, now, and married to an ex-Army man. Her daughter's fifteen."

"Beautiful, like her mother, I'm sure." The only person Katie considered more beautiful was her friend Winnie, but then that's why she was in the field of modeling. It was a requirement in that line of work.

"I'm sure. That girl had beautiful genes, and I've no doubt she passed them on. I told her about you and Jeff getting married, and that there was a baby on the way. When I said you were rebuilding the Point, she promised me she'd be here for the opening day of summer."

"July. The fourth." That was something else Katie remembered. She'd always shown up in June, as soon as she could get here, but the official "season" didn't ramp up until the first of July. People wanted to be in place for the Fourth Parade that wound through the middle of town.

512

Katie wondered if the baby would be there by then. At her last prenatal visit, they had it pegged about the first of the month, but had let her know that it wasn't unusual for a baby to run two weeks over. Katie didn't want it to run over. She wanted it out and done with. Women in love with being pregnant? No, not her. She'd love the baby, but she was ready to sleep at night.

Then, when the baby came, she probably wouldn't get much of that then, either. Having a baby, she was discovering, wasn't a win-win situation. It was a "pick your moments to treasure," and let all the bad times go.

Letting bad times go reminded her. Archie Coombs. If her back kept hurting, she might have to get a lasso after that man. She had to administer some Christian love, and he was going to listen to her do it, if it was the last thing she did.

Unavailable. Ha! No one was unavailable where Katie Ragsdale was concerned.

17

"Thank you, Connie. I understand Mr. Hickox also intends to offer medical and dental coverage to his employees. If we can work that into the deal, how do you think ALDMass will respond to our application?" To Katie's job prospects, she really meant. She'd made sure the two were indelibly linked. They couldn't have one without the other. Then, she suggested, with multiple policy discounts, she might be able to get ALDMass a toehold on the island auto insurance market. With her on the island as a full time representative, that alone would be good motivation for people to sign up.

She thought it was working. She had no doubt that Connie was rooting for her, but Maine was outside ALDMass's target clientele. Upper management had to be convinced an agent this far north would earn her way, along with a good margin of profit for the company, to boot.

Katie just wanted a paycheck. Every week, every two weeks, or every month, she didn't care. An island boy had come by to look at Jeff's Jeep. He'd lusted with his eyes, but Katie had refused to let Jeff drop the price low enough for the boy to afford it. She couldn't tolerate the thought of seeing the Jeep on the island, knowing it was being abused by someone who had gotten it for a steal. Besides, Jeff loved that car. Katie appreciated he was willing to give it up for her, but she didn't plan for him to give it up at all.

Connie, she silently pleaded, come through for me. Now!

Connie left Katie on an upbeat note, telling her that with the new store policies lined up, as long as Mr. Hickox followed up, it looked like they might be shaking hands before long. She also wanted Katie to let her know how the progression on the renovation was coming, and she expected to see pictures of that new baby the minute it showed its cute little face.

Katie sent her love to everyone at the company, and she hung up the phone, very pleased. She had handled it all very business-like, refusing to call on any special favors because of her friendship with Connie or her past employment at the company. She hadn't known she could act as an independent agent, but she had pulled it off masterfully. Now, though? She had dinner to prepare, and little Jeffie was complaining.

Inside the fridge, she pulled out two covered trays. Jeff was so good to her. He was on his boat today, pulling pots, and he came in tired on days he fished. Yet, he went out of his way to gather the things for the next evening's meal, prepping the meat and vegetables so that all Katie had to do was put it in a pan and let it go. She had about five hours until she expected Jeff, and that was just enough time for steak, potatoes, and vegetables. Pulling the foil off, the steaks were trimmed and waiting, the potatoes peeled and sliced in half, and the veggies were rinsed. She dumped them in the crock pot Jeff had pulled down the night before, added two cups of water, and hit start. By then, her energy was gone, and she tossed the pans in the sink and headed back to the living room.

Her heart went out to Janine. How had she managed babies two, three, and four? Katie could barely get through the day with no children, and just one in the oven.

She must have dozed, because the next thing she knew Jeff was kissing her on the cheek, and saying, "Hey, beautiful. Dinner smells wonderful." And it did, meaning she had been out the entire afternoon.

"I'm sorry, Jeff. I must have fallen asleep." She started to stand, only to feel the tug of the sofa pull her back down.

"No, you don't. You stay right there. I'm headed to the shower, and I'll take care of the rest afterward. You're looking after two of you, and that's the most important thing."

"You lovely, lovely man." She reached for his face, to brush it with her hand. "I called Connie today. She thinks we might have a deal."

"A deal?"

That woke Katie. She forgot she wasn't telling him until it was certain. She used her elbows to force herself into a sitting position. "With Ritchey's new store. He asked me about insurance, and I'm brokering a deal with my old company. If it goes through, I might have my old job back."

"Katie!" He sounded distressed. "You don't need to work. We're okay on money. Sure, it's a little tight right now, but the Lord provides for his own. I've never had a bill I couldn't pay eventually."

"I love you, Jeff. Ritchey does need insurance, though, and he's getting it somewhere. Why not me?" She smiled at him. "Why else would our heavenly Father have sent him our way if not to help us out? Winnie meeting up with Ritchey, then Ritchey buying the store in town? He doesn't need this store to be successful. Trust me in this. Me, Ritchey? God's got a plan, and we're part of it, so plan to enjoy the ride."

"I don't know. With the baby coming, and the house out on the Point, can you manage both?" He held one of her hands in both of his, and he lifted it to his lips and kissed it.

"Oh, you are a male, to your bones." Katie was fully awake, and she laughed. "I'm a woman, Jeff. I can do anything. Haven't you heard Peggy Lee sing her trademark song? Or anyone that's sung it since?"

"But, I'm your husband. I'm supposed to support you."

"Support, shumort. I'm finishing up dinner. Help me stand." She held out one hand.

"If you're sure." He stood and took hers in his.

"I've been on that sofa for five hours. If I can't stand now, I'll be bedfast until July. No way am I giving up this early in the game. You, shower. Me? I'll have steak and potatoes when you show back up." Once she was on her feet and stable, she waved him off, and she headed into the kitchen, stopping on the way to rest her hand on a barstool sitting against the wall. Getting to the sink, she was aware of how braggadocios her remarks to Jeff had been. She'd been covering a gaffe, but he was more right than he knew. She'd felt pretty good off her feet. Walking into the kitchen? She already needed to sit and rest.

Well, she could do both. She pulled the stool up to the sink, and she nestled onto it. Flipping on the water to let it warm, she set the stopper in place and added soap. See? she thought. There are ways around every obstacle in life. You just have to find a happy medium to bridge the scary gaps in between. That's what Connie Rivera was helping her put together, a bridge, one that would help Jeff and her make it from year one to year two, leaping across and catching a falling baby along the way.

And if things didn't work out? There was always God's safety net underneath, made up of Nina and Kent, Janine and Al, Jess and Roker, and all their other friends on the island.

Katie was pegging her hopes on ALDMass, though. Insurance was her thing, and she could do this, no matter how many stools she had to line up along the way.

18

Katie stood on Neil Foote's stoop, and the soles of her feet hurt. The sun had been warm on the way out, but Neil's small place was buried against a moss-covered granite rise, a good eighth of a mile from where she'd parked her car. It was little more than a cabin with a metal stack and a stained propane tank off to one side. The towering trees kept the sun at bay, and the water washing the rocky shore not two hundred feet away had the rising breeze decidedly chilly.

She was here at Nina's request. Rather, Nina had told her if she wanted to meet face-to-face with Archie Coombs, then Neil was her avenue. The two men had a connection way in the past, although Nina didn't know what it was, but if one was having a cantankerous spell, the other could always get through.

To satisfy Nina, and to resolve Archie's differences with the rebuilding of Carver Point, Katie raised her hand and rapped sharply three times on the edge of the screen door. It banged louder than she intended.

"I saw you when you drove up. Nabbit, give me time to get my suspenders on." The words filtered through the thin walls of the old cabin.

The door jerked open, and there stood Neil, more

wizened than old, with a three-day growth of beard, and still snapping suspenders onto the waistband of jeans that looked like they had seen better days in the previous century. He hadn't yet glanced up.

"Excuse me, Mr. Foote?"

"Eh?" He growled at the snap before finally clicking it shut. He lifted his head, squinting and working his face for a moment. "Oh, it's you. Let me get my teeth."

Katie watched him totter off, holding to the edge of a battered blue chest-of-drawers she could see just inside the room. His feet made a shuffling noise as he moved away. After a minute, she called after him, "I don't mean to be a bother, Mr. Foote."

"Eh?" He reappeared, standing deeper into the room. "Well, woman, come on in. Don't know who told you to call me Mr. Foote, but most people know me by my given name. Don't see how it should be any different for you. In, woman, and close the door after you."

"Thank you." She stepped through and pushed the door to, aware of the intense smell of wood smoke permeating the place. The woodstove looked cold, and there was an oil heater to the side. She'd seen propane out front, so there was that, too. She supposed he enjoyed having a fire most days in the winter. "Do you mind if I sit? I tire easily." She laughed nervously and patted her stomach.

"Suit yourself." When he motioned to her with his hand, she moved towards a chair. Neil was already in an upholstered rocker, one with oversized doilies on the arms. "Thought you looked in the family way. You the preacher's new wife?"

"Katie. I spoke to you at church." She was about to sit, but she caught herself and offered her hand to shake.

"Done know your name. It's my eyes not so good, not my memory. Wasn't sure you weren't that Amiro woman. Always coming by, wanting to help me out. Don't need no help, nabbit. I'm not an old man."

Katie wasn't too sure about that, but who was she to disagree with his self-assessment? She looked at her hand, and as it was still empty, she pulled it back and let herself sink into her chair.

"What'cha here for?" He began pushing with one foot, and his chair rocked. It squeaked, too, like a floorboard might be loose.

"Nina Vinson sent me out. My husband and I are rebuilding my grandmother's house out on Carver Point—"

"Eh, so that's it." Neil didn't let her finish. He stopped rocking, and he reached into his mouth and pulled out his teeth. He ran his fingers around the top where it fit against his gums, then he shook it over the floor and slipped it back into his mouth. "I told that husband of yours it was no business of that fool Archie. What's he want to complain about that for? When Old Mrs. Carver went, the man should'a let go, and he never could. Pardon me. I gotta get something to drink. My teeth make my mouth dry."

He pulled himself up with several squeaks from the boards under his chair, and he slid his feet towards a sink Katie could just make out on the far wall. She hadn't been sure it was really a sink before, as it had a gathered skirt covering the area underneath, and there were no other cupboards nearby. The tell-tale faucet, in battered chrome, gave it away.

He pulled a metal glass from a shelf attached to the wall, filled it from the faucet, and took a long draught. He returned the glass to the shelf and headed back towards Katie.

"What do you mean he should have let go? Did he and my grandmother have a falling out?"

He chortled until he coughed, and as he sat, he hit the arm of his chair several times until he got his throat cleared. "It was no falling out. Those two were in love, from the time they were knee-high to a root."

"In love?" Her grandmother had never said anything about being in love with a man on the island, and Katie had spent the first fourteen summers of her life with her. "My grandmother was Polly Carver—"

"I know who your grandmother is. All the boys on the island knew Polly Anne Ellison, or the lucky ones did. The most beautiful girl on the rock, and we all vied for her hand.

Archie almost got it." His eyes twinkled, and he showed a liveliness he hadn't let through before. He rocked, too, faster than earlier. "Made him mad to come back from the war and find her married to that Carver chap, no more'n a rich summer boy. I done told him, over and over, no summer girl marries an island boy. It don't work out. Like marries like, and that's the way it is."

"Perhaps she didn't really love Archie . . ." Katie let her voice die away. This was a surprising side of her favorite grandmother she'd never heard about, and she hadn't known Archie existed until she'd married Jeff at the end of the summer.

"She did, and that's the truth of that. As I told Archie, like marries like, and that's what Polly did. Archie always hoped, after your grandfather died, but Polly was set in her ways by then, out in that big house, and even love couldn't cross that barrier."

"But if he loved her, why would he complain about the house being rebuilt."

"Now, woman, what'cha building out there? The same house?" He'd stopped rocking, and one eyebrow was askance.

Katie was startled by the question. "We can't. There were foundation issues, and a survey dictated a different design altogether. But why would that matter?"

"Archie's still in love. You building something that's not your grandmother's? You're killing her a second time. That's how Archie sees it."

"Oh, my word. I had no idea." Katie's eyes burned, and she glanced toward the door, compelled to find the man now and clarify the situation to him. "If I explain, surely he'll understand."

"Done done that. Nah, what we've got to do is get the man on your side. Think of that, woman. How we going to do that?" Neil began to grin.

"I don't know. He won't meet with me. He hasn't shown up for church since construction started. That's why I'm talking to you."

"Young people these days." He cackled. "That Archie,

he's good with his tools. Likes woodworking. Likes babies, too. You might get to him with a baby, if you know where you can find one, 'specially one that needs a crib round about summer time."

"Oh, Neil. You are wonderful. Can I give you a hug?" This was going to work out wonderfully.

"Been waiting on that since you walked through that door."

Katie couldn't wait to tell Jeff. Nina had been her guardian angel, stepping in at just the right time, with just the right advice, and setting everything right. One thing she didn't see fit to correct Neil on was his pronouncement that like marries like. You see, on one hand, it was very true, so he was correct. Jeff and Katie were made for each other, as alike in soul and spirit as any two people had ever been created. Yet, Neil's statement wasn't true, either. Katie was as summer as they came, and Jeff was her island boy. She'd printed and framed that old picture Jeff had posted on Facebook, the one of the pack out digging for clams in the mud flats at low tide. Jeff, all covered with mud, proudly holding a clam in the air, and her, looking at him with admiration-filled eyes. He was her muddy island boy then, and he had been beautiful to her, and he was her handsome island man now. Yes, like married like, and no, like didn't have to marry like. It was, indeed, the love that counted.

She wished her grandmother had known that. Would her parents have been happier if they had been Coombs instead of Carvers? Her grandmother would have been, Katie was certain. Now, though, she suspected she knew why her grandmother had come to the island so early each year and stayed until the first hard freeze. She bet it was for love. Even if she couldn't hold it in her hands, to be on the same island with it must have been the next best thing.

Now, though, she had Archie to corral into her plans. A man that had loved her grandmother enough that he wanted to keep her memory alive, even almost fifteen years later? That was a man that any woman would want to know.

19

The melody was unmistakable.

The calendar had turned to April, Katie now drove with the steering wheel tilted as far up as possible, and the roadsides were littered with spring ephemerals, those first flower blossoms that would soon die back when the hardier summer growth took over.

Of course, a late-spring snow might kill them back even faster. Now, though, to hear *Oh, Christmas Tree* whistled along Main street made Katie's heart sing.

It was Jeff. Come May, Roker told her the song would start to disappear, but to Katie, it spoke of love, flyaway hair, and a wonderful lobsterman in her arms every night.

Today they were together to put love back on track for Archie Coombs.

"Hey, Katie. How's my little bump?" He kissed her, and at the same time, he ran his hand over the massive protrusion that extended what seemed three feet in front of her.

"Your bump is fine. The bump carrier has swollen ankles. At the clinic, they said I was to spend two hours every afternoon with my feet elevated. I asked them if preparing dinner counted, and they laughed."

"That shows they find you as entrancing as I do. Has Archie gone in, yet?"

They had a scheme running. Archie had still refused to meet with Katie, and he had, indeed, complained at the town council meeting. To his frustration, his complaints had been taken "under advisement" and promptly ignored, but that had just made him more vocal. Now, Ritchey had been recruited to hire the man to do some woodwork carving in the new store, and they intended to corner him there.

Katie had her insurance proposals, already vetted by ALDMass, in a leather satchel to turn over to Ritchey. The reason for their visit was very legit, and there was no way Archie could fault their presence in the store.

"About five minutes ago. Are you ready?" Katie had been, but now that the moment was here, she felt her backbone softening. She was about to decide she liked the color yellow, and yes, to avoid this confrontation, she would replace her entire summer wardrobe.

Her eyes had even begun to burn.

"Not chickening out, are you?" Jeff squeezed her, and he chuckled as they began heading that way. "I see those tears. Archie's a pussycat. We both know that. We just need to bring him around. Neil's idea is perfect."

"Okay." She took a deep breath, and she stood taller. "I'm strong. I'm a woman."

"Peggy Lee, right?" He chuckled again.

"Or Bette Midler, even Raquel Welch and Miss Piggy, once. I think one of the Judds, and half a dozen other people." She smiled. "The distraction is helping. Thanks, Jeff."

"Sure. Coming up, one hand-built crib on the way, Dame Carver." That was the plan, to get Archie involved in doing something for the baby, so that he'd feel included in the love he'd lost out on so many decades before.

"Ragsdale." She jabbed him with her elbow and laughed. "I'll never live down the Carver name, will I?"

"You laughed, which was my intention. Feeling better?"

"Sure. A kiss would help." She tiptoed, and he planted

524

one on her lips. "Now, I'm energized. Let's hit it, Sam."

Stepping through the door, they saw Ritchey at the back wall standing before a large pad of paper hanging on two hooks. He wore a dark blue suit, with the coat unbuttoned, and his tie loosened around his neck, looking every part a successful businessman, instinctively involved in every aspect of opening yet another branch of a money-making business. He held a marker in one hand, drawing in a design as he talked. It looked like a shelving project. Archie stood beside him, in rougher island clothes: a plaid flannel shirt, suspenders, and dark jeans that were too dark not to be new. His shoes were distressed leather lace-up boots with unevenly worn heels. A soft leather bag of tools was on a low table beside him.

"Ritchey!" Jeff called loudly and waved an arm.

"Jeff, Katie!" Ritchey called back, and he closed his marker and set it on the same table they'd used the first time Katie had visited the store. He put one hand on Archie's arm and spoke to him, before striding across the building, calling loudly, "Katie, did you bring those insurance quotes? My accountant needs to see how much damage you're doing to my bottom line." He laughed.

"Right here." She held up the satchel and patted it on one side.

"Oh, and do you know Archie?" Jeff took the satchel and headed back across the room. "Archie, this is Jeff, my very good friend from the island, and do you know Katie? She's been on the island most summers of her life. She's taking care of my insurance on the old place, here. If we go up in flames, she's the one I'm calling. After the baby comes, but you can see that, I guess." He grinned, backing away.

"Yep." Archie cleared his throat and kept his attention on the paper.

Ritchey winked at Katie, and he pulled Jeff to him, speaking with one arm over his shoulder. "Tell me about that antique crib you found off island. With my new godson being born in a couple months, I don't know that I'd trust some old thing put together with chewing gum and bailing

525

wire. You say you can't find anyone to build you a better one here on the island?"

"We've been looking." Jeff made a sound with his mouth, and it came across as disappointment. "Now, Bean's has one—"

"Bean's." Ritchey slapped Jeff on the chest, as if to make him see the light. "That's the sturdiest you can get. How much to get it shipped up here?"

"Too much." That was from Archie. He still watched the paper, with one finger tracing a design Ritchey had drawn.

"What's that, Archie?" Ritchey called to him. "Do you have another option my friends could consider?"

Archie flicked his eyes to Katie for one brief moment. "That baby coming about June?"

"Closer to July." Katie hoped, just hoped Ritchey had broken the ice.

"Might could have one ready about then." Archie cleared his throat. "Good design here, Mr. Hickox. I never told you, but I knew your daddy. He was a fine man. I'll get you a quote for this." He rapped the paper with his knuckles and turned, reaching for his bag, and walked in a slouching clomp toward the door. He turned to look at the three friends just before he opened it. "Sunday, Jeff. Katie." He nodded and stepped through outside.

Katie laughed as relief poured over her. At the same time, tears poured down her face, and she tasted the saltiness pooling at the corners of her mouth.

"Is that good or bad?" Ritchey smiled as he looked between Jeff and Katie, with his hands in the air, and his palms raised. He shrugged.

"Good, I think. Katie?" Jeff put his arms around her.

"I was afraid he'd yell at us, even after what Neil told me. I want to fit in and get along with everyone. This has been months, and I didn't know how much it had me stressed." She laughed, pushing away from Jeff and wiping her eyes. "Neil was right, though. You said baby, and he melted right there."

"I don't know about melted." Ritchey laughed. "I was

surprised to hear my old man was fine. I didn't know Pops as well as I thought, I guess. My dad, a fine man. Two thumbs up, Archie Coombs."

"I told you Archie's a pussycat. See? I know my island people pretty well." Jeff pulled Katie to him and kissed her on the forehead before turning to Ritchey. "Thanks, man. You are the best friend I've ever had."

"Thank your wife. These are the best insurance quotes I've ever had. Oh, and Katie, I don't need these copies. My legal department contacted ALDMass directly last week, and we're all set to go. I talked to—" He looked thoughtful for a minute, then snapped his fingers. "—Connie Rivera, I believe, and she tells me you're returning to the company as, how did she put it, head of their northern New England division. She had nothing but praise for you. Let me be the first to congratulate you on your promotion."

"Jeff, you can keep your Jeep!" Katie threw her arms around him. "I have a job, now. We don't have to sell it."

"You guys!" Ritchey put one hand on Jeff's shoulder, and the other on Katie's. "With that house going up, I thought you two were set. I had no idea money was tight for you. Hey, all you have to do is ask. I mean, now that you're working, but if you weren't, I would have bought it and let you keep it, just so I could drive it when I'm here. Think about that." He thumped Jeff on the chest.

"Thanks, Ritchey." Jeff gave him a one-fist punch on the arm.

Katie couldn't say anything. She was too filled up with love to get any words at all out. Spring was here, the flowers were blooming, and she had a job. She had a job!

And now she had a crib on the way. What more could she ask for? Nothing, and to quote Neil Foote, that was the truth of that.

20

"Jeff, I need you. Let's go, now!" Katie was nearly in tears. She lay in bed, her stomach was so cumbersome that she could barely turn over, and little Jeffie had kicked constantly for the last twenty minutes.

And the sun wasn't even up.

"What? Is the baby coming?" Jeff jerked awake, and he fumbled with the bedside light. His clock toppled to the floor before he found the switch. His hair was a tumbled mess, and his eyes were swollen and red.

"I wish. Then this would be over. I need you to help me to the bathroom. I can't get up."

"Again?" He fell back onto his pillow, groaning. "I'm sorry, Katie. Of course. Let me get around there."

Jeff rolled off the bed and stood in a v-neck tee and orange Texas A&M boxers, a gift he'd received in the mail from Ritchey. Normally he'd tout flannel pants, but this May hadn't exactly been normal. The first of the month had brought blinding thunderstorms they had thought would never end, even to the point of keeping Jeff off his boat. It had stalled work on the Point for two weeks, and with the thunder wracking her already sleepless nights, Katie had wanted to scream.

Then, the weather had broken, and she had sweltered.

Jeff had consoled her that the heat was the baby, but the skies had dumped unending sunshine on the island, and it felt like July. Hot afternoons were broken only by the grip of nightfall, when the heat eased enough to pull up a blanket for warmth.

This night had barely cooled at all, and Katie was damp with sweat.

"It's Rockhaven," she muttered, as he helped her stand. "How can it be hot at four in the morning?" The window at her side of the bed was open, but Jeff reflected the truth of the temperatures in his chill bumps.

"Here, beautiful, let me get the bath light." Jeff steadied her with one hand as he felt along the wall.

"Leave it off. I don't feel beautiful, and I don't want to see myself in the mirror. Oh, oh, hurry, Jeff. I need past now." Katie shoved him out of the way and scrambled to ready herself for her pending emergency.

That had been her nightly routine for the past week, and she was tired of it. Now, she lay sprawled on the sofa, the sun washed the inside of the room, and the sound of the ocean on the rocks lulled her into a welcome drowsiness. Anything that needed doing wasn't getting done today.

Her phone set off a chirruping sound. Jeff had reset the ringer, thinking this wouldn't disturb her as much as a rousing chorus of *Hallelujah!*, but it found its way in her head and jarred her awake anyway.

"Five more weeks!" She held the phone for a moment with her eyes closed, as it began its chirruping chorus once more. On the third set, she knew she had to answer, or she'd lose her caller. Looking at the display, she took a deep breath. It was Winnie. She brightened herself and tapped the phone. "Honey, I'm so glad you called. What's going on with you?"

"Hi, Sweetie! Guess where I am!" In the background came the sound of tinkling glass, like crystal tapping against crystal.

"In an airplane having lunch." Lunch. Just the thought of it turned Katie's stomach. Breakfast had not stayed down.

"Close. I'm in Monaco. Well, not in Monaco, but I can see it from my chair. Listen." Something high-pitched came through, falling off, then repeatedly rising in volume. "Can you tell what that is?"

"Um, your hairdryer?"

"Oh, you are such a goof! It's Monaco. Think that, and you'll know." She laughed, and she said something sotto voce to someone on her end of the line.

"Who's with you?"

"Stephanie."

Before Winnie could explain, the phone beeped several times, and it went dead.

"Oh, Stephanie," Katie muttered, and she looked at the screen, shaking her head, totally clueless who Stephanie was. However, Monaco told her why she hadn't heard from her friend in the past few weeks. Glancing at the phone told her it was nearing eleven. "I might as well try for some food. Maybe I can keep something down."

She dropped the phone beside her and rolled to her side, crawling as much as anything to her feet. People from the church had been coming by to offer their help on a daily basis, but she'd told Jeff she needed one day to herself. She hadn't even had a break from the new house out on the Point. John had been calling regularly with updates, and there was always something new to put her stamp of approval on. She learned it was called a timber-framed structure, and last week, John had needed to know if she wanted the exposed steel joining plates painted black or shellacked in a natural state. She hadn't known what joining plates were, but she did now.

"Just tell him to build it," she'd told Jeff, almost in tears. "It doesn't matter if it even has joining plates."

He'd been more reasonable, assuring her that it did matter, and next year, she'd be glad she'd taken the effort to involve herself in the construction. He'd also rubbed her back, and they'd discussed how after several easy months of carrying this baby, it had decided to fight her tooth and nail the final six weeks. Jeff acknowledging that had helped. Katie didn't feel so alone.

About the time she'd waddled into the kitchen, the phone on the sofa started to chirrup at her yet another time. Taking a deep breath, she retrieved it to discover it was Winnie back on the line.

"Hey, Honey. The call dropped. Sorry. What were you saying?"

"Did you guess yet?"

"I think I said your hairdryer. Was that it?" She worked on the bright voice, hoping Winnie wasn't paying close attention. She didn't want to be forced to try to explain the state of her day.

Winnie giggled. "Here, talk to Stephanie."

"Bonjour. I am very glad to speak with you. Katie, correct?" The speaker sounded very educated and proper. A ship's horn or something similar went off in the background.

"Katie Ragsdale, yes."

"I understand you are having your first child soon. Congratulations. Do you know yet, boy or girl?"

"Thank you. A boy, we think, but we haven't been able to tell for certain. He won't turn the correct direction."

"Ah!" She laughed. "With my son, it was the same. Louis never did as we wished. I wish to express my sympathy for Nicolette's illness. She has been a close family friend all my life, and she is like a favorite aunt to me. I am so glad she shares her final years with her American relations. Give her our family's love when you see her next. Au revoir."

"Hi, Sweetie. I'm back." Winnie giggled. "Isn't Stephanie so sweet? She's let me come on her boat to enjoy some peace and quiet. Since you won't guess, it's the Grand Prix. Nobody can get a minute's peace in the city with those cars making noise all day. You can't so much as carry on a conversation at any of the cafés."

"Am I getting this right? You're in Monaco for the Grand Prix? Why are you in Monaco for the Grand Prix?" Even more, Katie was trying to place Stephanie. Had her cousin ever mentioned someone by that name, especially in the context of an old family friend? Not that Katie remembered.

"Oh, you know. Jeffie's friend." Winnie made a remark to Stephanie about something Katie couldn't see, and an air horn blasted. It was loud.

"What was that?"

"They have this thing called paparazzi. Everyone wants our pictures. One of Stephanie's little men is chasing them off in a tiny boat. Oh, this is so much fun!"

"So, why did you call?" Katie's chipper brightness was about worn to a frazzle. Her hunger was real, now, and Winnie's conversation was all over the place.

"Sweetie, I'm coming to see you, once my photo shoot is done. Ritchey wants lots of pictures of me with the race cars. I'm going to be a calendar!"

"Sure. You're going to be a calendar. And Stephanie? I can't place her. Is she the photographer?"

"Oh, Sweetie! That's rich!" It sounded like she covered the phone and told Stephanie Katie's question. "Katie! Stephanie's the princess, well, one of them. I bumped into her, all by accident. She asked me what the pictures were for, and I told her about Ritchey and you and Jeffie, and we became best friends. Isn't it funny she knows Nikki, too? She thinks Nikki owns an apartment here in Monaco. I knew Nikki had money, but not real money. Oh, Sweetie, how's the house coming along? Stephanie wants to know. She was at your grandmother's once, when she was a girl. Of course, you weren't around then, so you wouldn't have met her." Winnie let out another giggle, and she spoke to someone on the boat with her, although she didn't call them by name.

Katie sighed, her energy totally depleted. "The house is framed in, but the roof's not on, and there are no windows, yet. Tell Stephanie she's welcome anytime. Call me when you know you're coming in, Honey, but it sounds like you've got a lot going on, and I'm about to have lunch."

"It's dinner time here. We're eating on the boat. We have a real dining room. Who has a boat with a real dining room? Oh, oh, before I forget, here's why I called. I got a

532

picture of me standing next to Princess Grace's picture. Stephanie took it. That's her mother. You know who Princess Grace is, don't you?"

"Grace Kelly?" It had to be. There was no other Princess Grace.

"Of course! I love you, Sweetie. See you this weekend!"

Katie watched the display on the phone return to its standard wallpaper, which was of Jeff on his boat, with a green buoy bell in the background. He wore sunglasses, and his hair was rumpled by the wind.

Grace Kelly, she thought. Cousin Nikki knew Grace Kelly, and she's like a favorite aunt to Grace Kelly's children. Oh, my. There was more to Nikki than Katie knew. And an apartment in Monaco?

Oh, my, indeed!

21

"Jeff, how was the party?" Katie was in bed with the covers piled over her. She had roasted last week, but this week she was freezing. Even though the phone had rung twice, she hadn't had the energy to answer it.

Winnie had been waylaid, thank goodness, in Boston. She'd stopped by to give Nikki a small present from Stephanie, and had called Katie to tell her there was a change of plans, and if Katie didn't mind, she thought she'd keep Nikki company for a few days.

Katie was grateful a new connection had been made, and she was more grateful she didn't have to entertain. She'd been ill the entire weekend. Now, she had doctor's orders to be off her feet at least one hour out of two. Actually? Three hours out of four was more practical.

"You would have loved it." Jeff came into the bedroom, wearing a bright tee with an ice cream stain on one sleeve, and baggy cargo shorts. One leg had grass stains down the side. He held a cell phone in his hand. "Did you survive all alone?"

"I wasn't all alone." She pushed the bedding back to sit, only to realize how cold it was in the room. "Aren't you freezing?"

"It's warmer in the sun than it looks from in here. I talked to Nina. She left the party early, and she said she'd stop. She made it, then." He leaned in and gave her a kiss on the cheek.

"She dropped off a pineapple cake. It's in the kitchen, and maybe a casserole. She tried to tell me, but I was half asleep. Sorry. Do you have pictures?"

"Remember that dead raccoon?"

"The one Kevie was carrying, the one we almost had in our car? How could I forget?" She smiled.

"Look at these. Keithie wouldn't take it off the entire time. I'm thinking I might have to have one." He chuckled, holding the phone out to her.

"Don't make me laugh." Katie was half-sitting, and she fell back onto the bed. "No, no laughter. That hurts my back."

"I'm so sorry. Is there anything I can do?"

"Not get me pregnant next time. Other than that, you're doing fine. I just have to get past the next month. Then I can give him to you and sleep in the guest room." She chuckled at that, wishing it didn't hurt so badly.

"I learned today why Winnie stayed in Boston." He clicked the phone off and held it in his hand, looking at her.

"Oh? Because I was sick? There was no way I could have been a good host." When he didn't laugh, she knew. This wasn't good news. "What, Jeff? Tell me."

"Your cousin. We knew there might be complications from her fall. Didn't we know that, Katie?" His eyes had gone red around the edges.

"Spit it out, Jeff." Katie's stomach was a rock, and it had nothing to do with food or physical illness.

"You were so sick Winnie and I agreed not to tell you, but she stayed in Boston rather than coming up here because pneumonia had set in. I knew she had that cough when we were there, but I didn't think much about it. Francois called me—" He chuckled, wiping at one eye. "—and I had the hardest time understanding. That man needs an interpreter. Well, he called last week, so I already suspected something had happened. Then when you were sick in bed, I knew you couldn't go down. With Winnie flying in, she agreed to stay at the hospital with her. Even the doctors didn't expect her to go downhill so quickly."

"How downhill?" Katie heard the ragged edge in her voice. She couldn't help it.

"I'm sorry, my love." Jeff took her hand in his. "It was this morning, early. I got the news while I was at the party."

"No. Jeff, no. The house isn't finished, and I so wanted her to get to see the baby. No." She let herself sink into the sobs that rushed over her in waves, consuming her.

"Baby, baby," Jeff crooned. "No, no, don't cry like this. Winnie was holding her hand when it happened. The last thing Nikki said was how much she enjoyed getting to know her family again. She wished she'd done it sooner."

"I wasn't there, Jeff. I should have been there." She couldn't look at him, and guilt washed over her.

"She loved you, Katie. You loved her. That's all that matters."

"Did Winnie tell her about Stephanie?"

He wiped one eye and gave a snort of a laugh. "She said your cousin laughed and said she wanted to whip that girl once when she poured a whole bottle of Chanel in the bath. She couldn't, though, because she was a little princess."

"What happened?"

"When she found it didn't make bubbles, she drained the tub and came back with kitchen soap. She poured in the whole bottle and made the bubbles overflow the tub."

"Oh, Jeff. That's funny. She really said the princess did that?" Katie wiped her face with her palms. "Maybe we should hope ours is a boy. He might tramp mud in the house, but at least all my Chanel would be safe."

"I'd have to get you some, first." He took her hand. "Seriously, are you going to be all right? I'm sorry I didn't tell you. The doctors thought she was improving."

"Your decision was the best, no matter that I would liked to have been there. I couldn't have gone down, anyway, and I would have worried. How is Francois doing? Did Winnie say?"

536

"Remember those file folders?" He smiled, but it was a wait-till-you-hear-this smile, not a real, isn't-this-exciting smile.

"In the hospital?"

"Yes. Your cousin was pretty savvy. The three we didn't look at concerned her estate. It seems she only has one living relation." He did the smile thing again.

"Who?" The question came out, but even as she said it, Katie knew the answer. "Sorry, but what does that mean? For us?"

He placed a hand beside her face, and he leaned in and kissed her. "It means you don't need that job any longer. And when we go to France, we can stay in St. Moritz or in your apartment in Monaco. Free."

"But Francois, what about him?"

"He texted me a statement the attorney had prepared. Francois will stay at the apartment in Boston until the estate changes hands. That timing is a little bit vague. However, Nikki did give him a permanent income, for either thirty years or life, whichever comes up first."

"I'm so glad. I really like Francois. I want him to be happy. I suppose he's ready to head back to France to be near his father. Good for Nikki, taking care of her driver. What about, you know, services and stuff? Should we plan something here, or will she be interred in France? Did anyone say?"

"France, from what the attorney's statement says. Nikki arranged to give Francois power of attorney to handle her final needs. Your cousin was very thorough in her legal matters. Later, perhaps, we can do a memorial here on the island."

"I'd like that. I'll miss her, Jeff."

"I know you will, sweetheart. I will, too. Don't you want to know how much the estate is worth?" He grinned.

Katie sighed, and she looked through the windows out to Moffat Cove. "Will it buy you a new boat?" That would be worth a lot to her.

"A new one every year for the rest of my life. Do you think I need one?" He seemed very pleased at her question, and his eyes shimmered.

"Can I still work if I want to?" She tried to smile, but she wasn't sure what to expect. And she did want to. It was something she was good at, and she liked meeting people. She liked helping people, and she felt she was doing that when she helped them resolve their insurance hassles. One call. It was ALDMass' motto. She intended to adopt it as her own.

"You want to work?" He seemed puzzled. "Thanks to your cousin, you'll never have to worry about money again."

"But if I want to?" She felt her eyes filling up. "Please?"

"How can I say no to that? For the woman I love, you can work every day of the week, and I'll love you every one of those days."

Katie held out her arms, and even with the baby in the way, she pulled Jeff tight, and she hugged him for all she was worth. She might have cried for Nikki in there a bit, but it was all a package, filled with love, and wrapped and tied with the arms of a strong man who was hers forever and ever.

She was reminded once more of Neil Foote, who once said, And that was the truth of that.

Over the next four weeks, Katie discovered that her first trimester had been the easy one.

That ninth month? It beat her to death. Rather, it exhausted her, swelled her ankles until she thought she couldn't walk, and she only made it out to the Point once, then only stayed long enough to see that there were windows and a roof, and that the grass needed to be trimmed. She hadn't gone so far as to get out of the car.

Just shoot me in the head, she thought. Take the little stinker by c-section, and bury me in an old hole.

She didn't mean that, not very often, anyway. Then came the night she timed her contractions, to find they fit within the permissible timetables, and she felt the relief of the angels that it was here, and two days early. This was going to be over and done.

However, it didn't get better at the hospital. They knew she was coming up on her due date, so she was expected at some point. However, while the nurse practitioner was very efficient, an epidural was what Katie demanded. It was not to be so. He wasn't trained, he quoted, "in administering epidural injections under fluoroscopy." Katie wasn't sure what that meant, except that she would be screaming in pain for the next few hours.

"Winnie. Where's Winnie? She promised to be here." Katie squeezed Jeff's hand as a spasm coursed through her body. She was drenched, and she didn't know how pain could be so bad.

"She'll be here on the first ferry. She's on her way now."

"The crib. Did Archie finish the crib?" Another spasm hit, and she tensed, trying not to cry out.

"He thought he had two more days, but he'll have it before you get home. He assured me."

"He'd better. How long did they say these contractions might last?" She panted, and she looked at Jeff, jealous he wasn't the one going through this. She wanted to trade positions desperately.

"It's your first. They said several hours—"

"Oh!" Another spasm racked her body.

"Never mind. Not long, not long."

"Really? Not long? Did they really say that, Jeff?" She didn't want him waffling. She wanted him to spit it out.

"They don't know. Your first means they don't know." He looked like he might cry himself.

"You're sure Winnie'll make the first ferry?" It might be worth it if she had to wait that long. Then she could scream at Winnie, too.

"If not, Al's agreed to go pick her up in his boat."

"Tell me about the house. Anything. Distract me." When he didn't respond fast enough, she barked out, "Now, talk!"

"Um, we've got water." He hesitated, and when Katie screwed up her face, nodding hard and fast two times, he continued. "They put in a temporary sink, to put the well under pressure and check out the septic lines. Oh, and electricity. The rain the first of May means we can't be in by the Fourth, but it'll be weather tight."

"The fireplace. Tell me about that." She had her eyes squeezed shut. "Is it all river rock like I asked?"

"The fireplace is done, and the garage, it even has an opener. They have a toilet in already, so we have a functioning one of those." He grinned when he saw Katie glaring at him.

"Good." She spat the word. "I expect everyone we know to be out there on the Fourth. I plan to be there with this baby." She panted, as another wave of pain hit her.

"Breathe, Katie. Breathe."

"Don't tell me to breathe. Tell me about my house!"

"Papa, do what she asked. Don't stress out our new mommy." The nurse practitioner across the room called out his instructions with a smile. "We'll get that baby here, sooner or later." He handed Jeff a damp towel, suggesting he pat her forehead to keep the sweat soaked up.

Jeff had gone through a pile of towels, and a new nurse had come on shift, when there was a knock at the door. The front duty nurse leaned in, asking, "Visitors? I have someone who wants to come in."

Katie called out, "If it's Winnie, tell her to get in here!"

The nurse laughed, and in a few minutes, a familiar face burst through the door, with her hair and clothes swathed in hospital green. "Sweetie," she cried out. "Is little Jeffie here, yet?"

"You'd better be glad you made it. This baby's about to come, like right now." Katie spat the words.

"Now?" Winnie froze, as if seeing Katie prepped, Jeff at her side, and the nurse scrubbed and with gloves on for the first time.

"Yes, now!" Katie let out a yell, and Jeff's eyes grew wide. The nurse made a few coaxing sounds, and after a few moments, let out a sigh of relief, holding up a brand-new baby boy.

Jeff had just enough time to say, "It *is* a little Jeffie," when something crashed into an instrument tray, and they looked over to see Winnie, out cold, and on the floor.

"At least she got to see him born." Katie sighed. "Give him to me." She held out her hands.

"Dad still needs to cut the cord." The nurse clamped it off, and handed Jeff a sturdy pair of surgical scissors, as the baby began to wail as hard as he could with his little lungs.

"Wow, this is tough." Jeff sawed away, finally snipping

it through.

That done, the nurse handed the baby to Katie, and stooped to check on Winnie before calling in the woman from the front desk.

Katie wasn't paying any attention. She only had eyes for her son. He was the most beautiful thing she'd ever seen. She brushed his face with her fingertips, and when she touched his lips, he hushed and began to suckle the tip of her finger.

"I think he wants the real thing." Jeff chuckled.

"My turn." The nurse stepped in, taking the baby. "I have some procedures I have to attend to, and then you can have him back."

"You did it, Katie." Jeff squeezed her hand, as his eyes tracked the baby in the nurse's arms.

"Oh, Jeff. We really did. Can we truly be at the Point on the Fourth? I want to show him off." She smiled. Pain? What pain? She had a baby. A healthy baby boy. That's all she could think of.

"It's only four days away."

"Four days. That's just enough time. Get Nina and Janine on the phone. They can plan everything."

"What about Winnie?"

"Oh, my word! Winnie!" Katie twisted around to see. Winnie was attempting to sit up with the help of the nurse.

"Did someone call my name? Oh, Katie, Jeff, I thought you were having a baby. I drove all the way up here. Did I miss it?" Then she caught the sight of the nurse sucking mucus out of the baby's nose, and her eyes rolled into her head, and she slumped into the nurse's arms.

"No, Honey, you didn't miss it by much."

Jeff chuckled and gave her a kiss on the forehead. "I love you, Katie."

"You'd better. I'm the mother of your child, and now you've got two of us."

Now Neil's words were really true, because her words said exactly what Katie really felt, except for one final thing.

"And by the way, I love you, too, Jeff."

Then the baby was back, and there was no more room for talking, not for anything except wondering how anything under God's creation could be so absolutely perfect; and to think, he belonged to them.

God's love child, wonderful in every way.

23

It was the opening day of summer, true summer, the one that started with the Fourth of July parade down Rockhaven's Main Street. The turnout was spectacular.

Afterwards, Nina had pulled together a fried fish spectacular at the Point, with a massive vat of hot oil bubbling away in the Ragsdale's new garage.

Of course, the house was unfinished on the inside, and the outside was rough wood underlayment, but all the windows and exterior doors were in place, and temporary stairs had been installed, allowing easy access to the second and third floors, to admire the views.

Babes Baker was there, as promised, now Babes Fifield, and she introduced her daughter, Wish. Why Wish? Because she got her wish when her daughter was born.

The surprise Babes brought with her was none other than Apple Dumpling, now married to Donald Crisp. Donald was at her side, red-haired and covered with freckles. He was a builder, himself, and he pulled John Chetwynde aside to discuss the challenges of home construction in such a remote location.

Apple introduced her three children, Macintosh, Braeburn, and Newton Pippin. All three were as colorful as their father.

Keithie Peavey ran the length of the Point over and over, his raccoon tail hat bobbing behind him the entire time.

Katie was surprised to see Winnie bringing a nattily-dressed man she recognized to meet her. She handed Jeff Little Jeffie, and she reached to shake. "Welcome, Mr. Sorensen. I'm glad you could make it to the island, today."

"Thanks to your friend, here." He motioned toward Winnie. "She has a gift for you. Francois!"

From beyond the gate, Francois appeared carrying a large item wrapped in brown paper. As he moved around people, he repeatedly called out, "Excusez-moi."

"Right here, Francois." Winnie called to him, snapping her fingers. When he set it down in front of Katie, Winnie ran her fingers down the fabric of his suit on one arm. "For one of these, I might even learn French." She giggled, reaching to brush the touch of gray that graced his temple, before turning back to Katie. "Now, though, today is yours. Your gift. From me to you, Sweetie. Open it."

"Jeff?" Katie called to him, but he'd wandered off with Ritchey, who had convinced his wife, Tricia, and their two eldest, Allie and Mark, to join him for the grand opening of the new store. The baby was back in Texas. Tricia had agreed, as long as she didn't have to get aboard a boat, not even once.

"Remember," Quincy Sorensen cautioned with a smile. "This is for decorative use, only."

As soon as Katie had part of the paper removed, she knew what it was, the old crib from the antique store. "Winnie!" She jumped up and hugged her friend, crying with happiness. "I love you so much."

"Then open the rest of it."

There was more, too, because the crib was filled with baby things. The best part was a doll, specially sculpted to look just like Little Jeffie. It had child-like hands and feet, and a cloth body, and it was exactly the same size. It was dressed in baby clothes and even opened its eyes when Katie picked it up. Winnie told her they had put it on rush order just for her, and Francois had driven it up from Boston that morning.

At one point, Ritchey was on his phone, and as he walked up to Katie, he clicked off and slipped it in his pocket.

"How are you holding up?" He smiled at her. "I heard you were under the weather the entire last month."

"Ha! That's the easy version. Compared to being pregnant, I'm peachy. What do you think of the house?"

"It's breaking my heart I can't get Chetwynde to do me a house like this in Texas. The views from inside are amazing. Enough of the house, though. We've one last gift for you today."

"Oh?"

"It's arriving now." He pointed to Archie Coomb's rusty old delivery van backing up to the gate, with puffs of blue smoke coming from the tailpipe.

"Archie got my crib finished." That had to be it. Katie was excited.

"It's more than a crib. You're going to need that big house to put it in." He chuckled.

"What do you mean?"

But by then, Archie was out, and he was pulling out pieces. Several looked like tree branches carved out of polished spruce, pale in color, with a touch of a yellow cast. Two large sections were carved into tree trunks, with roots that spread out to provide a firm base. The final piece he removed from the van was a carved ivy trough, with the ivy branches reaching up the sides to form an open fretwork of vines for the ribs of the crib.

Katie had tears in her eyes. She could see what it would look like set up, a vine-covered crib suspended from two trees, carved from the island's native spruce. It must have taken unknown hours to craft such an amazing masterpiece.

Jeff joined her on the way to look at it, and by the time they were there, Archie had it assembled. It was quite simple. They watched him set the two trunks in place, fasten the branches on top by means of a large, exposed peg, and place on top a leafy bridge that connected both trees. The ivy crib slipped in between the two tree trunks onto pegs shaped like small branches, locking the entire masterpiece in place.

"Archie, this is beautiful." Katie ran her hand along the carved leaves. The detail was masterful.

"I'm impressed." Jeff grabbed Archie's hand, and he pumped it. "You let us know what we owe you, Archie. Anything. This, I'm just amazed." He sniffled, and he pulled Katie to him in a hug.

"I never got to make one for Polly. Your grandfather wouldn't have it." He looked at Katie, as if embarrassed, and he cleared his throat. "I, um, helped myself. I hope you don't mind."

"No, I don't mind. Helped yourself how?"

"This is wood from the old house. When it burned all those years ago, your parents hired me to clear it away. I saved some of the best parts, mostly the floor timbers. I should have told someone, I know, but I never did. I've had 'em in my barn all this time. The insides were still good, milled from the trees right here on the Point. It's fitting, I think, for them to come back to their home."

"Archie, I don't mind at all." Before she thought, she threw her arms around him and gave him a hug. Hesitantly at first, then firmly, he hugged her back.

From inside the van, a familiar voice called, its tone as irascible as the man who used it. "It's about time the old grouch got a hug from a pretty Carver girl."

"Neil?" Jeff stepped to the back of the van. "What are you doing in there?"

"What you think, nabbit? Old fool there wouldn't'a come out here if I hadn't'a made him. Someone's gotta light the fire under his breeches."

Katie threw her arms around Jeff this time. She laughed, telling him, "I've had the best Rockhaven spring there's ever been. I'm so happy to be your wife, Jeff Ragsdale."

"And I feel the same about you. Come on, Dame Carver, we've got a baby to show off."

"You, Preacher Jeff, need to learn my real name." She

jabbed him with her elbow.

He led her to the new crib, and he pointed to the inside. One end had the name Ragsdale carved into it, and the opposite end spelled out Carver. "That's me, and that's you. Take one Ragsdale, add in a Carver, and that makes a pretty good baby. The best of both worlds, summer girl and island boy. What do you think about that?"

Katie didn't get to answer, because Neil Foote called from the van, "Young fools. Kiss her, Preacher. That's what I think about that."

Jeff did, and Katie did back, and if Jeff ever did want to try for a little Katie, that would all right with her; and that was the truth of that.